I0594558

THE LAST
KEEPER

BOOK ONE
THE IMMORTAL KEEPERS

HM HODGSON

Copyright © 2021 by HM Hodgson

All rights reserved.

No part of this book may be reproduced in any form or by any electronic or mechanical means, including information storage and retrieval systems, without written permission from the author, except for the use of brief quotations in a book review.

This book is a work of fiction. Names, characters, places and incidents, other than those clearly in the public domain, are fictitious and any resemblance to actual events, locales or persons—living or dead—is coincidental and not intended by the author/s.

Print ISBN: 978 0 6451286 2 8

Ebook ISBN: 978 0 6451286 1 1

Front cover design by Amanda Pillar from Smoking Hot Covers

https://www.smokinghotcovers.com

Inside cover design by Jacqueline Hayley with Marina Farcic

https://jacquelinehayley.com

Edited by Sarah Proulx Calfee, Three Little Words Editing

https://threelittlewordsediting.com

Proofread by Libby M Iriks, Romance Book Coach

https://romancebookcoach.com

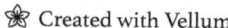 Created with Vellum

For Chance and Indigo. Dreams can come true.

PROLOGUE

One will come who carries the powers of all the worlds, and unto that power comes the strength to kill the World Tree. To kill you. And should the Tree fall on the rise of the black moon, none from the Higherworld, none from the Underworld will ever set foot again in the Mortalworld. You will be stranded. You will be at the mercies of any who dwell in your world at that time. Beware, Keeper, your world faces its most dire fight this night.

    ~ Freya, goddess of love, sex, and war

1

WARRAGUL, VICTORIA

A waning crescent moon disappeared behind storm-fueled clouds as India Jones shut the hotel room door and sagged against it. The bed was right there ... five short steps away. She just had to force her legs to take them.

Mustering the energy to move, she pushed off the door —and her stomach growled. Of course. Because she hadn't eaten since ... she scowled, when *had* she eaten? She forced her fatigue-fogged brain to think.

Huh. She'd stopped for petrol before the border, over four hours earlier, and had grabbed something greasy and quick to eat. She eyed the bed. Her belly growled again.

Food first, then sleep.

Except, right then, all-too-familiar goosebumps prickled over her arms, and the fresh green scent of her magic tingled in her nose. Her stomach dropped. *Oh crap, what next?*

She pushed off the door, darted into the small bathroom and grasped the edge of the chipped cabinet.

A dash of icy water hit the back of her hand. She jolted, automatically looking up for the leak.

A torrent of water smacked into her face.

Adrenaline shoved through her and she yelped, spluttering. What the hell? Shielding her face, she tried to make out what had to be a bloody big gaping hole in the ceiling of the tiny bathroom.

Except—the ceiling was perfectly normal.

India stifled another cry as more water poured down, echoing the driving rain from the storm outside. Holy crap, the storm might as well have been inside, beneath the perfectly fine-looking ceiling.

Shit, shit, shit. *Not again*. She needed a spell—needed something to stop this screwed up magic.

A knock sounded at her hotel room door. Her heart rammed inside her chest. *Oh no, uh-uh*. No way could anyone come in here.

She darted a look around the small room—towels, she needed towels. Lots of them. But first she had to stop the rain. If only she knew the spell for that. But, crap, India didn't even know the spell to make it start.

Then the rain ended as abruptly as it had begun.

The knock sounded again, slightly louder.

"India, this is Simone, the manager here." The muffled words filtered through the door. "I just checked you in."

"Ah, hi," India called out across the room. She swallowed hard, tried to calm her racing pulse. "Just a moment."

"No worries. I've brought you up an extra blanket. And I know the room's small, but I hope you find it okay."

Okay? *Okay?* India's chest rose sharply beneath rapid breaths. She swallowed and turned around.

The bathroom was covered in water, the small square

tiles slippery beneath her boots. The once neatly folded and fluffy white towels were now lumpy sodden messes. Water-logged carpet, where the bedroom floor met tile, squelched underfoot as she took a step toward the bed.

No, the room was not okay. *She* was not okay.

Though, thankfully, the water seemed contained—mostly—to the bathroom.

India tiptoed to the door, her dark hair plastered to her neck and shoulders. She slicked the long bangs off her face. With a deep breath, she opened the door a smidge and peeked out from behind it, making sure her drenched shirt and jeans were hidden even as she forced a smile.

Sure enough, the woman who'd checked her in earlier stood there, a thick woolen blanket folded in her arms.

"Hi," Simone said. "Hope you don't mind me coming up, but it gets chilly here at night, even in autumn, so I've brought you an extra blanket. And since the kitchen's closing soon, if you're hungry, I can take your order so you don't miss out on a hot meal."

India blinked. The easy, genuine smile on Simone's face was almost soothing, but India couldn't let her guard down. And she couldn't take the blanket without displaying her wet sleeves. "Thanks for the blanket, but I'll be fine. And I'm happy to come down to order something to eat."

Simone tucked the blanket under her arms and chuck-led. "No way, that's not how we treat visitors in the country. And hey, any chance you're related to Liz Jones? I source some of my produce from her and heard through the local grapevine—it's a reliable source of info here in town—that her granddaughter was visiting."

Butterflies took flight in India's stomach. She shifted her feet and ran a hand over her hair. The damp material of her sleeve brushed against her cheek, and she dropped her arm fast. But Simone's gaze only moved over India's hair.

"Oh, wow, you were having a shower," she said. "I'm so sorry for interrupting you. How about I save you a plate of tonight's special? It's chicken schnitzel with mash. The mash is made from Liz's potatoes."

"Um, that'll be great, thanks. I'll just finish up here and then come down." India managed to keep the smile on her face until Simone left. Closing the door, she sank against it.

Her grandmother—"Nan" to the family—was the reason India had reluctantly returned to her childhood home. Nan was India's only hope of understanding her magic. No way would she have come back otherwise.

Because, holy crap, did she need help with her magic!

Hot tears welled, but she dashed them away, stared up till they stopped. A single light bulb hung from an ornate ceiling rose in the center of the room. Her witchcraft used to be the polar opposite of that intricately detailed rose. Magic for India had always been an easy, minor, spell-driven part of her life. Magic-lite.

Until three weeks ago, anyway.

Now her witchcraft was wild.

Thunder still crashed outside, and lightning flashed through the window. India shivered, the cold of the night making itself known. Crap, she needed to get dry. But questions jammed inside her head, refused to go away—why had her magic changed so much? And how the hell was she meant to control it?

Her batshit magic had to have something to do with her mother. India wished for the thousandth time that she could ask for her advice. Her gentle, gifted mother would've known how to stop the rain—and how to start it.

If only there was a spell to raise the dead.

But even witches knew death couldn't defy the laws of nature.

The tears returned, as they had almost every day in the weeks since her mother's death. India knuckled them away. Tears weren't going to get her anywhere. What she needed were answers. That was why she'd driven twenty hours to this tiny town in the middle of nowhere, to the family that hadn't even bothered to come to Mum's funeral.

She pushed off the door. Worrying about magic would have to come later—right now she had to clean this room. No way was she leaving the wet, messy bathroom for someone else to clean. And she had to do it with manual labor, not magic, given how useless she was with spells.

The small hotel had probably once been grand, with a wrought iron balcony wrapping around the upper two levels. Her room was one of six on the first floor, and after locking the door behind her, she made her way down softly creaking, carpeted stairs, which were bordered by a dark timber balustrade. Just as India reached the last step, Simone walked out of the public bar, the black stenciled lettering above the door indicating its purpose.

"Perfect timing," Simone said, drying her hands on a dish towel with that same warm grin on her face.

India couldn't help the smile that spread over her own cheeks. Wow, she hadn't smiled in a long time. It was ... weird. And nice.

"Hi. Sorry I took so long," India said.

Simone waved a hand through the air.

"No worries there. I put a plate away for you. Come on through to the back room, it's the warmest at this time of night." Simone led the way to a dining room that had exposed brick walls and was filled with a mix of trestle and small square tables. "Here you go. Grab a seat anywhere you like, and I'll come back with that meal. Like I said, Liz's potatoes make great mash."

"Potatoes. I didn't know Nan farmed those," India said.

Simone tilted her head.

No magic was needed to read the question on her face. India swallowed hard, somehow managed an even expression.

"I grew up in Hill End but haven't been back in a while. It's a long story."

"Wow," Simone said, her grin becoming tentative. "So you don't know it's only an hour out to Hill End? Not that I want to lose the business, but this storm popped up out of nowhere. It's not even a blip on the radar, so it should pass soon. You could be out at your grandmother's tonight."

The butterflies returned, only this time with wings of lead. India forced a laugh.

"It's lovely that you're honest, but I'm almost out of fuel. I didn't realize petrol stations closed so early out here. No, I'd rather stay here tonight, fill the car up in the morning, and not risk getting lost on a stormy night in the middle of nowhere."

"Nah, absolutely don't want that to happen," Simone said, chuckling. "Well, I'll go and grab your dinner." But she stopped and turned around, held out her hand. "I really should introduce myself properly since you're practically a local. I'm Simone Morris, but call me Sim. I'm newish to town too, and I'm the owner and manager here."

India smiled and shook Sim's hand. A warm prickle shivered through her palm as a gentle spice tingled in her nose. The spicy scent of magic. For a split-second, India stopped breathing. She clamped her jaw to keep her mouth from dropping open. Her mother had taught her circumspection when acknowledging both her own and another's magic.

WITH HER STOMACH full and body warm, India locked her bedroom door with the simple hook and catch. A yawn rolled through her as she changed into leggings and a well-worn shirt.

Man, she needed this day to be over, but at least she was warm and dry.

She dropped onto the bed. Even if she'd wanted to think about the reason her magic was out of control, and how in the world she was supposed to contain it, she didn't have the chance, as sleep claimed her.

Her eyes had barely closed when she had the dream again.

She was riding the wind—no, she *was* the wind. Racing deep into a forest, she was pulled ever faster by an amazing force. She swerved around giant trunks, darted low under towering limbs, soared high over enormous boughs ... until she reached it.

The heart of the forest.

The dream wind surged like a roller coaster gaining momentum, only to stop with ferocious speed, sending her hurtling into space.

Then, for the first time, someone else appeared in her dream. Smelling of spicy musk and oozing masculinity. A solid torso and strong arms that caught her at the bottom of the surge.

The friction of warm hard muscles against her chest

ignited a wildfire. Her dream lover rubbed hot, capable hands over her breasts, her belly. Between her legs. Sent her blood to rise and boil. At her core, heat and pressure grew, expanded. The dream touch quickened. An orgasm began to build, stronger, stronger still—

India jolted awake. Heart racing. Pulse pounding.

The heat and pressure stopped. Right on the precipice of boiling over.

Her breath short, her body restless, India tried to recall the face of her dream lover. But no matter how hard she pushed, her memory halted at the hot, deeply tanned skin of his torso.

She took a deep breath, her pulse still racing. Dream lover aside, what did the dream mean? Every night for the past three weeks, her dreams had taken her into the forest—the one that had bordered her childhood home.

She hadn't seen that forest for eighteen years. Not since her mother had packed the two of them into their family car and driven for days and days, eventually arriving in Queensland.

A chill prickled over India's neck. She rubbed it away, rolled onto her side.

The dream didn't matter. The dream lover didn't matter. India had enough on her hands trying to figure out how to deal with her batshit magic without worrying about a recurring dream.

And with the rain hitting her window now a soothing patter, she gave the ceiling a cautious glance and sank back into sleep.

Hill End, Victoria

THRANE JOLTED AWAKE, his body taut, his heart racing. He whipped around, scanned his library.

The remnants of a fire gently crackled in the hearth. Soothing moonlight filtered through the large windows and played across the book-filled shelves. Their mellow tones were a stark contrast to the fire that raged inside him.

By the gods, that had been one hell of a dream.

He'd been working late into the evening and must've fallen asleep. But given the supple leather couch was one of his favorite places to write and he'd fallen asleep there often enough, that wasn't anything new.

Waking up on the verge of orgasm *was* new.

Thrane muffled a curse and stood up, tried without success to recall who else had featured in his dream. He couldn't capture her face, but the deep mysterious fire of her eyes stayed with him, and slowly, one by one, the hairs along the back of his neck rose.

Gods, this wasn't a normal reaction to a hot dream.

His mobile phone rang, and he scowled. Bloody late for a call. But when he saw the caller ID, he answered straight-away. A minute later he thumbed the end-call button, muttered an oath as he pushed dark curly hair out of his eyes. Fuck, that was one call he wished he'd never received.

A churning roiled through his gut. His gaze shot to the window, but he saw nothing except the silhouettes of trees —trees that stretched for days behind his house.

The same trees that hid the reason for his entire existence.

His first day here in Gippsland had shown him that the hardiness and tempered beauty of this land made it the perfect place for his mission. The deep forest was filled with ancient mountain ash and gum trees that speared tall and true into the sky, gentle foothills led to a sweeping mountain range, and rivers sang a silvery song as their waters slipped by.

On that day, as he'd packed down earth—his calloused hands more used to handling heavy swords than soil and fragile seedlings—he'd vowed to guard his secret, to see it safe for all the world's sake.

Thrane was not going to break that vow. The lives of all those who had gone before him deserved that honor, and the lives of all who would come after depended on it. But right now, that phone call meant he needed to get to Liz's, so he grabbed his car keys and a thick jacket, quickly locked up and jogged to his car.

He drove along the winding valley road for ten minutes, a blanket of stars his only company, to get to the Jones's farmhouse. Once there, out of habit, he ignored the formal entry and entered through the kitchen door.

Illuminated only by the dim light of a lamp, Liz Jones, wrapped up in a thick cardigan, stood at the island bench and held a cup of tea to her mouth. Her papery cheeks were drawn tight and her brow was furrowed. Thrane gently placed a hand on her arm.

"Your family confirmed they sense her?" he asked.

"They have all felt her," Liz said, well-worn creases deepening about her blue eyes as she met his gaze.

"Then others will have as well." Thrane scowled. "They'll come for her, Liz. Any of them—maybe all of them."

"We need to get her here as soon as possible." Liz shot him a glance. "A black moon rises in six days."

Ice slithered down Thrane's spine. He bit back a curse. A fine tremor shook Liz's hand as she placed her cup on the kitchen island.

"I knew going to Annette's funeral wasn't an option. But, damn it, if someone else had gone, maybe they could've talked India into doing this our way. She's just so ... so damned wary. Though who can blame her?"

Thrane blew out a slow breath.

"Calm, Elizabeth," he said.

"Don't tell me to be calm. And *don't* call me Elizabeth."

He cocked a hip against the counter. "*Liz*, focus on what you can accomplish here and now. What can you do?"

He straightened to his full height, his gaze steady, but she didn't back down. No surprise there.

"India's made it to Warragul and insists on staying there tonight, then driving up in the morning," Liz said.

"What? Why?"

"Apparently my granddaughter is worried about running out of petrol in the middle of a storm. Her words. It's not even raining here—how much of a storm can there be in town?" Liz snorted. "But she's Annette's daughter, and mercy knows Annie was the second-most stubborn person I've known."

"Well, she's come by that honestly, at least."

"You don't know India. Don't try to guess her motivations."

"Liz, neither do you anymore," Thrane said, forcing his voice to remain even. "You know I have one task only. *Nothing*, not even your granddaughter, is exempt from what I have to do to fulfil that." The ice returned to his veins. "And you said it yourself, there will be a black moon in less than a week."

"Bah, you won't harm her."

Thrane shook his head, but Liz was back to ignoring him. Her brow furrowed once more as she stared out the darkened window.

"But I agree we need to find out what's going on," she said. "If Annette was right, India is in terrible danger."

Thrane bit back the urge to argue the alternative. His view that India was as much "*a* danger" as "*in* danger" had been a constant point of conflict between them.

"All right, Liz, what do you want?"

"She's alone, Thrane. Right now, in town. You need to go in. Keep an eye on her."

"She's what, twenty-seven? I'm sure she'll be fine for one night."

"She's twenty-eight. And Thrane, this is India. Jev's daughter."

Thrane's chest tightened and he stared at Liz for one moment. Clenching his jaw to avoid cursing, he forced himself to exhale slowly.

"Fine. I'll go in." He shoved a hand through his hair. "I hate going into town."

"I know, I know. We just need to get her to the farm safely and keep her here until I can cast a shrouding spell like Annette's. And pray that with the strength of the second new moon, my magic is strong enough."

Those damn hairs on the back of his neck rose once more. But he hated seeing one of his oldest friends clearly worried.

"Liz, I'm sure she'll be fine."

2

India's eyes snapped open to a near pitch-black room. The hairs on the back of her neck spiked. Was someone else th—

A man's silhouette rushed into view. She screamed, but pressure, hard and fast, wrapped around her neck, cut her cry short. She pulled at the arms choking her, tried to wrench them away. The man straddled her chest, crushing the breath from her.

She bucked her hips, her legs, frantically clawed and grappled at his hands.

Her blood iced. Her mind blanked. And a punch of desperate energy spiked within her. She opened her mouth to cry out, let the force free, but couldn't make a sound.

Dark spots—darker than even the room around her—splotched at the edge of her vision. *Oh God, this can't be happening.* She gathered all her strength, then pitched onto her side. The roll dislodged the compression at her throat, gave her room enough to draw a panicked breath.

"Bitch," the man snarled.

She continued rolling, plunged off the bed, and onto the floor. Thuds and thumps echoed through the room as the man tried to catch her.

"Nowhere to hide, bitch," he called through the darkness.

India scrambled to her feet.

A dark shape rushed at her. She screamed, and the cry hurtled up her throat, echoed into the space. Then the man hit her full on, pushing her backward, bashing her head into the window frame. The curtain dislodged. Weak light from outside spilled into the room.

Harsh breathing grated on her ears, puffs of hot air hit her cheek. Thick arms wound around her torso, moved up toward her neck again.

"Told you. You can't hide. Not from us."

India screamed again.

An icy shiver shook her body right before a fresh scent bloomed in the room. *Magic.*

Within her, something dark twisted hard, fast. Over and over it rolled and churned, and then the twist released like a spring letting go, and a surge of energy hurtled through her. Exploded right as she shoved her arms outwards.

Her magic-enhanced strength broke the attacker's hold. She rammed her knee up, hard. Her attacker shrieked, shoved her sideways. She bounced off the bed.

And the door burst open.

Splinters of wood sprayed as a massive figure flew into the room. It—he?—rammed into her attacker, then the two bodies crashed into the window, shattering the glass, and tumbled in a tangle of limbs through the opening.

India ran to the window, peered through the dim light to the balcony. Her breathing too fast. Too sharp.

A man turned to face her.

Wild, thick hair shadowed a face with hard planes and a long straight nose. Blades of eyebrows tightened. Dark eyes, afire, met hers. Drew her in, captured her in their glittering heat.

Magic. But nothing like she knew. Magic that enticed, beguiled with a dark dangerous cutting edge. Magic that hit her low in the gut with a fist of lust. She would've reeled from the impact but was utterly trapped within that gaze.

Suddenly the room lit up brightly. She blinked against the abrupt glare, shielded her eyes. The spell broke.

Something touched her shoulder and she jolted, whirled around.

"India," Simone said, red hair tousled, her face tight with concern.

India caught her breath, turned back to the man. His fists were clenched at his sides, his gaze locked on her. Gathering her wits, she turned again to Simone.

"India, I heard crashes and screaming, and—are ... are you hurt?" Simone asked.

India tried to speak, but her throat was too tight. She swallowed gingerly, finally managing a strained sound.

"Ah, I'm not sure. About any of it." She winced. "Sore ... my throat's sore." Her heart beat hard and fast, so loud in her ears. Surely Simone could hear it. She ran her hand tentatively over the back of her head. "And my head hurts."

"What happened?" Simone's eyes widened as she looked around the room.

"Ah, I don't know. A man was here, in the room. And then another man crashed into him."

India slowly looked around the trashed space, shook her head. What time was it? She stumbled to the side table where her phone had been—it was now on the floor. Luckily, it hadn't been damaged.

It was 1:03 a.m.

Simone guided India over to the chair. "Here, sit down. I called the police when I heard the crash and your scream. Nate's coming now. Um, can I get you a water or something?"

India stared at Simone, and for one moment all she saw was the figure of the man who'd attacked her, but she saw it from afar, disconnected, like watching a scene from a movie, not living it. She blinked, shook her head to clear the cobwebby sensation.

"Water"—she swallowed again—"would be good."

A handful of strangers had gathered in the doorway, some blinking sleep from their eyes. Her skin crawled beneath their stares, and she had to say something. "Please ... ah, please leave the room. I'm okay."

"All right, everyone, thanks for checking on us," Simone said as she returned with a glass of water from the bathroom, "but you need to head back to your rooms or go downstairs. I'll make tea or coffee in a few moments for anyone who needs it."

India took a sip.

"Thanks. For the water and the ..." She waved at the people leaving the room.

"No worries," Simone said. "But before I make everyone warm drinks, I'm going to run upstairs and check on Tara, my daughter. She slept through it, but I ... I need to make sure she's okay. I'll check whether my mum's awake and see if she can keep an ear out for her, then I'll be right back. Will you be okay for a moment? Or you can come with me?"

"She'll be fine."

Simone yelped, whirled around.

The man from the balcony stood in the doorway. He was stunning. And tall—he filled the splintered doorframe. The wild hair India had glimpsed earlier was chocolate brown. Tousled from the struggle. His long nose gave him a hawkish appearance, tempered only by firm lips and mesmerizing dark eyes. His face, too harsh to be pretty, was utterly captivating.

"Go on upstairs, Simone, I'll wait with India."

India blinked. How did he know her name?

"Thanks, Thrane, but did you have to scare the hell out of me?" Simone gave India's hand a quick pat and ran out of the room.

Ah, *should* she stay with this man? Had Simone called him Thrane?

But a thrum of energy had poured off Simone—the woman clearly wanted, *needed* to check on her daughter. India didn't go after her, though she held her breath, flattened back in the seat as the man stalked into the room.

He kept his distance, which she was grateful for, and steadily moved to the broken window. He darted his head out and looked both ways. Apparently satisfied with whatever he saw, he stepped back and stood beside the shattered glass.

"How hurt are you?" he asked.

His voice was pitched low, but a faint accent tinged his words. Not so strong that she could place it but there nonetheless. Like his scent. She tried to pin down the origin of the warm musk that spiced the air. It was vaguely familiar. Although ... it wasn't the scent of a witch.

He was staring at her. Why?

Finally, she recalled his question.

"Ah, I'm sore. Here."

India touched the skin at her neck. Hissed. Crap, she was going to be one bloody big bruise. She took another sip of cool water.

The bed was at an angle, its tangled covers strewn over the floor. The curtain had torn on one side. Shards of glass littered the carpet beneath the shattered window. Of course. The man who'd attacked her—and the stranger here now—had gone through it.

"Who ... who was that guy? Where did he go after you ...?" India gestured to the broken window.

The man—Thrane, Simone had called him—peered closer at her neck but didn't answer.

Abruptly, the shirt she wore became too thin, too revealing. He would easily see the pebbles of her nipples through the flimsy material. A shiver skittered through her, and she gave in to the urge to cross her arms. No way was she letting this stranger see such a private part of her body.

Even if he'd, maybe, probably, helped save her. Even if he was the most physically stunning man she'd ever seen. Even if she seriously wanted to jump up and grab hold of him. Which had to be the craziest reaction anyone had ever heard of after being attacked.

And still Thrane didn't respond.

She tightened her arms around her chest.

"Hello?" she asked. "Did you see that man? Where he went?"

This time Thrane shifted to look out the window, as if

that was his reply. He even hunched his shoulders, as if he were trying to minimize his size. Which was impossible. He was tall. Very tall. Her mind rewound to the dream she'd had—where a faceless man with a hard torso and muscular arms had featured in her own X-rated movie.

She eyed his chest and shoulders—his cream cable-knit pullover had a rip in the side, but his size was obvious, even with his hunched body posture. Oh no, this was not the time to be impressed by a hot body, especially when the owner of the hot body was ignoring her question.

Her patience disappeared beneath a hot, razor-sharp rush of blood as temper outweighed pain.

She placed the glass down and jammed her fists on her hip. "Hey, you. Thrane, right? Are you always this rude?"

Thrane stiffened, and his gaze cut to hers. Then he shifted fully toward her and straightened to his full height.

He had to be well over six and a half feet.

Her mouth dried up and she tried to swallow. The breadth of his chest made her want to full-on body tackle it, to be wrapped up in those strong, safe arms.

Oh no, not again.

She forced her mind from where it obviously wanted to go.

THRANE STILLED, utterly captivated by India's sass, that she was giving him attitude despite what she'd been through.

He tried to appear unthreatening. He knew the impact of his size, and given what had happened, India wouldn't want a strange man too close. But he also had to make sure the attacker didn't come back.

Thrane had landed one strike on the bastard as they'd grappled on the balcony. That alone would have felled a mortal instantly. But a touch on Thrane's back—sizzling, inviting—had jarred his focus enough for the man to make a break for it. He'd lunged over the balcony before falling onto the road, then had raced off into the dark.

Instead of pursuing the attacker, Thrane's instinct had compelled him to turn around. Make sure India hadn't been hurt. Check if others were lying in wait.

Fucking hell, even now he should follow the attacker.

But he didn't want—couldn't leave India.

Because the sizzling touch had been *hers*. Her *gaze*. Setting his senses alight. And without doubt, it had been her gaze that had touched him in the erotic dream he'd had hours earlier.

Back on the balcony, after he'd decided not to chase the attacker but to go back to *her* instead, he'd risen from the floor and turned. Had seen her for the first time.

Adrenaline had surged. His heart had kicked hard in his chest. His blood had roared.

And now, back in the bright light, as she stood up to him … *Mine*.

By all the gods, this wasn't right.

This was the wrong place for lust. But more than that, he'd never let emotion—let another *being*, period—interfere with his vow.

A chill hit him. Could India be a weapon for the Order?

Gods, what if she was? He eliminated every threat. No matter who. No matter where. No matter if he had the world's biggest hard-on for her. He had to find out if she was a danger, intentional or not.

But right now, her hands were still on her hips and her eyes were narrowed.

"Well?" she asked.

A shaft of heat speared through him and he almost growled.

Fuck, now was not the time for this! He stabbed a hand through his hair, tried to say something. But staring into that amazing face, he couldn't speak.

Her eyes were a deep, fathomless green, filled with a fire that spoke of lightning and danger. Her face was arresting in its unusualness—a pointed chin below a wide mouth. A nose that was prominent in a librarian-look-down-your-nose-over-your-glasses way. Sexy.

Thick, straight dark hair. Mysterious.

Mine.

His whole body shuddered. He clenched his jaw. Shoved the drive to go to her far, far away.

He was the Keeper. First and always avowed to guard the World Tree. No one could get in the way of that. And if India knew the truth of him—the whole story—she wouldn't want him anywhere near her, period.

Yet he pushed off the wall, was about to move closer—

Simone rushed back into the room, Nate immediately behind her.

Thrane forced his muscles to relax, somehow wrangled his body under command. No other female in his existence had caused him to react like this. Not even Serephena, and she was a lord of the Underworld with the face of an angel and the body of a Valkyrie.

The unease that roiled in his gut solidified.

Thrane tensed again as Nate looked around the room, probably cataloguing everything and everyone there. But

Nate was a cop, and he had a job to do. Thrane respected that, as long as it didn't interfere with his vow.

Nate rested a hand on Sim's arm. "Thanks for calling me," he said. "I'll need to talk to you further, maybe everyone in the hotel, too, but first I need to speak with India."

Sim bit her bottom lip. "If you really need to talk to everyone, Mum's upstairs with Tara—"

"Let's leave them for now, hey? We'll have plenty of time to find out if they noticed anything. I called the ambo's just in case, and they should be here any minute. Could you wait downstairs and send them up when they get here?" Nate cut Thrane a glance. "Actually, why doesn't *everyone* but India head downstairs?"

Thrane snorted. *That* was interfering. He wasn't going anywhere.

INDIA RECOGNIZED her cousin Nathan immediately. Visually he was an older version of the boy she remembered. But it was more than that—she recognized his witchcraft.

Although his magic-scent had matured, developed, it was definitely him. When they'd been children, his witchcraft had smelled like a glass of grape juice. Now, it was like a good shiraz—powerful and not to be messed with.

"You grew up." She smiled up at him, realizing she had really, really missed him.

They'd been close as kids. While Nathan was a few years older, as the two youngest of their generation, they'd gone through every family get-together and school event—it was such a small school their classes had been combined—side by side. In fact, almost every major occasion of their lives had been shared. They might be cousins, but back then they'd been more like brother and sister.

She took in the physical changes—he was taller, his body had filled out, and his face had grown comfortably into its length.

She jumped up, hugged him. Fire flashed through her neck. She stiffened and couldn't contain a gasp.

He let her go immediately. "Shit, sorry. How bad are you hurt?"

Thrane pushed off the wall. "Careful," he muttered. He frowned at Nate, then India.

India tensed. Menace poured off Thrane ... but was it toward her, or Nate?

"I'm sore," India blurted, then filled Nate in on what had happened, including what she could recall of the man, eyeing Thrane as she did. He crossed his arms, but she was aware his gaze stayed on her.

"How did you manage to escape him?" Nate asked when she was finished.

The memory of her magic winding up, then exploding outward with enough force to break the man's hold on her replayed through her mind. But she didn't know how she'd done it. And she couldn't exactly talk about witchcraft in front of Thrane. She crossed her arms over her chest.

"It just happened. I didn't really think about it—I guess I knew what to do ..." She slid a look at Thrane. Did he believe her?

"How?" Thrane demanded. "How did *you* get away from *him*?"

"Don't snap at me," India whispered as loudly as her throat let her. "It's been a—well, a long night. And you haven't exactly been Mr. Nice Guy, although I suppose I have to thank you for helping—"

"Help? *Suppose?*"

Before Thrane could say another word, the ambulance team appeared in the doorway, one carried a large navy-blue duffel bag, the other a collapsible stretcher.

"Ah, I don't need that," India said, nodding at the stretcher.

"That's good to hear, love," said a paramedic, a lovely looking woman—maybe in her fifties, clearly of Polynesian ancestry. Her thick hair was wound up in a large bun, and she had a friendly face. "Hey, Nate."

Nathan nodded. "Steph, Alex, thanks for getting here so quickly."

The young man behind Steph was tall, almost skinny, with short yellowish hair. He smiled too and placed the collapsible stretcher out in the hallway.

Nate explained the situation, then Steph took over, and India found herself poked and prodded and measured and checked.

The whole time Thrane stayed, completely silent, and it was as if everyone but her had forgotten he was there.

Simone came back with a mug of tea and handed it to India, right as Steph and Alex were packing up their gear.

"There are coffee and hot cinnamon buns downstairs when you're ready," Simone said.

India blinked, cradling the warmth of the mug against her chest. "When did you have time to make those?"

"Reheated only," Simone said, giving her a small smile before she headed back downstairs with Steph and Alex.

Then India was left in the room with Nathan and Thrane.

The tension rose by a million degrees. India wanted to tackle the questions that were on her mind—there were *a lot* of them—but she was suddenly exhausted.

Would she make it to the bed? She didn't want to embarrass herself by pitching forward and passing out. Plus, both men looked ready to call Steph and Alex back, and then she'd end up in hospital.

Not her preferred outcome.

She placed the mug on the floor at her feet and ran her palms up and down her thighs a couple of times.

"All right, boys," she said, "I'm officially done. It's cold, and I'm exhausted. Why don't you continue this—*thing* you've got going on—downstairs, and I'll go to sleep."

Nathan said, "India, you can't stay here."

Thrane said, "This isn't a secure—"

They stopped, stared at each other.

And then Nan walked into the room.

India's stomach clenched. Holy crap, she wasn't ready for this.

"Nan! How did you—you shouldn't be here," Nate said, scrubbing his hand tiredly over his face.

"Nonsense, young man. Your cousin has come home, and this is the welcome she's received? I'm telling you, I'm taking her home with me, right now."

Now? India balked. She wasn't ready to face her grandmother. Not yet. Not now.

"Ah, Nan, I'm already checked in for the night. It's no trouble to stay and drive up—"

"My dear, I've already spoken with Simone and made the arrangements. No arguing."

India folded her arms. Thought about debating her sleeping arrangements. Except it'd take way more energy than she had. And it would only put off the inevitable for a few more hours.

She slumped back in the chair.

Nan nodded, then turned back to Nathan, though her gaze cut to Thrane for a long moment. "If you need to speak with India further, you can do so in the morning. At the farm."

3

MELBOURNE, VICTORIA

In the icy predawn air, Ri'Kiant pulled the shadows in around him to slide unseen through the back door of the inner-city building. Melbourne had ample such warehouses, with laneways and alleys in between that he could use to his advantage.

By comparison, the interior was lit with cool white globes and afforded him no shadows to cloak himself. Not that it mattered. Only his soldiers were inside. Nineteen of them raised their faces as he entered. They knelt in a large circle—a twentieth person lay inside it. He crafted concern on his features.

"Will he live?" Ri'Kiant asked, his own voice grating on his ears. It was nothing like the voice he was used to from his world. Not that these mortals would ever know the difference.

"Unlikely," Sean, one of the oldest recruits, said from his position at the dying man's head. "How Adam has survived this long is a miracle. Clearly our god is with us."

Ri'Kiant nodded. Sean was accurate there; a god *was* behind the survival of the soldier so far.

He made his way into the circle and knelt, placed his hands on the prone soldier's chest. The mortal heart barely beat beneath the rib cage. Remnants of stolen magic, given to the young male days earlier, was waning already. What a pathetic waste of death magic.

Ri'Kiant reined in the urge to slam his foot into the now useless body, to shake the life from the pitiful being with his own hands. Rage, the urge to destroy, to kill and maim, boiled up inside him.

But he forced it down. For now. None of these soldiers knew the source of the power they received—only that their "miracles" gave them speed and strength unlike any other human.

He could have performed the rite to remove the power, allow it to be passed to another. But once removed from its true owner, stolen magic—death magic—rapidly degraded.

With no need to squander the energy required for the rite, Ri'Kiant stood and said a prayer for the benefit of the kneeling soldiers. Their emotions responded in a positive surge at his words. His lips curled—he barely hid his contempt.

But soon enough the body and life force parted. The whisper of the force moved through the room, dissipated back into the universe, unnoticed except by him.

Ri'Kiant allowed his soldiers to cleanse the body in their customary ritual, and to send more prayers for a safe passing to the final world, before he redirected their focus.

"Where did he go, and what did he find?" Ri'Kiant asked.

"Trackers from our chapter in Europe reported sensing magic that belonged to a witchling thought lost years ago,"

Sean said, speaking again. He'd become their chapter's spokesperson of late. That would bear watching in the future. "It wasn't strong enough to determine an exact position, so we thought it prudent to send someone to her last known location. A place called Warragul."

Warragul. The child.

Ri'Kiant stifled a shout—from the thrill of hearing of one long-thought lost to them, and at the fucking incompetence of his own chapter.

But then his heart leaped, and he ignored everything and everyone as he rapidly calculated the dates.

A black moon would rise in six days.

His plan was working. His ice blood—courtesy of his Underworld heritage—surged, and a hiss of excitement carried to every single part of his body. But he forced himself to breathe low, deep.

He had to play a role of two parts, and at this time in the game he needed to ensure his fighters were perfectly trained and ready to execute the next phase of his plan. He barely maintained his crafted veil of empathy.

"Good work, Sean. Do you know what happened to Adam?"

"No. In our last contact he stated that he was in position in the town, then he turned up here a couple of hours ago. He'd been dealt a deathblow. I don't think he even expected to make it back here. No one else has ever withstood such a strike."

Ri'Kiant's lip curled. He turned away, unable to hide his contempt any longer. "And the witch?"

"We didn't hear from Adam again until he got back here. He could barely breathe, let alone speak. But surely he found something, right?"

Ri'Kiant clenched his jaw and nodded, allowed his soldier to deliver the rest of his report, including details of new witches they'd found. Finally, he sent them to meditate, his preferred conditioning to ensure the mind was as strong as the body. His soldiers needed mental strength as much as physical to fight the Keepers.

But the killer in *him* demanded appeasement now. Rage surged, bladed with the driving need to destroy. To hurt and maim and cut.

He cast his mind over the witches his team had under surveillance. Selected a mark to sate his thirst.

4
_____

HILL END

India woke up the following morning to the squawk of chickens, and holy crap, was that a rooster crowing?

A pale sliver of light rimmed the window from behind a heavy curtain. The rest of the room was dim, almost dark.

She lifted her head—stiffened as an ache throbbed through her neck—and tried to recall where she'd left her phone. Where was it?

Her heart calmed when she spied her phone on the bedside table.

She groaned. 6:10 a.m. Bloody chickens. Was their coop right outside her window?

Gingerly, she sat up, hissed as chilled air hit her.

Pulling the blankets back up over her chest, she rested against the headboard as questions tumbled on top of each other. Who was the attacker from last night? Why had he targeted her? Was it an attack on *her*, or had it been random, like a robbery and she just happened to be the mark? How had he even broken into her room? She *knew* she'd latched the door.

And where had the strength in her magic come from? No way could she have broken free from the attack without the aid—albeit unbidden aid—of her magic. She had no experience to understand the nature of the magic she'd used last night. The more she thought about it, the more the questions piled up.

She wanted—no, she *needed* answers.

Which was why she was here.

As fast as her sore muscles allowed, she pulled on black jeans and a long-sleeved T-shirt, then her favorite thick green jumper. The knit was so soft to the touch she'd had to buy it, even though Brisbane only got cold enough to wear jumpers a few times a year.

She ran a comb very, very lightly through her hair. She still had a sore spot at the back of her head, so left the thick mass as it was.

Finally dressed and feeling a bit more normal, India pulled aside the window blind and found that her room faced the inner yard, which had huge sheds on the other side. A childhood memory surfaced of clambering over, under, and all around the haystacks with her cousins. Man, they'd had fun.

With a sigh, she dropped the blind, left her bedroom, and walked down the long, narrow, darkened corridor that connected the bedrooms and baths in this wing of the house.

The hallway was separated from the living areas by a timber door. Another sliver of light, this one golden and warm, shone with welcome between the door and the floor. Low sounds echoed through the timber from the other side—more than one person was talking in the next room. She listened for a moment, making out three distinct voices even if she couldn't make out their words.

The butterflies roared back into her stomach. This was it, the moment she'd see the family she hadn't seen—well, before last night, anyway—in eighteen years.

She took a deep breath. Opened the door.

Nan, Nathan, and—crap—*Thrane* were in the open-plan kitchen and living area.

Thrane sat at a six-seater timber dining table, which was pushed close to the wall near her. She froze mid-stride— what was *he* doing here? And at this time of day?

His dark gaze was locked on her, as if he'd known she was going to walk through the door. His kind-of-curly hair was a little neater than it had been last night, the ends hitting the collar of his red-checked shirt.

Wrenching her gaze from his, she forced her legs to move, and almost walked into the dining table.

At least the stumble took her attention off Thrane. She quickly glanced up—right as Nate swiveled toward her. He sat on a stool at the kitchen bench, hands wrapped around a mug, a grin tilting his lips.

"Morning, cuz," Nate said, lifting his mug. "Watch out for the table. You might not have noticed it there, seeing as how it's so big and all."

"Ah, sarcasm. My favorite way to start the day," India said with a low laugh. "And good morning to you too." She looked past Nate, to where Nan stood in the kitchen, her small frame mostly hidden behind the bench, her silvering hair swept back from softly rounded cheeks.

"Nan," India said.

"India." Nan's soft blue eyes crinkled at the edges, and the smile that lit up her face made India's heart melt.

It was her mother's.

Tears warmed India's eyes. She'd never thought to see that smile again in this world. She walked past Thrane and Nate, went straight to Nan, and enfolded her grandmother in her arms. Or maybe she was the one enfolded. Regardless, she held on tight.

Nan's magic-scent washed over India. Brought with it memories of freshly baked scones. Lavender from the garden. The leather and tang of horses and tack. And it spoke to India, somewhere deep inside, of home. Of family. Of power.

Nan might be seventy, but her magic was clearly as strong as ever.

And in that embrace, something expanded in India's chest, a connection to Nan that she'd never expected to feel. Maybe it had always been there, just waiting for India to return?

The butterflies that had been whipping around her stomach slowed down—still present, but not nearly as sharply winged.

She didn't realize tears had spilled over her cheeks until she saw them mirrored in Nan's.

India eased back, suddenly hesitant to give so much so soon.

"I didn't expect to be crying on my first day back," she said, scrubbing the tears from her cheeks.

Nan smiled, though her eyes stayed serious. "Words will never convey how happy I am, we all are, to have you back. Welcome home, my dear." She leaned in and kissed India gently on the cheek. "Now, no more making *me* cry. I'm going to make you a tea. Or do you prefer coffee?"

India swallowed the lump in her throat that threatened to rise up again. "I'd *kill* for a coffee."

"Your voice is still so strained," Nan said. "Here, sit down. How are you feeling? And no murder needed for the coffee. How do you like it?"

"A little milk, thanks, no sugar." India stood still for a moment. "Are you sure I can't help?"

Nan waved her to the table. "Sit, sit. And no, dear. Nate insisted we get a machine last year. Apparently, our instant brew wasn't good enough. I can manage a pod and milk. Now, please, sit down. Let me make it for you."

"Well, okay," India said and rubbed her hand over her thighs once, before she took a seat. "And thanks." She looked around, suddenly aware of Thrane and Nate both watching her intently.

Their regard made the back of her neck itch. Looking for something to say, she nodded to the prep area. "I have the same model. Next best thing to an espresso."

"That's what Nate says." Nan smiled.

In the next moment, a cold, wet sensation butted against her hand. India yelped, then laughed—a blue heeler, one of Nan's farm dogs, sat under the table, its big brown eyes staring up.

"Hello, there," India said. She reached down and let the dog nudge her again with its soft nose and take in her scent before she scratched beneath its tan short-haired chin.

"That's Smokey." Nathan gestured with his mug. "He's Nan's oldest, part of the family."

India smiled, at least this was one family member she could be easy around. "Hello, Smokey. You're beautiful, aren't you?"

Still smiling, she glanced up. Met Thrane's intense stare.

Was suddenly trapped in that fierce melted-chocolate gaze. Finally, he dipped his head once.

"Morning," he muttered.

"Ah, morning to you too."

Thrane looked to be in his mid, maybe late thirties, though it was hard to be certain. And while his otherworldly scent teased her senses, she still couldn't pin it down. It wasn't magic exactly ...

A shiver of awareness coursed through her, along with the urge to walk over and get close to him in any way possible. Exactly the same urge as when she'd first seen him.

So much for last night's effect being a fluke—a stress reaction or something. Clearly not. She'd never been pulled —reeled in—like this before. She forced herself to think of something else.

"Nan," India asked, "who do I thank for bringing my bags in?"

Nan looked up and over at the dining table. India followed her gaze.

Chocolate eyes crashed back into hers.

"Oh, thank you." India held his gaze, refused to back down, even as her cheeks prickled and flooded with heat.

Even as his eyes narrowed and his jaw ticked.

Nan came over and handed her a mug of coffee.

"Thanks." India smiled, grateful for the interruption. She took a sip. The warm, smooth bite hit her, and she sighed in true appreciation.

Nan brought another cup over to Thrane.

India let out a pent-up breath, surreptitiously eyed Thrane over the rim of her mug.

Strong, tanned forearms, revealed beneath the turned-up sleeves of his shirt, flexed as he held his mug with two hands and lifted it to take a sip. He visibly sighed too, and his carved jaw unclenched.

India mentally shook her head, forced her eyes back to her own drink. This infatuation, or whatever it was, was seriously bizarre.

She'd made the trip to Victoria because she needed answers, information. And in the few hours she'd been in town, her list of questions was already bigger, more urgent.

Becoming spellbound by a stranger—even if he was the hottest man she'd ever seen—didn't feature anywhere in her plan. India forced herself to focus on her goals and took a small breath, hoped no one noticed her nerves.

"So, I'm India. Nice to officially meet you. Who are you, and what happened last night?"

"Thrane."

A current of unseen tension crackled, and the hairs on India's arms stood up. But she wasn't going to be put off. She took another sip of coffee.

"Is that a last name? First name? Even a name at all?" she asked.

He chuckled. "Do you doubt me?"

"Well, you didn't answer my question."

"*You* didn't answer mine."

Rolling her eyes, India leaned forward. "That *was* my answer. Now, who *are* you?"

"Well, I've already answered, but as you don't believe me, what would you like to hear this time?"

She sat back with a huff. "Still a non-answer. Let's move to the next question. What happened last night? And don't try to fob me off. I'm too sore and have an egg the size of a"—she ran a hand gingerly over her scalp—"well, an egg, on the back of my head."

No sooner had she touched her hair than Thrane stood up and moved behind her, ran his hands over her head.

"Hey." She tried to turn around and shrug him away. "No touching the person who doesn't know you."

"Ah, but you do know me. I'm Thrane, remember?" He pressed firmly on her shoulder. "Keep still, I'm checking it out."

"How about asking permission next time?"

"There'll be a next time?"

Warmth prickled through her. Oh no, not that again. She tried to shrug him off once more. "Not the point. You don't just touch a person's head without asking."

"Fine, may I please look at your injury to ascertain if you need more medical treatment?"

She rolled her eyes. "I was checked last night, remember? They gave me the all-clear."

"Let him look, dear," Nan said. "It's better to make sure that we don't need to call the doctor out."

India almost growled but instead pursed her lips and sat down. Shot Thrane a look. "Be careful."

"Of course."

"You know that mild tone is annoying, right?"

"I do now. Thank you for telling me."

Nathan snorted from his seat at the bench.

India rolled her eyes—at both of the men. But Thrane's hands gently parted her hair at the scalp. He lightly probed the knot on her head.

"Ouch—that hurt!" She flinched and he stopped immediately. "What's the verdict?"

"Any dizziness, nausea this morning?"

"No."

"Then you'll live." His hand lingered on her shoulder.

India blinked. How long was he going to stand there?

"Great, thanks for that," she said and rolled her shoulder, dislodged his touch. Ignored the chill that followed where his warm palm had just been.

"No trouble," he murmured.

"So, back to my question, Thrane—what happened last night?"

"That's more my question. How did you fight off the attacker?"

"You know that's twice you've managed *not* to answer my question? And yes, I'm counting."

"Stop bickering, you two," Nan said as she took a packet of frozen peas from the freezer. "Here, India, keep these on your head for a few minutes. Now, please, humor an old lady and tell me how you managed to get away?"

India glared at Thrane—who was he to boss her around? She wasn't about to explain in front of him that a surge of her uncontrollable magic had been responsible, but she also didn't want to start a fight—yet. She moistened her lips.

"It was instinct, Nan," India said, "that's all. I kneed the guy in the balls—groin. I got lucky."

A look passed between Thrane and Nan and her heart sank. Her lie of omission hadn't convinced them.

India held the bag of peas against her head. The hairs on the back of her neck rose—and not because of the frozen vegetables. Something was up with her family and Thrane. What was it, and how did it involve her?

Clearly, she was going to need a plan to get her answers. Just as well she was a good researcher—she had to be as a communications manager. She mapped things out until they made sense, so that's what she'd do now.

Nan was in the know, undoubtedly, but she was clearly very, *very* stubborn—there was no guarantee she'd open up. India put her last on the list.

Thrane was definitely a good option—the way he'd dealt with that person last night, and the fact that everyone accepted him, especially her family, put him in a position of knowledge. The problem with him, though, was that she really didn't know him; she had no idea if he'd be open with her—he certainly hadn't been so far. So she'd try him for info, but he wasn't at the top of her list.

She could try Nathan, but as a cop he might be even harder to extract information from than Thrane.

Maybe Simone from the hotel? She'd seemed genuine, and clearly had some form of witchcraft, so it might be best to start with her. If India planned it right, she might be able to get some one-on-one time with Simone today when she went into town to get her car.

With a plan in mind, she decided to hold off on interrogations for now. She removed the peas from her head.

"So, Nathan, when did you start going by 'Nate'?"

"I don't know," Nate said, glancing at Nan. "Around when I finished high school?"

"It suits you," India said. "There are so many things I've missed, and I'm only now realizing just how many."

Nate and Nan seemed to take that as an opportunity to fill her in on all the changes around the farm and with the family over the last eighteen years. The chat was lovely, but India sensed they were glad to be talking about anything other than the attack.

Only Thrane didn't participate. He nodded occasionally and accepted another coffee from Nan. While he didn't stare outright at India again, she knew his gaze kept coming back to her. Every time it did, warmth prickled along her skin, as intensely as if he'd reached out one of those large, strong hands and run it straight over her.

This awareness of another person—of Thrane—was on an entirely different level to anything she'd known before.

And look at how everyone else had responded to him at the hotel last night. The paramedics hadn't batted an eyelid at having him there. Nate hadn't been able to get him to leave the room, even though he'd practically ordered him to go. And now Nan treated Thrane as if they were in some secret society, for just the two of them.

What was going on here?

"Hello," a feminine voice called out from the front door. A woman, perhaps in her fifties, walked into the room, followed closely by a man of a similar age.

"Mum, Dad," Nate said. He stood up, hugged them both. "What are you doing here so early?"

India's mouth went dry. More family? That meant more people who hadn't come to Mum's funeral.

"We're here to see our niece, of course," Nate's mother said, peering over Nate's arm. "We can't stay long today, but I promise we'll be back for a longer visit soon."

"Ah, hi. Lovely to meet you—that is, see you again, Aunty, Uncle," India said, trying not to look relieved at hearing they couldn't stay for long.

Nate's mother smiled easily. "No, no, please, call us Vera and Jack. Now, may I give you a hug?"

Before India knew it, another person she barely remembered was hugging her. Her uncle Jack followed suit, though he was more reserved. India returned their hugs, awkwardly half-sitting, half-standing, and registered their magic-scent. They were both witches, though not as strong as Nathan, and certainly nowhere near as strong as Nan.

Vera explained that Jack was an accountant—he had an early meeting with one of his clients—and Vera was a vet's assistant and helped out with the farm animals. She was headed out to Nan's stables to check on a mare and her foal before going to work.

Both Vera and Jack treated Thrane as if he were part of the furniture.

Nan walked Vera and Jack out when they left, and India took the diversion as an opportunity to set her plan in motion.

"Nathan—Nate, if you're heading into town could you drop me at Simone's place? I need to pick up my car and also want to check in on Simone, she had a pretty rough night as well, and I'd really like to say thanks in person."

"Well, I was going to take your statement formally," Nate said, running a hand over his hair. "That needs to be done this morning. And you know, one of the guys from the police station can drive your car out here. I'll take them back into town with me afterward, save you the drive."

"Thanks for the offer," India said, "but I'm—"

"I can drive you into town to get your car," Thrane said, shrugging his shoulders. "It's no trouble."

Nate's eyebrows flew up, but he didn't say anything.

India paused. Thrane's offer would give her a chance to probe him for information.

Her belly tightened and her body warmed. An hour beside all that muscle ... that delicious scent ...

Crap, maybe getting a lift with him wasn't such a good idea. Answers, she was here for answers. And look how hard it'd been to get a straight response out of Thrane so far—

plus the way he and Nan traded weird looks. Something funky was going on.

She'd have more luck with Nate. No doubt. And that was *not* a flash of disappointment zinging through her.

"Thanks," India said, forcing a bright voice, "but surely I've taken enough of your time already."

She tried a guileless smile but must've botched it because his eyes narrowed. Clearly, she needed to get rid of him if she wanted to make progress.

She pivoted to Nate. "Do you want to get started on this official statement now? I'll head into town with you once we're done."

Nate's gaze briefly landed on Thrane, then cut back to her.

"You always were stubborn," Nate said with a sigh. "All right, let's get started."

"You're off the hook, Thrane"—India gave him another bright smile—"but thanks again for the offer."

Thrane muttered something as he rose from the chair, his body unfolding, then rising to his towering height. She blinked. He was every bit as tall as she remembered. He held his lips in a straight line and pierced her with his glittering gaze before saying goodbye and leaving.

India barely held in a sigh, somehow managed not to shake her head as his seriously impressive body—even from the back—disappeared from view.

The warmth in the room disappeared and she rubbed her arms, suddenly cold.

Nate left too, and India took the time to simply sit. She'd reclaimed her equilibrium by the time he came back with his laptop.

"Okay," Nate said. "I'm going to type up your official

statement, then get you to sign it. We can start with what you said last night, but you might have remembered some more details between then and now, so I'll also ask you some further questions."

India reflexively touched her neck. Suddenly her throat was too tight—and she couldn't get the words out.

The kitchen door opened, and Nan came back inside.

Nate filled her in on the statement process, which was just as well because India still hadn't found her voice.

Then Nan sat down and placed her hand on India's. India flinched, then bit her lip. "Sorry, didn't mean to jump. I wasn't expecting the ..." she wanted to say touch, but thought better of it, "the support."

"Don't worry, dear." Nan kept pressure on India's hand, and the tension that had bottled up in India's throat released enough for her to speak.

Nate let her explain everything for the first time. Then he started asking questions, occasionally referring back to the handwritten notes he'd taken the night before. How tall was the offender? What did he say? Did India recognize him at all? Did he have any identifying features or tattoos? Did she know anyone who would want to hurt her? Had she told anyone she would be staying at the hotel?

She worked out her attacker's height by recalling where his head had been as they were against the wall.

But apart from remembering that he had short hair, she didn't recall enough details to answer the rest of his questions.

Each time she gave a negative response, Nate's shoulders tensed. His lips tightened.

"I know I can't tell you much about what he looked like,

it was so dark I barely saw his face, but what do you think?" India leaned forward. "Was he a local?"

"Not sure yet. The description you've given, height and hair, will help us sift through anyone known to us." Nate's jaw ticked, but his voice stayed even. "But it may also be that he was passing through town, opportunistic, you know? I'll print this off then get you to sign it. Nan, can I use your printer?"

After India signed the paperwork, Nan turned to Nate. "Nate, dear," she said, "could you pop out to the stables? I left my hat by the goat's shed, and you know what happened to the last one I left there. Would you mind bringing it in?"

"Can do, Nan. Enjoy some time with India."

India held in a snort. What was her grandmother up to? That had been the most obvious "give us some privacy" request she'd ever heard. She sat back, eyed Nan, and waited.

As soon as the kitchen door closed behind Nate, Nan leaned forward. "Now, what are you up to, young lady?"

"Nan. I think that's my question. Why did you just get rid of Nate?"

Nan's smile tightened. "Because I wanted to get you alone and ask you what you're up to. We might not have seen each other in a lot of years, but I can still tell you're hiding something."

India contained a scowl. *She* was hiding something? Fine, if Nan could keep a secret, so could India.

"I'm not up to anything," she said with a shrug.

"Dear, don't think that just because I'm your grandmother you can pull one over on me."

India sighed and crossed her arms. A truth slipped past her lips before she could catch it.

"I wanted to reconnect with the place Mum called home. I miss her." India swallowed the lump in her throat. She wasn't ready to forgive Nan—didn't know if she could—for the lack of contact. Slowly, she met her grandmother's gaze. "You must miss her too. At least I'd spent time with her recently—you hadn't seen her for eighteen years."

Nan closed her eyes for a long moment. When she opened them, their soft blue-gray depths were awash.

"I missed her so much," Nan said. "Every damned day. She's—she was—my daughter. For every breath I breathe, I will always hold a love for her like nothing else. And for you." The tears gently welled over and tracked softly down Nan's cheeks. "You need to know that your mother left here for a very good reason, India, and she didn't take you away from your family lightly." Nan used the back of her hand to wipe her cheeks. "But she had my full support, and she knew it."

"I know it was a long way to go, but, well, no one came to the funeral." India cleared the lump suddenly filling her throat, forced her voice to remain steady. "I—ah—I wasn't sure how welcome I'd be here."

Nan's face paled, and her eyes filled with more tears.

"Crap." India unfolded her arms. "I don't mean to upset you, Nan. I'm, well, I'm really just trying to understand it, that's all." She took a deep breath. "I have questions, so many questions about magic. About Mum."

"Oh, my dear, you are absolutely welcome here. This is your home. And I wanted to be there with you, with Annie, one more time—so very, very much. We do have a lot to talk about, don't we? Maybe you could humor your grand-mother, take a couple of days and settle in. Take the time to reconnect with this old farm and with your family's magic."

Nan squeezed India's hands before she let go. "The bla—the new moon is seven days away. Let us make a family circle and bring you in, then you can ask your questions—and have your answers—in safety."

India wanted to ask why they needed the circle, why she needed safety to ask her questions, but she didn't push any further. In fact, she'd heard the most important answer she hadn't known she'd been seeking. Her grandmother cared.

The emotional wall that had surrounded India's heart crumbled a little further.

But her resolve to get answers strengthened. What had compelled her mother to leave her family? If Nan wasn't the reason, who or what had been?

5

Needing fresh air, India ventured into the yard. The morning was still crisp under the autumn sun. She shifted on her feet in the gravel driveway, which wound all the way from the road to the front door, and tightly crossed her arms to find some warmth. Tried to find some level of calm, too. Recounting the attack for Nate, and then having the conversation with Nan, had left her raw. Edgy.

She purposefully took a deep breath, made herself look around.

The lush green grass—more carpet than lawn—in Nan's garden invited her to wander between the elegant flower beds. Some bushes bore blossoms that hung like little white bells, while others grew heads of lavender-colored petals as large as her hand. It was a riot of colors and shapes. Magical.

She was tempted to wander between the enchanting beds, but ... there was something else she wanted to see, so instead, she remained on the driveway. Gravel crunched beneath each footfall as she followed the path toward the cottages. To the one at the end—the one that had been her childhood home.

Would her memories be close to the real thing?

She picked up her pace.

Rounding the garden, India halted in the soft, springy grass that separated the cottages from the driveway. The two little buildings must have undergone extensive changes, because no matter how hard she tried, she couldn't find anything familiar. The cottage from her memories was gone.

A chill wind swept around her.

She pressed her lips together, held in the sob that wanted to escape.

Memories. That was all she had left. Images flitted, movie-reel fast, through her mind—their little dining table, the pot-belly heater, the cozy kitchen. Love. Laughter. Warmth.

Right then, with every ounce of her being, she wanted to reconnect with her past. Her father and mother.

Both gone now.

A hollowness, bone-dry and bone-white, grew within her. She hugged her arms tighter to her chest, swallowed the sudden constriction in her throat. They were memories of a lifetime ago.

The wind picked up, swirled around her ankles, nipped at her heels like Nan's blue heelers.

What the—? Wind had never done that before.

She turned around, half expecting to see an actual dog at her feet, but no, it was only the swaying grass that tickled her ankles.

The wind pushed harder, and she almost laughed at the comical sensation. Her spirit lifted, and she let the wind dog her steps. It propelled her forward until she found herself in the side paddocks, well beyond the cottages and completely out of view of the farmhouse.

Here, the land gently fell away in a series of paddocks that had been used in rotation for decades. Autumn sunlight filtered through the clouds, casting a warm glow over distant hillcrests. She stopped after several paces, breathed in the crisp, sweet air as it swept in over acres of land.

In front of the farmhouse, horse paddocks ran down the slope of the hill to the road, which wound through the gully, but here, the field before her appeared empty—the word "fallow" came to mind. In the far distance was a gray timber fence, barely visible—the property boundary.

India stilled, closed her eyes. Without conscious will, her magic welled up from within, reached out and touched the energy of the land around her.

The cool long green grass. The rich dark volcanic soil. The gum trees that towered into the sky, with limbs gently swaying and creaking, their leaves breathing life into the air.

And then a soft magical touch—a kind of magic she'd never known before—brushed her mind. The touch was a statement of life and love and history and *knowing*. This *was* her land. This *was* her place. The land *was* magic.

Goosebumps prickled up her neck, and so, so slowly she opened her eyes—stared out over the land.

How on earth had she, a born witch, never known that magic wasn't only in her will but in the world around her?

Holy crap, she had a lot to learn. But one thing she knew now, the magic of this land was in harmony with her—or, more accurately, she was in harmony with it.

She scented more magic in one place than in any she'd ever been in before. As if all the magic ever practiced here had left traces of itself—perhaps even of the practitioners—forever embedded into the land.

And then a different magic brushed her mind. Distinctive. Warm and gentle. Yet enormous. It bespoke an age and a depth of purpose far beyond the land.

India followed the direction of the touch, slowly turned north toward the back of the farm. The land ran on for over a hundred acres until it melded with the state forest.

Nothing unusual stood out, but that calm touch stayed present, a patient knock on the door to her mind. Waiting. Waiting for her to do something.

But what?

Absently, she rubbed the sensitive skin at her neck, and the magic-touch on her mind moved too. To the very spot beneath her fingers.

Warmth bloomed where the magic-touch lingered on her neck. The soreness drifted away. The sense of emptiness eased.

Even the jagged wall of fear and hurt and anger that had emerged and grown stronger every day since her mother's funeral began to soften.

"India!"

The shout broke her concentration, and she dropped her hand. Holy crap. The ache in her neck was gone. And it's disappearance was due to the presence that called to her from the forest.

Whoever it was, she was grateful for their help.

"India, can you hear me?" Nan's voice rang out again from the direction of the house.

India went to head back, except ... she hesitated, her gaze drawn back to the vista of the valley and distant hills. She didn't want to leave such peace and acceptance.

Determination flowed through her—she would discover how this magic had been lost to her.

"I'll be back," India whispered to the land and to the unknown touch, smiled at the answering whisper of the breeze on her cheeks.

How wonderful, how amazing, was this? She inhaled one last deep breath of sweet, crisp air, then slowly walked back.

"India!" Nan's voice carried over the breeze from where she stood in the middle of the driveway.

"I'm here, Nan, no need to yell. I was looking around," she said. "So where's Nate?"

"Oh, he got a call, dear. Work, he said. He had to leave right away."

India stared at Nan for a beat. "He was going to take me into town. To get my car."

"Well, I'm sure he'll take you in when he comes back. And wouldn't that be better, that way you can get some rest? Oh, and, India, dear, the farm has changed since you were here last. Why don't you wait until one of the family can show you around before you do any more exploring?"

"Nan, I'm an adult. I can look around by myself, and no one will want to babysit me, I'm sure. How much trouble can I get into, after all?"

6

The next morning, Thrane was transplanting a tray of bulbs in one of the greenhouses—or at least trying to concentrate on the task—when the rumble of a motor and the heavy crunch of tires on gravel announced a visitor.

He sighed. What the hell? He'd hardly managed to get any chores done, given all he could think about was India. Might as well see who it was. Few people had the code to his front gate, so at least it would be someone he knew. Small talk with strangers was not his thing.

He packed in the potting mix, wiped his hands on his khaki cargo pants, and left the greenhouse right as Liz's truck pulled to a stop in front of his house. He walked over and opened the driver's door, offered his hand to help her out.

"Bah, I'm not that old yet, Thrane," Liz said.

"Liz." He steadied her as she stepped down to the ground. "Don't be an arse. You're one of my oldest friends in this world. You know these hands have been used for fighting—only the gods know how many fights they've been in—but they're good for more than that. Like being lent to a friend when needed."

"Ha, don't think I didn't hear that reference to *this* world. I know you've got a few Otherworld friends, remember? Wasn't there something about a special lordette of the Underworld, maybe Serephena?"

Thrane groaned.

"Only you would be able to ferret out that old tale. Let me guess, Elaine told you?" But he didn't deny the charge. "Drop the lordette, though. Serephena might not take kindly to having her rank subjugated."

"I'll take that under advisement." Liz's blue eyes grew steely. "India insists one day of rest is enough. She's going into town to get her car."

"*Liz.* You were supposed to keep her at the farm. What the fu—"

"Thrane." Liz glared at him.

"Who's taking her?"

"Nate's driving her in after lunch. But he'll stall until I return."

"That's something anyway. His magic is almost a strong as yours."

Liz's lips tightened. "The black moon will be here at the end of the week. The family can come together then and perform the ritual to re-shroud her magic, but I'm worried it's too late."

"*Too late*? I'm still seriously concerned she *is* the danger, remember? You need to explain this ritual. Come inside while I wash up and tell me about it."

He led the way inside and cleaned up as quickly as he could. By the time he walked back into the kitchen, Liz was pouring boiling water into two mugs, Irish Breakfast tea bags already in the cups. He kept a supply of her favorite blend.

Thrane waited for Liz to sit at the kitchen table before he took his own seat.

"Liz, I've known you since you were a babe," he said. "Gods, I've known all of your family since your grandparents came to this land. The only one I haven't known from the cradle is India—and that's part of my issue here. I don't know her." He tried to gentle his voice. "And she's been gone for eighteen years ... so neither do you."

"Thrane, I know this is hard for you. You weren't here when India was born. But Annette absolutely believed the attack that killed Jev was meant for India."

Thrane dropped Liz's gaze, stared down at his mug and curled his fingers tightly around it. The familiar burn rose in his chest. His best friend had died—had been *killed*—for helping him.

Thrane was the one who was supposed to have been in danger—he'd been fighting an unknown army in the Underworld—yet Jev was the one who'd gotten fucking killed.

"Jev's last words were that India's magic was the danger," Liz said.

Thrane's blood instantly iced over.

"Liz, we've been over this before. Surely you see the other possibility. I don't like it any more than you do, but Jev's words are what they are. India and danger. And look at her this morning—clearly she's hiding something."

Liz again glared at him. Again, not a new reaction.

"Don't start, Thrane. Just because Jev said India's magic was the danger doesn't mean it's a danger to the Tree."

"Jev was a Keeper, Liz. He might've only recently joined

us, but his foremost duty was the safety of the Tree. It makes sense that he would be concerned with anything that endangered it."

"I know you put your duty above all else," Liz said, shaking her head a little, "but I believe, *truly* believe, that Jev's duty included protecting India as surely as the Tree. Trust me, being a parent changes your perspective."

"That's not the issue. I'm saying that Jev's words indicated India and a danger. It's not something I can ignore, you know that."

"Thrane, listen to me, please. Annette believed India was *in* danger. Annie was a spellcaster like no one else in our family—it made sense that she turned to a spell to keep India safe. She cast a shrouding spell every new moon to hide both of their magic from all supernatural sight. No magic tracker, no scryer, no dreamer, could find a trace of India's magic. Annette told me years ago that the spell was so strong, it hid India's magic from everyone, including India."

"So how strong is she? And does she know her power?"

"I'm trying to work that out. I—I don't want to push her too hard. She was so wary about coming back that if she runs now, she may never return."

"Liz, now's not the time to sanitize the truth. India needs to know—whatever we're willing to share, anyway. And *we* need to know what's going on. Look at what happened last night."

Liz closed her eyes and drew in a shaky breath. Thrane rested a hand on hers for a moment. She was one tough lady —the gods knew she'd been through more than her share of tragedy, yet she kept on going.

She opened her eyes, the steel in her gaze still present, and he nodded in approval.

"Last night's attack only makes me more certain that India is the one in danger," Liz said. "Do you think it was someone from the Order? What about her father's family? Could it have been Freya or Evine trying to find her?"

"India's Higherworld family won't try to hurt her. They might want to claim her—gods, not might, they *will* want to. And that means they'll take her back with them, have Fate record her in their codex. But they won't hurt her."

Liz paled. "Jev's family *and* Freya will claim her?"

"No, Freya is a god—she's only ever interceded when the Tree was in dire need of her help. But Evine ..." He grimaced. "She's not a god, so she doesn't have to stick to the same rules. And she's not just a warrior in her own right, she leads the house. As India's grandmother, if Evine knows about India, she *will* try to claim her."

"Evine can't claim her. India's only just come home. And she knows nothing about them."

"Jev's family don't understand the meaning of no, Liz."

"Bah, Jev was easygoing."

"That was Jev." Thrane shook his head. "His brother Oev and his mother Evine—well, they're something else. Let's hope they gave up trying to find India when Annette left."

He didn't hold much hope, although he didn't say as much. Liz was already upset enough. But given how rare supernatural children were—and how the Heavens worked —India, even as a mortal, was a commodity Jev's family wouldn't want to squander. But they weren't his immediate problem.

"Liz, we need to know more about the attack. Why India? Why that hotel room? I was downstairs when she screamed. Scared the shi—hell—out of me. And I landed a strike after we crashed through the window. No human could've walked away from that."

"Well, thank the lord you'd gone into town."

"You ordered me to." Thrane cut Liz a glance. "And it illustrates my position. If India knows the danger she *may* be in, she'll be far more likely to heed my—your—requests to stay at the farm. At least there she has the protection of your magic."

"Thrane." Liz's tone indicated patience, but he knew she was more stubborn than the bull she had in her paddock. "I might be older than everyone, except you, of course—and don't roll your eyes at me—but I'm still the head of my family. And I'm doing what I believe is best."

Thrane considered Liz for one more moment before taking their mugs to the sink to rinse. "I hope your course is the right one, although I don't believe it is." Drying his hands, he turned back to Liz. "I'll take her into town to get her car."

"You hate town."

"I know."

Thrane saw Liz off, then quickly changed out of his work clothes. Because he needed to move. Because his interest in India was about more than just the threat she posed to the Tree.

And hell, interested was too tame a word to explain his driving need to be wherever she was. Ants crawling under his skin would've been more comfortable than the itch he felt to get near India, from the moment he'd seen her. No, that wasn't even right—from the moment her eyes had landed on him.

India Jones was proving to be a stubborn—hardly

surprising given that Liz was her grandmother— compelling, intriguing woman. Who placed the Tree in deadly danger.

Which frustrated as much as it worried him. Desire never swayed his actions. Why now? Why with this one mortal woman?

He locked his house, jogged to his car.

And the gods help him if India was as attracted to him as he was to her—although ... if she was, it would be the perfect excuse to keep her close.

Because that was his job. His vow came first. Always.

7

India hopped into the cab of Thrane's pickup truck, shaking her head at the abrupt change in plans. Nate had finally been about to take her into town, then Thrane had pulled up to the farmhouse and commandeered the role of her driver.

And, crap, she was both annoyed and pleased about the change. From the moment she'd met Thrane, he'd been ... intense. Bossy. Way too sexy. Dangerous.

Something inside her screamed at her to run away, fast. Probably her primitive hindbrain being totally sensible. But the rest of her screamed the opposite. Get as close as possible.

It had to be her hormones, although why they'd chosen now to go into overdrive, who knew?

She buckled her seatbelt as Thrane hopped into the driver's seat. The moment the car doors shut, his warm sent filled the cabin, teased at her senses.

She cut him a surreptitious look as he drove away from

the farm with his jaw set and his hands gripping the steering wheel so tightly his knuckles were white.

Clearly the man didn't like her. So why the big effort?

And damn it, she'd planned on getting answers out of Nate on the drive. Well, Thrane had decided to take over the role of driver, so he could be a replacement for questioning, too.

She crossed her arms and purposefully turned away from the patchwork of rich browns and reds and greens as the countryside raced outside the car window.

Thrane glanced at her at the same time.

"Have you seen much of the farm yet?" he asked.

"Not really. Although I did go looking for the cottage we used to live in. I hadn't seen it since—" A hot lump rose in her throat. Crap. She turned to the window, swallowing the lump before looking back at him. "I hadn't seen it since before my father died. I was just a kid when it happened."

Thrane glanced at her, and his gruff voice lowered. "Sorry, didn't mean to make you upset."

"It's okay. I've had a long time to adjust to Dad dying." She didn't mention her mum. She took a deep breath, maybe if she kept their conversation easy, he'd open up. "So, tell me about yourself. You seem pretty comfortable at Nan's, almost like a member of the family, but I don't remember you at all."

Thrane shrugged, his shoulders pulling at the seams of his work shirt. "Well, I've been around the area for some time. I do a fair bit of business with Liz, plus help with her garden."

"So you're a gardener?" she asked, pulling her gaze from his shoulders.

"Technically, I'm a horticulturist."

"As in, you have a nursery?"

"Yep. And I write a little."

India sat up a little taller, looked at Thrane's profile a little closer.

At first, the idea of this fierce man-mountain being a gardener, let alone a writer, jarred. But then India recalled the intelligence that had blazed from his chocolate eyes. Maybe the idea wasn't so jarring after all. A zing of interest arrowed through her.

"Where would I have read your work?"

"Do you read about gardening?"

"Ah, no."

Thrane shrugged.

India hid a frown. This was like pulling hen's teeth. But she wasn't about to give up.

"Nan mentioned your land borders hers. Is it the land at the back of her farm?"

Thrane's grip tightened further on the steering wheel.

"We share a small boundary. What's with the interest in me?"

"What? No. I'm not interested in *you*. I'm just getting to know Nan's neighbour."

Prickly heat worked over her cheeks, and she opened the window, pretended to enjoy the view until the crisp air cooled her cheeks.

Except, even as her cheeks cooled, that darkly warm scent seemed to wrap around her more snugly. And the heat in her belly coiled tighter.

"What about you? What's Brisbane like?" Thrane asked.

"Brisbane?"

"That's where you live, right? What's it like? Any boyfriend pining for you to come back?"

"What? I am not discussing my boyfriend situation with you."

Especially since there wasn't any boyfriend situation. Her last relationship had ended maybe two years ago. He'd been an office coworker, but he'd moved to a different company and eventually they'd parted ways. No animosity. No regret. Relationships had always been that way for her— ho-hum. Take 'em or leave 'em.

India blinked. Holy crap, how had she missed that it had been such a long time? No wonder she was having hot dreams about a fantasy man. Her gaze drifted back to Thrane's chest.

She quickly looked away. *Focus, India*. Answers. She was here for answers. Not a hot-bodied man. And she needed to play nice if she was going to get anywhere. She rolled her shoulders, forced her body to relax.

"Brisbane is lovely," she finally said. "Great weather most of the year, although it gets so humid in summer it's like you're walking into a wall of sticky, consuming heat."

"Well, you won't have to worry about humidity here. So what exactly do you do for work? Liz mentioned freelance-something."

India resisted the urge to bare her teeth and growl—did he really think he could turn this interrogation around?

"That's right," she said, forcing a smile. "I started my own business a few months ago. Actually, I thought I'd talk to Simone about her business experience while I'm in town. She seems pretty accomplished. Look at how she managed what happened, right?"

Unbidden, memories of the attack flew past her vision. She shivered, had to swallow the lump that suddenly lodged in her throat.

Finally, she moistened her lips. She wasn't going to be distracted from her questions.

"Were you staying in town the other night? The ... attack happened very late. And you were right there."

His lips tightened. "I was in town late, happened to be walking by when I heard your scream."

"You just happened to be walking past the hotel at that very moment."

"Yep."

"Right," India scoffed. "Then everyone, even my cousin, lets you call the shots. The gardener bossing the detective?"

Thrane's jaw clenched tighter. "I told you, I was just there."

She turned toward him as far as her seatbelt allowed. "You 'were just there.' That's your explanation?"

The cold bite of tension ratcheted up inside the car, but India folded her arms, set her chin. Refused to be put off.

Thrane might as well have put a stop sign over his forehead as a giant frown tightened his face.

She saw red. Goosebumps rippled up her neck and her magic scent hit the air.

Lightning exploded right by their car. Thrane ducked, and the car swerved.

"Fuck!" he shouted.

"Holy crap!" Heart thumping, India searched the sky. "I didn't know there was a storm."

"There isn't," he said, eyes narrowed.

"Well, don't glare at me. I don't control the weather."

India resisted biting her lip. *Had* that been her doing? It had been way too close. If it *had been* her doing—unconsciously—it needed to stop because she didn't fancy being barbecued. And no matter how annoying Thrane was, she didn't want to fry him with an errant lightning bolt. Yet.

She took a slow, deep breath. Focussed on the road ahead. Thankfully, no more lightning scared the crap out of her, and her heart gradually resumed its normal rhythm.

Outside the car, the paddocks and pasture gave way to houses and small shops. And then they were driving through the outskirts of town, a little patch of rural suburbia.

Thrane tried to engage her with a running monologue of how the town had grown, changed, over the years. But India saw his conversation for what it was—a distraction. She swore under her breath. This interrogation had gone nowhere.

The moment Thrane pulled the car to a stop outside Simone's hotel, India unbuckled her seatbelt, opened the door.

"Give me a call when you're heading home and I'll drive behind you," Thrane called as she got out of the cabin.

"You've got to be kidding."

Thrane's eyes tightened. "Don't want you getting lost on the way home, that's all."

"The farm is not my home." Something tensed in her stomach. She pushed the sensation away. "And there are about four roads to get to the farm, so I'm *not* getting lost."

"But I have to head there anyway. Why not drive together?"

She rolled her eyes—clearly, Thrane and her family didn't want her going off on her own. She pinched her lips and she swallowed the urge to yell, *what the fuck is going on?*

Deep breaths, India. Deep breaths. Now was not the time

for more batshit magic. Except playing nice had gotten her zero information from Thrane so far.

"Thrane. Enough is enough. Are you going to tell me what the crap's going on?" she asked between clenched teeth. He stiffened and India snorted. "Never mind. I'm going to see how Simone's doing. Get my answers another way."

She managed—barely—to avoid slamming the car door behind her.

India was still boiling when she walked into the hotel's small guest lounge, but when she spotted Simone sitting on a sofa with a little girl in her lap—they were reading a book together—her anger dissipated.

Instantly two separate minty magic-scents—one mild, one potent—tangled in India's nose. She picked them apart as easily as nutmeg and lemon.

Simone looked up, and a smile brightened her face.

"India, hi," she said.

"Morning, Simone." India smiled back.

"No, no, please call me Sim. I wanted to call but wasn't sure when would be a good time. How are you? Have you heard any news about—?"

Simone bit her lip, dropped her gaze to the child. India understood immediately.

"All good," India murmured. "Hi, you must be Tara?"

"Oh my gosh, you haven't met yet, have you?" Sim smiled and looked into her daughter's face. "Tara, this lovely lady is India. She's Liz's granddaughter. You know Liz, don't you? And India, this is Tara, she's my four-year-old princess."

"Very nice to meet you, Princess Tara."

"Thanks," Simone mouthed.

"No worries," India mouthed back.

"Tara and I were about to head upstairs and have a cookie," Simone said aloud. "You can meet my mum, too. She lives with Tara and me in the residence on the top floor. Would you like to join us?"

"Absolutely."

INDIA FOLLOWED Sim and Tara up to the second floor and into their apartment. Sim's mother, June, was sitting at a chunky dining table, close to a wall of windows. She turned her lovely gray eyes to India, but after one slow nod and a quiet greeting, she stared back out the window.

Sim nodded toward the kitchen. "Coffee?"

"Sure." India picked up the hint and joined her.

Sim chewed at her lip for a moment, then quietly said, "I just wanted to let you know that Mum can be ... withdrawn. Please don't worry though, that's just how she is. Tara and I go about our business as if nothing's amiss."

India nodded. "Of course. No worries at all."

"So, how did you say you have your coffee?"

Sim made instant coffee when India insisted there was no need to go downstairs for an espresso. India accepted the mug with a smile, and they sat at the table with June.

India glanced around the open-plan kitchen and living area. "How awesome that you live right here above your business. I wasn't expecting such a large space."

"Yep, it's way bigger than what we had when we lived in the city. And I love being so close to the business, especially since I do most of the check-ins and check-outs myself." Sim grabbed a tin from the center of the table and removed the lid with a flourish. "Now, I promised choc-chip cookies. Help yourself."

India didn't wait to be asked twice and nabbed a chunky cookie. After one bite she held the cookie up to inspect the lumps of chocolate goodness. "These are delicious. Did you make them yourself?"

"Thank you," Sim said with a grin. "And yep, I made them. I don't do a lot of baking, but making cookies is a pleasure and I get to eat the end product which is even better."

India chuckled. She took in Sim's magic-scent again. It was mild, but definitely there. Hopefully she was open to answering some questions.

"So, how did you end up in Warragul? Did you say the other night that you're also newish to town?"

"That's right. God, you've got a good memory, especially after what you've been through. I'm actually one of the luckiest people you'll ever meet, or at least I was about eighteen months ago. I won the lotto."

India sat back in her seat. "Wow. Wasn't expecting that."

"Nope, not many do." Sim laughed

"Huh. You're the first person I've ever known to have done that."

"It's incredible, isn't it? I was walking past a news agency, and I had this feeling something amazing was in that store. The next thing I knew, I'd bought a ticket—the cheapest one you can get, you know? But it was weird, because I can clearly recall, as I walked out of the store, feeling as if a door was opening in front of me, and I could never go back. The next day I checked the ticket, and well, here I am."

"That's amazing. And you're right, that story is the luckiest I've heard. You won the lotto because of a feeling." India took a small breath. "Can I ask a personal question?"

Sim nodded.

"This might sound odd," she continued, "but have you always listened to your intuition?"

"Intuition?"

"Mm, that sensation you had about buying the ticket. That was your intuition, right?"

"Well, yeah, I guess." Sim took a sip of her coffee. "And yeah, you could say I have a good intuition. I'd like to say I *listened* to it more often. Why?"

"Mine rarely leads me wrong, either. I'm listening to it right now actually." India took a deep breath. She'd never broached this topic with anyone other than her own mother. "Because my intuition is more. More than normal. More *other*."

Sim stared quietly for a moment, her whiskey-colored eyes assessing. "What do you mean?"

India moistened her lips. Was Sim being evasive, or did she really not know about magic? How could that be, given she and her daughter were clearly witches? India's heart thudded hard against her ribs.

"I'm a witch," India said.

"Oh." Sim said, her smile dimming.

India held Sim's gaze. "Yep."

"You're not kidding, are you?"

India's heart sank.

Then Sim's phone beeped. "Looks like Thrane's here to check on the door," Sim said. "Do you mind if we pop down and see him? He's in town for the second time in two days— that's practically unheard of."

India trailed Sim downstairs, still absorbed by their brief

chat. Sim was aware that her intuition was strong but clearly had no knowledge of her witchcraft. Which was odd given her age—witches were born with their power and it usually grew with them—well, except in India's case.

Sim looked over her shoulder as they rounded the last turn in the staircase. "India, what you just said—"

"What's that?" A deep voice called up the stairs.

Sim jumped and whipped around.

"Hell, Thrane," she said, "you bloody did it again."

Thrane stood in the doorway to the office, his wide shoulders filling the opening. "What? Me?"

His words were for Sim, but as India met and held his gaze, she was drawn once more into a sea of decadent, silky hot-chocolate. She forced herself to blink and cut the connection. She didn't—suddenly, couldn't—say a word.

"Scared the hell out of me," Sim said.

"I was simply standing here." Thrane held out both hands. "Nothing scary in that."

India snorted.

8

As India brushed past Thrane and entered the cozy room, the scent of hot spice bloomed in her nose and her body clenched. She stumbled over a side table that she swore hadn't been there a moment ago.

Thrane's heavy-duty cargo pants hugged his tree-trunk thighs. His flannel work-shirt strained across his wide chest, leaving no question that ripped muscles lay underneath.

India's heart kicked, and heat slowly burned through her.

"Be back in a few minutes, India," Sim said, disappearing.

India took a deep breath. Had she been staring at Thrane this whole time? She walked over to the bookcase-lined wall, trying to find her equilibrium. Something she'd struggled to do around this mountain of a man ever since she'd first seen him.

Had it only been two nights ago? There was no way she'd known him for less than two days. Everything, every single atom of her being yelled that she knew this man on a far deeper level.

She turned around. "Thrane, I have to ... no, I *need* to ask you a question. And you need to be honest—no more evasions—this is important."

Thrane's eyes tightened, and for a moment he regarded her silently. Finally, he nodded. "All right."

India blinked. That had been easy. Too easy.

"How about we have a seat?" She gestured to the sofa nearest him, then sat on the other—only he sat beside her. Of course he did. Settling his massive frame into the cushions as well as he could, he shifted slightly toward her.

Again, that dark and spicy heat brushed her with invisible fingers, and a tingle shimmied from her head to her toes. Taking a quick breath, she reached out with her magic —which was surprisingly easy to do—and pushed it toward Thrane. Searched for the hum of energy as she'd done the night before with Simone.

Sure enough, there it was—a pulse, an electrical hum so full of energy that it almost zapped her. That tingle shivered through her again, and she barely contained her excitement. India could read Thrane's ... well, she didn't actually know what it was, but it had a razor edge that belied his seemingly relaxed state.

Her eyes narrowed. Why the calm facade?

More questions to add to her evergrowing list.

But she did know one thing—whatever she'd picked up, she'd *consciously read another person!*

Oh crap, he was staring at her. Probably because she was staring at him.

"Er, right. Well, I actually have a few questions, quite a few. Can we start with"—she wanted to say "who you are" but the words that came out were—"why do I feel like I've known you forever?"

THRANE WAS ON FIRE. By the gods, all he had to do was sit beside India and his blood heated. What was it about her that got to him?

She wanted answers, and he honestly believed she should be given a version of the truth. He—*they*—needed to keep her under control. Having India asking questions all around town, which clearly, she was hell-bent on doing, was the exact opposite of that. So he'd use their obvious mutual attraction—hell, he was the Keeper, he'd use any and every advantage possible—to protect the World Tree.

But then a delicious, sizzling heat and a fresh crisp scent spiraled closer and closer. Wrapped around him. His mouth watered for more of that sizzle, more of that scent on his tongue, on his body, around him, in him.

He met her gaze, and her green eyes captured his. His heart began pounding. Heat flooded his groin and all he wanted was to drag her across his chest and ...

He swallowed hard.

Fuck. This did not bode well.

When India had descended the hotel's old staircase minutes earlier with a smile on her face, seemingly relaxed and happy, he'd stopped and stared. His words had frozen. Something alien had spread through him, his heart picking up, his body warming. A smile had fucking curved the corners of his mouth. A *smile*. Just from being in her vicinity.

Now she'd asked why it felt as if she'd known him forever.

He wanted to roar with satisfaction. To know she felt the same—to not be alone in this storm of emotion and sensation raging within—incited his desire further.

"I have no idea what's going on here," Thrane said, "but I can't get you out of my head."

Her pupils dilated. Her mouth opened. But she didn't back away from him, and by the gods that delighted him even more.

"But you don't even like me."

Like her? Like was too tame a word for this overwhelming need. This craving that crawled under his skin and sent his blood pounding.

"Not true," he growled. His gaze dropped as the tip of her tongue moistened the smooth, lush skin of her curved lips.

Lips he wanted under his.

Blood surged in his veins. He leaned down—careful not to touch her. Lips a breath above hers, he paused and searched India's emerald eyes. She nodded once, her gaze full of permission for the caress.

Thrane gave in to the urge that had ridden him hard since he'd first seen her. But at the last moment, he reined in his ferocity and reached out to cup the curve of her cheek. Then, lightly, ever so softly, he touched his lips to hers.

Attuned to India's every move, he registered the stiffening of her jaw beneath his palm, her indrawn breath, and somehow steadied himself to withdraw—

But then she moaned. Her lips pressed into his.

Silky strands of her dark hair brushed over his skin. Heat coursed through him. Gods, he needed ... more. Needed to band his arms around her. Drag her onto his lap. Push inside her. Needed *her*.

Thrane forced himself to enjoy the pure touch of her lips, to hold back any other contact, still conscious of her attack the night before. But he may as well have been holding back a wildfire. An inferno raged inside him, and his penis pounded in rhythm to his heartbeat. He slanted his mouth hard over hers.

Devoured her.

He wanted to spread her jean-clad thighs over his erection, palm the hot curve of her buttock, shape the curve of her breasts. Somehow, he had the presence of mind to release her cheek and clench his fists at his sides, unleashing his desire through their kiss alone.

Again and again, he molded his lips over hers.

Her tongue tangled with his. Fire raced through his body until every nerve, every layer of his skin was ready to burst. If he didn't get his hands on her, he was going to explode.

HOLY CRAP, she—they—were going at it hard and hot. This wasn't the plan. They needed to stop. India needed to stop this now. She tried to focus on why she was here. She'd been after answers, not pleasure so enticing it clouded all reason.

Except, it was.

It was exactly what she wanted. With the guy she'd met less than forty-eight hours earlier. The same way-too-sexy guy who wasn't even touching her. Why wasn't he touching her?

Touch. She needed touch. His.

India grasped his arms, and solid muscles jolted beneath her grip. His growl echoed in her ears, and she wanted to lift her eyes and see his face, but all her thoughts, all her concerns, submerged beneath a layer of desire so strong her hips shifted forward. To hell with the reasons you shouldn't kiss a mysterious, sexy almost-stranger—

A panicked cry echoed through the hotel.

The thin shout cut razor-sharp into India's skin. It arrived on a distorted current of energy, the blurred lines of the cry an immediate call to action.

She wrenched back. Thrane's eyes glittered down at her. His lips slanted in a feral curve, and his chest heaved. He was the hottest, most dangerous thing she'd ever seen. And everything inside her clenched for him.

But then the desperate cry came again on razor wings, and like lightning, adrenaline replaced desire. India pushed Thrane to one side and ran out the door.

Goosebumps raced up her neck, the tang of magic—hers—flooded the air. And suddenly, a visible trail of energy, the energy that had carried that cry, snapped into view.

Instinctively, her magic revved in a spike of power, moved from an unconscious state to complete awareness. And in that state, she fully recognized the currents of energy that abounded everywhere she looked.

They swirled, they darted, they languidly danced and rolled, but everywhere, they *moved*—and they were colors, and they were noisy, and she knew that they were, somehow, alive.

Everything in her wanted to stop—to take in the majesty of a world she'd never seen before—but the currents that had brought the cry still rippled and distorted from all the others. Still carried a sense of desperation that made India's mouth go dry.

Those currents were so dark a red they were almost

black, with jagged edges that sawed the air around them. And in that moment, she was so aware of the energy currents, so in tune with their message, she could've followed them even with her eyes closed.

Thrane ran behind her, and the currents made way for his energy as it leaped ahead of him, a racehorse biting at the bit.

They raced through the ground floor area into the kitchen and out the back door.

Sim's voice echoed from somewhere—she was yelling her daughter's name. And then India saw where the currents led.

A small form lay huddled on the concrete driveway at the far end of the lot. In a burst of speed, Thrane moved ahead of India and reached the figure first. India stumbled to a stop, fell to her knees beside Thrane and ...

Tara. She was on her side, curled into a tight ball, wrapped around a small bundle of dark fluff. The currents around Tara were sluggish and pale. Quiet.

Thrane gently placed his hands on the little girl's shoulders and then pushed her midnight hair away from her face. As he did, the ball of fluff—just a pup—opened its eyes and licked Tara's chin. Tara stirred, and India expelled the breath she hadn't known she was holding.

The paleness of Tara's face was broken by a large graze on her temple, which was speckled with beads of blood.

Sim arrived, fell to her knees.

"What happened?" she demanded.

"Sim." Thrane grabbed her arm. "Don't move Tara yet. We need to check her over. Just hold her hand, try to keep her as quiet and still as you can. That's it."

The puppy began to wriggle, so India scooped it up.

"Do you sense anyone else here other than us?" Thrane asked, looking straight at India.

She quickly looked around. "No. No one else is—"

"No, not with your eyes. Like you did before. Use your craft. I know you can do it. Gods, I saw you inside. We need to know now."

And she knew what he meant.

She tried to see the energy currents again, but her normal sight was back—she couldn't see or hear or feel anything that wasn't actually in front of her.

"I'm trying."

India closed her eyes, forced out any other sound or sense. Focusing on the center of her body, and using the memory from her earlier mad dash, she visualized her energy. It was bright, made up of millions of crystalline drops in shimmering hues of greens. The crystals spun around and around.

And then she was connected.

When India opened her eyes, the currents of energy were all around her once again. Tara's energy currents were crystal-shaped like India's, but they were pale, their colors muted, the currents slowly spinning.

Sim's were also crystals. They threw off sparks that threatened to become a firestorm, furiously spinning in different directions, only to be jerked back into a semblance of order. Somehow, Sim was holding herself together.

Even the pup had currents of energy moving around it, although they weren't crystalline in appearance.

Then there was Thrane. His crystals were cold and hard like diamonds, with a bright-gold inner fire, but glacial on the outside. And they were ruthlessly held in order—not one stray orbit, not one stray color or flicker.

And there was one more trail, different to all others. The currents that created it were frozen in midair. While every other energy current moved, these were absolutely motionless. They created a perfect line out through the back of the lot, disappearing from sight behind the surrounding property fences.

India wanted to get up, follow the trail on foot, but that would be totally reckless. No way was she doing that.

Maybe she could use her magic to follow the trail? She closed her eyes again and focused all her attention on pushing her energy currents toward the trail, but her first push sent them in the opposite direction. Luckily it was a weak push, and her currents hit the back door of the hotel before she corralled them back into herself.

Drawing in a steadying breath, she tried again and this time sent her currents in the right direction—for a minute. But then she lost control and her currents rushed in all directions, like a deflating balloon zigzagging through the air. She scrambled to bring them back together and got them under control right as the world started to spin around her.

India opened her eyes. Her head swam as if she'd held her breath underwater for too long. At least she'd been able to determine one thing before she'd lost control.

"No one else is out the back. Now. But someone was there, that much I can tell you."

Thrane gave a short nod. "Can you call an ambulance?"

"Yep." India wobbled to her feet. Where was her phone? Crap, it was upstairs with her handbag, in Sim's apartment. She forced herself to run—stumble—inside.

She ran up the two flights of stairs, gasping for breath by

the time she reached Sim's apartment, and pushed the door open.

Sim's mum, June, still sat at the table staring out the window, exactly where she'd been earlier. India's handbag was on the table beside her.

India quickly found her phone and called Nate. He promised to be there soon—apparently he'd come into town too.

India was about to tell June what had happened when she realized Sim's mum had a full view of the courtyard below.

June suddenly grabbed India's hand. India jumped.

"You ... shouldn't send yourself," June whispered. You'll get ... lost."

"Crap. You scared me. Ah, Sim–Simone's down there. With Tara." India pointed out the window.

She glanced back, but the older woman continued to sit and stare out of the window. A new shiver, wholly unrelated to Tara, crept up India's spine. She pulled her arm from June's grasp.

"Right, well, I've got to go. Back down, that is," India said.

Rubbing a hand over the tender point on her arm, India ran downstairs right as Nate entered in a rush through the main door.

His jaw was tight, his normally sparkling eyes flat. "Where?"

"Out the back."

"Wait here for the ambulance, then bring the medics through. They're coming now."

India nodded, and by the time she turned around, two paramedics were entering the building. She led them quickly through to the back yard, then stood back while they took over from Thrane.

Thrane stood up, and as he did the black pup let out a whimper. Thrane picked the pup up, looked it over, then tucked it into his chest.

Then Thrane looked right at India. Into her. Without a word, he stepped to her side, close. His heat seeped into her, warded off the cool that threatened, even in the midafternoon sun.

Eventually the paramedics told Sim that while Tara had no obvious serious injuries, they wanted to take her to the local hospital for further assessment. When Sim crumbled, Nate placed an arm around her shoulders and walked her out with Tara and the paramedics to the ambulance.

In the now quiet back lot, India blew out a steadying breath and looked up at Thrane.

"You're not a witch. So how do you know about magic?"

9

R i'Kiant staggered as he reached the car he had stolen in the very early hours of that morning. It was parked at the farthest end of an abandoned shopping complex that reconnaissance had shown had no CCTV monitors. The concrete was cracked, uneven with scraggly weeds. The perfect place to stash a vehicle.

He fumbled with the handle, lurched into the car. Didn't even close the door.

Dropped his head back against the headrest, cursed as more barbs of fire lanced through him. What the fuck had gone wrong? His plan was one he had utilized immeasurable times in the past and always with success: find an animal, use it to lure his target to a secluded place, sacrifice the target, steal their magic, and slake his burning thirst for death.

The witchling had fallen for the lure. He had placed a hand on her chest to commence his ritual. And then he had known pain on a level he'd never experienced before. His very skin had bubbled and blistered where it had made contact with that ... that *thing*.

Agony pulsed throughout his limbs. He'd let her go instantly, but the fire and barbs had stayed—only to grow and grow. He'd staggered to a patch of shade, using the space to cloak himself.

Amid calls for the witchling and the sound of boot steps pounding toward him, he had run, staggered, and fallen all the way back to the vehicle.

Sweat drenched his skin, the first experience of it his body had known.

A knock cracked on the vehicle's window.

An unfortunate young man appeared at the open door. Ri'Kiant sprang up and reacted with all his rage and violence feeding on the pain of his earlier encounter. His fists flew, met the giving flesh of the chest before him.

Minutes, maybe many of them later, he stopped his assault and looked at the bloody, pulpy mess leaking on the broken concrete. He darted a look around him, but he had no reason to be wary—this end of the old complex was dead.

As dead as the body at his feet.

His rage over, Ri'Kiant surveyed it. The body didn't contain witchcraft, but since blood continued to spill, the heart must still be beating. After such an attack, it was somewhat remarkable.

He decided then to perform the rite of sacrifice. His current physical state dictated the need for more strength. This vessel held a pittance, but any aid in the pursuit of the final goal was warranted. He spared another glance around the lot, made sure there was no other being in sight.

With that, he withdrew his ritual knife and went to work on the only patch of skin not reduced to pulp.

10

———

Thrane sat at Liz's kitchen bench, staring into the bitter black depths of his coffee.

"By the gods, Liz. It was out of this—any—world. India knew exactly where to find Tara. Then she knew no one else was around. And I swear, she didn't call a spell. It was as if she just fuc—just knew it." The fine hairs on the back of Thrane's neck pricked to attention. "I've never seen anything like it."

He rubbed his neck. India's magic the day before had been impressive. And scary. What else could she do?

Thrane didn't mention the kiss. Hell, he couldn't believe it had even happened, let alone how powerful one fucking kiss could be. The urge to get back to India—and this time get his hands on her silky skin—surged right along with his blood. But it cooled just as quickly.

Look what had happened the last time the Order found the Tree with their stolen death magic.

What if they got India's?

What if India was an agent for them? It was clear she was hiding something.

The black moon was four days away, and his role was absolute. Protect the World Tree against *all* dangers.

Oblivious to his internal struggle, Liz braced her arms on the sink and stared out the kitchen window.

"It must be from her father's side," she said. "We don't have anything like that in my line."

This was what worried him—it would take strong magic to kill the Tree, even with a black moon on the rise. The kind of magic that India seemed to wield. He took a careful breath.

"Annie was a strong witch, though," Thrane said. "And look at you and Nate. You all have the strength in your genes to pull the big spells."

"Yes, but those are spells. We can't just call on magic out of nothing."

"Is that what India's doing?"

Liz shook her head but continued to look out the window. "I don't know."

"We have to watch her closely, Liz. If her magic is as strong as it seems ... well, you know the danger she poses." He waited for her to reply, but Liz stayed focused on the view outside the window. "What are you looking at?"

He joined her at the sink. Out by the stables, wearing blue jeans and a green jumper, India held the reins of a fully saddled bay horse. Nate appeared a moment later, leading Liz's largest horse, Timothy.

"Where are they going?" He shook his head. "Never mind, let's pick this up later, Liz."

Thrane headed outside, ignoring the crisp air that greeted him as he strode over to the horses.

India looked up first. Her hair was pulled back in a ponytail that swung with her movement, the dark locks brushing her shoulders. The sun picked out blue highlights that Thrane itched to stroke. He knew how silky her hair was—recalled vividly the cool slide of it over his hand.

His body tightened. Gods, he had to get himself under control. He cleared his throat, more forcefully than he'd intended.

"Where are you off to?" he asked.

"India wants to see the farm," Nate said. "We could all do with a little break from the worry of the past few days, so I offered to take her on a guided tour."

Thrane read the message—Nate wouldn't let India get near the World Tree.

But as much as Nate understood the need to ensure the safety of the World Tree, he wasn't the Keeper—not that Thrane didn't think he was fit for the role. But Nate was being bloody stubborn, and if the World Tree was calling him, he hadn't let on.

But that didn't matter now. Only one thing did. And no way in fucking hell was Thrane letting India roam about the farm without him right by her side. Looked like he was going for a ride.

"Nate, I wanted to check out our border fence today anyway. Why don't I go instead?" Thrane said, rubbing a hand over Timothy's shoulder. "Tim and I know each other well enough, and it'd be good to get a ride in."

The truth rang inside him for a moment. He really would like to take Tim for ride. He loved horses, but in this age, he'd found less time—and need—for riding on horseback.

"Ah, thanks, but I'm going to spend some time with Nate," India said.

Thrane threw a fast look at Nate.

"Listen, India," Nate said, "I'd really wanted to get some work done on the case today and then head into town, see if Sim needs anything. If Thrane's free to show you around, that works for everyone."

"Of course," India said. "I called Sim this morning already, but if you see her, please let her know we're all thinking of Tara. Thrane, I don't need to take up your time. I'm sure I can get around the farm okay on my own."

"When was the last time you were on a horse?" he asked.

India lifted her chin. "Eighteen years ago."

"Right, so probably not a good idea to head out on your own, then. Even with gentle Gemma here." Thrane gave Gemma a light pat. "I've got this, Nate. You take care of whatever you need to."

Nate handed over Tim's reins. Along with one hard look. Thrane read it easily—don't hurt India.

"Do I get a say in this?" India asked, folding her arms.

"Let's see. Do you want to ride or walk?" he asked. Not that it mattered. He'd be India's shadow wherever she went.

She scowled up at him, fire igniting in her emerald eyes, then opened her mouth as if to say something but a moment later shook her head and turned away. "Fine."

Thrane stared hard at her back for a moment. That had been easy.

India ran a hand over Gemma's neck. "Okay, sweetheart, let's do this. Hope you live up to your name, though."

She lifted one foot into the stirrup and hoisted herself into the saddle. Her legs were long enough that she straddled Gemma easily. And the rounded curve of her backside, visible as she slid into the leather seat, had Thrane's pants growing instantly tight around his groin.

He bit back a groan. This was going to be torture. Especially since the woman seemed to have no interest in going back to where they'd been yesterday.

INDIA HAD to bite her tongue to stop from demanding answers from Thrane right there. It was either that or throw herself at him, and that wasn't happening.

Yesterday's kiss had been an aberration. Seriously, even if the guy was a walking wet-dream, she wasn't getting liplocked with him again any time soon. Not only had the maddening man-mountain not answered her question yesterday, now he was acting like she'd never even asked it. And what was with the weird authority he had over her family? Nate had been perfectly willing to go for a ride until Mr. Maddening came along.

But damn it, she did want to see the farm and she did want to go for a ride. From the moment she'd seen Gemma, memories of sitting bareback on these gentle giants had surfaced.

Gemma shifted slightly, forcing India to focus on the here and now.

It was obvious her family thought they were managing her—well, she'd let them think that while she went ahead and found the answers she needed. On her own. And keeping Thrane at arm's length was the best course of action. He had too much sway over her family already. Letting him have any sway over her too didn't seem like a good idea.

But that didn't mean she couldn't grill him. And this ride was the perfect opportunity.

As Thrane smoothly mounted Timothy, the big gray horse danced a few steps. Thrane tightened his thighs and reined Timothy in, patting the horse's proud neck.

"Steady on, lad. I've got you." Horse and man steadied together. Thrane looked straight at her. Heat and liquid-chocolate combined. "Let's go."

Oh man, she was a goner.

The clip of hooves rang comfortably in India's ears as Thrane led them down the aisle of the small stable. The tang of hay and tack and horse tingled in her nose. And a little tendril of warmth uncurled from deep inside her—that scent, it connected her to years earlier in this very place. India took a deep breath and absorbed that knowledge; this farm was her heritage.

The veil of time moved as more childhood memories flowed back, countless days spent running around the stable and being shushed by adults. Of her mother bringing horses in from the paddock to saddle up right here, brushing them, feeding them, tending to them. Her mother had loved those horses.

A lump formed in India's throat—her beautiful mother. Tears pricked at India's eyes, but they didn't fall. She took a deep breath, forced the lump down.

India owed it to her mother to discover why she had left this—her family, her horses—behind.

Gemma lifted her head and gave a soft whuffle. Drawn out of her reverie, India smiled, leaned forward, and rubbed Gemma's neck.

"Good girl," she said.

Thrane pulled ahead of her, but he looked back over his

shoulder, dark eyes mysterious. Assessing. He waited until she'd caught up.

"Are you all right?" he asked.

"Yeah, I am. Just had a moment. The stables ... well, the scent, it reminded me of something. From a long time ago."

Thrane eyed her again. What he was looking for, she had no idea. But eventually he nodded.

"I wanted to check the lower paddock on the other side of the hill, that's where Liz and I share a border fence." Thrane gestured up the rise to the north. "Are you okay with that?"

"Of course."

And then a playful breeze caught the end of her hair before darting around her shoulders and trailing off and over the paddocks. The same wind that always carried her into the forest in her dreams.

The forest that waited on the other side of the hill.

She considered asking Thrane about it but decided not to say anything. The only reason she knew about the forest was because of her dream—and that was one dream she wasn't willing to share with anyone. No need for anyone to think her unhinged. Yet.

As they crested the hill, India forced herself to not dwell on her memories or dreams, even when the land called to her with more recollections. Liz's farm lay spread out; cattle grazed in some paddocks, while others were clearly for crops.

Eventually, Thrane and India rode into a large open paddock, a small dam visible in the distance before farmland gave way to scrub, bush, and then forest. The scrub was a mix of earthy greens and browns, then farther in, where the forest grew true, the dense foliage was a deeper green again. Not vibrant, but strong and tested. Tall rambling bushes were dotted here and there around the bottom paddock. Another memory surfaced, and India turned quickly to Thrane.

"Are those blackberries?" she asked.

"Yeah. Why?"

"I remember them, this place." India laughed. "We used to come down here, I'm sure of it. We used to bring buckets so we could pick blackberries for Nan to make jam, but we'd end up eating them straight from the bush. Although there were a lot more bushes then. Or at least it seemed like it."

"Yeah, I suppose there were. Most of them have been cleared, because even though the berries are absolutely delicious, they're considered a pest."

"Why a pest?"

"They grow like nothing else," Thrane said. "If you're not careful, they'll take over a paddock or spread into the forest. We've got management plans for them, but somehow I doubt we'll ever eradicate them completely."

"You sound like you don't think that's a bad thing?"

"Like I said, blackberries are delicious. Want to see if any are ready to pick?"

"Yeah. This is one childhood experience I want to relive as an adult."

India dismounted and, as she did, glanced toward Thrane's property and the endless forest beyond. The wind rushed in behind her.

The presence she'd sensed on her first day back was with her again. And the presence was excited. India's heart picked up—she was close to it, closer than ever before.

Thrane clapped her on the shoulder, suddenly right beside her, and the force made her stumble.

He grabbed her arm to right her. "Sorry," he said.

The presence from the forest retreated—and the memory of yesterday's kiss flowed through her. Heat flooded her, low in the stomach.

"Ah, I'm okay," India said.

"C'mon, I'm going to write an article about current management techniques for blackberry bushes, so we might as well get a good close-up look."

"Where do we secure the horses?"

"We don't. They can't get too far, the paddocks are fully fenced. Besides, they'll come back when we call, if they leave us at all. They're more likely to hang around and eat some of this fresh grass."

A smile teased Thrane's lips, and his hair hung over his brow. He looked comfortable and relaxed as he led the way.

India eyed the head-high brambly bush. Between red- and black-tipped leaves, thorns clearly spiked out from the stems. And hidden behind the leaves, perilously close to the thorns, were berries. Some were red, but a few were black.

"Did you say you're writing an article about these?" India asked.

"Yeah, I write freelance for a few horticultural magazines. You write too, don't you?"

"I do copywriting and editing for corporate communications and just opened my own freelance editing agency. I can work from home, and the work has loads of variety, which I like."

"Is it hard to get clients?"

"Not so far. The corporates I've worked for in the past like it because they only have to pay me per piece but I'm already acquainted with their operations." She looked closer at the bush. "So, why this plant?"

"Well, blackberries have a bad reputation with their pest status and all, but there are some great thornless and non-invasive varieties available now. Writing about those could really change people's perception about them."

"Change people's perceptions?" India couldn't help but smile. "That sounds pretty ambitious for a thorny berry bush."

"Uh-uh, not just any thorny berry bush. Here"—he deftly picked a glossy black berry—"try this."

India eyed the berry and let Thrane place the fruit in her mouth. A sweet tang burst on her tongue.

His melted-chocolate gaze caught her, held her utterly spellbound. His mouth tightened. A tinge of color hit high on his cheeks. Those masterful lips were a breath from hers once more. That traitorous warmth expanded, hit her breasts, her core.

But she wasn't going there. No way. She needed information—not kisses. No matter how bloody amazing those kisses were. She swallowed hard and turned away. Took a deep breath. Finally, she cleared her throat.

"Yep, that was delicious. Let's have some more." She reached into the bush and hurriedly picked the first berry she saw, though she wasn't as deft as Thrane, and a thorn grabbed her on the way. She shook her hand. "Ouch."

"Let me see," Thrane said.

She couldn't let him get any closer, or she'd lose every sane intention she had and throw herself at him.

"No, no. I'm okay, see? Just got bitten by the blackberry bush trying to nab this morsel." She held up the large berry she'd scored and showed the scratch along her hand.

Thrane grabbed her forearm. "You might not want to eat that one."

"Hey, no grabbing!" She tried to jerk her arm away. "Of course, I'm going to eat it. I earned it."

"You earned a spider?"

India came to a halt. Her attention zeroed in on the berry—and on the black spindly legs she now saw creeping around it.

Her heart leaped. She screamed, dropped the berry. Jerked back even harder. But Thrane still held her arm, and her feet flew from beneath her, sending her tumbling toward the thorny brambles.

"India!"

"Holy crap!"

She tried to fall away from the thorns, grabbed Thrane right as he pulled her into him, and then the ground rushed up to meet her.

Thrane hit the dirt first, then she collided with his chest, her breath whooshing out of her lungs.

"Bloody blackberries," Thrane groaned.

She finally managed to wheeze in a breath and a giggle escaped her.

"By that laugh, I take it you're not hurt?" he asked.

India shook her head. "You took the brunt of the fall, I'm afraid." She pushed herself up—no choice but to press her palms into his chest to find purchase.

A sizzle worked up her arms. She licked her lips, hyper-aware of the hot hard muscles beneath her.

"Ah, what about you? I'm not crushing anything?" she asked, voice husky.

Thrane stared at her. "Nothing that doesn't want to be crushed right now."

The moment he spoke, her gaze flew to his lips.

Heat pooled in her groin. Oh no, uh-uh. She'd only been

in town for three days and had already locked lips with Thrane, though he'd practically been a stranger. She was *not* kissing this deliciously hot man again. This was insane.

Except, under the welcome warmth of the late autumn sun, with the tang of blackberries in the air, pressed along his body—

"Everything okay here, you two?" Nan's voice rang out.

Thrane groaned, dropped his head to the ground with a thud.

India blinked, rolled to the side, elbow digging into Thrane's side. She ignored his second groan and shielded her eyes as the silhouette of a horse and rider moved into view.

Heat flooded India's cheeks. "Nan. This isn't what it looks like."

"Of course, dear. It never is."

11

L ed by the whispering dream wind, dark gleaming leaves swished to a silent beat, beckoning India closer, ever closer. Over and over, their fine tips called her to them. To the heart of the forest. Her feet followed the call, taking her over Nan's property, into the forest beyond. Then the dream leaves stiffened, darkened, until one by one they crumbled to ash, and suddenly every branch was bare and only a dark, withered trunk remained. A curdling scream hurtled through the forest.

India jolted upright. Heart racing, she shoved her hair out of her face, looked around the forest for where the scream had come from.

Except she was in her bedroom. And judging by the sliver of warm light showing around the edge of the blinds, the day was underway.

A shiver shook through her and she gathered the blankets around her. What the hell had that dream meant? For the first time, the tree in her dreams had ... died. And now she knew where her dream tree was. In the forest beyond Nan's property. On Thrane's property.

As if her thoughts had conjured him, the deep rumble of a familiar voice coming from the living room made India's stomach drop even as her pulse picked up pace. Crap. He was here again.

How was she meant to get this weird attraction out of her system when he was always around?

Maybe she could stay in bed, pull the blankets over her head until he left. Let the world—her dreams, the magic, the questions, Thrane, *all* of it—pass her by. Just for a day.

And really, maybe ostriches had the right idea by burying their heads in the sand. It would make it so much easier to ignore the world ...

A knock rapped on her door.

"India? Are you getting up now, dear?" Nan called.

India groaned. So much for being an ostrich.

"Up now, Nan. Be out soon," India called back.

After a shower she pulled on black denim jeans with a warm black knit. She was able to put her hair back now without any discomfort so tucked it into a ponytail, then pulled on her low-heeled black boots.

She might not look like she was ready for a day on a farm, but she was ready to face her fourth day here.

She opened the door to the kitchen and living area with purpose. Today. *Today*, she was going to get her answers.

"Good morning," Thrane said from the dining table. He had a laptop set up in front of him, its power cord plugged into the wall.

India eyed him for a moment. He wore a black fitted top that moulded to the ridges of his chest and biceps, and his hair was pulled back into a knot. He looked too hot. Too urban. Nothing like the rough physical man he'd been so far.

"Morning," she replied, skirting around the dining table and going into the kitchen. She didn't need another whiff of his delicious scent.

"Nan knocked on my door not too long ago. Do you know where she's gone?" India asked once the kitchen bench separated her from Thrane.

"She's out checking the harvest equipment with the mechanics and said to let you know she'll be back in for lunch."

"Oh." India looked through the window. Sure enough, a giant machine was lumbering off in the distance. Crap.

Chewing on her lip, she cut a glance at Thrane. He started tapping away on his laptop.

"Don't you have a home to go to?" she asked, tapping her own fingers on the bench.

Thrane held his hands over the keyboard for a moment before he resumed typing. "Are you referring to the fact that I'm *here* working on a piece, or are you genuinely asking if I have a home?"

India crossed her arms. "Just calling it like I see it. You've been here every day."

"What can I say, *Liz* is good company."

India narrowed her eyes, ignored the implied insult. "So you must know Nan pretty well then?"

"You're full of questions this morning, aren't you? Why don't you make yourself some brekky and sit down to ask them? I can't talk to you while you're over there and type easily, and I'm on a deadline with this article."

She snorted, ignoring a zing of interest at the mention of

writing. "Sure, would hate to get in the way of your deadline."

Actually, she hated missing a deadline. She could procrastinate with the best of them but had learned the hard way that things happened, life happened, and she'd end up rushing her work. Another thing she hated.

"Are you making coffee?" Thrane asked, his head still bent over his laptop.

"Yep," she replied, grabbing a mug from the beneath the counter.

"Can you make me a refill?"

"You want me to make you a coffee?"

Thrane held up his mug and grinned. "Mine's empty."

"You've got two legs, right?"

"Yes."

"Well then?"

Thrane sighed. "You are one tough woman. Haven't you heard the way to man's heart is through his stomach?"

"That's for food."

"Coffee should count. It's the most important meal of the day."

India snorted, even though she agreed with Thrane about the coffee. Not that she'd say so. "It's a good thing I'm not here for any heart stuff then," she said, and went about making her breakfast. And coffee.

At the last moment she took the lid off a small glass pot filled with crushed purple petals and sugar.

"What's that?" Thrane asked.

India added a pinch of the aromatic mix to her coffee. "Lavender sugar. I picked some edible lavender from Nan's garden and mixed it up the other day. Makes a great treat." She didn't tell him that the action of being in the garden, of mixing and making something even as simple as the lavender sugar had grounded her.

Plus, lavender promoted healing and peace. Two things she desperately needed.

She took her breakfast to the table and carefully sat opposite Thrane. *You can do this, India.* She was a strong woman, she could ignore the warmth of his scent, the heat of his body, and enjoy her breakfast.

Thrane cut a look from his mug to hers, and his lips twitched. But he didn't say anything before standing up and making one for himself.

He plunked it down on the table just hard enough to make a noise.

"Careful, would hate to see you spill your precious brew," India murmured over her coffee.

He laughed outright. "Thanks for the tip." He raked a hand over his hair and jerked his chin at his laptop. "I'm struggling to articulate my point, and I really need to finish this morning."

An urge to see his work surged through her. "Want some help?" The words came out before she could contain them.

"You're offering to help ... me?" Thrane asked, one eyebrow raised.

"It's no big deal. I'm an editor. You're a writer. I might not have worked on garden-y stuff before, but I can try." India rolled her eyes and shrugged. "Or not. Up to you."

Thrane leaned back in his chair, locked his gaze on hers. Whatever he was looking for, he seemed to find it, because he swivelled the laptop around.

"Well, Ms. Editor, I'd be grateful for a second set of eyes."

India ignored the little surge of pleasure she felt at

having him accept her help. At least she was on the other side of the table from him. Keeping him at arms' length seemed the best course of action right now.

They worked—bickered—over the piece for some time, and when they'd finished India sat back in her seat with a laugh.

"I never expected I'd work on an article about plants, but I enjoyed it. Who would've thought I'd find a new branch, pun intended, to my business by coming back here?"

Thrane smiled and stood up, stretching his frame as he did.

India's mouth went dry, and she looked at her now empty mug. It was either that or risk drooling. Really, how could anyone be so sexy?

"Can I get you another coffee? It's the least I owe you for your help here," he said.

"Ah, sure." India pushed her mug over the table. "Thanks."

"So," Thrane spoke over as his shoulder as he moved about the kitchen, "what *did* bring you back?"

A lump lodged in India's throat. Crap, how to answer him?

She eyed him for a moment. How much did he know about witchcraft? After what happened at the hotel, he clearly knew something, and given how much time he spent with Nan, he had to know about the family's craft. But he wasn't a witch. So what was he?

And why was the tree from her dreams on *his* land? Was it all connected?

India was here for her magic; absolutely. She had to get control before she washed out any more bathrooms or fried anyone with lightning. But the echo of her dreams played over in her mind, and her eyes drifted to the kitchen window, where the view of the farm led unerringly toward the forest. Thrane's forest.

"Before I answer that, you need to answer something for me," she said.

Thrane raised one brow. "Ask away."

"How do you know about witchcraft?"

Thrane's features tightened for a moment, then he busied himself with the coffees before returning to the table.

"I'm not a witch, if that's what you're asking," he said as he handed over her mug.

"That's not my question," she said, shaking her head. "I know you're not a witch."

"What? How?"

"Uh-uh. I'm not saying anything more until you tell me. How do you know about magic?"

Thrane stared into his coffee for a long moment, then finally lifted his gaze to hers. "I've been around Liz for some time," he slowly said. "You could say I've learned most of what I know from Liz and her family. Now. How do you know I'm not a witch?"

A shiver trickled through India at the intensity in his gaze.

"Well, this will sound odd, but I can sense witchcraft by smell, all witches have a scent. It differs in intensity and perfume, but it's there. And you don't have it."

Thrane's hands tightened on his mug.

"Ah, why did that make you upset?" India asked him.

"I'm not upset."

"Sure you're not," she said, rolling her eyes. "Thrane, the reason I came back to Victoria, why I drove for two days to the family I haven't seen in years, is because I don't understand my magic."

The urge to tell him the rest—to ask about the tree—boiled up within her. But no, the dream tree was too personal. Too important. Too ... out of this world to mention.

"And you think Liz can teach you?" Thrane asked.

"I hope so."

Only, what if Nan never showed her? What if she never learned what this magic part of her actually was? What if she never came to fully understand who *she* was?

Goosebumps prickled the back of India's neck, and the faintest of tangs bloomed around her.

She jumped. Oh crap, what next? She darted a look up at the ceiling. Nothing. But the goosebumps kept prickling —and she knew what that meant.

"What are you doing?" Thrane rose to his feet, like liquid in motion. His eyes narrowed. "India?"

"Ah, look around." India hugged her arms to her chest as a full-on chill shook her. "Does anything seem off?"

"Apart from the fact that it's turned cold, really cold, you mean?"

Suddenly the kitchen door opened, smashed into the wall. Icy wind streamed into the room, swirled around her.

India shivered again.

"Crap, Thrane! What's going on?"

He strode to the door and tried to shut it. It didn't budge. He pivoted to her.

"India. This is magic. Is it you? Because if it is, you have to stop this."

The swirling wind sent the pictures on the wall rattling.

Picked up papers and tossed them around. Her heart began to pound.

"I don't know how it started," she said through chattering teeth. "How the hell do I make it stop?"

Thrane strode back to her, grasped her shoulders. "Think, India. Something is causing this."

Instantly, his dark spicy scent wrapped around her. His body heat, more welcome than ever, curved delicious fingers around her.

An answering heat coiled low in her belly. Her gaze dropped to Thrane's lips.

"India," he murmured.

"Mm?" She didn't—couldn't—keep her gaze from his lips. She knew their taste. Rich, exotic. Knew their texture. Luscious, silky. Firm.

Knew she wanted them on hers again.

She lifted up, led to him by a storm of warmth and spice. His lips hovered above hers; so close. Not close enough.

The icy wind subsided, as if the heat of their kiss had melted it.

A snick ... a creak ... another snick cut through the sudden silence. The kitchen door shutting.

India stepped back as Nan walked into the kitchen, slowly taking off her farm hat.

"India. Thrane. What happened here?" Nan asked, looking around.

India blinked. What *had* happened? That was the billion-dollar question. At least the polar vortex had stopped. Pictures no longer rattled on the walls. Loose papers slowly drifted to the ground from where they'd been tossed into the air.

"India's magic went haywire," Thrane replied smoothly.

"Again," India added.

"Again?" Nan asked, her eyes sharpening. "When else has it happened?"

"It happens all the time. When I first came back ... that night at Sim's hotel. In the car with Thrane." India snuck Thrane a look. "That's why I need to know how to stop it. How to control it. I need to learn my craft."

Nan shot Thrane a look, which he returned with a raised eyebrow, then straightening her shoulders, she sighed.

"India, I need some time to think this through. To find the best option for you, for all of us." Nan picked up the hat she'd thrown onto the counter.

"What? You need more time—after what just happened?" She turned to Thrane. "What about you?"

He shot Nan a look, but Nan's steely gaze remained steady. He ran a hand over his hair before nodding at India.

"Right, well, I've got to get back," he said. "Work to do and all. Thanks for your help with the article."

"I have to head out as well, dear."

India blinked as Nan and Thrane left the kitchen one after the other. Crap. Looked like it wasn't the day for answers after all.

12

Later that afternoon, India walked alone to the east paddock behind the cottages. When she reached the long grass, she rested the tools she'd gathered on the ground and deeply inhaled the crisp, sweet air. Tilting her chin to soak in the last rays of the sun, she closed her eyes for a moment and simply existed.

Her mind calmed, her heart eased.

Connection. Peace. No wonder she'd been out here each day since she first arrived.

Opening her eyes, she picked up her ceremonial knife. It was the only one she owned and had been a gift from her mother for her sixteenth birthday. The silver weighed comfortably in her palm. Her other tool was a sprig of calendula that she'd taken from Nan's herb garden.

The sun was saying goodnight slowly behind the hills at her back, and in the valley below, the sky was a riot of indigos and lilacs.

As the cool of the grass and soil seeped through the

denim of her jeans, she took another deep breath and consciously cleared her mind. No room for doubts.

"May I join you?" Nan asked.

India whirled around. "Nan, you scared the crap out of me."

Her grandmother wore jeans and a sweater, with a sleeveless puffer jacket zipped all the way up. Incongruous with the woman who called everyone "dear." She held a plant in one hand.

"Sorry, dear," she said. "I saw you pick the calendula and thought you might be going to cast a rite for Tara?"

"I was." India paused. "I didn't think you'd mind the calendula, though?"

"Oh, I don't mind. In fact, I brought the whole plant. Do you know why?"

"No, I have no idea actually."

"Well, I've been thinking about what you said earlier, about needing to know your craft. Maybe I can start now by sharing my knowledge. And then I could join you in the ritual?"

India swallowed, still unsure of her family's motivations. Who to trust? But she'd come back for this very reason—to learn about magic. And one thing she'd already discovered was that Nan did care about her.

"That would be nice," India said. Now came the hard part. "But first I have to tell you something. I'm not a very strong spellcaster. Mum was though. She cast her rites every new moon. But I never had Mum's magical skill."

Nan pursed her lips and said, "India, dear, help me sit down."

India automatically reached out and steadied her grandmother as she settled in the grass.

"Are you sure you're comfortable here?" India asked. "We can go inside."

Nan shooed the idea away with a wave of her plant.

"Where do you think I do most of my rituals? This place has been a special spot for many, many years."

"Ah, now that makes sense. It was like I was called out here when I first got back. And when I stood right here, the land spoke to me. There's this scent, an echo of all the magic that was here before me."

"Scent? And you were being called?"

India suddenly wanted to tell Nan about her nightly dream. It was so much stronger since she'd been on the farm. Every night, the dream wind whispered around the farmhouse, sang a luring tune, beckoned her up and over the hill. Toward the place where Thrane's land bordered Nan's. To the forest.

And every morning, she woke up more certain—she *had* to go into that forest. It was *almost* as important as learning about her magic. But she also couldn't bring herself to explain it. It was too personal. Too important. Too vital.

Would her family think she was unhinged? Worse, would they boot her out? Because then how would she learn about her magic? About her mother? And would she ever find what was calling her into the forest? No, she wasn't risking sharing that part of her. Not yet. But she did address the other question.

"This will sound ... silly," India said, "but I've always sensed other magic like that, as if each witch has an individual scent when they cast a spell. And that scent sometimes lingers where the spell was cast." She rubbed her hands over her arms, trying to find a little warmth. She swallowed her uncertainty. "Have you heard of a skill like that?"

Nan chest rose sharply, but she didn't respond.

"Nan. Please answer me. I need to know what's happening. I need to learn more about my magic. This is ... this is important."

Nan sighed, looked down over the valley. When she turned back, her face was pale.

"India, I know you've had a hard time with everything that's happened. But I need to ask one thing of you, just one."

India stilled, eyed her grandmother carefully. "What?"

"I want to wait till after the new moon, tomorrow night, when the whole family will be here to perform a magic circle. We'll bring you formally into our family, and then once your magic is truly part of us, we can cast one more spell. After that, you should be able to have all your answers. In safety. Can you—will you wait till then?"

In safety. What did that mean? The wait, the mystery, the secrets—it was all driving her antsy. Why couldn't they just be truthful about everything?

"Please, India?" Nan asked. "This is—well, I can only say this is really important."

India glanced at the forest. Two more nights—could she wait that long? She eyed Nan, took in the creases that tightened further around those soft blue eyes.

"India, I know this has been hard for you. I didn't come to Annie's funeral, and with everything that's happened lately, I know I haven't given you any reason to trust me. To trust us. But I can't put into words how important this is."

India snorted. That was one hell of a guilt trip. Though the strain in Nan's face was real. She didn't *want* to add to

Nan's worries, but she couldn't just give up either. She'd have to find her answers, especially about her dream, in secret. She glanced down at her hands even as the lie sprung to her lips.

"Okay, Nan," India said. "But can we talk about normal, everyday spells?"

Nan smiled, and relief shone from her eyes. "Thank you. And yes, we can talk about everyday spells. Because you're right about one thing, you do need to use your magic. Wilfully use it."

"I feel it too. I get goosebumps right before something batshi—ah, weird happens."

Nan held out a hand. "May I?"

India placed her hand in Nan's.

"India, a spell comes to life when we consciously decide to enact it. But the magic comes from us. From within us. Possibly, because you haven't used your craft enough, it's finding a release, likely when your emotions are heightened." Nan turned India's hand over. "The more you use your craft, the less your body will react without your will. Instead, you can channel it, like many of us do, through your palms."

India titled her head. "Can you show me?"

"Of course. This is a spell for witch-light. It's a good intermediate level spell." Nan curled her hand. *"Ward the dark, cleave the night, strike the flint, reveal the light. Heed my words, make it be."*

Slowly, Nan opened her hand. A tiny kernel of light shone in her palm. India rocked back in the grass. Nan closed her eyes, and the light-ball grew too bright for India to look at.

"Holy crap," she whispered.

"If you don't have control over your magic when it releases ... well, the results can be ..."

"Catastrophic?"

"That's a possibility." Nan waved her fingers, and the witch-light disappeared. "Which is why we need to work on your craft every day, just small steps, simple spells." She shot India a sideways look. "Maybe we should discuss Thrane, too?"

Heat prickled India's cheeks.

"He is a very nice specimen of a man, my dear, but he's rather older than you are."

"Nan, there's nothing to discuss. I'm here for a visit. He's the giant, frustrating neighbor who seems to be very at home on your farm."

The hot and sexy, darkly dangerous, mysterious stranger, who, even at the mention of his name, sent her heart racing and made her tummy tighten with desire. Whose company she ... enjoyed. India pursed her lips. Firmly.

"Hmm." Nan regarded her closely for a minute. "Well, you know how small towns are, dear. One rumor of a kiss, and the next thing you know, we'll have you off on a great romance, moving down here permanently." Nan chuckled.

"Oh no. There's no great romance. I'm not here for that." *You are not lying, you are not lying. You. Are. Not. Lying.*

"Let's talk about the spells, thank you," India said. "And I do want to try something for Tara." She looked closer at the plant Nan had brought with her. It was the same as hers. "Do you want to use my calendula?" She held up her sprig of the herb.

"That's fine if you want to help someone heal a paper cut, dear. But for anything requiring more energy than it takes to blow out a candle, you should always go for the whole plant. Roots and all. The whole plant, after all, is what this world connects with."

"I didn't know that. Why the hell didn't Mum ever tell me about this?" India snapped her mouth shut. "Sorry, Nan. I didn't mean to sound so … angry."

"Don't say sorry, dear. Your mother had her reasons for limiting your level of magical education, and God knows when Annie made up her mind about something, it was impossible to change it. But why don't I start at the beginning?"

"That would be perfect."

"When you use a plant for witchcraft," Nan said, "you bring an essential element of this world into your spell. A small amount of the element will produce a minor effect, and a larger amount of the element produces more of an effect. Looking at this calendula, what part of it do you think is the most important?"

India frowned. The weed-like plant had straggly roots, long fine green stems, and leaves with small flowers.

"Um, I'll take a guess that it's the roots? Isn't that where plants absorb water?"

"The roots are important, yes. But without the flowers to pollinate and go to seed, there will be no new life. Without the leaves, there will be no oxygen and carbon dioxide, and without the stem, the flowers and leaves can't get high enough to catch the sun and wind."

"Are you saying that there is no one part more important than the others?"

"Yes." Nan beamed.

India had to grin. She loved seeing that smile.

"Now, let's do some magic," Nan said.

"Okay, but, Nan—please remember, I'm not very good at this."

"India, stop wasting time."

Nan rose to her knees, shooting India a glance that definitely said no assistance needed. Then she nodded, and India knelt too. They faced each other. Nan to the south, India to the north—where Thrane's forest lay.

India took a deep breath, once more calmed her mind, and took up the blade by its hilt. The contact with the pure metal sent a happy tingle through her arm. She touched the tip of the blade to the earth.

Life coursed into the blade, through the silver, into her hand. Into her. India touched the blade to the calendula and warmth poured into her. Then she touched the blade to the inside of her wrist, and her energy joined the combination. Finally, she touched the tip of the blade to Nan's extended hand, and her grandmother's energy joined the mix.

The scent of magic erupted in the air, a potent blend, seductive, enticing—it beckoned her senses to let go and flow with it. But it was more than an invisible scent. The magic spoke to her on every sensory level.

Wow. All these years, whenever she'd smelled magic, she'd really been sensing the energy currents that magic created.

The ethereal currents moved whisper-quiet but with such force that they—at least the ones here—pushed all other currents out of the way. Was this normal? Or was this exceptionally strong magic?

She didn't ponder this for long, as more energy rose from the earth, from the plant, from Nan, and from within herself. The energy currents gained strength, both in clarity and momentum, as they joined to make the spell, until she could easily identify all four energies—and now the fifth result, the magic itself.

The earth's energy was a rich red, a lava-like flow of bubbling, tumbling energy. The calendula was white-hot energy with its beads pulsing along a delicate string. Nan's energy currents, while at first even-paced, began to spin erratically, and then even India's spun faster and faster.

Something told her to complete the spell now.

India closed her eyes and pictured Tara's face from when she'd visited her in the hospital—pale and pinched. And then she pictured it rested and rosy, and she gathered the currents close to her. She visualized the earth and the calendula combining their energies, and sent them flying together into the universe.

Nan still knelt with her eyes closed, but she was pale and wobbled in the grass. India shot out both arms, steadied her.

"You didn't use words," Nan said.

"Are you okay?" India asked, helping Nan to her feet.

"I'm fine, India. Well, maybe not exactly okay—more like rather tired. Your magic called up more of mine, more than I have ever done." She swayed on her feet for a moment. "Come, dear, I think I do need to go back the house. Can you walk with me?"

India held Nan's arm. "I'm so sorry—I didn't know I could do that to you. I would never have intentionally taken more than you could give, even if I knew how."

"Hush, dear, your magic is different to mine, that's all." Nan sighed. "You really do need to get to know your family, India. Thankfully the new moon is close. Perhaps you should wait until then to try any more spells."

Stop doing magic? Now?

She'd finally begun to discover what her magic looked

like, felt like. She pursed her lips. No way. Nan was moti-
vated out of fear—that was clear. What she was afraid of,
India couldn't tell. Yet.

But India wasn't scared, not of her magic anyway. What
was scary was the thought of never knowing how her magic
operated, why her dreams called and beckoned her into the
forest, of never finding out who *she* was. And she'd only now
discovered that last question even needed an answer.

She had to learn the truth. The pull toward them was a
physical imperative that she couldn't—wouldn't—ignore. It
was important. No, important was too light, too non-
compelling.

It was vital.

Nan patted India's hand, an absent gesture that seemed
out of habit, which made it all the more important. "Don't
worry, dear. You'll be fine."

In that touch, Nan's genuine care became apparent. And
India cared back.

Surprise! On both counts.

It seemed like an age ago when she'd thought Nan and
the rest of the family wanted nothing to do with her. And
now—well, now she knew they did care. Clearly something
was going on, something none of them felt they could
explain until this bloody new moon.

But as the knowledge that they cared settled inside her, a
little more of her raw hurt and bitter anger drifted away.

India patted Nan's hand in return. She'd try to not upset
Nan, but no way was she stopping now—she'd just keep her
investigations to herself.

They walked back to the house in a not uncomfortable
silence.

13

Early the next morning, thrashing, rhythmic gusts of wind beat at India's bedroom window. The glass panes rattled nonstop until India jumped out of bed and opened them. The release of pressure sent air howling into the room. It rushed around her legs, gathered at her back. Ahead of her, the mist-shrouded forest filled her view.

A knocking, followed by a touch, jolted her out of the dream.

India rolled over and looked straight into Thrane's face as he stood above her.

Was this another dream?

She'd seen him every day this week, and every time she'd had to resist the urge to burrow into his warmth. But if this was a dream ... she could do what she wanted.

India gave in, placed a hand on his sexy square jaw. But he didn't come closer. Frustrated, she tugged him down—her dream lover finally had a face.

Warm, sweet air hit her lips. His skin tightened beneath her palm. Oh, crap. Her stomach dropped.

"I'm not dreaming, am I?" India said.

"If this is your dream, I'm sad to say you're not. Perhaps we could pretend?"

Lips touched hers in the gentlest caress she had ever experienced. Heat stole across her body, like a cat rolling over and stretching after a sun-drenched nap. She jerked, pulled the quilt up to cover her mouth.

"Thrane, what are you doing? I haven't brushed my teeth. And why are you in my room?"

"Well, I was kissing you. And as I just woke you, it wouldn't be logical to expect your teeth to be brushed." He dropped a kiss to her forehead. "That was a lovely good morning, by the way. Everyone else is out and about, and I have to head over to the vet and pick up the pup today. Thought you might like to come for a drive before the bonfire tonight?"

India groaned and pulled the covers up over her head. Bonfire day. The day she was going to meet all her family, and Nan was going to cast some circle and do some spell.

"Coffee's on," Thrane said before leaving and closing her bedroom door with a snick.

She pushed the covers off. Maybe a distraction would be a good thing.

It was the coldest morning yet, so India got ready quickly. Holy crap, how cold would it get in winter? Not that she would be here long enough to find out.

When she emerged into the living room, a cup of coffee sat on the kitchen bench alongside a fresh slice of toast and breakfast condiments—butter, jam, honey and Vegemite.

Thrane was at the bench with a coffee already in hand and munching on his own slice of toast. "Coffee's hot."

"Thanks."

"You're welcome."

Shaking her head at the conversation—or lack of—India sat beside Thrane. Subtle warmth emanated from him, tempting her to forget everything but his physicality. But she forced herself to ignore it, took a sip of hot, wonderful coffee.

"So, since today's outing is your idea, it might be nice to talk a bit, don't you think?" she asked.

Thrane's chocolate gaze slid straight to hers.

"What do you want to talk about?" he asked.

"Um, right now?" India forced herself to see past the swell of desire that rippled through her core. "How about your age? I've been told you're too old for me."

Thrane's eyebrows rose, and he laughed.

"Let me guess—Liz?"

"Huh. And how come you get to call Nan 'Liz'?"

"So why 'India'?"

"What? Are you seriously ignoring my question and asking one of your own? You know you keep doing that—answering my question with a question, right?"

"But I really am curious. Your name's pretty unusual—do you know why your parents picked it?"

"Ha. You're one to talk, *Thrane*. Fine. I'll answer your question and you answer mine." She looked at him hard. "Promise?"

"You want to know how old I am?" Thrane asked.

"Ah no. I've got something more important to discuss than your age. So?"

"All right, I'll answer your question—one that's more important than my age." A rueful smile gradually curved his lips. "Promise."

"Deal. My name's pretty simple. Apparently, Mum and

Dad were huge fans of these movies where the main character—an archaeologist who runs around with a whip on his hip—had the same last name as us. Dad especially got a kick out of them." Thrane spluttered on his coffee and India grinned. "Yep, that's right. Mum said they couldn't help themselves with a last name like Jones. It was too good an opportunity to pass up." She waited until he'd stopped laughing. "Now it's your turn."

Thrane's phone beeped and a message lit up the screen.

"Hey, where are you going?" India asked.

"That was the vet," he said, slipping the phone into his pocket and jingling his keys. "The pup's ready. Do you still want to come with me to pick him up?"

More time with Thrane—something she really should be avoiding—especially because she wanted it so much.

Thrane placed his mug in the sink, leaned his hips against the kitchen counter.

"Come on, Jones," he said. "We can 'talk' while we're out. I'll keep my promise."

India eyed him. Something was different—the tension in his shoulders, the way his arms crossed over his chest. Was he was finally going to be honest with her?

"No sneaky kisses," she said, waving her mug.

"No sneaky kisses."

"And I've got questions about more than just your name. Don't make me regret this."

Thrane nodded and took the empty mug from her hand, placed it in the sink with his.

"No regrets," he said.

"Thanks. One of those questions will be about why you're so at home in my family's house."

INDIA HAD the pup in her lap as Thrane drove them out of the animal hospital parking lot. She gently rubbed the furrows over its brow and couldn't help but smile when the little guy yawned.

"Do they know what breed he is?" India asked.

Thrane competently steered them onto the highway.

"They think he's a mix—probably mastiff and Bernese mountain dog—the cross is known as mountain mastiff. They don't know anyone who breeds them around here, though."

"And he's okay?"

"Yeah," Thrane said, "he was dehydrated, but they fixed that up quick enough. Sadly, he's not chipped. The vet called all the local breeders, but no one claimed him, and now that he's well they can't keep him at the surgery indefinitely."

"Where else could he go?"

"If no one takes him, he'll go to the pound or a shelter."

"Can you take him?" India asked.

When Thrane didn't answer, she looked up from the pup. Thrane's face was in profile—his straight, proud nose perfect for his angular face and strong jaw. His grip tightened on the steering wheel and his lips tightened.

She cradled the pup closer. "If it's too much trouble, maybe Nan can take him?"

Thrane blew out a short breath. "It's not about *trouble*. And maybe Liz could take him, but I won't spring him on her. I guess ... he can come home with me for now." He waited a beat before saying, "My place isn't too far away.

Why don't we get him settled and then grab something to eat?"

"Have you heard anything more from Nate about how this little guy came to be at the hotel?"

"Not yet. They think the most likely scenario is that the pup was used to lure Tara outside. Nate said it's actually a known tactic with child predators. Tara hasn't been able to give them much of an explanation of what happened. Either she's blanked it out or she really didn't see much."

India shivered and cuddled the pup closer.

"We did a ritual for Tara yesterday afternoon. Nan and I, that is. God, I can't get over seeing her crumpled on the ground."

Thrane reached over and briefly laid a hand on her thigh. She would have liked it to stay longer, for both the lick of warmth it triggered and the reassurance.

"I spoke with Sim last night," India said. "She's happy to have Tara home, but she's nervous about being at the hotel until they find whoever was involved."

"She and Tara could stay at the farm with you. There's a cottage free now, right?"

"There is. I had a look through it and it's clean, ready to go. But it only has two bedrooms, and with Sim's mum as well, I'm not sure if they'd all be comfortable."

"It would be easier for Nate," Thrane said.

"What do you mean?"

"Hold on, we're here."

He slowed the car, and they turned into a formal entrance. An old stone wall bordered the graceful driveway. Jonquils and daffodils stood at attention, guarding the gray stones. A far more modern gate, made from vertical black iron bars, opened.

India's mouth dropped. "Thrane, this place—your property—it looks old. And grand. Has it always been in your family? Did you grow up here, too?"

The crunch of gravel beneath the car's tires was the only sound for a moment.

"It's technically correct to say it's my family's property," Thrane said.

"Well, it's amazing." India sat back, stunned by the formal, beautiful entry.

At first, the formality seemed a total contradiction to the rough-edged, brusque man she was getting to know. But as she looked at his strong profile, she began to see he carried an innate grandeur all of his own, and actually, the formal, structured entry suited him perfectly.

Was this formality another facet of his intriguing personality? Maybe an outward sign of his inner barriers? He certainly hadn't been easy to get to know over the past days.

The straight driveway was lined both sides by liquidambar trees, their bright green foliage turning to amber and chocolate. A carpet of deeper green lawn spread out to frame perfect plants and beds of flowers.

But India's gaze was drawn from the stunning garden to the true woods beyond.

Recognition speared into her. She was close.

The fine hairs on her arms prickled to attention, her magic lit up without direction. She connected with the energy around her.

The car stopped suddenly. But that didn't halt her reaction.

The very air around her seemed to be holding its breath. The only thing that wasn't still and quiet was Thrane. He was talking, his words present at a distant level. But what they were and what they meant she had no desire to discover.

All of her focus, all of *her,* was connected to this land and the energies that lived here. Because the dream wind that had been pushing her, pulling her into the forest, was now an energy current that held her in thrall.

It wasn't a dream now. It was real. It was excited—as if it couldn't believe she was so close. Her energy currents made contact with it, and as the wind energy receded into the forest, hers instinctively followed.

A SUDDEN SHIFT in the air alerted Thrane that something had changed. As if the molecules had been rearranged. Every muscle in his body tensed. His fight or flight instinct engaged. Protect the Tree. Protect India.

He pulled the car to a stop, ordered India to stay in the car, was halfway out when he realized India had obeyed his order far too well. He leaned back inside.

"India? India, talk to me." He grabbed her arm. She didn't react to his touch at all. She stared, unblinking. He waved a hand in front of her eyes. "India, this is not the place to do this. Can you hear me?"

She didn't respond.

A shiver of ice raced through him. The instinct to protect raged, pushed him hard to take action. But against what? Who? He turned to the forest. Was the Tree in danger? Was India? Or was *India* the danger?

He'd never been in this predicament before, had never been so strongly connected to another being as he was to

India. In any world, in any age. Not even to Serephena, the lord of the Underworld, who'd been his last real romantic liaison.

In the space of six days, India had made him laugh. Made him mad. Made him lust after her with an all-consuming desire. Made him happy to be in her presence. It was as if she existed in this world on a different plane to everyone else. But if she was the danger, what might he have to do?

Protecting the Tree was everything. Gods, so many had sacrificed themselves so that the Tree might live. He simply could not let India endanger the Tree.

The hairs along his arms and neck rose, and his blood iced over. The unease that had ridden him since that first night coalesced into an all-encompassing awareness of what he might have to do.

But he thrust the physical reaction away, opened the car door on India's side. As he reached in to unbuckle her seatbelt, he had an idea—if he kissed her, it might bring her out of the ... the vacant state she was in. He paused for a second. India had said no more sneaky kisses. But this didn't seem sneaky, this seemed necessary. He gently pressed his lips to hers.

After a moment, her lips pressed into his.

Thrane's instinct to protect waned. Which told him a great deal. His instinct to grab her and make love to her reared up.

India was the one to pull back, lips parted, green eyes watchful.

"That wasn't sneaky," he said.

"Thrane, we need to work this out. Now," India said and slowly moistened the lush curve of her lips.

He gripped the edge of the car door. Hard. India probably wasn't having the same thoughts as he was. He gave her room to get out of the car.

"I agree," he said, glancing at his house.

Heading inside right then was more temptation than he needed. Her body brushed his and he stifled a groan. He stepped back quickly—one look down, and she might decide to go home immediately.

"Why don't we take a walk in the garden?" he asked, taking the pup from her. "This little guy must need one."

14

To keep her thoughts off the energy of the land around them, India focused on the pup's joy as it leaped about the garden beds and rolled in the lush lawn. But still that energy called to her, beckoned her to walk away from Thrane and the pup and straight into the forest.

Batshit. She must be full-blown batshit. India blew out a slow breath, forced herself to focus.

"This is beautiful, Thrane. Nate told me you're a horticulturist. And that you helped Nan with her garden?"

"That's right. I have an affinity for gardening, I guess you could say."

"You run your business from here?" India asked.

"Yeah, those buildings over at the far end of the garden are the greenhouses. Do you want to take a look around?"

"Absolutely. I've always loved gardens, even though we didn't have a big one in Brisbane. We didn't have nearly the variety of plants you have here."

"I think that's one of the things I love about the climate

here. We can grow some really beautiful plants that won't thrive in other parts of the country."

"Which ones?"

"Come for a walk, and I'll show you."

Thrane scooped up the pup and stepped in close to place him in India's arms. Her focus snapped back to Thrane, on the play of his lean hips and wide shoulders as he walked down the gentle slope.

Bubbling along at the bottom of the slope, a meandering creek ran into a large pond. On the other side, the bank rose sharply to a higher elevation. Spanning the creek was a stone bridge, its sides draped in a dark-green–leafed plant covered in stunning purple flowers.

Thrane must've seen her awe because he walked to the edge of the creek and touched a hand to the delicate purple flowers.

"This is wisteria," he said. "It's one of my favorites."

"It's beautiful. Like something out of a fairytale. And one of my favorites now, too."

"I knew we'd have something in common."

A teasing smile spread over Thrane's face, and he took her hand—or maybe she gave it to him—and then he pulled her onto the bridge.

As he looked over the ponds, pride filled his eyes. India made herself shift her gaze from him to the view.

"See the bottom ponds?" Thrane said. "You can see the water lilies growing. They're another of my favorites."

"I'm getting the sense you really do like your plants, Thrane."

He chuckled and she looked up at his face. His curved lips slowly tightened, and the heat kindled once more in his gaze. The pulse at the base of his neck beat faster, harder.

But he didn't move.

India eyed the dangerous curve of his jaw, inhaled the heady musk of his scent. Descended into the physical, went past all thought and gave up fighting. She rose up on her toes, pressed her lips to his.

Heat bloomed.

Surprise flared in his eyes, then his arms banded around her, even as his lips slanted hard over hers.

Need exploded within her, and she pressed harder into his hard, hot chest—until a sharp yap and the scrabble of tiny claws got her attention. Thrane and India leaned back at the same time and looked down at the small bundle in her arms. The little face was indignant, and she had to laugh.

"I don't think he liked being left out," India said.

Thrane gave the small head a soft scratch. And a thread of emotion unfurled within her, slowly reached out, attached to him. Her stomach clenched. What in the hell was that?

"Sorry, little guy, I don't think I want to share." Thrane looked up from the pup, straight at her, into her. "Do you still want to look around—or would you like to come inside?"

If they went inside, they'd be having sex within minutes. She knew it. He knew it. He was leaving the choice to her. She moistened her lips, and her heart kicked when his gaze dipped to watch the movement. Holy hell, her body clamored for her to take Thrane's hand and run into the house.

But she'd only known him a few days.

He'd gone from being the most dangerous and maddening and frustrating man she'd ever met to ... well, to someone who liked puppies, was gentle with little girls who were hurt, laughed when he fell into blackberries, and loved gardening and writing. Talk about a walking contradiction. Not to mention, she still had the bewildering desire to run into his forest.

"I'm very, very close to saying yes to that question," India said. "But everything—this week, I mean, has gone so fast. I think, let's look around a bit more. And actually, I want to ask that question."

If disappointment entered his gaze, it was gone in the next instant. Instead, Thrane took her hand and led her to the other side of the bridge. Shallow stone steps with moss-covered edges took them in a slow curve up the gentle slope to more greenhouses.

They walked in silence to the top of the rise before Thrane stopped. "So I promised you an answer. What's your question?"

He appeared genuine. She took a deep breath, prayed that he could actually answer.

"Do you know what magic is?"

Thrane regarded her as closely as she had him. Finally, his eyes left her face, and he walked over to a stone bench that overlooked the creek.

"We might need a seat for this," he said, sitting down and shuffling to one end.

India joined him and placed the pup on the ground at their feet.

The midday sun warmed her face and hands, the sweet tang of the flowers teased her nose. For a moment, she closed her eyes and lifted her face, simply bathing in the autumn rays.

"Magic like your mother's was a connection with the world that most humans don't have," Thrane said finally.

"Your mother felt the world—that is, I've been *told* that your mother felt the world in a way that let her interact with it, kind of like a duet, where she could ask, sometimes softly, sometimes powerfully, to have it work with her to achieve something.

"She couldn't *make* the magic happen, but she understood the currents of life that make up every single thing. And those currents can be shifted, manipulated even, by someone who has knowledge of them. But it's more than simply knowing, otherwise everyone would do it. Witches have a spark within them that opens a door to communicate.

"In your family, that genetic spark has been passed down for generations. Some ignored it. Some used it casually with no great fuss. And some of them, like your mother, used it to its absolute limit." Thrane sighed, looked over the land again before meeting her eyes. "You have that spark, India. You can choose what to do with it."

India stilled, remembering her mother's laughing blue eyes and sweet rounded cheeks. Her throat tightened and tears burned her eyes. She took a deep breath, shakily blew it out.

"I found her," India said. "The night she died."

Thrane picked up her hand, rubbed her palm with his thumb. Concern shone in his eyes.

"Liz mentioned you had to deal with everything on your own, so I guessed you must have. Do you want to talk about it?"

India sighed. "That's nice of you to offer. But I've dealt—no, more like I'm dealing with it. Though, well, I find it interesting that my magic led me to find her."

"How's that?" Thrane asked.

"Before Mum died, and this will sound weird, but my magic was a really minor part of my life. I used to joke about it being magic-lite, but mostly it was all based on intuition. And that was what led me to Mum. I'd been out with friends, and suddenly I had this urge to check on her. I called, but she didn't answer. Which was odd. So I went straight home. When I got there, I didn't knock, just pushed her bedroom door open. But she was already gone."

Thrane stroked her hand. "That must have been truly awful."

She drew in a shuddering breath. "Yeah. The coroner found she'd had a massive stroke in her sleep. It explains why I found her in bed. I ... I wonder, if I'd been with her that night, instead of out at dinner, whether I could have got there in time, you know?"

The tightness in her chest eased, as if by speaking those words aloud she'd finally faced something she hadn't been able to before.

"Hey," Thrane murmured. "You know you couldn't have stopped it from happening, right?"

She gave him a small smile. "Thanks for saying it. And yeah, a logical piece of me knows that. But ..."

Thrane squeezed her hand. "Yeah, I get the 'but.' Have had enough of those during my life."

"My hope is that Mum and Dad are together again, somehow, some way." India said. "Do you know anything about my father?"

Thrane's eyes hardened and he tensed, then sighed, and his massive body sagged. "Yes. Your father wasn't a witch though."

His words jarred in her brain, and she recoiled. "What did you just say?"

"Jev was not a witch, but he was supernatural. He was a Herald."

"A ... a what?"

"A Herald. Heralds are the protectors of the Heavens."

India waited for him to say more but he didn't. She replayed Thrane's comment in her mind.

"You're shitting me," India said.

"No, I'm not shitting you."

"My father, who lived on our farm, who worked as a farmhand, right here in Hill End, was not from earth?"

"Well, I wouldn't say not from earth. After all, the Heavens are earth, only not as we know it. But yes, you have the correct idea."

"And did he—do I—have more family in the Heavens?"

"Yes, you do."

"What does that make me?"

"A witch," he said. "A daughter, granddaughter, niece, cousin. But there is something more, India. You are your father's daughter—a child of the Heavens. While it hasn't meant much till now, your grandmother fears that it may be an issue. And I fear that you may be more of a danger than any before you."

"What do you mean?"

"Eighteen years ago, your father died."

"Yeah, he was killed in a tractor accident, up in the back paddock." Thrane's jaw tightened. A frisson of awareness tingled up India's spine. "Thrane?"

When his gaze returned to hers, something turbulent and dark washed through it.

"India," he said, "your father died of his wounds in the back paddock, but he wasn't in an accident. And the injury that killed him didn't happen on your farm. Your mother found him before he died. In his last moments, Jev told Annette something that made her believe you were in danger, because of your magic."

India's breath released, as if she'd been punched in the gut, and a chill raced through her body. She dropped Thrane's hand, tightly folded her arms to find some warmth, a barrier, from the icy storm inside her.

"Do ... do you mean Dad was murdered?"

"Yes, India. And after that, your mother used every ounce of her magic to craft and cast a spell each new moon, month after month, one that had never been achieved before—she shrouded your magic from all supernatural sight."

India's stomach roiled. She folded over, breathed swiftly through her nose until the queasy sensation passed.

All the while, her mother's beautiful face littered through her mind. Her smile. Her laugh. Her ease with magic. The way each and every new moon she went into their private little garden and cast her spells.

No. Surely not. Surely her gentle, beautiful mum hadn't lied to her for her entire bloody life.

India shot to her feet and faced Thrane. "This is crap. Why on earth should I believe you? You, practically a stranger, say that my own mother lied to me for most of my life."

"I keep trying to tell you, I'm not a stranger, but regarding your father and your magic, you don't have to believe me. According to Liz, the spell your mother cast had an unexpected side effect. It effectively shrouded your magic even from you. And with your mother's passing, and the spell with her, your magic has been coming to life. You said it yourself, magic used to be a minor part of your life. Now look at it."

India recalled her childhood magic—immature, often unpredictable, and very much based in emotion. But it had definitely existed. Then, for the last eighteen years, her magic had been a song played underwater—muted, softened, garbled. Inconsequential.

And now, in a mere three weeks, she wielded power like she'd never known.

Thrane's story had moments of plausibility. While she absorbed his comments, she looked around the garden. It reminded her of Nan's. Of her childhood. How was she meant to make sense of all this? A half-sob, half-snort escaped her and she slouched back beside Thrane.

"Do you know, when Dad died and Mum moved us to Brisbane, it made perfect sense to me? That she'd want to start fresh, I mean. I remember their love, like it was a tangible thing. They'd hold hands, they'd laugh together. *Be* together, and they always included me in that love."

Thrane picked up India's hand again, holding off the oncoming chill with the warmth of his skin.

"I've heard from Liz how much Annette and Jev loved each other. And you," he said.

"But why keep lying? I can understand protecting a child, but I'm twenty-eight. What possible reason could Mum have had for lying to me all that time? She *lied* to me."

The sense of betrayal that stole over her seemed wrong, and hot tears stung her eyes. She knew her mother would only have done what she thought best. But India had spent eighteen years—*eighteen years*—not really knowing her family's story. Anger rebuilt with ferocity.

"I'm so *sick* of the lies," India shouted.

The words were daggers thrown into the sky, and with them a wind whipped up and caught the ends of her hair.

The raw energy of a storm rolling in over the mountains called to her. Any moment now the wind would answer and bear her aloft to run wild. The rain would drive and spear the ground. The lightning would scorch the earth and set the trees ablaze. The power at her command would decimate this puny place. These elements were hers to command. Hers to bend and shape, and they'd scream her fury and rage and pain.

The softest touch of warmth on India's lips broke her communion with the storm. And then Thrane's lips moved on hers. They slanted hard, and the heat of her anger changed in a staggering rush to warm her innermost being.

India returned the caress, their tongues mating and tangling. She breathed him in, the tang and spice and heat of him pouring into her. Thrane dragged her onto his lap. His rock-hard erection slammed into her softness.

Needing connection, needing *him*, India wrapped her arms around his shoulders, pressed hard against every answering hard plane of his body. Her hands learned the shape of his biceps, the flex of his back.

Need and want and fear and anger filled her, fueled her, and she ground into him. Poured her tumult of emotions into their kiss, into his body. As hard as she could.

Oh God, she needed more.

Strip she was about to say, just when surprisingly warm raindrops pattered on her heated skin.

She let go of him.

The storm that had been threatening minutes earlier now rushed toward them, bruising the sky beneath billowing clouds. The wind called to her, reached out and sang through her veins along with her ire. Sheets of rain raced the wind, threw off clouds of steam, as hot as the fire that heated her blood.

Holy crap, had she caused the storm?

"Gods, what the hell is that?" Thrane asked.

"I think I can ... I may have ... talked to the elements."

She tentatively, consciously, reached out with her will and found the storm's energy. With her emotions under *slightly* more control, she might be able to influence the tempest.

"Ah, India, what are you doing?"

"Sh, I need to talk to the storm."

"That's what I'm worried about. Do you know what you're—"

"Shush. Not sure if you've noticed, but that rain looks hot—as in steaming—and I don't want to get boiled alive right now." She was pretty certain the rain wouldn't hurt her. But Thrane ... "Let me be a witch."

She worked hard to dilute the rage that had been in her emotions earlier, whispered the storm back to the mountains.

Right as she was satisfied with her efforts, a thought struck, and she awkwardly hopped off Thrane's lap and stared down at him.

"Hold on, you fear *I'm* the danger?"

15

"India, at least let me drive you back. I can have you home in ten minutes, otherwise it's an hour's walk up and over the hill."

India opened her mouth to say no but couldn't get the word out. Nothing was getting past the ball of anger sitting high in her throat. It was the kind of ball so hard and hot it might turn to tears. Just as well—if she did say anything, the boiling rain from earlier might come back. Ha. That would serve him right.

A heavy weight coiled tight in her stomach, and the grass sped beneath her as she strode up the hill toward the farm. *She* was the danger? Why? Because she had some weird form of magic?

Thrane spoke again, but she tuned him out. Like she needed more to worry about. She was going to meet her whole family tonight. Some circle was going to be cast that she was going to join, and who knew what that meant?

Thrane's news about her father, his family, and some supposed danger was too much.

The stables came into view, and she stalked through them.

Thrane cursed behind her. "India, wait," he said. "Let me talk."

But India didn't pause till she reached the farmhouse. She wrenched the front door open.

"I think you've talked enough for today, thanks. Make up your mind—I'm either *in* danger or *the* danger."

She slammed the door behind her. Glared at it hard. Would he follow her?

The door handle moved.

"India. Let me in."

Her witchcraft flared and a blast of air struck the door. The handle continued to rattle, and Thrane called her name again, but the door didn't budge.

Her magic had made a solid airlock—she'd have been impressed if she'd actually tried to achieve that outcome—but it did the job. Thrane was not coming in. And while he could have tried another entry, he didn't. Which she grudgingly appreciated.

She stomped through the house to Nan's office, cocked a hip against the doorframe. Nan swiveled in her chair, and her face lit up.

"Well, something's got your knickers in a knot," she said.

"How did you know?"

"Apart from the stomping and slightly murderous frown, you mean? You might not be aware, but you have a little whirlwind swirling around your hair."

"Huh. So that's what that is. And only slightly murderous? I was going for outright death and mayhem."

"Thrane?"

"How did you guess?"

"I think it's time for a cup of tea. Why don't we have a break and head into the lounge?"

India didn't want a cup of tea, was already sloshing from the amount of tea and coffee Nan insisted they consume on a daily basis, but she didn't want to hurt Nan's feelings.

"I'll make it," India said.

Making the tea actually settled her a bit; she was calmer —at least her hair wasn't caught in a whirlwind anymore— by the time she took the teacups and saucers into the formal lounge.

Nan already sat on one of the couches, several albums and papers in front of her on the low coffee table. One document was covered in illustrations of the moon's phases drawn in lead pencil.

"Put that down here, dear," Nan said. "I've got something I'd like to show you. It's only fitting given tonight's the rise of the new moon."

India looked sharply to Nan, recalling Thrane's words from earlier. Somehow, she managed to keep her voice even.

"You've mentioned the new moon a few times since I came back. What's so important about it?"

Nan took a sip of tea, then slowly, carefully, placed her teacup back on the table.

"India, the new moon is the first phase of the lunar cycle. The moon is hidden from our sight because it comes into alignment with the earth and the sun."

India shrugged. "And?"

"When all three celestial bodies are aligned, all magics are enhanced. Strengthened. It's the perfect night to make magic."

Crap. The way her magic was behaving, that didn't sound good at all.

"Nan, are you sure this is a good idea? My magic hasn't exactly been under control as it is."

Nan's jaw hardened—a sign India was becoming increasingly familiar with.

"India, this is the night. This is the only night where your family can do something for you. For Annette. Now, come, please sit beside me. I want to share this with you." Nan gestured to the papers in front of her.

"But, Nan, this new moon, why is it so important that we have to do this now?"

"India, I know I've—we've—asked a lot of you. But please, just wait."

"I know, I know. One more night."

"Not even, dear. A few more hours. Then you can ask your questions and we can answer them."

Not upsetting her grandmother was becoming harder and harder. India gritted her teeth, somehow managed to keep from swearing and demanding more answers, and took a seat on the floral-patterned sofa beside Nan. Through the glass sliding doors, the garden filled her view, a riot of colors, sizes, and shapes.

"The garden looks so beautiful from here," India said. "It's like we're in the middle of a botanical garden."

Nan leaned forward and patted India's thigh. "Thank you, dear. That garden has been a labor of love for me. When I was your age, it was a vegetable patch, but I'd seen Thrane's garden and dreamed of having something like that for myself."

India's gaze flew to the garden. She slowly turned back to Nan.

"*You* were inspired by Thrane's garden? But your garden looked like this when I was a kid."

"Yes, dear. I started to build this when your mother was a little girl."

India's heart stuttered. Thrane's comments about her mother and father, how he knew so much about them, rushed back into her mind.

Her stomach dropped.

"Nan, how old is Thrane?"

"Well, I don't think he'd consider it my place to tell you. But I did mention he's a lot older than you."

"*Nan*. I thought you were talking about years older not ... well, not decades. Holy crap. But he doesn't look—he couldn't be—more than what, mid-thirties?" Her heart began to pound over and over. She frowned at the garden, tried to assimilate what Nan was saying. "So, what, Thrane doesn't age somehow?"

"You have the general idea, dear."

"Seriously, holy crap."

"I know," Nan said, "but now, it would be good for you to have a little insight into your family before tonight. After all, this is your first family circle. Most witches go through this ritual when they reach their witchcraft maturity, not some ten years after."

"What exactly is going to happen tonight?"

"Your witchcraft will be 'familiarized' in the truest sense of the word. Once within the circle, all your family members who are also of age—and mind you, that's based on physical and emotional maturity, not chronological age—will join their magic, and yours will be welcomed in. Your magic will find its level within our family circle. Based on your level, your magic can be called upon, or you can call upon others in times of need. This is where your full potential is realized, my dear. Where your strengths are recognized, your weaknesses identified. And there's a blood rite, of course. After all, blood is our connection. It's only a little blood, I promise."

"Nan," India said, "once again, this is the first time I'm hearing about this."

"Well, that's why we need to have a good chat. It might be helpful if you know who's who, before all the family arrive."

Nan reached over and opened a photo album. As she did, a very old sheet of paper inside a clear plastic sheet protector slid free. India stayed Nan's hand.

"What's this?" she asked.

"Let me look. Ah, this is the original title to this property. My grandmother and grandfather came out to Australia in the very early 1900s. They were farmers back in Ireland, but with little land to till, they decided to bring their crops—potatoes, of course—with them to start afresh here. Did you know they started out with a little over one hundred acres? Back then, land was measured in hectares. They were granted twenty-five, and so they came here and settled."

"Were they witches?"

"Oh, my grandmother definitely. She was very much tied to the earth. I think her magic probably guided her to this valley. Heaven knows there could not be many more fertile places on earth. But then, I know she also used her magic to give back to the land. She even taught me how to use my magic to nourish the soil so that the crops would be hearty. I imagine that her family back in Ireland were witches too."

"Have you ever been there," India asked, "to Ireland?"

"No. Maybe one day."

India looked at the first image in the album. It was a

small black-and-white photo, yellowed in places with age. It featured two young children—identical twins.

"Who is that?" She looked closer, raised her eyes to Nan's in astonishment. "Is that you? And if so—who is that?"

"Elaine. My twin sister. Your great-aunt." Nan smiled softly. "I miss her."

"How long since she passed?"

"Oh no, dear. She's alive—she lives in the Underworld."

India went to shake her head, but resisting the tide of information about to flow her way was impossible, so she put aside her disbelief and opened her mind.

"You know," Nan continued, "my grandmother was the first witch of our line here in Australia. And that magic has bred true in all of my family, except for my twin. Each of us have been through our own circles, like you will tonight."

"Who, exactly, will be here for the circle?"

"All of us, dear. Every direct member of my family. Let me think, your uncles and aunts, their children—your cousins—and some of them are married with very young children too. So, in total, let me count, it makes eleven direct family members, and then six in-laws. Plus, three young-sters who aren't of an age yet to join the circle."

India began to laugh. Why was she nervous? Thrane was some kind of ageless being. Her aunt lived in the Under-world. She'd gone from having no family to having more than she could count—and she was joining her magic to theirs tonight.

16

R i'Kiant knelt in the center of the circle created by the prostrate bodies of his chapter. He hid his contempt and the unending desire for death beneath a calm facade. He was a soldier, yes, but these fighters had to see him as more than that—they needed to see a leader they would follow to the death.

Even if that death was at his hands.

After they had practiced enough mindfulness, he raised his head and sent his people to their tasks for the evening ahead.

Once the room had emptied, he removed his will from the spell that had hidden the altar.

It rose in a mangled mess of bleached bones from the center of the room. Had his soldiers seen it, their faith would have been tested; therefore he kept it hidden, using stolen magic to pull the shadows in the windowless room and hiding it in plain sight.

As the structure was revealed, a form materialized atop it.

The creature began as a mist, then within moments molecules solidified into the shape of a woman, lying on the altar. Her breasts were studded and tipped with steel claws, and her naval and crotch were connected with razor-sharp platinum chains. She had hair so black it sucked in all light.

When her forked tongue licked over her deep-red lips, Ri'Kiant's cock engorged, pressed painfully against the restraint of his clothes.

"Ri'Kiant," she said, uttering his name in a purr that stroked his scaly skin and sent his demon into a fever. "The black moon rises this eve. Have you success to report, my first?"

The interwoven lines that had been clawed into his forehead cut deeper again. Blood welled along the already raised scar tissue. And with every purred word, claws raked over his mind even as heat suffused his groin. Ri'Kiant shuddered.

"As your honored first," he said, "I bring news of great import, my god. Our plan is proceeding as expected."

Ri'Kiant had been his god's first follower for hundreds of years, since he had done away with the one who had come before him. His measure was not to be second.

At the time of his succession, the marks scored into his forehead had been amended with a single slice down the very center—adding one vertical to the two horizontal cuts. The two horizontal lines represented the lands under his god's dominion within the Underworld. The vertical cut announced him as her first soldier, her most important, most trusted follower.

And when his Order finally took the Mortalworld in her name, they would add another horizontal line to their scars.

Ri'Kiant dropped to his knees, imparted the news of the witch's return.

17

"By all the bloody gods," Thrane said and rested his forehead against the front door of Liz's house. Finally, he stepped away—that door wasn't budging, no matter what he did. "Bloody witchcraft."

Thrane continued muttering as he looked around Liz's garden, a view that usually calmed him. He could've kicked his own butt over the way he'd handled things with India.

By the gods, she was amazing. Strong-willed and feisty —traits he admired and had always been attracted to—but also unpredictable, and funny, and intelligent. The combination fascinated him. Meant he'd been unable and unwilling to do anything else but follow her up and over the hill. But would he follow her anywhere?

It was a staggering question but also alien because he could never remember feeling this way in his entire existence—as a mortal for thirty years, and as an immortal for some five hundred more.

He needed to clear his head. After that, he needed to figure out what to do with the pup that was currently sitting in his arms as if it belonged there, and then what to do with India. And since he'd walked—hell, he'd practically run up the hill after her—he was going to have to either walk back or catch a ride. Luckily Nate's mum Vera was in the yard, and she had the keys to one of the farm quad bikes.

"Remember the bonfire tonight," she said as she dropped him off and waved goodbye.

As if he could forget it.

But he had the sickening sensation that the spell wouldn't work. Plus, it was probably too late. If a scryer had locked onto India's magic, India would have to leave here and travel a long way under the spell before she could be free and clear again.

Though to his mind, the bigger issue was India's magic. If she was the strongest in her family, none of their magic would influence hers. And worse, if her level was above that of anyone else in the family, she could influence *their* magic. And what then? With her witchcraft, she could outright destroy what he'd dedicated his entire fucking existence to protect.

And the black moon would rise tonight.

Freya's words, given over a century ago, rang again through his mind. Her warning had been delivered right before she bade him depart the fight for the original World Tree and hide a seedling in the farthest reaches of the known world.

What if her warning hadn't been for that night?

A shiver shook him from deep inside, spread slow icy fingers through his veins and over his skin. India could still be the gravest danger the World Tree—he—had ever faced. He dared not ignore that fact. He forced himself to focus on what needed to be done here and now.

Firstly, he had to see to the pup. Even as he had the thought, the pup balanced two soft paws on his chest and, leaning up, placed a soft lick on his chin. Thrane sighed, hugged the little bundle close for a moment before he went to the car—pup still in his arms—to get the supplies he'd purchased while at the vet.

In the kitchen, he found two Tupperware containers, filled one with water and added some food to the other, then let the little guy eat. Afterward, they took a trip to the grass, which led to some rough-and-tumble exploring of his garden. When the pup began to flag, Thrane took him inside, grabbed his laundry basket, and lined it with an old blanket as a makeshift bed. He'd keep the pup in the kitchen until he figured out what to do with him in the long term.

But the pup had other ideas and started to whine as soon as Thrane walked away. In the end, Thrane lifted the pup into his arms, took the basket into the library and sat down on the couch. The pup lay down on his lap. He softly rubbed the furrows over the pup's brow.

"What are we going to do? I haven't had a pet here in many, many years."

And he had a good reason. As an immortal, his life was immeasurable but for one thing—the lifecycle of humans and animals in this world. He'd learned with time to balance the loss and sorrow and hurt of seeing friends pass on with the pleasure of knowing them during their existence. But it had become easier and less painful to stop keeping pets.

And that was one more reason to restrain himself with India. He was wild for her; however, he'd never been in love with a mortal. Perhaps he'd always held back from taking that step, knowing what would ensue. And yet, he had the foreboding thought that it would not take much to fall for her. Hard.

Once the pup was asleep, Thrane lowered him into the basket, then looked out through the windows to the garden beyond. The sun stood low in the afternoon sky. There was one place where he could find clarity.

THRANE WALKED BRISKLY through his garden and into the low scrub beyond. Lilly pilly, bottlebrush, wattles, and smaller natives created an effective demarcation between the garden he tended and the garden he protected.

The scrub grew thicker, the foliage denser, and the plants hardier, but his practiced steps took him quickly into the forest's interior.

Here, gum trees speared out of the earth, their dappled trunks straight and true, their graceful branches lifting long sharp-tipped leaves into the sunshine high above. These trees had seen little danger in their long lives. Though wildfire had threatened, he'd worked hard every year to build firebreaks throughout the surrounding gullies to reduce the risk. So far he'd been successful.

Rocky outcroppings and low shrubbery dotted the ground, and the gums grew taller and wider the farther he ventured into the forest. Eventually, even the shrubbery dwindled until only large patches of forest grasses and leaf litter existed beneath the evergreen canopies. Here, there was enough room to walk with ease, and if cavalry and armaments were ever needed, it wouldn't pose a problem.

And then Thrane was at the clearing.

The World Tree was enormous now. The girth of its dark trunk measured easily fifteen feet, and Thrane estimated its height to be approaching one hundred and fifty feet. Its limbs rose like giant arms with elbows that pushed richly hued leafy fingertips high into the sunlight. The World Tree could stand in this very place for thousands of years if given the chance.

And Thrane would be there to see to it.

Since he'd been called to this fight all those years ago, the Tree had touched his heart and mind. It communicated not with words but with intent and energy. He supposed its language was akin to witchcraft in that way. For Thrane, his connection to the Tree had only deepened since he'd taken oversight of this one as a seedling.

He made his way to the Tree's massive trunk and touched the smooth bark. As soon as he did, the Tree's consciousness connected with his. Acceptance. Love. Guidance and trust.

It was a mental connection, and yet it carried the weight of three worlds. Thrane had conversed with gods who carried less weight in their words than the Tree did with a gentle touch of its consciousness. He sent the Tree his thoughts, his love, commitment, concern.

And his concern for India.

Instantly he was bombarded with images, impressions, and sensations.

Thrane had hundreds of years' experience in deciphering the Tree's messages, and while they could be subtle, today they were not.

A sense of urgency hit him first, followed by interminable waiting, a million eyes watching, and of Fate, standing at her spinning wheel. He saw an image of heavenly warriors—not of the Order and not of Keepers—in this very clearing. Next, he saw Jev, and Jev's ancestors. These images were followed by another.

In which India lay, eyes shut, at the foot of the World Tree.

His heart wrenched from his chest, and in the fading light of day, he sank to his knees. The Tree withdrew its consciousness from his.

Thrane forced himself not to react, instead he took precious minutes to add context to the Tree's message. Time was nonlinear to the Tree, and it often sent messages on different timelines to those he normally dealt with. But he also respected the first sensation he had received. Urgency.

India was in serious trouble.

18

I n the sweet late-afternoon air, looking for a distraction from her thoughts of the night ahead, India made her way through the stables to the back paddock, where a pile of timber was stacked high.

She found Sim sitting on a massive, weathered tree stump, turned on its side like a giant's chair. Sim stared at the stack of wood, ready for the bonfire ahead.

"Some view, hey?" India said, taking a seat beside Sim.

Sim nodded, and slowly a smile grew on her face. "It's amazing."

"Are you settled in the cottage?" India asked.

"Yeah. Liz told me you'd gotten it ready for us. Thanks for that."

"No worries. Happy to do anything that makes things a bit easier for you, Tara, and your mum."

"Tara's loving it. And she's better for being here, I think. Liz and Mum have her eating cake up at the main house." Sim sighed. "Actually, she's much better than okay. She seems completely fine, as if nothing happened."

Sim shuddered and tears welled in her eyes.

"Hey, need a hug?"

"Yeah, I do. Thanks." Sim wiped her face as India wrapped an arm around her shoulders. "Sorry for the tears. It gets to me every time I think about it. How close it was to ... to ..."

"Go ahead and cry," India said. "God knows I've done my share since coming here. Maybe it's this place."

Sim hiccupped but turned it into a laugh.

"Thanks for that. Nice to know I'm not the only basket case in town."

India squeezed Sim's shoulders. "Definitely no need to worry about that. But seriously, I'm here if you want to talk about it some more."

"Thanks. I'll probably be talking about this for years to come, trying to process it all. But for tonight, I could do with some down time, you know? Put it out of my mind and enjoy the bonfire. How about we talk about something else?"

India thought about broaching the whole witchcraft thing, but Sim had said she wanted a night of enjoyment, so India shelved the topic for now, since after tonight's rite Sim would no doubt be asking a lot of questions.

Instead she chose another, still interesting, subject.

"So," she asked, "how long have you known Nate?"

Sim's gaze jolted up to India's, and she let out a chuckle that seemed to surprise her as much as it did India.

"That's a guilty look if I ever saw one."

"Sh."

India laughed. "Sim, we're alone. Who are you worried about overhearing you out here?"

"Ha. I've learned you don't have to worry about the walls

having ears in the country, it's the seemingly quiet, only-person-in-sight, eerie openness you have to worry about."

"Wow. So why did you move out here?"

"Warragul's still a town, but this countryside is a completely different thing."

"Hmm, you wouldn't be stalling, would you?" India said. "If I'm completely off base, or if this is too personal"—she held up a hand—"say the word, and I'll change the topic again. To something totally impersonal—um, how about the giant pile of sticks over there waiting for a match?"

"Well, I'm truthfully very interested in this bonfire and really honored to be invited. It's the first time I'll have been to anything like this since we moved here."

"Oh." India swished her feet through the grass, tilted her face up to enjoy the last warming rays of the sun. "Who did the inviting?"

"Nate—that is, he mentioned Nan had offered for us all to stay here for a couple of days. And that it was a perfect night to come out with the bonfire happening and all."

India held in a smile. "Nate?"

"Mm. He's been really amazing after what happened to Tara. Mind you, Tara's had a crush on him practically from the day we moved here."

"Tara?"

"Yes, *Tara*, smarty-pants. But you can't deny that he's a handsome hunk of man-flesh."

"If you say so."

"Well, I do," Sim said. "He was really good to us from the day we came here. My mother can be ... well, let's say with-drawn. But Nate talks to her and she smiles, every time. You'd think she was a young girl again.

"And speaking of girls, Tara—oh my God—she talks and

talks about him"—India noted the look of bemusement and something else, a different level of interest, in Sim's face—"but as I said, he's been really good to us. To me. He stopped by the hospital every few hours, and believe me, I definitely got as much—no, way more than Tara did out of his company.

"He was a rock," Sim went on. "And he even helped set up someone to look after the hotel for me for a few days."

"Nate's pretty special," India said.

"Thrane stopped in as well. Did you know?"

India jerked at the sudden mention of Thrane's name and fought to regain a calm facade.

"Mm, he mentioned that today."

"Oh?" Sim said.

"So, it's my turn to be grilled?"

"Well, it's only fair right?"

"You're as nosy as I am."

"Yes, yes, I am."

They laughed at each other, then India shook her head.

"Thrane is ... he leaves me speechless. I swear, every time I see him, I get lost in those chocolate eyes. I can't believe I've only known him for a week."

"Wow, that's not what I was expecting. You are talking about the giant, serious man who keeps to himself—mostly—and who lives next door to Nan, right?" Sim asked.

"Okay, we're not talking about the same man here. Thrane, whose property is at the back of Nan's. The man who teases me nonstop and tries to boss me around. *That* Thrane?"

"Mm."

"The Thrane who kisses like wildfire and has a hard, hot

body that sends me to fantasy land every time I look at him?"

Sim laughed until her eyes teared up, then said, "Well, they say there's someone for everyone."

"I'm not sure our different takes on Thrane is that funny." Pursing her lips, India tried not to laugh. "But why don't we head inside? I think we've grilled each other enough for one day. And I'd like to grab a jumper. It's gotten cold so quickly."

"Well, this is Victoria."

India tilted her head to one side as they walked back toward the stables.

"You know, four seasons in one day?" Sim said.

"I've heard that before. I thought it was a joke?"

"Oh no, it's real."

When they passed through the stables and emerged into the yard, several cars were coming up the driveway, one after the other.

India's stomach muscles tightened. But then Sim's shoulder brushed hers. At the contact, a wave of reassuring energy eased over her, dissipating her nerves.

Whether Sim realized it or not, she was emitting strong empathetic magic.

Nan met them at the kitchen door.

"Sim, India," she said, "perfect timing. Can you come and help with the platters?"

As a mellow indigo sky deepened above the farm, Nan stood barefoot in front of the woodpile in jeans and a sleeveless parka, her silvering hair falling loose to her shoulders, the fading light gilding it white gold. She brandished a rolled-up newspaper like a sword, the top end of it alight, and tightly wedged it into the center of the stack.

India stood back a little from most of her family, almost at the stump where she'd sat earlier. Right now, though, that stump was occupied by Sim and her family. Nate stood to India's left, but he didn't watch the bonfire—his eyes were on Sim.

Like Nan, all the adults were barefoot. Some of the older children were too, but the younger ones were still in shoes or gumboots.

The grass was cool beneath India's feet. Surely once night truly fell, the ground would be uncomfortably cold. But apparently this was how the family practiced their magic.

At last, the fire's warmth reached out with slow flicks of heat as the flames spread across the stack, the small burning core gradually consuming the whole, until eventually the fire leaped high into the deepening indigo sky. Behind the dancing flames, the dark of the new moon gave way to scattered pinpoints of starlight.

A cold shiver trickled down India's spine.

The children enjoyed the bonfire for some time with marshmallows staked on long twigs, and damper, too, which they'd either rolled in foil or mashed around long sticks before setting it into the outlying coals.

The atmosphere was surreal. The chatter; the warmth on a cold night; the dancing flames, mesmerizing in their beauty and ferocity. Eventually, the younger ones were taken back to the house. A movie was set up in the lounge with the oldest underage cousin supervising.

Nan came over and took India's hand. The smile on her

handsome face was tinged with sadness. This must be hard —all her children present bar one. India's palms began to sweat.

"Nan," India whispered, "I'm really not sure about this."

Nan's mouth curved down for a moment. "Hush, my dear. This is one place where you are safe." A steely look entered Nan's eyes. "And after tonight, you will be even more so."

India surveyed the faces of everyone in her family. They'd all moved closer to the fire as it started to burn deeper into the felled tree. Sim, who'd stayed, stood beside Nate with a thoughtful expression.

"So what happens now?" India asked.

Nan looked around at her family before smiling at India. "Now we conduct our business," she said.

India raised one eyebrow.

"Sorry, dear. That's what we call it when we make magic."

India allowed Nan to lead her closer to the fire. To her family.

"Jack, Henry, Steven," Nan called to her sons. They all stopped their conversations and looked up to their mother. The matriarch. "Would you take the first three points? Nate, would you take the fourth?"

"We"—Nan gestured to her sons and Nate—"will be the five points of the star, five points to guide the five elements. We are the strongest and will help the rest of the family to join their magic to ours. Once we're all joined, we'll have a complete circle. By holding your hand, India, I can then bring you in. And from there, your magic will find its level." Nan smiled softly. "And that's it. After that, we can begin our rite."

Nan, Nate, and India's uncles took their places. In the light of the flames, India studied their faces, which were occasionally claimed by shadows, occasionally illuminated with a golden glow. Determination rang true in all of their expressions.

"Simone, dear, would you take a seat at the log?" Nan asked.

A curious frown crossed Sim's face, but she moved to the log and drew her knees up, under her chin. Nan, keeping a firm hold of India's hand the whole time, eventually directed every family member at a specific place around the fire until a full circle had been formed. India took a deep breath, battled the impulse to wrench her hand away and run to the safety of the house.

But her mother had clearly made a life-shattering choice to protect her. If Annette could do that, India could do this.

She squeezed Nan's hand. She wasn't going anywhere.

19

India opened up her magic as Nan closed her eyes. Her grandmother was five-and-a-half-feet tall, but in this setting, she dominated her family. Not through size, but through the weight of her magic.

Energy currents swirled in all directions. Nan and the others glowed in a kaleidoscope of hues, and the fire radiated energy in sparkling gold and reds.

"Mother Earth," Nan said, "we thank you for receiving our house. We thank you for your water." Jack's energy levels increased, and suddenly, his swirling waves formed into a single line that leaped from him into the fire, and from the fire into Nan. "We thank you for your wind." Steve's energy poured into the fire and then into Nan. "We thank you for your earth. We thank you for your fire." Steve's and Nate's energies joined too. "We thank you for your magic." Nan's own energy combined with the four others and poured back into the fire.

The fire erupted in a giant flash of flame and pushed a single strand of the combined energies into all five family members. With the fire in the center, their energies created a perfect five-pointed star.

Every inch of India's skin tingled. She shut her magic down and looked around with human eyes. She could still see her family, still scent the magic that had occurred, but couldn't detect the star-shaped strand of energy.

And then Nan spoke again, asked the other family members to join their energy to the fire. India opened her magic up once more, watched in awe as each family member did so. Once they were all joined, their combined magic created a circle of fire-lit energy, the star nestled within, and connected at each of the five points.

At first the crystal beads seemed still, an unbroken connection between each of the family members. But no, the beads still moved, only at a pace that must have approached the speed of light because they created an illusion of one continuous beam of energy.

And their colors changed. Each family member gave the ribbon of light a different color, and once the energy passed through the fire it was tinged with a gold-red glow. It was clear who the stronger witches were—their energies rode at higher levels in the ribbon. Nan's were at the top. Entranced by the energy, and how it transmuted between the fire and the family, India almost missed the squeeze on her hand.

She looked up, startled.

Nan watched her with a half-smile and held out a silver-hilted ceremonial knife.

"And now," Nan said, "we thank you, Mother Earth, for welcoming the next of our house to this circle."

India stretched out her free hand, the prick of the knife on the pad of her thumb a minor sting as it broke the skin.

Next, Nan took the knife and broke the skin on her own thumb.

Something gave an almighty tug on India's energy. Her crystals simply spiraled out from within her, the delicate beads spinning faster and faster as they arrowed into the flames. As they—*she*—hit the fire, a wash of sensations flowed through her.

Right before India's vision was overtaken, an enormous arc of green and gold flame burst from the fire and lit up the sky. And then the fire was gone, her family were gone, the hills and land were gone. Instead, she raced through a cosmic landscape, its darkness absolute but broken in bursts with worlds being born, supernovas exploding, atoms spinning in perfectly synchronized formations.

Her eyes finally acclimated to the strobe-like effect, but then, jerked into a primeval landscape, she was sent flying over towering trees and rivers and gorges and volcanos. The earth opened, and she fell through a giant crevice to a molten core, which spun a million times faster than anything she knew to be possible. The white-gold core pushed her up and out into an ocean teaming with life and color and tastes and sounds.

Next, she was at the foot of a giant, familiar Tree, its gnarled, blackened trunk—which should have been frightening—instead pulsed with love. With life.

In the blink of an eye, she was returned to the hillside.

As the vision fell away from her magic-sight, her family were once more visible to her, their energies combined with hers now. The gold-red circle and star now held an inner emerald core. Another tug came, not on her body but within her, and she followed the pull to find the energy strand attached to it.

It was the color she associated with Nan.

No sooner had she completed that thought than she followed the strand right back to her grandmother. Could have, if she wanted, followed it *into* Nan. Instinctively, she balked at going farther. Instead, she withdrew her mind and returned to her body.

It was then that she looked at the circle of other energies combining with hers. They were all there—the energies of each family member—in neat layers.

And hers was at the very top.

It was the lack of warmth in her palm that drew her attention away from the circle of energy, back into the human world. A fluttering hit her belly.

"Nan? Why did you let go? I thought we were going to cast a spell."

Nan's mouth opened, but no sound came out. Her arms dropped to her sides. The ceremonial knife fell softly to the grass. The rest of India's family lowered their hands too. With the physical connection gone, the circle of energy disappeared, and the fire also winked out. What had been a phenomenal sight was now simply a waning bonfire.

The butterflies dropped, deadweights, to the pit of India's stomach.

"You need to tell me what's going on, Nan," India said. "Now."

Nan's shoulders slumped.

"You can tell me. Nan, you can trust me."

"India, no, it's not about trust. That's not the problem, or at least it wasn't. Dear lord, I don't even know how many more problems we have now."

Nan sat beside Sim on the stump.

"Maybe I should go," Sim said and shifted.

"That's not necessary, dear." Nan patted Sim's knee, even as she sighed again. "It looks like it is indeed time for truths."

India sat down on her grandmother's other side.

"I've been gone for eighteen years, Nan," she said. "I've gone from having almost no magic to more than I ever knew existed. Please, tell me. Tell me what I need to know."

Nan sighed and then straightened her shoulders. "India, your magic is tri-dimensional. You know that there are the three worlds—our Mortalworld, the Heavens and the Underworld.

"Your mortal maternal line brings you witchcraft—our family tree has always produced uncommonly strong practitioners. Almost everyone born from our line carries a gene that enables them to influence the world around them through their energy. But we can only *influence* the world. In fact, we use ritual to ask common requests, sometimes even harder, rarer requests, but we always ask the world to work with us."

India nodded. "Go on."

"Your Higherworld gene comes from your paternal line, your father's people. I know Thrane told you that today. But what you don't know yet ... well, you also have an Underworld gene, as do all my children, through my father's family. He was once a lord of the Underworld."

India stared at Nan, then at the rest of her family.

"Your father?" she asked.

"Yes, dear. And your heritage is why you need—needed—our protection. You're my granddaughter." She paused. "Annette's baby. I would try anything to keep you safe."

"But why, Nan? What on earth am I in danger from?"

Nan moistened her lips, seemed to be trying to find the right words.

Nate stepped forward. "Your mother was afraid your magic would get you killed," he said. "We think the spell she crafted to protect you began eroding after she died. Bit by bit, your magic has been regaining its strength. Which means that, potentially, you could now be located by other supernatural beings. Anyone who is trained to track witch-craft will be able to see yours easily because it's so strong."

India looked at her cousin for a long moment. "The attack at the hotel?"

"That was likely an opportunistic attempt given there was only one attacker and you didn't plan to stop in town for the night."

"Who?" India asked. "Who on earth is trying to kill me, and you still haven't explained why they want to?"

"That secret is not theirs to tell, India," Thrane said, emerging from behind the bonfire, his massive silhouette backlit in red and gold.

Heat flared through India's belly. She forced herself to ignore it and stood up, waited as he stalked toward her. The carved planes of his jaw tensed. Steely strength menaced from his body.

Everything feminine in her wanted to run and jump him.

But she also recognized the danger pouring off him. Her magic flared, and his energy—made from diamond-hard crystals—formed a barbed wire fence surrounding him. His control was absolute, and not one bead moved outside of their tightly contained orbit.

"And why not? For the same reason you think I'm a danger?" India asked.

"He doesn't think you're a danger, India," Nan said.

"You're wrong, Nan." India didn't look away from Thrane, because she'd caught the expression on his face—he absolutely disagreed with Nan.

India regarded Thrane as he did her. Finally, his eyes widened and his mouth tightened. He whipped around.

"You cast the circle? Elizabeth, what the fuck—"

India jumped up, pushed a hand against Thrane's chest. A sizzle of heat curled through her skin. She ignored it through sheer force of will.

"Don't try to intimidate my grandmother, Thrane."

"By the gods, you still don't know do you?" he said.

"Oh, for crap's sake, of course not. Because no one ever tells me anything, except in bits and pieces. Which only raises more questions!" India sensed the tips of her hair rise as her magic rushed through her, igniting in a wild torrent. "So why don't you sit the hell down and tell me?"

Wind roared into the paddock and crashed into Thrane like an invisible wall. He flew backward onto the grass. Tried to get to his feet, but the wind kept him pinned, and India relished the flow of power that allowed her to keep him right there. At her command.

Then Nan was at her side, and their family watched, in various states of disbelief— wariness, nerves, horror.

"Let him go, dear," Nan said. "We will tell you."

"Fine. You can get up," India said and released her energy. The wind dissipated with a sharp sigh. "So, you were up to the part where you tell me who wants to kill me and why."

Thrane rose fluidly to his feet, which was amazing given his size.

He towered over her, but when he spoke his voice rose

gently into the air. "Your magic, born of the three worlds, might be the strongest ever known. And there is an Order who we believe want to kill you so they can steal your magic and use it themselves."

The juxtaposition of Thrane's hard body and soft voice sent a shiver through India, but she held her ground.

"An Order wants to kill me, steal my magic?" India raised an eyebrow. "That's pretty out there."

"You wield magic like it's silk, India. *You* are pretty out there yourself."

"So why do they need my magic? What are they trying to do? Take over the world or something?"

Thrane's eyes narrowed.

Her own narrowed in response. "No way."

"Yes, India. Only magic born of the three worlds has the power they need. And yes, they seek to take over the Mortalworld."

"What's your part in this?" India asked. "And stop telling me you're only a family friend."

"I'm here to protect—"

"Nate!" The yell echoed through the stables. "Nate!" The cousin who'd stayed with the youngest children came running toward them, brandishing a mobile phone. "Nate, you need to take this call. It's an emergency."

"Thrane," boomed an unknown voice, "Keeper of this region within the Mortalworld. I hail you with advice from the Heavens."

A man—dressed in a leather vest and skirt that each showcased the bulging perfection of sleek, deeply tanned muscles—materialized out of the darkness. Roman sandals of black leather wound up and around his calves. A black helmet with a green plume sat on top of midnight-black hair. The ensemble was finished with a forest-green cape that brushed the ground, and a scabbard, presumably holding a sword, which was peeking through the folds of the cape at his hip.

Respect flashed through India for any being who could wear that outfit. He was a punk rock Roman gladiator.

Thrane launched forward—a panther springing at its prey—and then he was pointing a massive, fierce sword under the gladiator's chin.

India blinked. She'd never seen Thrane move with such deadly grace and speed.

20

"Holy crap. Where did that come from?" India glanced around at the others, but no one else seemed perturbed by the sudden appearance of the sword.

Nate was talking on his phone, his body tense, though his eyes were fixed on the newcomer. Nan and India's uncles had formed a rough circle, and the rest of the family had moved inside it.

And India was in that circle. Surrounded by family.

"I'm the matriarch of this house," Nan said. "To what do we owe this pleasure?"

"Hail, Elizabeth, witchcraft maker and house matriarch," the man said and inclined his head by the slimmest fraction. Any farther and he'd have impaled himself upon Thrane's sword. "I am Oev. Herald to the House of Freya, and I come with a missive for India, daughter of Jev."

Thrane dropped his sword. His massive body shuddered.

India frowned. What was that about?

Nan stepped directly between India and the gladiator, so

India waved at the gladiator over her grandmother's head. "That's me," she said.

The rock-gladiator's gaze locked on her, and he regarded her for a long moment before he inclined his head deeply. No risk of impalement now.

"Your Higherworld family will travel henceforth to this place," he said. "They will bring you home for your fate to be recorded within the codex."

"Huh?" India blurted. "Fate? Codex?"

"Cut the formal talk, Oev," Thrane growled. "Who's coming?"

Oev shrugged. "Evine. Perhaps Jona if he wants to travel and see his *granddaughter*."

"Evine." Thrane shook his head slowly. "By all the bloody gods ... how long?"

"They'll be here when they're ready. Which could be any time."

"He's right," Thrane said, turning to Nan. "The Heavens always think they own the worlds. They could be here already, or they could be here in two weeks."

"But they will come?" Nan said.

"I'm sorry, Liz. If Evine claims India as a child of the Heavens, then they will come for her."

"Hold it right there, Thrane, Nan. You," India said and glared at Oev. "Everyone, stop talking like I'm not right here. Did you say granddaughter?"

"That is correct, daughter of Jev. Evine is your grandmother and Jona your grandsire. You are of the family of Freya, one of the oldest, proudest houses of the Higherworld." Oev's chin lifted. "It is an honor to be of our family."

"What the crap?" India said, and Nan alone met her eyes, fear blazing clear and strong in her gaze. But India was overwhelmed. "Wow. I mean, this is unexpected. Obviously, I know Dad had parents, but this wasn't how I thought I'd find them—meet them—whatever." Another thought hit her and she froze. "What if my other family try to claim me, Nan's father's family? They could lay a claim too, couldn't they?"

"What is this?" Oev asked Nan.

Nan scowled, then finally sighed. "My father," she said, "gave up the Underworld when he chose to live here in the Mortalworld with my mother. His wish was to be known only as the farmer he became. We gave him that wish. Only his children—and Thrane, of course—are still alive to know differently."

"But, Nan," India said, "if he was a supernatural being, isn't he, um, meant to be immortal?"

"Immortality is a bit of a con, dear, but in any event, Father allowed himself to pass from these worlds after my mother died."

"And you're not immortal?"

"I'm not," Nan said.

"So, are you saying, they—your father's family—could try and claim me too?"

"Of which domain was he lord?" Oev asked.

"Domain?" India said.

"The Underworld is broken into domains in which each lord carries total dominion," Oev said. "Clearly, India, your training has been as poor regarding the Underworld as it has the Higherworld."

Oev looked at Nan. Waited.

"Father was from the Helkin," Nan said.

There was silence around the bonfire. Everyone's faces were caught in varying stages of shock. Except Thrane's.

"That means something?" she asked.

"Yes, India," Thrane said. "Your grandmother and, there-fore, your family are descendants of Hel. One of the founding families of the Underworld."

"So we've got some history. Why is that so shocking?"

"Wait," Oev growled, glaring at Nan. "Are you in line for dominion?"

"It is a possibility," Nan said. "However, neither I, nor any of my children, nor their children—pending India's development—have been immortal. It has been a nonissue up until now."

"Elizabeth," Oev asked, "how could you have kept this a secret, for all of these years? They could come for her—any minute, any second. And they would have rights."

Nan shot a glance at Thrane.

"Uh, what does that mean?" India looked around. "Anyone?"

"Technically," Thrane said, "your familial lines from both the Underworld and the Heavens could claim you. They have different methods. It's very rare, but there's an accord that the first claiming family carry the claim."

"You realize that makes me sound like a commodity, right?" India said, crossing her arms. "Nan, you saw my magic in the circle. Did I read it right that my level is the highest in our family?"

"Oh, my dear, you did. And I'm so, so sorry. I thought we could recast the spell to shroud your magic. But it would only have worked if you were weaker than at least one of our house. We can't influence your magic."

Tears gathered in Nan's eyes; her skin was waxy, pale.

"Nan, sh. Here." India placed her arm around her grand-mother's shoulders.

"Elizabeth, you should not have tried to shroud her," Oev said softly, hands on his hips and a frown on his face that marred its perfection. "India's obligation to the spinner's codex is absolute. She is a daughter of the Higherworld."

"You say that like I know what you mean," India said.

"Elizabeth," Oev said in a strained voice, "how does your granddaughter not know of her obligation?"

"Bah, your definition of obligation differs to mine. And it's irrelevant. India doesn't know who you are, or why you're determined for her to see your spinner's book, or whatever you call it."

"Spinner's codex."

"As I said, whatever you call it."

India squeezed Nan's hand, pleased to see her grandmother had recovered her asperity.

"Wait, Oev—is that your name?" India said.

He nodded.

"Well, *Oev*, you keep talking about the Higherworld, and Thrane keeps talking about the Heavens. Are they the same?"

Oev cut a look at Thrane. His top lip curled. "You would listen to what *he* has to say?"

Thrane shouldered Oev aside to stand before India. "Don't pay any attention to Oev, India."

Firelight played on Thrane's muscles. His eyes were steady on hers, and she lost her train of thought the moment his gaze collided with hers. Heat. Fire. Beads of energy spinning and colliding.

India almost reached out to touch his chest, feel his hard warmth again. Only the physical sensation of her muscle movement recalled her to her surroundings, and she barely avoided the intimate contact. Holy crap, this man got to her.

Thrane placed the sword tip in the grass before he spoke. "Only beings from there call it the Higherworld," Thrane said, "the rest of us know it as the Heavens. But yes, they are one and the same."

She clamped down again on her desire and focused on his words.

"Okay, that kind of makes sense," India said. "Wait—when did you get a sword?"

"Now. It was hidden."

"Where?"

Silence.

"Right, clearly trust isn't one of our strong points here," India said. "Anyway, so you're saying that because my dad was not from earth—" She held up her hand when three people seemed about to launch into a rebuttal of that statement. "Sorry, not from *this* Earth, I have to have my fate recorded. Is that it?"

"As succinctly as possible, my dear, yes," Nan said. "But there is more—"

"Thrane, Nan," Nate said. He held up his mobile phone. "You need to hear this." He looked around at the family, all still watching the tableau playing out in front of them. "Let's get everyone back inside, as quickly as possible."

"Tell me," Thrane said, shooting Nate a hard look.

"That was the station. A body's been found in town. A young man who went missing on the same day as the attack on Tara." Nate rested a hand on Sim's shoulder. "He was almost unrecognizable from his injuries, but they found a mark cut into his forehead. Two horizontal cuts inside a circle."

A roar of wind whipped through the paddock; the fire funneled to life. Astounded that Thrane could generate such a reaction, India turned to the source. Thrane's head was bowed, then he raised it and leveled his gaze on her.

"The Order," he said.

BLOOD SURGED through Thrane's veins, but he ruthlessly kept himself in check as he clinically reviewed every possibility, every outcome.

"This is my Keep, and as heads of your respective houses you will obey me in this," Thrane said, looking at Liz and Oev. "Do you acknowledge my authority?"

Oev nodded immediately. "My house will recognize your authority."

"Of course, Thrane. We all know you're in charge." Liz's eyes cut to India, though.

Fuck, Liz was right, but he'd deal with that last. He swiveled to Nate. "Do as you said, make sure everyone's secure in the house." Confident Nate would execute the order, he placed a hand on India's arm, said, "I need to talk to you in a minute," then swiveled back to Oev. "Your people are coming this way soon, but we are prepared to fight. You either leave now and warn them, or stay and be prepared to fight yourself."

"I've known of you for centuries, Thrane, and while the occasion has never risen for us to fight side by side, I would stand with you for the World Tree if I ever had cause. However, my first allegiance is to my house, and I must warn them of what they advance into. Can you hold your Keep?"

Thrane growled low in his throat. "I will."

"Then I will depart," Oev said. With a final glance at India he pivoted and strode into the darkness.

"What do you need from me, Thrane?" Liz asked.

"Liz, I never wanted to purposely place you and your family in danger. I promised myself that a long time ago, and I haven't had to break that promise. But now, if the Order is here, then they're coming for the Tree or for India. You and I know they're probably coming for both." Thrane clenched his jaw. Hard. "The only way to protect your family is to cast a circle, and it needs to be a big one to contain the house. Thank the gods it's a black moon and you're strong enough to do it. But I need one more of your family. I *must* be with the Tree. And that means I can't be here. If they come here first, I need to know."

Comprehension bloomed in Liz's expression and her cheeks paled. "You need someone to remain outside of the circle."

"I do, Liz. The Tree does."

"I'll do it," India said.

"You can't, India." Thrane vehemently shook his head. "They're probably coming *for* you. And if they get you, they get your magic. That is an unacceptable risk."

"I should do it," Liz said.

"That won't work either," Thrane said. "You need to hold the spell."

Liz glanced at India.

"India doesn't know how to cast the spell, Liz, and you know it. She might have the raw power, but she has no experience in this type of magic. Plus, your family will have to accept her, and by the gods, their faces tonight didn't exactly shout a warm welcome."

"Who then?" Liz asked.

"Nate."

"No! Thrane, he's not—"

"He's a powerful witch in his own right. The next most powerful to you. I know this is frightening. I know you would put yourself in front of him every time. But we need to do this. And Nate can do it."

Liz looked at him like the matriarch she was. "Tell me what you need him to do."

That was an order, but Thrane understood her position and didn't fight her.

"At the first sign of activity here, I need Nate to push a spell into the fire, shooting it high and white, to make a flame big enough that I'll be able to see it from my place. I'll be watching out for it. And if I see it, I'll take position on your side of my property. I can fight the Order, but every advance warning makes it less likely that they will prevail."

"I'll head in and tell him," she said.

Thrane rested a hand on her shoulder. "I can do it."

"No. He's my blood, my responsibility I know you will do everything in your power to protect us. All of us." She touched his arm before striding back to the house.

"Which leaves you," Thrane said, looking down at India.

She stood as tall as his chin, an unusual occurrence given his height. He stepped closer—one more step and their bodies would touch. He couldn't seem to back away. Her green eyes bored into his. A flush rose high to tint her incandescent skin. Her desire, her confusion, as evident as his own. Thrane couldn't help himself; he cupped one smooth, vitally alive cheek.

"By the gods, India." A short, bitter laugh escaped him. "You should be running as far away from me as you can. You don't know what I have to do. What I have done. But I'm so hot for you, I swear I could explode right here. I want to sink so far into your heat I never come out."

Thrane dropped his hand, needed to turn away from her because his own words lit his desire even further. What the fuck was he doing? His first, his only, reason for being was to protect the World Tree. His people. A sliver of ice staked into his heart when he realized India was a distraction he could not afford.

"India, you need to go with Liz and your family. You must stay inside and do not leave your house for any purpose."

"What?" Her beautiful eyes widened, chilled.

"Do not argue. You are not allowed to argue with me. I am the Keeper. This is my fight." Why in the hell didn't she understand this? He wanted to roar his frustration. "Do as I bid in this, India. I'm begging you. Do not put your life at risk—it's far more vulnerable than you know."

The sliver of fear turned into a massive spike as he recalled the image the Tree had sent him—India on the ground. Thrane closed his eyes for one moment. By the gods, do not let that image be her death.

21

I n the house yard, India swallowed hard as Nan handed her a blanket.

"Here, take this," Nan said. "It's going to be a long, cold night. Now, you'll take the middle cottage. Between us all, we'll make a rough circle around the buildings, each of us at different points in the circle. You need to wait until you feel my magic cast the circle, and then join us." Nan paused, worry etched on her face. "This will be hard because your magic will try to rise above mine, which will disrupt the spell, or worse."

"What should I do if it does?"

"If you can't join, sit it out. With the new moon, we can create and hold the circle without your magic. But we should try to use you if we can. Wait till you hear my invocation."

"Okay."

"Good girl." Nan quickly squeezed India's hands. "We'll get there, dear. And don't worry about your uncles. This has been a shock, and I swear these men deal with surprise worse than anyone. But you're blood. They'll come around."

India jogged along the driveway, gravel crunching underfoot until she reached the cottage she'd been allocated. She hugged her arms tightly to her chest, shivering even under a thick jumper.

The lights in all the buildings were banked, and with the new moon emitting no light, it was hard to tell exactly where the front door to the cottage was located. She ran her hand over the timber-clad wall until she reached the doorway.

India was grateful her magic wasn't actually needed to make the spell work. Although she'd try joining the circle, no way did she want her unstable magic disturbing the spell, or worse, blowing back and hurting her family.

She couldn't see her grandmother, but as soon as Nan's voice carried the Latin invocation, India opened up her witchcraft.

Nan's energy spiraled out to meet the rest of the family, through the stables to the barn, then the first cottage, purposefully slipping around India, before returning to Nan.

The circle was cast.

It was a woven pattern, blues and purples and indigos, even gold. The circle didn't have a star at its heart this time as there was no internal focus here.

The circle thickened and grew, the energy currents pushing outward, past the cottages and the barn, until even the house and stables were enclosed within it.

India gasped. The combined energy rose in supplication to the wind. Lend us your strength. Feed us your will.

And the wind answered.

A gale howled up the hillside from all directions, racing faster and faster until it surrounded the circle.

The same wind that had knocked Thrane down in the paddock earlier was now an immeasurably stronger barrier —somehow working in all directions, at all angles.

India found herself caught up in the beauty of the witch-craft dance. Nan's magic continuously called to the wind, and the family supported Nan's energy to feed her request.

Even with the new moon, if Nan had been alone, surely her energy couldn't have lasted much longer. The strength needed to call the wind, bend it, shape it to the desired outcome was phenomenal.

Wow. This was why family acceptance was so crucial—it was her family that held Nan up to the spell. If they didn't trust her, or didn't support her, then their energy would never meet the demand either.

India took a deep breath, pushed the nerves away, and raised her energy. Holding her breath, she directed her currents toward the circle.

Maybe it was because she'd been holding Nan's hand, or because they'd just performed the blood exchange, but joining the circle had been much easier at the bonfire. Right now, her energy wanted to veer off, head toward Thrane's land.

She forced her focus back to Nan, finally corralled her energy into the direction she wanted until it met the circle. Joined it.

Her breath whooshed out.

But in the next instant, her energy picked up, spun faster, the angle growing steeper and steeper till her currents were riding up and through the circle—not in line with it.

Additional energy poured into the spell as Nan exerted more and more strength to maintain its equilibrium—barely holding it together. Tension rose, hard, buffered India from all directions.

She had to leave. Now.

India shut down her magic. The circle of energy disappeared from sight, as if a light had been switched off.

The tension subsided.

As India slid down the door and met the cold porch floor, its timber creaked beneath her weight. She raised her knees up, under her chin, wrapped her arms around them.

Back at the bonfire, in that one amazing moment when her magic had met the circle and placed her with the family —albeit on top—she'd been *part* of something. She'd connected with them.

And now, here she sat, again on the outside. Could she break back in? Would they even want her? Their faces, when she'd called the wind to hold Thrane down, said otherwise. And although Nan said they'd come around, what if they didn't? What if they never accepted her? Would she be a circle of one? Nan would support her, would push the family to do so. But Nan wouldn't be there forever, and what then?

India's head dropped forward and tears washed over her cheeks.

She scrubbed a fist over them, pushed them away. What the hell had she been thinking? She wasn't ready for any of this.

Pulling the blanket around her, she wrapped herself in the little warmth it offered. Was wrapped too in the scent of magic that steeped in the air, in the echoes of the gale as it growled and howled.

And she sat there. Alone.

Her eyes drifted toward Thrane's land.

He'd been mesmerizing up at the fire. Suddenly and completely in charge. But then, he always had been. Though never so overtly.

He was still a mystery though—was clearly holding something back.

Why all the secrets? Not that she could talk. She hadn't told anyone about the dream wind that called her into the forest.

Secrets and distrust on all sides. That was her issue. India didn't trust her family or Thrane. And they didn't trust her. Otherwise, there'd be no need for all the secrets.

But was that really it? Because she did trust Nan, in some ways. Her grandmother loved her, was clearly trying to protect her, just as Annette had.

And she was coming to trust Thrane—at least, she had been until he'd let it slip that he thought she was a danger.

A danger to what? India snorted. She wasn't nearly in control of her magic enough to be a danger to anyone.

So what was she? *Who* was she?

She was a witch—although, not one like her family knew or seemed able to comprehend.

She was determined—after all, she'd pushed to find her answers. Even when the world seemed hell-bent on getting in the way.

She was powerful—even without full control over her craft. And she was a child of three worlds. Of three families.

Energy surged through her. Holy crap. Now was the time to find out more about who she was. Suddenly, India knew what she had to do.

She eyed the gap between her cottage and the next. In the sky above, stars pinpointed a straight line to the north.

To the heart of the forest.

A familiar, sensory knock on the door to her witchcraft had her jumping to her feet. An image swept into her mind, the wind reaching out with a beckoning hand to call her over the hills into the forest.

She was a witch. She was determined. And she was powerful. She'd follow the dream that had called her here and find the heart of the forest.

Slipping away was easy. The wind was a roar keeping everything out but nothing in. Darkness veiled her movement as she stepped between the cottages. Within a minute, she stood behind the cottages.

The only thing between her and the forest was her family's spell.

India considered the magic circle carefully because she couldn't disrupt the spell. But her energy had spun at her command. Could she tamp it down on command as well? It was risky, given her lack of experience.

But the wind called her, and the vision from the dream was clear in her mind. She had to try. And so, she tightly reined her energy in, imagined a tiny ball of light locked in a chest held within herself. With a deep breath, she took a step into the energy that formed the circle.

Stepped out on the other side.

Her breath whooshed, and she looked back to check the circle's magic—it still pulsed and spun.

She *could* do this. Every new experience showed her yet another way her magic worked. And now, she was finally going to find the heart of the forest.

Anticipation prickled up her spine.

With one last glance behind her, she headed toward Thrane's property.

Moving in the general direction wasn't a problem, but it was so dark, she could easily go off course. While she'd walked this path once before, it had been from the other direction.

As the hillcrest rose above her, the sky that met the horizon was a rich black velvet studded with diamonds. She could keep going and hope she got there, or she could trust her witchcraft to guide her.

The decision wasn't hard.

Her sense of sight transmuted, and the landscape surrounding her changed, drastically, fantastically.

Rich brown swirls of energy spiraled low over the earth. The grass rolled beneath her feet, pushing a spring into every step. Deep emerald sparks glinted in the starlight wherever trees speared out of the ground. Tiny beads rushed past her, filling the air as the wind was called to the house. Even the sky was a living, breathing masterpiece of galaxies.

Finally, she reached the crest of the hill.

Far below, Thrane's property lay nestled in the early flora of the forest. From her vantage point, the forest was alive with great swells of greens and blues and browns, rolling back and forth, in and under the tips of the trees.

Deep within the forest, Thrane's crystal currents were readable, even across the night sky, but along with it a different energy glinted. Like stardust. Tiny beads of gold diamonds that lifted up, dissipating into the sky in an unending symphony of life.

India bounced on her feet and her pulse picked up. That had to be it. The heart of the forest.

One more energy trace caught her eye. A series of black beads so dense no light escaped at all, so dark they stood out even in the moonless night. Motionless in a suspended orbit. Alien to every other living thing.

She'd seen that before—the day Tara had been attacked.

And there were so many of them. All converging on Thrane's house.

The hairs on the back of her neck rose. How many people could Thrane take on all by himself? He was dangerous, capable—of that she was sure. But one man against many? No way.

Thrane needed help. Crap! She could run back down the hill to warn Nate and get help, but that would take forever. Or she could yell and try to warn Thrane, but that would give away her position.

Shit. Her only other option was to skirt around the beads and warn Thrane herself. She swallowed hard. Instinct warned her not to get anywhere near the owners of those energy beads.

But Thrane needed her.

She blew out a breath. She was a witch. She was powerful. She could do it.

With her magic activated, she knew where Thrane was in relation to the colorless energy beads, so if she skirted around the lower side of his house, she could get to him that way.

Her magic would guide them to escape and get help.

"Move," Ri'Kiant said, "you four, through the garden, single formation, search the abode. You two, with me. We'll clear the outside."

He looked at each of his fighters, each given the additional strength of witchcraft stolen earlier that day from a witch he had sacrificed in the city.

"The goal is the daughter of Jev." Ri'Kiant bit back the urge to cry out his glee. "You contain her. I will deal with her. Remember. You *must not kill* her." That was his purview alone.

He waited until all six had nodded. "The daughter of Jev was tracked to this location." Ri'Kiant shivered; he could taste his success now. "She is an enemy of our god. She is evil."

Trust shone in the young, impressionable faces before him. Absolute belief poured out of their honest eyes.

After eighteen years of humiliation, of failure, of his god's disappointment, Ri'Kiant was about to complete his mission. He was sure of it.

A black moon had risen. The witch had returned. Fate had finally smiled on him.

A vibration growled, trembled through the ground beneath Thrane's feet. It was a warning he'd received only once before in his existence. When the original World Tree had been attacked.

He'd been on patrol deep within the forest, surrounded by pine, fir, and birch when a tremor had shaken the earth. By the time he'd reached the Tree, it had been under full attack. Wave after wave of fighters from the Order had been throwing all their might to break through the ranks of Keepers who stood in their way.

The screams of his brethren, falling beneath death magic and Underworld weapons, had assaulted his ears. The acrid tang of smoke from fire grenades had stung his eyes and permeated his senses. But at that stage, the Order hadn't yet encircled the Tree, so Thrane had joined the rank closest to the World Tree.

And, he had later deduced, that was why he'd been the one the goddess Freya had summoned to her side.

The summons of a god is no light thing. The weight of

the call had taken him to his knees, and if he'd been fighting an immediate foe, no doubt he would have perished.

Instead, he'd staggered to the Tree. The summons had been unequivocal in its outcome, and the Tree had delivered him straight to the goddess.

In that brief moment, transported to the Heavens, Thrane had understood that it was the Tree that had made the earth tremble. It had radiated its power through its roots in the direction of all Keepers, alerting them to imminent danger.

That night had changed Thrane's life. And now, that same tremor had shaken the ground.

His heart skipped a beat. Was he once more on the wrong side of the Tree?

From his vantage point, he checked the fire on the hill for Nate's sign. No white flares lit the night sky. India and her family were safe within the circle.

The trembling ground signaled a different danger. The Tree.

INDIA PASSED through the side gate to Thrane's property and paused behind the first tree she came to. The energy traces were harder to discern among the plants and trees surrounding the house.

While she didn't know their cause, her innermost core of knowledge screamed "wrong."

What could she do to stay away from those energy traces? She bit her lip, thinking. She could call up the wind to keep them from reaching her, but that might impact Nan's spell, and she didn't want to risk her family's safety. She could cast a spell to hide, which sounded good, except she didn't actually know how to do that. The one thing she could do well at the moment was detect the energies around her.

And so she poured all of her energy into her magic.

The energies around her flared brighter, hotter in patterns and rhythms, and while her mortal vision strained to see anything at all in the darkness, her witch-vision picked up movements void of any color. The black beads.

The closer she looked, the more voids she identified as they flickered in and out closer to Thrane's house.

Hunched over, India darted between the larger plants and established trees at the outer edge of the garden and took the longest path possible around the house toward Thrane.

The ground crunched underfoot. She'd found the tree-lined driveway. A row of rolling energy currents tempted her to follow the trees up to the house, but a quick check of the black energy beads told her that whoever owned them was still too close for comfort.

The greenhouses she'd seen on her first visit here were to her right—if she got to them, she'd have another layer of buildings between her and the dark beads. Then she'd skirt around them and get to Thrane.

That was motivation enough.

India didn't look back. She got to the tree on the other side of the driveway and pressed back into the foliage.

Her heart thudded in her chest, so loudly it was all she could hear. She inhaled a shaking breath, tried to calm her heart.

The hairs rose on her arms and on the back of her neck. Perhaps it was the absence of sound, the stillness of the air, but suddenly she knew, something, someone, was right behind her. Instinct pressured her to check the area.

Then something else—something not of this world—cried out in awareness within her. Shouted, screamed, *"Run!"*

She jumped. Ran.

A form materialized to her right.

Cries and yells, the furious crunch of gravel under many feet ricocheted through the garden.

India pushed her magic farther, harder, to easily guide her steps. She darted around plants and garden beds. The glowing currents dimmed. What the—?

She poured every last inch of her energy into her magic to keep the garden lit, ran down the grassy embankment to the creek, darted over the wisteria-draped bridge and back up the cobbled steps.

All the while shouts and cries echoed behind her.

They were coming, fast, but her magic and knowledge of the garden gave her an edge, because they hadn't caught her.

The greenhouses loomed out of the swirling energy currents. India raced headlong for the last of them and ran inside.

She focused more energy on her magic—but the energy currents sputtered, faded ... reappeared ... completely dropped away.

Stygian darkness met her gaze. The air was moist. Thick.

India almost cried out but swallowed the sound. She tried to push more witchcraft only to find—nothing. No inner core of energy. Her magic was gone.

Her stomach dropped.

Think, she had to think. Was there a door at the other

end? Trembling, she reached out. Cold metal met her hands —the workbenches. She knocked over small pots and plants, cringed with every clang that shattered the silence as she felt her way to the end.

Please, please let the door be near. She stretched out both hands and stepped away from the workbench.

She tripped over something, barely swallowed another scream as she fell against the glasshouse wall. She caught her breath but didn't stop—instead fumbled her way to a handle.

Her breath let out. She pressed down and the door swung out. A shape moved into the frame.

"So nice to meet you, daughter of Jev."

This time her scream let fly.

WITH HIS SCABBARD slung over his shoulder, Thrane reached the World Tree in moments, touched the smooth bark. Instantly, the Tree sent him an image of the Order—at his house.

Ice-hard, ice-cold, his blood froze in his veins.

Thrane ran.

Emerged into his yard minutes later, instinctively blending his form with the plants along the edge. Voices and the sounds of movement clearly came from the other side of his house, from the direction of the greenhouses.

He smoothly drew his sword from the scabbard, silently placed the scabbard on the ground. Then bringing his sword to the ready in a two-handed grip, he slowed his speed, slowed his heart, until he was nothing but precision, purpose.

No stray thought, no errant emotion, no wasted movement.

For a century, he'd strategized and practiced plans for attack and defense from every angle, from one foe to many, and so he confidently, silently stepped toward the far side of his house.

The dark of the moonless sky kept the Order hidden from his sight—and him from theirs—but they made enough noise to alert the dead.

A smart assault would leave scouts on the perimeter, so he angled his attack between his conifers and spruces, left no line of sight from the house. Began to stalk his prey.

He came upon the first soldier from the side. One view of the lined circle tattooed into the skin, and Thrane sliced his sword in a swift, efficient arc, taking the fighter down in one movement.

He caught the body, soundlessly lowered it to the ground.

Sword still held at the ready, Thrane stepped over the form, followed the next sound. Two voices signaled soldiers ahead, moving fast. He made swift work of both.

Blood splattered, the warmth of it hit his face even as more shouts came from closer to the house. He stilled, calculated three different fighters from the voices ahead. Based on the location of those he'd dispatched already, the Order were in an arrowhead formation, so he'd—

Glass shattering and a curdling scream rented the air.

He knew that scream.

Everything in him stopped.

"India!" Her name was torn from his throat. He ran straight for the last greenhouse.

The three Order fighters appeared and fell beneath his

sword, one after the other. He reached the door and shoved through. At the other end, India lay on the ground by the door. A figure bent over her.

Thrane's heart thudded hard in his chest, blood rushed to every single part of his being. A roar hurtled through him.

"India—light!" he shouted.

He raised his sword high, thundered down the aisle. A sliver of illumination appeared. Lit a face he knew only too well. The demon responsible for the last deadly attack on the Tree. A furnace blasted away the ice in his veins.

"Ri'Kiant!" Thrane said and brought his sword around.

The demon reared back, its human face recoiling for an instant. Then his eyes widened, and he cursed, spun and fled. Thrane leaped over India, sword still raised, and followed Ri'Kiant into the night. He threw himself through the air and, sword extended, lunged with everything he had.

His blade caught the arm of the demon, cleanly slicing through flesh and bone. The severed arm thudded to the ground. Blood spewed, dark and wet, from the demon's shoulder.

Ri'Kiant screamed, spun, and threw a knife straight at Thrane's head.

Thrane dropped to his knees, skidded though the gravel and threw his head back. The knife sped through the air above him, its blade glinting in the starlight.

With a curse, Thrane launched to his feet, used the sound of Ri'Kiant's heavy footfalls to follow him. But as Thrane reached the road, a car screeched around the corner, and the demon leaped in through its flung-open door.

Thrane hauled in a breath, stared at the taillights as the car fishtailed, then disappeared into the night.

"By all the fucking gods." He whirled around, ran back to the greenhouse.

India.

He reached the greenhouse as she staggered to her feet, ethereal cheeks pale, washed out against the ink of her hair. Wide eyes stared up at him.

He grabbed her arm to steady her when she wobbled. The instant her cool skin touched his, his blood boiled. He clenched his teeth—tried to contain the bitter burn inside but failed.

"What the fuck, India! What the fuck are you doing here? By the gods, woman, you should be—you were almost—"

"Dead?" she whispered.

He hauled India into his arms, crushed her to his chest. Gods, he never wanted to let her go. His heart pounded, hard, fast, and he swore it suddenly beat right in time with India's.

His arms tightened even as he struggled to gain his equilibrium.

"Squishing me, Thrane, you're squishing—"

He immediately loosed his grip.

"—me."

"Hush, India, hush. I need a moment." Thrane closed his eyes, and he held her. Gods, the demon had been bent over her. Her life had been about to end—and the truth of that shattered him more than the knowledge that the next death after hers would have been the Tree's.

How, by the gods, had she come to mean so much to him so quickly?

Abruptly, he realized she wasn't struggling, and he opened his eyes.

"India, are you hurt?" He didn't wait for an answer. "Use your magic, you need to tell me now if there's an injury."

"I'm not hurt. But I can't use my magic."

"Are you sure?"

"Yes, I'm sure. I used up all my energy. The light I made when you came in took everything I had." India rolled her shoulders, winced. "Apart from that, I'm okay." Her voice wavered, and a tremble ran through her, into him. "But I think that if you hadn't arrived when you did, I would definitely not be okay right now."

"That's an understatement." He picked up his sword, pulled her with him. "Come on, I need to check the bodies."

"Bodies?"

"By the gods, what did you expect?" he said and grasped her wrist firmly. "I told you—I fucking told you—not to leave the circle. And yet here you are."

"Hey! I was coming to warn you. I saw a heap of these, these weird beads of energy. They didn't even move, and I was coming to tell you they were at your house."

"We already knew that was a possibility, India. That's why we had the plan. The one where you were meant to stay at the farm inside the family circle, remember?"

"Ouch, ease up, Thrane. Let go."

Thrane looked down at her wrist held within his hand. He loosened his grip. For a moment.

"Not a chance in hell. You're staying right beside me while I check every one of these bodies. And then, you and I are going to have the completely honest talk you've been wanting."

"Wow, great," India said. "Now you want to talk."

"I've never had an issue with talking to you."

Accusation clearly settled over her features, but he

didn't have time to deal with it. He set about the grim task of checking each of the bodies, five in total, all killed with one strike from his sword. His skin was sticky, and he frowned at the bloody smudges streaked across India's clothes and face from where he'd held her.

"I need to take care of these bodies. Then I need to wash." He pulled India along behind him—she had to jog to keep up, but he didn't care. As far as he was concerned, she had placed herself in danger, in life-threatening danger, and she was going to get some home truths as soon as he wasn't covered in bloody gore.

"Is that man, that thing, going to come back?" India asked.

Thrane growled. "Of course." Bitterness coated his voice —but he couldn't keep it at bay. "Not tonight, but yes, he'll be back, with more fighters and more determined than ever."

"Should we get help?"

"India." He had to stop himself from shaking her. "I *am* the help. Now come on."

Thrane took a large bucket of salt from his storage shed. The salt, imbued with the World Tree's energy, came from the Heavens. He scattered it over the remains, even the demon's arm, and let the salt work its magic. It would completely consume the remains, and then the souls would be returned to the Heavens. He and his brethren Keepers had always undertaken this cleansing rite for the souls the Order left behind.

After the grim task was done, he looked hard at India, standing mutely at the greenhouse door. Her face was pale in the moonless sky, but he easily made out smudges and scrapes.

He looked down at himself—his clothes were covered in even more gore now. He grimaced again and battled for calm. Adrenaline pushed him to keep up the fight. Rage threatened to consume him at having come so close to losing everything.

Finally, he took a shattered breath, his exhale visibly dissipating into the icy air. Shit. He picked up India's limp, cold hand.

"It's close to freezing out here," he said. "Come on."

He led India into his house, didn't bother with the main lights but went straight into the bathroom. He flicked two switches and the bathroom lit up in a golden glow, revealed his walk-in shower and the claw-foot bathtub opposite.

"The floor tiles will warm up in a few minutes." He struggled to manage a calm voice, refused to give in to the utter rage that still pulsed through his veins.

"Sit." He practically placed India on the edge of the tub. "Stay."

"Thrane, I can wait outside."

"No. You are staying right here where I can see you."

24

The splatters and streaks of blood and gross matter that covered Thrane shone wetly in the mellow light. India should've been repulsed, but the heat emanating from his body, the intensity of his unwavering regard, had India's gaze fixed firmly on Thrane's massive form.

She sat numbly where he'd placed her, apparently unable, maybe unwilling, to move.

A wave of ice poured through her veins, and suddenly she was alone, though Thrane was only a step away. Where had their closeness gone? Back in the greenhouse, after ... after the attack, Thrane had held her so tightly they'd been almost one being.

They'd connected in that instant.

And she'd come very, very close, right there in that greenhouse, to losing her life and missing out entirely on that connection.

Thrane opened the shower door. A tremor shook his body as he reached in and turned on the spray. It was a reaction she'd never seen him display. He was always so sure, so confident, the master of every situation. His hands trembled again as he adjusted the temperature. He stood back as the water started to stream, his hands clenched and his eyes closed.

She instinctively reached with her witchcraft to understand his feelings but still had no power to call on. Why had it gone? Was it temporary ... or .... or—

Her mind blanked, her throat closed. She forced a breath in and out.

"Thrane," she said and cleared her throat. "Thrane, ah, I need to ask you something?"

He glanced over. Eyes guarded. "What?"

She bit her lip. The sting helped cut through the panic.

"Can ... can witches drain their magic? To the point of no return?"

"It hasn't returned yet?"

She shook her head.

Thrane stared at her hard.

"India, your magic is so different that I don't think anyone knows what to expect."

Her chest tightened, and she inhaled sharply.

"Hey, breathe, India. There's no need to panic. I know of others, not only witches, who have exhausted their powers only to have them return after sustenance and rest. It's a function of your body and needs your energy, right? So, if you overuse it, it makes sense that you'll need to rebuild your reserves."

India hauled in a shaky breath. Her shoulders dropped.

"Thank God. It doesn't feel permanent, but, well, I've just found my magic. I guess I'm not ready to lose it yet."

"By the gods, India. You pushed yourself hard. Too.

Fucking. Hard," Thrane said, staring at her, his eyes tainted by something dark, deep. "And risked it all."

Hope at the knowledge her magic would return warred with worry over Thrane's obvious tension. And without her magic, she was on her own with only her human senses to guide her. Adding to that, she was overwhelmingly tired.

Thrane's muscles were drawn taut. His jaw ticked. He looked as if he was on the edge of a precipice with no way to keep himself from falling. Those capable hands clenched tighter, and he exhaled through flared nostrils before finally inhaling. A heartbeat later, he drew his gore-covered shirt up and over his head.

His body was a masterpiece of beautifully carved, deeply tanned skin that flowed from his abdomen to his chest and up to his shoulders. A leather necklace with a medallion was fixed around his neck. His biceps bunched and released as he reached out and dropped the shirt into the bathtub beside her.

Nope. She wasn't numb. She was on fire.

She followed his every movement, and when he touched the button on his jeans, her mouth went dry. Was it appropriate to watch him undress? Should she shut her eyes? She could always turn around. And since when had she been attracted to such overt muscles? Never before had the sight of such—

Okay, he was undoing his jeans.

Lean hips, an indent of muscle that absolutely invited someone—her—to follow it down to his groin, where a pair of black trunks covered his dick. His legs were long and muscled like the rest of him.

He tossed his jeans in the corner, gripped the edges of his trunks. Then he paused.

What was he waiting for?

Oh crap, she was still staring—maybe he didn't want to undress in front of her.

She licked her lips. "Thrane, I'll, ah, wait outside if you'd prefer."

"No." Gravel strained his voice. "India, you could've died tonight. *Everyone* could've died tonight. You are staying right here where I can see you. Turn around if the blood of your enemies is too much to stand."

Another shiver racked her.

"Are you cold?" he asked.

She shook her head, unsure of the reason she was shaking.

"You're shivering. If you're not cold, it will be the adrenaline wearing off. It's normal, all you can do is ride it out."

"It's like I've had too many coffees, but I'm still wiped out. Is your adrenaline wearing off? Is that why you were trembling?"

"I wasn't trembling. I was shaking. With anger. I'm *still* angry. But yes, my adrenaline is waning too. Although, I've had plenty of practice riding out the wave."

"Okay. Shaking, not trembling. Got it."

As he drew down his underwear his eyes flared, heated with desire. But behind that heat, the ocean of his internal struggle broke through.

"Thrane," India said and almost reeled from his visible pain. "I didn't want, never wanted, to hurt you."

Thrane ducked his head, but when he looked back at her, only the heat of desire blazed from the chocolate depths of his gaze. And suddenly, his desire was urgently, clearly evident. India couldn't help herself—even if she'd wanted to. She stared at his hard, thick erection. Desire mixed with anticipation to pool in the pit of her stomach.

"Your actions today were more reckless than I can even begin to say," Thrane said. "But yes, I want you. Still. As I have since the night I first saw you at the hotel."

He stepped into the shower enclosure then, and closed the glass door behind him. The water streamed over him, caressed, that hard, amazing body. India wanted to be that water. Steam billowed and rolled and began to fog over the glass, hiding more and more of that wonderful sight.

The break in her view caused her to look down. Her hands were scraped, crusted with soil and beads of blood. Even more blood stained her clothing from where Thrane had held her against him.

That moment might've been the closest she'd ever been to another person. He'd held her so tightly, as if she were an essential part of him—maybe, even, essential *to* him. She'd relished being wanted, needed. At least until she'd needed to breathe.

India had known in that moment that he was a decent man. He'd been maddening, frustrating, autocratic, but he'd also been kind and gentle. And tonight—tonight he'd been vulnerable. The tendril of emotion that had unfurled within her and attached to him only yesterday, now pulsed with a whisper of something special, past the physical.

Need. Want. Desire. *Connection.*

Holy crap—it wasn't possible.

Her heart leaped in her chest, and she jumped up from the bath, as if she could run away from the thought. She wasn't looking for any emotional entanglement. And come on, she'd known him for, what, seven days? And those seven days had been filled with secrets, danger. Hurt.

But she saw more, saw something she wanted more than anything else. Could she take this moment? Experience what Thrane's darkly dangerous body now promised?

India looked over at the shower.

Met Thrane's heavy-lidded gaze through the steam.

She'd almost missed this opportunity. If Thrane had arrived one second later, she'd be dead now.

India's stomach tightened. How dare anyone—anything —try to get in the way of this feeling? This driving, raging need.

For him.

"Thrane, I'm covered in grime too. I should shower as well." Not wanting to lose her nerve, India quickly undressed, dropped her clothes in the tub with his. Opened the door, met his hot, hot gaze. "I think I should tell you— that is, to be clear, I feel the same. Since that first night at the hotel. I don't want any miscommunication."

The fire in his eyes burned deeper.

"Can I?" She gestured into the cubicle.

His nostrils flared, and he paused.

Was he going to let her in? She searched his eyes, found the mirror of her own rage, her own search for meaning, blazing back at her.

Finally, he stepped to one side, made room for her under the spray. Steam billowed, surrounded them, wrapped around and entwined them. Turned the glass opaque. And then they were alone, together, locked in a world of warm gray mist.

Thrane reached around India and took a bottle of something from an inbuilt ledge in the marble wall.

"Your hair will get wet. Can I wash it?" he asked.

Words that had once come easily suddenly dried up, but

she locked her eyes on his, nodded. He poured some of the amber liquid from the bottle into his palm. A fresh scent, tangy with blossom, bloomed. He rubbed his palms together briefly, then placed his warm, strong, capable hands on her arms.

Her skin erupted in a sunburst of heat beneath his touch.

India swayed, somehow kept her gaze on his hard, fierce face. Thick dark eyelashes, spiked with water, framed his melted-chocolate eyes. Wordless still, she searched their depths, could've sunk into the sea of desire that filled them.

Their connection pulsed again, and even without her magic, the visceral tug sent a thrill inside her. Thrane's hands caressed up her arms to her shoulders. Color hit high on his cheeks and his lips tightened.

Everywhere his hands swept, deep, drugging heat beckoned her closer. Her head fell forward under the onslaught of sensation, and she caught sight of the disk-shaped pendant lying flush to his chest.

Somehow, she raised her head. His proud, strong face was so close. All hard angles and dangerous planes. Planes she wanted to touch. She finally gave in, reached up to cup his clenched jaw.

As if her touch was the permission he needed, he ran his calloused hands, blissfully hot and firm, over her shoulders and around her back. Down her arms to her fingertips.

He warmed her up from the inside out.

Aches and pains, present earlier, now melted under his touch. She groaned, and yet again, he seemed to understand her unspoken thoughts because he turned her, so her back was to his chest. Pressing harder now, he spread his fingers over her skin, deeply kneading her tight muscles.

For long minutes, he worked over knot after knot, and her body responded. Strain dissipated beneath a tide of hot, relaxing pressure.

Her desire mellowed, the earlier fire now a bed of embers tingling at her core, lazy under the blanket of comforting, warm sensations.

And then his palms swept down to the flare of her hip, around her waist. Dipped into the hollow at the top of her bottom, up and over her stomach. His hands skirted the sides of her breasts, her nipples tightening into flushed red nubs before he finally cupped her breasts.

She inhaled sharply, pushed the swell of her breasts into his palms. He thumbed her nipples, and sensation spiked, raced from the tips of her breasts, gathered in a firestorm at her core.

Desire punched hard and fast, and the bed of embers caught aflame.

A growl rumbled from Thrane, then he let her go.

Swaying, India almost moaned at the loss of his touch. Only inhaled again when he turned her to face him. She waited, breathless, as he poured more of the amber liquid into his palm, then he knelt down and massaged her hips, her thighs, her calves, her feet, her toes.

And then he swayed, pressed his face into her groin.

His hot breath hit the junction of her thighs. She gasped, tilted her hips into his heat. Her fingers clenched in his hair, held him to her. Slowly, Thrane blew out one more breath, then rose to his feet. A dangerous god rising from his steamy ocean.

India would remember that image forever, of water streaming over his hard, deeply tanned muscles, the predatory gleam in his chocolate eyes.

"India, by the gods, you are mine tonight."

Emboldened by the hoarse rasp of his voice, she gave in to temptation, grasped the shaft of his penis. It was satin over steel, hard and hotter than any other part of him. He throbbed in her grasp. India wanted to drop to her knees and run her lips over it, wanted to impale herself on its length.

"India."

At the tone of his voice, she looked up, perplexed at the interruption.

"Let me take you to bed," he said. "I want to be inside you. Need to be inside you. I *need* you."

Heat flooded, and her core clenched at his words, at the intensity that shone from his eyes. India imagined him pushing into her, dragging through her inner muscles. Her breath came faster, and she instinctively tightened her grip.

Thrane shuddered, and his eyes closed. For the first time in her life, a feminine sense of power filled her. Control over his pleasure was a heady thing. His hand came up and covered hers, and he pushed himself within her grasp once, twice.

Opening his eyes, he gently, firmly, removed her hand.

"India, you'll undo me right here. But this time, our first time, needs to last longer."

India dropped her hand, with one last caress along his rigid erection.

He inhaled sharply, then turned off the water. Effort-lessly, he picked her up. Cradling her, wet and naked, to his chest once more, he carried her out of the bathroom into an adjoining darkened room.

25

Thrane set India down on her feet, onto thick carpet, and turned on a bedside-lamp. It cast a muted glow. Warm. Intimate. A large bed dominated the room, topped with a heavy quilt in hues of blues and greens.

"I'll be right back," Thrane said and quickly returned with two towels.

India dried herself briskly, noted Thrane's eyes on her, hot and full of promise, while he did the same.

"Here, it's freezing." He held up the quilt.

Grateful, she slipped beneath the thick blanket.

Though it was cold, India's internal furnace was on the rise. And every time she looked at Thrane, she wanted to jump straight into hot, sweaty, earthy sex. With *him*.

And yet, what was this force that reeled her to him? Why Thrane? Why now? The questions made her pause—but no, she wanted this. She wanted Thrane. No way was she turning back now, no matter what else was going on in her life.

And then he joined her under the covers, lithe, graceful.

His body heat warmed her up instantly. His eyes arrowed to her face, and he stilled.

"India, are you okay? Is this okay—us here, in my bed? If this is happening because you were almost killed tonight, and you're not ready ... it might undo me but"—his mouth twisted, half-smile, half-grimace—"if you need to stop, we'll stop."

Who wouldn't fall for someone so virtuous? India almost smacked her forehead. Uh-uh, this wasn't about emotions—this was about physical release. About desire. And she absolutely had that. She didn't have to think twice about what she wanted. Though now *he* clearly needed convincing.

"Thrane, remember when we stood in your garden, and you asked if I wanted to come inside?"

He nodded.

"I wanted to, but everything was moving so fast that I wanted to wait. Then tonight, I realized I never want to miss out on this. This experience, right now, with you. So, yeah, the timing is partly because of what happened tonight. But being here, being right here in this bed with *you*, is what it's all about. Because it's something I've wanted since the moment I first saw you."

His mouth twisted.

India willed him to see her, really see her. "I'm in charge of what I want here, Thrane. I'm doing what I want."

The burn ignited in his melted-chocolate gaze, and he picked up her palm, drew it to his mouth. Pressed a hot kiss to its center.

Fire flashed through her.

She didn't hold back, met him in the middle of the bed. He rolled them till he was on top, and she arched her breasts up to meet the muscled expanse of his chest. Pleasure swept through her at the heat, the press of his body on hers. Legs tangled. Hips pressed close.

And the fire fully reignited.

She hungrily accepted his tongue as he stroked it into her mouth, rubbed it against her own.

He tasted, retreated, invited her to follow, and then returned to taste her again. He tongued his way along her jaw. Pressed hot, hard lips to the hollow of her neck.

"Gods, India, I want you. Need to be in you. Now."

He laid searing kisses on the sensitive skin below her ear, down her neck to her breasts. His hot tongue swirled around one tip. He suckled her hard, and another flash of fire speared to her groin.

She pushed her hips against his hardness, undulated against him, desperate for pressure. Gasped again as the tip of his penis slipped into her slick folds for a brief moment.

More. She needed more of him inside her.

A groan tore through him, but instead of filling her, he drew back, shifted to kiss his way down her body.

And then he kissed her core. She drew in a broken breath—once—moaned as his tongue speared through her delicate folds, rubbed her clitoris.

Her hips rose, and he placed a warm hand on her stomach, held her down before he licked her harder, rasped against her sensitized flesh, over and over. Drew a firestorm inside her.

Her back bowed, her arms stretched above her head, trying to hold on to some invisible force as pressure, heat and need, coiled and coiled inside her.

Then he tasted her deeply. Drank her in and pressed

hard against her. The heat of his breath, the pressure of his tongue lashed against her, again and again.

An uncontrolled keen poured from her lips.

The coil crested in a surge she couldn't hold back, and she cried out as sensation after sensation pummeled her body.

He licked her hard through her orgasm, kept going until she was reduced to a quivering mess of limbs. He raised his head. The hard curve of his lips gleamed in the lamplight, his bright eyes focused on her core.

"More," he growled, a man starving. "India, I need more."

He pressed his mouth hard to her entry once again, pushed his tongue deep and hard within her in a hot velvet invasion. Feasted over and over. Her inner muscles clenched, and once more sensation spiked, crested, sent her flying to the stars. Only once she was back on earth did he shift, his huge form filling her vision as he crawled up her body, eyes locked on her core.

"Wait," India said. "Wait." Aftershocks ricocheted through her, and though she hadn't yet caught her breath, she managed to raise up on her elbow. "Condom."

"Right." He jerked a drawer open and rummaged through his bedside table.

Finally, he reared back onto his knees between her thighs. India's mouth went dry. The low lamplight lovingly gilded the sweeping curve of his deeply tanned, ropes of muscles. Unable to stop herself, India ran her hand over the ridges along his stomach, down, down farther. Helped Thrane cover himself.

Then she dropped back onto the bed, shifted her thighs. Let him see her.

His jaw tightened.

Her whole body clenched. Need, fierce and hot, swamped her.

"Gods, now, India," Thrane said and his large calloused hands took hold of her thighs and opened her wide to him.

She watched with him as he fed his thickness into her depths, inch by inch by inch. So large and hard and hot. She was impaled, stretched, filled. Only her earlier release allowed him to get this far.

She shifted her hips, a tiny keen escaped her.

"Sh, India." He steadied her, then inhaled a shuddering breath. He took another, his ribs expanded, and he pushed in farther.

Her body stretched, clamped tightly around him, and she moaned as he ran one hand up to palm her breast, caressed the still sensitized, tender flesh.

"Let me in, India." Thrane's voice was low, guttural. "Let me in."

Panting, she gradually relaxed, adjusted to his invasion.

"Look at me, India, let me see those emeralds."

She shifted her focus from the undeniable, incredible sensation to his eyes, to his mesmerizing gaze.

"That's it, love," he said.

His body shook, and India realized he was holding himself back, waiting for her to be comfortable with his size.

"Are you shaking now?" she asked.

Thrane barked a surprised laugh, even as his muscles shook again. "No, India."

The gravel in his voice, the utter sexiness of him, made her entire body clench.

"No, this is a tremble. For you."

She laughed, a throaty sound that matched his desire,

and with their gazes still tangled, she flexed her hips, an intrinsic feminine reaction.

He shuddered, arched his back, and pushed in even farther, pressing so deep she wanted to scream.

Utterly entranced by him, by the sensations wrought by his body, she flexed her hips again, this time on purpose, and placed the soles of her feet flat on the bed. She lifted her pelvis to take him all the way, gasped as he finally slid home and she was filled with heat.

She ran her hands over every inch of his body, delighted in the tremble that still quivered through him. Savored his heat, the utter luxury of having him inside her, around her, all over her.

"India," Thrane said, clutching at her hips. His teeth gnashed. "Can't—can't hold back."

He drove himself into her. Over and over, his length withdrew, pushed in. Dragged along her sensitive inner tissue, drew another firestorm of sensation with every inward and outward stroke.

Her back bowed again, her muscles tensed with every stroke. Pressure built higher and faster, until, with eyes locked on him, she convulsed on a scream.

And he shouted with her, pushed harder and harder, and then stilled. Held himself deep.

THRANE SHUDDERED as he emptied himself into India's silken hold. Her sheath still rippled from her orgasms, and the clasp and release of her body wrung him until he was dry.

Pleasure—pure, unadulterated pleasure—sang through

him in wave after wave. On his final thrust he held himself still, savored the exquisite sensation for as long as possible. Finally, he heaved in a deep breath.

India's dark hair was a shining pool on the cool linen. Her eyes, an emerald fire, slowly veiled as she closed them; her lips curved in a sated smile. That, the perfection of her, completed the moment. Sealed it in his memory, he sensed, forever.

He withdrew his hands from her hips with a soft caress, found no energy for anything else, and unceremoniously collapsed on top of India. Braced his weight on his forearms at the last moment to avoid crushing her.

He'd never encountered sex like this before. His entire body hummed with an electrical buzz. Urgency had demanded he get inside her, but then she'd somehow connected with an element of him—a place deep inside that no one else had ever found.

His world had shifted.

What by the gods was he meant to do now? The strength of India's magic meant she still posed the gravest danger the Tree had ever faced. And she was a mortal—he'd never had a romantic connection with a human.

Gods, he was in serious danger of forging an emotional bond, the kind he'd never thought to have. Apart from the kinship he had to his brethren Keepers, he'd not had a true emotional bond with another since his own parents had left this world hundreds of years ago. Yes, he cared for people. Look at Liz and her family. But they too would pass—he was ready, always, for that outcome.

He wasn't prepared for the depth of feeling, the connection that threatened—hell, had already forged ahead with

India. He knew only how easily a mortal could perish, all the dangers they faced in this world.

And what if it was him who was the danger to her? No being that represented a true danger to the Tree had survived Thrane's hand. But never before had a danger been innocent, as he believed India was.

And what about his involvement in Jev's death? India wouldn't want anything to do with him when she learned the full story of how her father had died. The weight of concern and guilt battled with the utter satisfaction that still rolled through his body. He exhaled long and low.

"Gods. That was incredible."

India opened her eyes. Their brilliance stole his breath, and as she placed one hand to his chest, his heart picked up pace. He knew he should move, should get up, out of India. Figure out what to do next. But he was utterly, physically happy—replete—right there. All he wanted was to sink down into her softness and hold her close.

But India set her stubborn, determined chin. He groaned.

"You're itching to ask questions, aren't you?" he asked and dropped a fast, hard kiss to her lips. "Let's get dressed. I'll make something to eat. You must be famished, I know I am, and we can talk."

"Well, that would be nice, thanks. But can I have something to wear?"

26

India cleaned up in the bathroom and pulled on a shirt that Thrane had given her. It hung to her knees, thankfully, because she had nothing else to wear. The shirt was a black long-sleeved jersey, soft from wear, and she lifted her shoulder to rub her nose in the fabric, inhaled Thrane's sexy scent.

She looked at herself, really looked at herself, in the bathroom mirror. Holy crap, so much had changed. Past the physical, India wasn't the same person she'd been a week ago. She knew her power—well, was learning about it at least—but more importantly, she *knew* she had power.

She'd come to Victoria looking for something. She'd thought all she'd wanted was answers, and to learn about her magic, but what if she'd been looking for more than that? Maybe ... maybe she'd been looking for connection. For emotional, unbreakable bonds. The kind that she'd had with her parents but had lost.

Could it be that somehow she'd formed such a bond with Thrane?

A shiver trickled down her spine.

Nuh-uh, no way. She glared at herself in the mirror. This wasn't some happily-ever-after love. She barely knew the man—and she was only visiting Warragul for heaven's sake. There were still too many unknowns for her to have made such a strong connection.

This thing with Thrane, it was physical. A bodily need. That was it. After all, the man *was* hotter than hell. Who wouldn't want to get naked with him? So what if sex with Thrane had been spectacular, tender, powerful—everything sex had never been for her before him?

Unique, a whisper echoed in her heart.

She pushed the voice away.

As she did, Thrane's reflection showed in the mirror. He scanned her legs, the shirt that covered her from neck to thigh. Desire flickered in the warm depths of his chocolate eyes.

"Tea's made," he said. "Thought you might like to sit in the library. When you're ready it's down the hall on the left."

"Thanks." She turned off the faucet and met Thrane's gaze. "Won't be a moment."

India finished up and padded down the corridor, the floorboards creaking with her steps and chilling her bare feet. Light spilled from an open doorway, and as she approached Thrane's muted voice sounded from within.

"Nate," he said, "I promise you, she's okay but tired, and without clean clothes."

India stepped into the room. Thrane held his mobile phone to his ear as he knelt in front of a large stone hearth, cajoling a fire to life. He was focused on the task but must have sensed her presence because he turned to face her.

She nodded in greeting and his eyes didn't leave her.

"Nate, I've got to go," he said. "Believe me when I say that Ri'Kiant is not a threat tonight. And he'll have to gather new fighters before he can fight again."

India barely noticed Thrane's words as he ended his conversation—her attention was captured by the room she'd walked into.

As large as the main living area at Nan's, the library had two full walls covered from floor to ceiling with bookshelves. The exterior wall was glass, and looked out at the night sky.

"How many books do you have?" she asked, finding one volume that looked really, really old.

Thrane stood up from the fireplace. The crackle and the dancing flames drew her closer. The faint smell of woodsmoke made her nose tingle. One look at him, warmly lit in the glow of the lamps and spreading fire, made her tingle in another place too.

She had the increasingly familiar urge to run and throw herself against that hard body. And now she knew just how hard and hot it was. She swallowed, unsure of what to say, do.

"The view from here during the day must make this a wonderful, beautiful place to be," she said.

"It is. It's my favorite room in the house. I do most of my writing here."

A small table at the end of the couch held two mugs of tea and a dinner-sized plate with a couple of sandwiches piled up. Thrane leaned over and handed her one of the mugs.

"Here, come and have a seat. The tea and the fire should warm you up."

She did as he suggested, relaxed back into the supple

leather of the couch. But how close do you sit to a person with whom you just had incredible, brain-numbing sex?

India shivered at the thought.

"You're still cold. I'll grab a blanket and be right back."

Thrane left the room before she could correct him. She took a sip of her tea. It was strong, with a dash of milk and no sugar. Exactly as she liked it. She hadn't yet taken a second sip before Thrane came back with a thick knitted blanket. He covered her lap with it before sitting beside her.

"Is the tea okay?" he asked.

"Mm, you remembered how I drink it. Thank you."

Thrane shrugged and nodded but didn't reply. Instead, he took the plate of sandwiches and held it for her.

"Would you like to eat something? They're only ham and cheese, but you should try to eat if you can. You've had a big day."

She had to smile at that, and he did too.

"And that was an understatement, wasn't it?"

She shrugged, then took one of the sandwiches. "Thanks."

They ate in silence, which she found surprisingly comfortable, and once they'd finished the sandwiches, he laced his fingers through hers.

"Well, I guess now is a good time to talk," Thrane said. "I'd like to know more about you. And you must have a lot of questions."

India looked down at their hands. Another connection.

The crackle of the fire was slow and languorous, and she focused on it while she sorted her thoughts. Suddenly, one question topped all others.

"Are you really centuries old?" she asked.

"Centuries?"

"That man at the fire—Oev—said he's known you for centuries."

"Ah, you are observant."

"Editors—we're always listening to what people say."

He smiled at her, and she found herself grinning back. She tucked one leg onto the couch beneath her.

"So?" she asked.

His smile slipped, and he looked intently at her. "Are you sure you want to know the answer?"

She nodded, and Thrane's grip tightened on her hand.

"Just remember, you asked for this. I'm approaching seven centuries on this earth. I was born in the Middle Ages."

India stilled, took in his words. Took in this man who was healthy and fit—she knew just how fit. She frowned.

"Well, you look like a man in his prime, somewhere in your thirties. Forties at the most."

His smile slowly rose again. "Prime? I'll take that, thank you very much." The golden tongues of the fire's flames reflected in his eyes. "I was a human warrior, India. And I was good. Uncannily good, but at that time, it was rare for a man in my profession to live to be three decades or more."

"Your profession?"

"I was technically a mercenary. I trained and led a small contingent of men who went with me to fight for lords and knights, sometimes royalty."

"So how are you still alive? Are you supernatural, the child of someone supernatural, like me?"

"No, I was the fourth child of a blacksmith and his wife, one of many children. Early in my youth, my size was apparent, and a knight who served the lord of our land offered to take me and train me."

"You were taken from your parents?" India asked, wincing. "How old were you? That must have been awful."

"I would've been six or seven. But that was the practice of the time, and my parents were recompensed for my removal."

"Do you remember them?"

"My parents? Yes, but I'd say I recall them more as feelings than direct memories. I had such few years with them as a mortal, and I think the memories of children are steeped in emotions more than details."

India's heart broke for the little boy Thrane had been, leaving his mother and father behind.

"So how did you become immortal? And, holy crap"— she sat up straight—"am I immortal because my father was supernatural?"

"The path to immortality varies, but no, you don't automatically become immortal just because you have a parent who is. Your genealogy is complex, India, and there is the possibility of immortality. Normally, you'd know when you reach the maturity of your power."

"How would I know? What are the signs?"

"When you're immortal you don't age, you don't need to eat food to survive as a mortal would, and you're resistant to disease and illness."

"Can you die?"

"Yes. Immortality is a stretch of the truth. Most supernatural beings, barring perhaps the gods, have the ability to die. The cause would have to be extreme, as supernatural bodies will regenerate from most injuries, but death is possible—complete removal of heart or head, even bleeding out can do it. I've even heard stories of some ancient immortals regenerating from wounds even at that level."

"What's it like? Immortality, I mean."

A pensive look crossed his face. Drawn to comfort him, she curled into his side.

"It has been long," Thrane said, "and lonely in differing ways. My relationships are dissimilar to what you would expect as a mortal. Certainly, I've never had this"—he gestured back and forth between them—"with a mortal."

"Are you saying you've never had ... ?" She mimicked his gesture.

"I'm not talking about sex. India, you've been the catalyst for many changes in my world. No mortal has ever held me in such thrall. No one has ever tempted me to the point of forgetting my life's fight."

A thrill went through her. Thrane's gravelly voice was a drug, and she was quickly becoming addicted. And the way he combined old and contemporary language ...

She suppressed a shiver, made herself focus on his words. "What does that mean—*your life's fight*?"

Thrane's lips tightened, and he broke their gaze, stared at their joined hands.

"I fought often throughout my first few hundred years, but in recent decades, my focus has been on growing things, not killing them. And I wouldn't have thought it possible, but I've enjoyed having a reason for living that exists outside of fighting. Not having to kill or be killed."

A sliver of ice edged inside her. "Has that happened— have you almost been killed, I mean?"

"Surprisingly, not when I was a mortal, no. But as an

immortal, I've certainly sustained major wounds, have had to regenerate portions of limbs and organs. But as I said, that all happened such a long time ago. I haven't thought of those times for many years."

"And you fight the Order? Why?"

27

Thrane clasped India's hand tighter as she nestled into his side. *Mine.* This moment, right now, was everything. His entire being shouted it, knew it with complete certainty.

But how, by all the gods, it had happened, he had no idea. Because as much as he'd been drawn to India—nay, compelled to be near her—he'd thought he could manage the temptation, the desire, even as he kept her close. Using their attraction to keep in constant contact, he'd thought he would be ready for whatever danger she posed.

Yet the tables had turned. He was the one in danger of losing his heart to a mortal—a *mortal.*

And she still didn't know the truth of him. He was a Keeper. His mission put him at direct odds with what she represented. How he was meant to resolve that, he had no idea. And then there was Jev.

Maybe Thrane should just tell her the truth out about her father, let this thing between them end before his heart was engaged permanently. Should he be honest, ending any chance of a relationship now? Or see out his mission, keeping her close until the risk she posed could be removed ... and risk his heart instead?

India snuggled into him. He sighed, hoped to the gods he was doing the right thing.

"You've opened me up like one of these books," Thrane said, "when I wanted to learn about you."

"I didn't mean to be evasive, honestly. I'm really interested in your story. Frankly, everything about you amazes me."

He laughed, brought her hand to his mouth and kissed her palm. Desire stirred, low, languorously through him. "Your honesty undoes me."

"Ha. I doubt much could undo you, Thrane."

"Now, that's where you're wrong."

He studied her as she sat beside him. Intelligence shone from her eyes, and a level of inquisitiveness that rang as genuine.

He rubbed the back of his neck. Could he trust her? Was he really a man who would—could—forge an emotional connection with someone if they posed a danger to his reason for existence? What if, by extending that trust—especially if it were influenced by his attraction—it resulted in disaster?

The last serious attack on the World Tree had led to the demise of his brethren Keepers. And it had nearly resulted in the destruction of the Tree, which would have opened up the Mortalworld to a fate of horror.

And his sense now was that any danger to the Tree would spill over to India's family, simply because of their proximity to India *and* him.

The stakes were higher than he could stand if he was wrong about India.

But as he considered her now, he realised she was a contradiction of stubbornness, shyness and honesty. Power and a lack of worldliness. He'd seen her remain calm and work through what needed to be done in two different stressful situations now. His life's experience had taught him one thing—pressure brought out the true colors of an individual. And he honestly did not believe she intended harm to the Tree.

By the gods, he hoped he was right. Risking his heart was one thing. Risking the Tree was unacceptable.

"India, I am the Keeper, the last of my kind here in the Mortalworld. I guard the World Tree against all threats. I've fought—still fight—the Order who have sought its destruction for eons." He watched her face carefully with each word, looking for any sign of recognition. Her confusion was evident in the tilt of her head, the narrowing of her eyes, but there was no twitch, no flicker of gaze to a different location, no tightening of her muscles. She was either an astounding actress, or she really had no knowledge of the Tree.

He exhaled slowly. "You asked what brought me to immortality? It was the World Tree."

"A tree made you immortal?"

"That may sound odd, but—"

"Uh-uh. I've found out I'm the daughter of a supernatural, have family who live in the Heavens, have more power than I ever knew, and you are seven hundred years old. A tree giving you immortality isn't that odd at all."

"When you put it like that, I guess it's not. But in all truth, the World Tree is the reason I exist in this world. I told you I was once a warrior in the Middle Ages. During that time, I started having intense dreams of being called to a giant tree in an ancient forest. I found the Tree I'd been dreaming of in central Europe—as a mercenary, the opportunity to travel was always present—and when I made physical contact with it, it passed to me the power of immortality. I share the Tree's immortality."

India stared at him. Her mouth dropped open.

"It's true. I am not lying to you, India."

"No, no, it's not that. I'm just amazed. So, ah, what happened then?"

"I became a Keeper. We, my brethren Keepers, men and women along with me, vowed to keep the World Tree alive. I protected the original Tree here in the Mortalworld."

"Does that mean it exists in the other worlds?"

"It exists in all worlds, in all times."

"What—"

"India, let me tell you about the World Tree from the beginning." Thrane smiled, recognizing how her interest had been pricked. "Otherwise, you'll only get bits and pieces not understand the whole. And by that look in your eyes, we could be here all night if you don't get the whole story."

"I'm not that bad."

"That was a very mild protest, but fine, you won't keep me here all night—only some of it." He cocked his head to one side, considered the press of her body against his. "And India, I'd much rather be otherwise occupied at some point tonight."

She swatted his arm and laughed. "Come on."

"Right, well here goes. The World Tree was created by the old gods at the very beginning of time as mortals know it. They created it in a unanimous bid to claim their territories. The Tree connects—but more than that, it is the *construct* for the three worlds. The Heavens and deities within its limbs and leaves, the Mortalworld within its trunk, and the Underworld within its roots. For thousands of years, the Tree existed as a corporeal being—both singular and all—in every world, in every time. And then some two thousand years ago, whispers began to abound of a sect, an order of warriors who sought out the World Tree so they could destroy it. One of the old gods, Freya, foresaw the danger this order represented. She called together the old gods and new—any who would answer her call—and they combined their powers with the World Tree to create—"

"Wait, wait. I can't help it. I have questions, a lot of questions. But firstly, differing civilizations? And why kill the Tree in the Mortalworld?"

"Yes, gods exist within all civilizations, their power derives directly from their worship—hence there are many gods. Each with varying levels of power and dominion, depending on the world in which they live."

"Wow. Okay. Definitely didn't see that one coming."

"Let me help you understand, India. Let me tell it my way. The gods and the World Tree combined their power to create a class of warriors whose sole duty was to protect the physical World Tree in every world and in every time. We were—are—called Keepers. Only the World Tree decides who will be a Keeper—and once you accept the call, you are tied to the World Tree. Irrevocably." Thrane paused, rubbed his thumb over India's palm. "And to answer your other question—while we don't know who leads the Order that wishes to destroy the World Tree, we do know that without a World Tree here, supernatural beings—even the gods, *all* gods—would be unable to travel to this world. The Mortal-world would be stranded."

"Can't the gods find out who's behind it?"

"They help as much as they can, but by their own decree the gods don't interfere here. You see, the Order disguise themselves and lure innocent mortals into their web. They turn the mortals into hunters and killers. All for the purpose of finding and destroying the Tree." Comprehension sparked in India's eyes, and he ran his thumb over her palm in reassurance. "They have tried for two thousand years, India, and haven't succeeded yet. Although they have come close."

"Close?"

Thrane exhaled. "This is not an easy tale to tell, India. But yes, one hundred and fifty years ago, the World Tree—then in Europe—came under the deadliest attack we had ever seen. If it weren't for Freya once again interceding, we would not be here today."

The clash of swords, the ring and clang of metal. Flesh splitting, the cries and chokes of the dead and dying.

Images and echoes rang through his library, as clear as if he were back on the battlefield. Pressure on his palm cleared the flashback, drew him back to the present—India had wrapped her hand tightly about his. He gave hers an answering squeeze.

"So," India asked, "this Freya, did she save the Tree?"

"In a way. Freya summoned me to her side. She bade me depart the fight, depart my brethren Keepers—warriors I had fought beside for centuries. She ordered me to take a seedling of the World Tree and find safe harbor for it to take root." Thrane looked out his windows. The night sky laid a blanket of shadows on his land. "I chose this place."

"What happened to the World Tree—the one you were guarding?"

"Gone. My brethren Keepers, gone." Thrane's blood boiled again, even as his chest burned under the lead weight of their loss—a weight he'd lived with every day since. He swallowed down the hot and heavy ball that tightened his throat. "I vowed, when I came here, that I would never let harm come to the Tree, or my people, again."

"You've been here for all that time?"

"Yes, that's why I know your family so well. When Liz's grandparents immigrated, I was here. And have been here for almost every member of your family's birth since then. Your family have been instrumental in helping me maintain my cover. And let me tell you, it's a challenge in this technologically advanced age."

"No wonder Nan lets you call her Liz. So, the men—that thing—who came for me tonight. They were from the Order?"

"Did you see the mark on their foreheads?"

"It was so dark. I could barely see anything."

"The Order tattoo a symbol onto the foreheads of their human fighters. It's a circle with two lines running across it."

"I've seen that before—on the man who attacked me, back at Sim's hotel. What does it mean?"

"The Order came into existence around the time Christianity began to spread across Europe. The Order took one of the earliest Christian symbols, the christogram, and created a version for their followers."

"Wait—I've heard of that. It's a monogram, isn't it?"

"That's right. And the Order has its own version. But it gets worse. We have found the mark on bodies the Order has sacrificed."

The bloom to India's skin paled. "Sacrificed?"

"That's what they do. They sacrifice beings—usually witches—steal their power, and use it for their own purpose."

"Holy crap. Is that what that man was going to do to me in the greenhouse?"

"Yes, and if he stole your power—" Thrane shuddered. "I'm hundreds of years old, but in all my time, I've never known anyone like you, India Jones. And this level of ... of —" He shook his head. "I'm struggling to find the right words here. What I'm trying to say is that I've never felt such a strong connection. From the moment I first saw you—by the gods, it's a compulsion to be near you. A desire to touch you." He stroked both of her palms. "To kiss you." He kissed her lips, her cheeks, watched her eyelids flutter closed. "Be inside you."

He pulled India up to meet him, chest to chest, and groaned as she wrapped her legs around him. Her feminine heat beckoned him in. His penis, covered only with his trunks, rose to press insistently at her core.

His voice dropped to a growl. "Can I? Be inside you again?"

Green fire blazed at him. She freed her hand from his, pushed hard against his chest. He willingly obliged the unspoken request and stretched out. She moved with him, her long, silken legs clasping him tighter, her heat in constant contact with his shaft.

The risks, the questions, the worry—the entire outside world—disappeared until all he focused on was the beautiful, erotic creature astride him.

India pulled his shirt over her head, and with every movement, the firelight gilded her skin molten gold. The moment her breasts were revealed, he leaned up, tasted first one and then the other. Drew their lush tips into his mouth.

She moaned and dropped her head back. Her dark hair swung as she undulated, pushed the head of his penis straight up and into her, through the flimsy material of his trunks. They both gasped. And then his need for her was suddenly, overwhelming urgent. They fumbled at each other's clothes. He found a condom, then parted her thighs, surged into the tight welcoming warmth of her sheath.

Thrane pressed his thumb against her clitoris as he edged his way in, farther, and farther still, until she had taken him all the way. Her head dropped back, he ran a hand up the column of her neck, down the glowing skin of her breasts as they rose with her shallow breaths.

Her inner muscles held him tight as he thrust high and long. Heaven. Pure, total heaven. She clasped him tighter still as he thrust again, and then she cried out, her skin gleaming, her midnight hair swinging as she convulsed on his body.

The need to move overtook him, and he thrust hard and fast, again and again, until he too came, crying hoarsely with each wave he rode.

28

M ore fighters, more sacrifice, more destruction. Ri'Kiant needed it all. Needed it now. Sean drove him into an abandoned factory. As soon as the car stopped, Ri'Kiant smashed his fist through Sean's throat. Shoved the man's trachea to the other side of his neck. Kept pushing till vertebrae crunched.

The body slumped to one side.

Ri'Kiant barely glanced at it. This one's fate had been decreed the moment he tried to step in and lead Ri'Kiant's team.

Death at his hands diffused his rage. Finally, he was able to reason.

How had that bloody Keeper found him? He'd been so close, so near to his goal after all these years. The intimacy of the sacrifice had been at hand. He could have licked the fear pouring off her, had been about to rip the skin from her body, when that—that foul stench of immortality had stopped him.

Ri'Kiant refused to look at the stub of bone and flesh

that protruded from where his arm had been. The wound had sealed, regrowth visible in the limb even now, but the fire pulsing at the site was a constant reminder of his defeat. Rage fueled his resistance to the agony.

And then a shudder racked his body as the summons of his god hit his mind. Without an altar she couldn't materialize, but he heard her as effectively as if she stood before him.

My first, what is your progress with the daughter of Jev?

Her mind invaded his. Ripped open every connection, every synapse in a roaring funnel of white-hot pain. The pressure pushed blood through every orifice. It slid and dripped from his nose, his eyes, his ears; he gagged on blood and heaved onto the floor.

The task must be completed ere the black moon's passing in the morn. You will go back and find the witch of the three worlds. Sacrifice her. Bring me her power. My first, my love. The voice crooned in his mind with anything but affection. *Sate my lust for the death of this one, and you shall be crowned king when I am god queen.*

She showed him an image of them sitting on dual thrones made out of prostrate mortal bodies. She held out her hand to him and parted her legs, and he saw himself slide to his knees, worship her with his mouth, then his cock.

The pleasure of the vision blinded him to the pain of the summons, and he staggered to his feet. The image melted away along with the presence of her mind. Ri'Kiant pulled the body from the car and dropped it to the ground. It had no magic of its own, and the stolen magic it had been given had long waned. He kicked it hard before he took the driver's seat and drove out of the town and toward his "church."

He needed more followers. Needed them now. And he had no time to find another sacrifice and give his followers stolen strength—who cared if they all fell beneath the sword of the Keeper as long as he killed the daughter of Jev?

Ri'Kiant felt the will of his god upon him and went to do her bidding. Willingly content to kill any and all of his soldiers in her quest for destruction and dominion.

29

Warm and content, still lying on the couch in the library, India roused to the gentle patter of raindrops on the windows and roof. The dream wind sang a soft song as it whispered along the garden paths, around the buildings, then into the forest.

Except she was awake. This was the real wind—and it was talking to her.

She lay beneath the blanket, not needed for warmth, really, wrapped as she was in Thrane. Their legs were tangled, her back to his chest, and one of his hands cupped her breast. Her head was pillowed on his arm, and his masculine scent had settled all around her.

The fire had died down to the embers, and through the windows, the coming dawn threw muted-charcoal streaks across the sky. Suddenly, the rain tapped more insistently on the window, and the wind picked up pace and volume.

A knock came at the door to her mind, and this time she thought she knew what it was.

Surely, from what Thrane had said, it was the World

Tree calling her. But why? She wasn't exactly a warrior of renown, so it was unlikely the Tree was calling her to be a Keeper. But she was sure now that it had definitely been calling her. Had been doing so since her mother passed.

And something else ... her witchcraft was restored. She didn't even have to ask the question, she simply knew it. Knew it like she knew how to breathe. And so now she could find the heart of the forest and figure out why her dreams, the land, the very wind was calling her.

And yet, right here, where she was warm and satisfied, she had another option—stay with Thrane and avoid whatever was going on.

As if aware of her indecision, the wind let out a howl before it subsided into song once more, continued to roll around the garden and house. Should she go? India glanced over her shoulder at Thrane; he breathed deeply in his sleep behind her. His task was clear, protect the World Tree. And while he also seemed determined to protect her, if she woke him now to take her out into the forest, her chances would be slim to none.

She glanced at him again. He seemed in a deep enough sleep that he wouldn't wake if she left. But she needed to be sure, so she reached for her magic and easily brought up a fraction of her strength. As she expected, the three-dimensional library turned into a four-dimensional landscape. Thrane's diamond energy currents moved in lazy waves that spoke of satisfaction and contentment. Even their hard edges appeared muted, softer somehow than she'd seen before. She could slip away, find the heart of the forest from her dreams, and be back before Thrane woke up.

India made up her mind.

THRANE WOKE as India broke their physical contact, watched as she ducked out the door of the library wearing nothing more than his shirt. Masculine approval rolled through him.

She'd handled this entire situation with amazing fortitude. Even with her localized knowledge of witchcraft, nothing could've prepared her for the onslaught of information she'd been dealt.

The creak of the bathroom door signaled where she'd gone, and he rested his head on his arm, pulled the blanket higher across his chest. He was cool without India's warmth tucked into him.

Gods, what a night. Though it had started as deadly and terrifying, it had ended as something out of his wildest dreams. And if he didn't know better, he'd have thought they'd bonded.

But that could not happen. He was immortal. She wasn't. Even believing she didn't intend harm to the Tree, even if she could somehow see past what had happened with her father, one day she would die. And then he'd be alone, for eternity.

Thrane sighed, no closer to figuring this out than he'd been last night—except now he knew how amazing they were together. Part of him feared it was too late, that their bond had been sealed last night, no matter which way he wanted it to be.

Another sound came from farther inside the house—a door opening, then closing. From the opposite direction of the bathroom. He slowly stood up, walked to the library door, checked the corridor.

No one was there.

"India?" he called out.

Nothing—no noise at all came from anywhere in the house. He padded softly to the kitchen. A movement through the large window caught his attention and he stared hard into the darkened yard.

He blinked and looked again. *What the fuck?*

With rain drizzling around her, India stared into the forest.

What was she looking at—or for? She must've found whatever it was because she took a step into the low-lying scrub.

He followed her line of sight. The Tree.

Thrane took a step after her, but he wasn't even wearing shoes. Fuck it.

He took hold of his medallion, registered the warmth of the wood, and as soon as he directed his will, he appeared in the cell where his weapon was stored. No more than a second later, he was back in his house, sword in hand.

He'd swept silently into the garden before India had moved far at all. While her direction was true to the Tree, her path took her through the thickest scrub. His knowledge of the terrain meant he moved effortlessly in parallel with her at all times. He easily reached the Tree first and stood behind the massive trunk, hidden from India's view when she emerged into the clearing.

While he couldn't see her, he could definitely hear her. She made no effort at all to hide her progress. What by all the gods was she doing? And what was he going to do about it? Blood pulsed through his veins, pounded until he could almost hear it ringing in his ears.

Was she the gravest danger he'd ever faced? Had she been fooling him all this time?

Yet his sword arm lowered, until the weapon tip touched the ground. How could he even think about taking action against her?

India's footfalls closed in on the Tree.

Protect the Tree. One vow. One mission.

With his pulse hammering harder than in any fight he'd ever been in, he stepped out from around the trunk, ran one hand across the smooth, resilient bark. The Tree. His life's fight for all these years. All the sacrifice and deaths that had gone before. He tightened his grip on his sword. The tip rose, slowly, surely. His worst nightmare.

India's hand flew to her chest, and she stumbled to a stop.

"Holy crap, Thrane!"

He almost brought her close to soothe her surprise, but he drove his instinct to comfort her away, forced himself to stand still.

"What are you doing here, India?"

"You were asleep. How did you get here so fast?" Her eyes dipped to his sword, widened. "Where did that come from? Is that man here—from the Order? You said they wouldn't be coming back tonight."

"He's not. They're not."

"Then why the sword?"

He didn't say anything.

"Me?" Her glowing skin paled. "Of course. I'm the danger. You actually believe *I'm* the danger, don't you? Don't you?"

It was an accusation he didn't correct; though in that moment he didn't—couldn't—bring himself to believe that the danger she posed was intentional. But he had to find out what was going on, so he hardened his resolve.

"Why are you here?" he asked.

The hand she'd held to her chest dropped, and her whole body slumped too.

"How could you have made love to me thinking I was—well, crap, it wasn't making love. It wasn't any kind of feeling." She laughed, a short bitter sound. "It was just sex, wasn't it?"

"This isn't about feelings or sex." His gut clenched at the hurt blazing from her. "You are the gravest danger to the Tree I have ever known. How can I think of—of an attachment—of feelings? I don't know if that's something I can ever, *will ever* look for. And with a mortal? Yes, you're a witch, and undeniably strong, but you're still mortal. You could leave this world, leave me in the blink of an eye."

"That's weak, Thrane. You're saying you can't have a relationship because of the Tree? Or because I might die? Hate to tell you this, but people die all the time. You even said it yourself, supernatural people can die, so don't give me that BS."

Thrane ground his teeth. India's words hit a nerve, but he refused to let that halt him.

"India, you speak of loss, eternal loss so easily. But you don't know—you haven't been there. An eternity of missing the people who held your heart is not some easy thing."

"I don't know about loss?" India said. "You're kidding, right? My mother, father, both gone. And you're telling me I don't know about loss? Come on, Thrane. I'm a big girl—I'm not looking for some great love, and hell, I'm heading back to Brisbane as soon as I've figured out my magic. But I sure as hell thought we had some level of mutual respect."

He shut down the prick of conscience her words brought. Focused on what he'd done for five hundred years.

"None of that matters, India. Even if this thing between you and I were possible, this is about the Tree. The Tree alone," he said.

"Bull crap. If this was only ever about the Tree, why have sex—?" Her face paled and she swayed. Once again, he stifled the urge to go to her.

"Now I get it," she said. "You really were being honest when you said I didn't know what you might have to do. So, this—us last night—was what, a convenient way to keep me close? Make it easier for you to keep an eye on me, just in case I'm the grave 'danger' you think I am?"

"India, don't confuse the issue. Remember my entire reason for existence? I'm here to protect the World Tree, and you have placed yourself in a position where it can come to serious harm. *You* are a potential threat that I can't, won't— even as much as I may wish to— ignore."

"Okay, what happens now?" India said, gesturing to his sword. "This is absurd, Thrane, I'm no danger to your precious Tree."

"Then tell me why you're here. Why you left me asleep, came unerringly to this place? Remember we spoke of trust? Tell me why I should trust you when you came right fucking here? Give me a reason to make sense of all this."

"Sense? You want me to make sense of this?" Tears welled in her eyes. "Thrane, I'm the maddest of us all, you know that? I'm here, because for weeks, I've been dreaming of flying through this forest, of coming here. To its heart. The heart of the forest. I swear it calls to me in my dreams." She looked around at the giant limbs soaring above them, bearing the canopy of the World Tree.

Even after centuries had passed, Thrane still recalled

those dreams. Remembered what had drawn him to the Tree all those years ago.

"India," he said, his stomach unclenching truly for the first time. Because now he understood. India wasn't a danger—she was the opposite. She had been *called* by the World Tree.

"And now," she said, throwing her hands into the air, "I have not one family—but two. Two families! Where the hell did that come from? But don't forget that there might possibly be a third. And, oh yeah, the thing that makes the least sense is that my mother, my beautiful mother, hid all this from me."

India crumbled, the tears now spilling over her cheeks, and Thrane couldn't handle it anymore. He dropped the sword, held her when she would've fallen. He supported her in his arms easily, but she didn't return his embrace. The rain pelted down and washed away her tears, replaced them with tracks of its own.

"India ..."

But what was he going to tell her? He'd dropped his sword when everything screamed at him to protect the Tree —from her.

"How touching," a droll voice said from behind him.

Thrane went cold.

He hadn't even heard the speaker approach, but he'd never let anyone hurt India. Not himself, not the Order. He spun around, maneuvered India at his back.

Oev was barely visible, standing at the edge of the clearing, his sword out of its scabbard.

Thrane's breath expelled. "You should announce yourself first, lest you end up on the tip of my sword."

With his eyes glued to Oev, Thrane slowly reached down

and picked up his sword. India tensed again behind him. Fuck, he needed to tell her.

"Hail, India, daughter of Jev," Oev said. "Your paternal house arrives anon."

"Cut the bullshit, Oev."

"Fine, fine." Oev waved. "India, your grandparents are at the Jones's farmhouse waiting for you. It's time to fulfill your duty."

Thrane stepped forward, registered Oev tensing as he did. "She's not going anywhere."

"Oh, but she is," Oev said. "You know this is absolute. Her family have claimed her, and she must submit. The gods will not allow any who have been claimed to forgo this."

"Fuck the gods."

Oev shifted one foot forward, raised his sword tip.

An attack stance.

The hairs on the back of Thrane's neck rose—Oev certainly wasn't about to hurt India.

"Why are you ready to attack, Oev?" Thrane asked, slowly mirroring Oev's stance.

"The better question is what are *you* doing, Thrane, *Keeper* of this World Tree. We have learned that our kin is a direct threat to the Tree. We know what you do with threats. I cannot let you hurt her."

"By all the gods, I'm not here to kill India."

"Really?" India asked.

Thrane shifted slightly at India's voice.

"If you're not here to kill me, why is your sword out? Where's the danger?"

Thrane wanted to turn to her but couldn't put Oev to his

back. Nor did he shift to India's other side as he didn't want India between himself and Oev.

"Answer that question if you will, Thrane," Oev said, stepping closer.

"Stay back. Do naught else to place yourself into this situation."

"He's only asking what I want to know, too, Thrane," India said.

She moved from behind him, raised both hands, and whispered something. Moments later, the rain ceased to fall and starlight illuminated their little patch of clearing. Oev's eyes widened at the display, and Thrane groaned. That act, small as it had been, cemented India's ability. And she clearly had no idea what potent power it took to turn off the rain.

Of course, they would claim her. They likely would have done so regardless, seeing as she was Jev's daughter, but now, with power like hers, they would not want to give up that advantage.

And India was a daughter of the three worlds. Her genealogy was a gift to them.

He had to talk to her. Now. Thrane took a gamble and turned to face her fully. Doing so placed Oev at a side-on position that gave him a much greater advantage—an advantage he'd recognize instantly.

India shoved her hands on her hips. "You actually believed I was going to hurt it, didn't you?"

Thrane stood facing her, tall, all masculine grace and heat, and a flash of energy pulsed between them, made her blood heat. Crap, she still reacted to his energy like it was her own personal current. Would she ever be able to turn it off?

His jaw ticked, and he nodded once.

"Why on earth would you think that? Am I the only one here who wouldn't have sex with a person I thought maybe, just maybe I might have to kill one day?"

"Kill you? By the gods India, I *saved* you last night. Remember?"

"Then why this? Answer me." Tears born of anger and hurt threatened to spill over. She refused to let them fall. "Answer me."

"India." His jaw clenched, released. "Okay, yes—when I woke and saw you leave the house, in the fucking rain, I did wonder. Why, by all the gods, would you leave the warmth, the safety of my house, and not even tell me?"

She glanced at Oev. "Would you give us a little privacy here? I'd like to have this talk with Thrane without an audience."

"That's not something I can do, India." Oev nodded at Thrane. "I'm waiting on his answer too."

"Fine," Thrane said and threw his sword at India's feet.

"Hey!" India jumped back.

"India. Ignore Oev."

Oev snorted but didn't say anything more.

"Go on," India said, glaring at Thrane.

"I watched you move through my garden like an arrow, straight and true, fucking right to the Tree. How? Why? You have a power that could obliterate the Tree. And for that you will always present a true and real danger. But from the moment I first saw you, I haven't been able to walk away from you. And then, when you got here, I couldn't hurt you." Thrane swallowed hard. "Even for the Tree."

"You're saying," Oev said, laconically, "that after centuries of fighting to save the Tree, now, all of a sudden, due to *this* mortal, you're forsaking your sworn allegiance?"

Was Thrane telling the truth? India's instinct was to believe him. But she'd given him her trust once and look where they were now. She needed to work out what to do, and the best way to do that was to get some space. From both of these men. As soon as she had that thought, the knocking at her mental door began again, harder and more insistent than ever.

India was forced to look away from both men and toward the Tree. It stood, barely illuminated in the coming light of dawn, the mighty trunk easily wide enough to hide four or five people. Its towering height ranging up and splitting into enormous limbs that soared higher still, forming a giant canopy of leaves, shaded silver and black in the last of the new moon sky.

Goosebumps prickled up her neck.

Thrane had said the Tree was over a hundred years old, but India could sense immediately that this Tree was not merely old, it had a soul of eons.

Holy crap. The Tree had a soul.

A whisper called as the breeze caught the leaves and bent them toward her. Even the branches swayed her way. The Tree wanted her. And she—she wanted to connect with it. To meet this being who'd watched over worlds for eons.

India recalled what had happened on her first visit to Thrane's property—that journey through, around, and over the cosmos. This Tree—this being—was the thing that bound the universe. She needed to touch it. Needed to physically connect with it.

"India," Oev said, his sharp voice cutting through her reverie.

He slunk toward her, but Thrane blocked him.

"Don't touch her, Oev," he said.

"You do not order my actions, Thrane. This isn't about the safety of the Tree—you've confirmed that. Therefore, this is about India. As a member of her claiming-house, I am reminding you that you cannot interfere with our business."

A deep growl rumbled in Thrane's chest and India glanced at him in surprise. His heated gaze caught hers, but he didn't say a thing.

"Thrane?" India looked from one man to the other.

"Okay, clearly there's more I need to know. Who wants to spill?"

"Spill?" Oev asked, eyebrows drawing together.

"She means who will explain what's happening."

"She is here," India said. "I mean, *I'm* right here. I can speak for myself." She glared at Oev. "What do you mean?"

Oev looked down his nose and said, "India, you are a daughter of the House of Freya. We have claimed you. Our world obligates all who belong to a supernatural house to come to the Higherworld and record their fate in the spinner's codex.

"You cannot forgo this requirement. And yes, while matters regarding the World Tree do take precedence, Thrane stated he is taking no action regarding the World Tree and you. Therefore, you are *obligated* to come to the Higherworld.

"The rest of your family is awaiting you at the farmhouse. And they will not tolerate any interference in a family matter."

"The spinner?" India said. "You said that back at the bonfire. What are you talking about?"

"The spinner guards the fates of all Higherworld beings by sealing them in the codex, an ancient book, held in the Great Library."

"Listen, this is an awful lot to take in." Not to mention this guy was loopy if he thought he—or anyone—could just come and take her anywhere without her permission.

She looked to Thrane for support. Met in his eyes a longing and depth of feeling she hadn't expected. It took her breath away.

"India," Thrane said, voice catching. "India, Oev is telling you the truth."

"You're serious, aren't you?" India said, pivoting to Oev. "Why on earth would I choose to go anywhere with you? And why in the hell would anyone care about my fate?"

"This is not about choice," Oev said. "The spinner weaves your fate into the codex, records your inherent supernatural ability, and what you may do with it."

"So," India said, "kind of like saying what type of job you want? Is that it? Well, I already have one of those, thanks."

Oev looked at Thrane, who shook his head.

"No," Thrane said, "a job is something you choose, which is why Oev doesn't understand your context, because the spinner will record the details of your super-natural powers ... and how they can be *exploited* by the gods."

"That doesn't sound very nice."

"Our gods do not exploit us, Keeper."

"That's not how I've heard it told," Thrane said. "In fact, isn't it right that the gods of your house have access to your power at any time? And they can trade your powers with that of other houses at their choosing?"

"What?" India gaped at both men. "Hold on, no one has said that before."

Oev didn't blink. Thrane raised an eyebrow at him.

"And this is something you thought I should only find out now?" India asked. "How about saying, hey, India—one small thing, once you get the Heavens and do this thing, you'll be *owned* by the family. Oh, and they can pimp you out any time, too."

India warred with herself to maintain a calm facade. The effort took her will away from her magic, and when she opened her eyes, the rain restarted. What the hell, she was already drenched. And it looked as if she'd have to sort this mess out herself. She managed, somehow, to keep her voice even.

"I'm going to Nan's house, right now, and getting to the bottom of this—this book, or codex, or spinner nonsense. Thrane, I don't even know what to say to you right now." He opened his mouth and she shot him look. "No. Don't talk. Don't use that voice to try to get out of this."

"You do not need to go anywhere, India of the House of Freya. Granddaughter. We are here," said a woman, emerging from the surrounding trees.

India sighed.

This most elegant woman, timeless in her beauty, had sleek golden hair—not one strand out of place. She rode a stunning white horse, and three men rode in behind her. They all wore the same garb as Oev, with forest-green cloaks pushed back over their shoulders. All of them had sword scabbards, either slung to one side of their saddles or strapped across their backs.

"Mother," Oev inclined his head to her. "Father."

"Fuck," Thrane cursed under his breath.

"Holy crap," India breathed. She cut a glance at Thrane, but he didn't meet her gaze. She tuned back to Oev. "*They* are your family?"

"*Our* family," he replied as the riders stationed themselves between India and the Tree. "Mother, Father, meet India, daughter of Jev. India, meet Evine, from the House of Freya, and Jona, affiliate to the House of Freya."

"I honestly have no words," India said.

Evine—her *grandmother?*—was scarily lovely, a very feminine version of her father, with the same patrician nose and direct green eyes that shimmered with an internal fire. Evine was also tall—maybe that was where her own height came from, India realized with a jolt. And at odds to the rest of her house, Evine was dressed in tight-fitting dark denim jeans and a green silky shirt.

Only the scabbard slung over her back stopped her from appearing like an expensive European fashion icon. Her age was impossible to determine—by complexion alone she could have been India's age—with few lines to mar the perfection of her face. But her eyes held a story of something different. They spoke of age, no, more like Ages. Those eyes had viewed countless years of actions and reactions.

And they now held India in close regard.

"Grandmother." India inclined her head as she'd seen Oev do, and then looked at the man, Jona, next. He had dark hair and deep brown eyes. "Grandfather, it's ... well, it's lovely to meet you both."

"You say that pleasantly, child, though I sense you do not feel that way." Evine nudged her horse closer. "However, thank you for your words." Her gaze cut to Thrane, and her eyes narrowed.

India was used to the heavenly manner of speaking now through her time with Oev. But with her grandmother, it was stronger, as if the other woman didn't spend much time talking to people outside of her own world.

"You're welcome," India said, "I guess. So, pleasantries aside, I'm very tired." India tried—failed—to stop the heat rising up her cheeks. "Last night's attack and all, you know? And I really want to get back to Nan's."

"We have claimed you in the name of our house," Evine said. "We will depart this place and undertake your obligation to the spinner's codex."

"Yeah, I've heard that before. But I already have a family,

you see, one of witches, humans, right here in Hill End. And a life, a job—all that jazz. So, no thanks."

"You are the daughter of a supernatural. And under our laws that generational link to the Higherworld requires for you to record your fate. Should we not claim you, you will be open to any attack and malicious action when in this world, and we will have little cause to defend or prevent such attacks."

"Not so fast, please. I get to decide who I belong to," India said. "And I'm not going to be given, or taken, at someone's whim."

"Evine, let me speak," her grandfather said.

He had piercing eyes, but they were kind, gentle almost. Only when he neared did India get a sense of another world lurking behind his gaze.

"Hail, Granddaughter. Long have we wanted to meet you, child of our firstborn son."

"Hi—ah—Grandfather. Listen, like I said, it's lovely to meet you and all, but I'm really tired. Let's all head back to Nan's, and then we can discuss this—this claiming thing —later."

"You can't ignore this, India," Thrane said, his voice was the gentlest she'd heard yet.

She turned to him, and he finally met her gaze. His eyes were narrowed, his shoulders stiff.

"What's going on, Thrane" she asked. "Why are you looking at me like that?"

"Stay out of this, Keeper," Evine said, nudging her horse between India and Thrane. "You have done enough, caused enough pain to this family."

India waited for Thrane to defend himself. But instead,

he stared at her, over the back of Evine's mount. True pain burned in his eyes.

"Thrane, what does she mean?" India asked.

Evine looked down her patrician nose, green eyes afire at Thrane.

"Don't you know, granddaughter?" she asked. "He is responsible for the death of Jev."

India went cold. Then the ground trembled beneath her feet.

31

———

Thrane whirled to check the Tree as the ground shook and groaned beneath his feet. Birds, screeching, crying, flew up into the sky en masse.

He pinpointed the danger immediately. Order soldiers poured into the clearing from where Evine and Jona had emerged.

And the new moon was not yet done.

"The Order!" Thrane yelled at Oev, even as he ducked to pick up his sword.

India's eyes flew wide, her face went white, right as the first Order fighter reached him. He struck the soldier with one sweep of his sword.

"India," Thrane barked, "keep your back to the Tree." His next step took him to Evine. "I am the Keeper, heed my orders here. India is their aim—send your guard to her—the rest of us will destroy the Order soldiers. Watch out for the leader, Ri'Kiant. He's the most dangerous."

Thrane cut down another fighter in midflight as Evine withdrew her sword. She leaned down, gripped his arm.

"Done," she said. "Do not let harm come to my grand-daughter, Keeper." She turned her horse in a time-honed move and charged toward the incoming hoard. Thrane raised his sword high and met the next soldier, felled him with the following strike.

He assessed his strategy swiftly. The larger trees blocked his view of all of the fighters, but Thrane knew this land—his land. He knew the layout of every plant and sapling, every tree and bush, and easily plotted the battlefield in his mind's eye.

As he did, another fighter, forehead clearly marked with the lined circle, rushed at him with a weapon held high. Again, the attack was weak, and Thrane dispatched the fighter with two fast flicks of his sword. The fighters were advancing in a wedge from the narrowest point of the simplest trail.

"Oev," Thrane said, "head left, for the smaller brush. Pincer them between you and Evine."

The immortal sprang to the side, and sure enough, India's paternal family began to pick off the Order fighters.

But it was too easy. Entirely too easy. Where was Ri'Kiant? He'd clearly regrouped with a new and poorly trained cohort of fighters. They had only mild stolen magic, for they offered little to no threat to him or Evine and her men.

Thrane darted to Oev's side, pointed at the trail. "Their leader isn't here—he may come from the other side, and I need to get there before him. He's the most dangerous of all. You have to hold this side of the Tree."

"Aye, we'll hold it," Oev said and grabbed Thrane's arm. "Protect our girl."

Thrane nodded and ran, darting between trunks, all the while moving toward the Tree.

His acute hearing picked up the crunch of footfall on leaf litter, and he came to a halt. Another crack echoed from ahead. Measured footsteps. No labored breathing, no sudden jolts or jerks, nor errant strikes of the surrounding flora. Thrane held his breath, allowed no sound to come from him, and listened for one heartbeat, then the next. Calibrated the trajectory of his opponent.

The footfalls came toward the Tree at a forty-five–degree angle. Even if Thrane moved straight for them, their maker would still reach the clearing first. Instead, he backtracked, took the shortest path to the clearing, erupted into the space. India was still protected between Evine's fighters. Good. Ri'Kiant couldn't kill the World Tree himself, he had to get to India first.

Thrane stood in front of her. And sure enough, the demon emerged. All limbs intact. He appeared with stealth in a whisper of movement. Rage suffused Ri'Kiant's face, twisting his cheekbones, pulling his eyes and mouth, flattening his nose.

"You," Ri'Kiant spat out. Then his gaze darted to India.

"You will not get to her," Thrane said, swiveling his sword and gripping with both hands. "How's the arm?"

A growl emerged from within the demon, but he didn't even flicker an eye to the regrown limb. Simply locked his gaze on Thrane and stepped forward.

Thrane took one of his own, started a deadly duet.

Ri'Kiant maneuvered toward India, but Thrane cut him off each time. No fucking way was he letting Ri'Kiant get anywhere close to her.

"Your men will be cut down, demon. And I will cut *you* down, too. Mark my words."

The demon's gaze cut from Thrane to India, then to the forest behind them. Cries and wet gurgling noises carried through the clearing. Thrane watched the demon consider his options.

And then Ri'Kiant charged. He whipped a dagger from a wrist scabbard, drew his sword from his back. The dual-weapon attack was smart and fast, and Thrane raised his sword in defense, had to work hard to press his own agenda.

Finally, Thrane picked up a pattern in Ri'Kiant's attack. After each rapid flurry of strike and defense, Ri'Kiant always led the next strike with his left side. Thrane could take advantage of the tell, and spin the demon.

Except that would place Ri'Kiant closer to India.

Thrane refused to take the bait. Instead, he pushed harder. A burning kiss from Ri'Kiant's dagger sliced across his side.

The dagger had to go. With swords alone Thrane could take the demon, was sure of his ability. Keeping pace, Thrane took a calculated risk—he whipped his sword around from high to low and kicked the demon with his offside leg. The demon reacted, brought his dagger down low and lifted his sword high.

Thrane used the downward motion of his own sword already in flight to slice down and true. Blood flew. Ri'Kiant's hand and the dagger fell to the ground. His howl rent the air, but the demon was eons in age, and the wound began to knit shut even as he raised his sword with his remaining hand and struck defensively across Thrane's chest.

Thrane pressed hard, rained blow after blow upon the demon.

Ri'Kiant cursed and his lips flattened. He ceased to push forward, took an unexpected step back, and Thrane's momentum took him close. Ri'Kiant swept Thrane's feet from beneath him.

Landing hard on the leaf-littered ground, Thrane focused on his two-handed grip, brought his sword up above his head. The demon's sword hit his in a furious screech that rang through the forest. The blow shook Thrane's hands, but he pushed through his core, arms shaking, withstanding the force, and held steady. He exerted more pressure, pushed his sword high, and forced Ri'Kiant's sword to glance downward.

India cried out—he knew she was watching—but he now had the better position, and he didn't let her shout interfere with his focus.

In the split moment where Ri'Kiant's sword hit the ground, Thrane sprang to his feet precisely between the demon and India and struck at Ri'Kiant's chest.

A pained scream echoed behind him. But he couldn't turn.

Ri'Kiant's eyes darted over Thrane's shoulder. The demon stiffened. "No, leave her to me!"

Cold fingers clawed at Thrane's stomach—what the fuck was going on? But his momentum propelled his sword into Ri'Kiant's side. At the last second the demon spun hard in the opposite direction, and Thrane's strike didn't cut all the way through.

Ri'Kiant hissed, pressed one hand to his side as blood spurted between his fingers. He stumbled backward, then turned and fled, still stumbling, away from the World Tree.

Thrane went to launch after the wounded demon, when a wet, gurgling cough sounded behind him.

By all the Gods, don't let that be India.

He ignored Ri'Kiant and spun around.

The guardsmen who'd been protecting India now writhed on the ground. Blood foamed and frothed from their lips and eyes and ears.

India lay beside them.

Time seemed to stop, and all thought fled. Thrane dropped to his knees beside her. His sword thudded to the ground.

Blood ran and splattered among the leaf litter, pooled beneath her as she lay on her side.

"India. Gods, India, hold on." Holding his breath, he reached out with trembling hands, drew the dark veil of her hair back to see the pale skin of her cheek.

Blood ran in a bright stream from the corner of her mouth. Her face was drawn, her eyes glassy. Unfocused.

"Thrane," India barely managed to whisper.

"Sh." He gently turned her—blanched when she gasped and cried out—but he had to check her wound. "Fuck!" He couldn't find words, hated the added pain he caused her. "I need to see. India, I need to see where you're hurt."

The sound of movement came from behind them. He reached for his sword.

"It is me, Keeper," Evine said, kneeling beside him. "I am no danger to her."

Thrane grunted but didn't shift his eyes from his task. Lifted the tattered end of India's shirt. A large puncture wound, several inches long through her side. Dark blood welled and ran from the injury. India's eyes locked on his. But they were hazy, their green fire dim.

His heart pounded inside his chest, harder than ever before. She needed care. Urgent care. There was no time to waste. She'd bleed out in minutes.

A sound, barely audible, escaped her lips.

"Sh, India, I have to bring you to the Tree. You need to get to the Heavens." He gathered her into his arms.

Every cry, each gasp, cut him like a knife, fast and hard. But he kept his eyes on the Tree ahead.

"Evine," he called out. "Come with us now. Your medics can treat her, right?"

"Yes—yes, but Keeper—*Thrane*—the Tree is not near our home. She is—"

"By the gods, we will get her there, and you will get your medics. Now!"

Thrane risked further damage and ran the last steps to the Tree.

India cried out.

Thrane was eerily aware of the blood flowing from her, down his own legs. He dropped to the ground, reached out, connected with the Tree. Took India's hand in his—met no resistance—looked sharply at her face. Her eyes, open still, held no fire at all now.

"India, stay with me," he yelled, his words echoing through the clearing. "Watch me, India. You're going to the Heavens. Evine!"

India's eyes closed.

He let out a gutted cry, only breathed again when she slowly lifted her eyelids. Her blood was everywhere, his palms were slippery with it, and he dropped the hand of hers that he held.

As her hand fell, pale and cold, it scraped the trunk of the Tree.

Her eyes widened, a gasp exploded from her, more blood pooled and welled from her mouth. She looked from the Tree to Thrane. Her eyes closed. Stayed closed.

Evine took hold of her, and they both disappeared.

32

Thrane knelt in a pool of India's blood. It stained his knees, the roots, and fallen leaves a garish bright hue. A ringing grew louder and louder in his ears.

What, by all the gods, had just fucking happened?

India was gone.

He shook his head. She couldn't be dead. Where would Evine go? Gods, he couldn't make his mind work.

India could be immortal. His heart picked up, then dropped fast as he took in the amount of blood around him.

Even an immortal could bleed out and die.

She was gone.

Thrane tried to breathe but couldn't seem to open his lungs. They burned and burned till he finally gasped, dragged air in. He had to ... had to ... he couldn't catch his thoughts. Knew he had to do something. But by the gods what?

A touch on his shoulder. Jona, it was Jona.

Jona gripped his elbow, and Thrane rose to his feet, vaguely aware of others coming toward them.

"Do not give up hope, Keeper," Jona said.

Thrane stared at him, unable to speak. Had it been minutes—or hours—since India disappeared?

Nate rode into the clearing. He dropped from the horse's back.

"Thrane," Nate said, "what happened? Where's India?"

Thrane ran a hand over his face, something sticky trailed over his cheek.

"India—" He cleared the thickening in this throat. "She's gone. To the Higherworld. With Evine. I think, hope, Evine got her there in time."

"What do you mean, she's gone? To do the codex thing?" Nate looked around the clearing. His face paled. "India?" Nate asked, his voice shaking.

Thrane caught his breath. "She was hurt, Nate. Bad. I don't know how. I was fighting Ri'Kiant"—Thrane gestured at two bodies on the other side of the clearing—"over there, when I heard India cry out. I got her to the Tree and then Evine took her to the Higherworld. To get help."

"How bad?"

Thrane tried to answer. But no sound came out. All he could see was India bleeding. All he could hear was her gasping.

"How bad is she hurt?" Nate asked Jona. "*Where* is she?"

Thrane exerted all of his will to focus on Jona and what he was about to say. He had to know exactly how to get to India.

"She was dying," Jona said. "My granddaughter was dying of her wound. However, Thrane may have saved her life. He got her to the Tree, and Evine will take her to the best place possible. India will get the help she needs."

"But how? Who hurt her?"

"One of our guards did the deed," Oev said, kneeling by the two dead men. He held up one of their bloody swords. "But, by all the gods, I cannot imagine any reason for that."

Oev's words cut through the haze. Thrane found enough control to take in the blood-soaked clearing.

"Look at how the blood has poured from every orifice," Thrane said, squatting beside the bodies of Oev's men. "Is there a chance any of your soldiers would betray you?"

"They wouldn't. Ever."

"And yet they did. And now they're both dead, bled out but with no visible wound."

Oev's eyes narrowed. "You have seen this before?" he asked.

"A very long time ago, yes. It happened when a god forced their will onto a being. The weight of the demand forced the blood from every opening."

"That would be the only explanation I would accept for our men to do such a thing." Oev stood. "Which god would interfere with our family? Risk Freya's wrath?"

Adrenaline flooded Thrane's system, sent his pulse pounding. But he reined it in, took the energy, the pain, the urge to fight and shout and fucking destroy everything, and channeled it into cold, hard precision. Whoever fucking did this would not get away with it.

He looked hard at Jona, Oev and Nate—all blood kin to India. They'd fight for her, but no harder than he would. Thrane clenched his hands at his sides.

"I'll find the thing that did this to India. And I will kill it. But right now, I need to find her." He swallowed the lump that tightened in his throat. "I *have* to find her."

With one hand, he touched the massive trunk. Instantly, images of India bombarded his mind.

His heart lurched. To find India, he had to leave the Tree.

A tiny kernel of warmth, of acceptance, flowed from the Tree to him. Swiftly followed by an image of him entering the Heavens.

Thrane sent back his determination to find India and protect both her and the Tree.

"I have to leave," he said, "but I need someone to look out for the Tree. And to clean up here."

Jona and Oev nodded. Nate's face was pale, but he nodded too.

"Go to my work shed," Thrane said. "Inside is a large bin, lid buckled down, filled with silver salt. There's only one like it. Spread the salt over the remains, it will take care of the rest." Thrane reached out with one crimson-stained hand and grasped Nate's shoulder. "I swear this, to you all. On India's blood, I will see her home."

"Are you going now?" Nate asked.

"Yes, I can't wait, I need the World Tree to take me to Evine, and she's already got a head start. Can I take your mount, Jona?" Thrane asked. "I don't want to waste any more time, and I give you my word, I'll look after her."

Jona looked hard at Thrane then nodded. "Resilience has been with me since she was a foal. Guard her well."

He too whistled and his mare came to them immediately. Jona spoke softly into her ear and introduced her to Thrane. As impatient as Thrane was to get going, he held a hand out to Resilience. Though she didn't shy at the blood's metallic scent, her muzzle twitched, and her ears flickered, but she steadied with a quiet word from Jona.

Thrane gave her a soft rub, spoke her name, and lifted himself onto her back. Not used to his weight, she danced a little as he settled into the saddle. Then, with a nudge of his thighs, the mare took him right to the trunk of the Tree.

INDIA OPENED her eyes to a ceiling of stars. Stunning gold orbs—some as big as her fist, others as small is a pinhead—shimmered in a velvet-indigo sky.

She was lying on a bed—a very comfortable, very large bed. Around her, walls of white met the horizon. They swayed, and a soothing breeze crossed her skin. Ah, the walls were curtains.

India turned to follow their billowing movement. Fire traced through her torso. She gasped, clutched at her side.

And she remembered.

The graze of her hand against the World Tree, a move involuntary and so slight, had revealed her true purpose. Why she was the perfect choice for this task.

The Tree had spoken with her. Their conversation—one of images and feelings—had lasted the length of time it took for her to transition to the Heavens.

That transition, similar to her experience when she first went to Thrane's, had been a kaleidoscope of galaxies and stars and worlds spinning past. No sense of up or down, or backward or forward. No sense of anything but space.

That had been the physical transition. Her mental transition had been filled with the World Tree's communication.

It had shown her how it had given the mortals a world where they could be free from undue duress, from those whose abilities to shape the will of others far outweighed any human's. And it had shown her the fight for its existence over the last two thousand years.

India understood that the Tree she'd touched was one World Tree, but it was also all World Trees. It was a guardian for their worlds, their lives, and their existence.

She'd seen Thrane, in appearance and physical form exactly as he was now, yet dressed as a knight in heavy armor.

Thrane! She jolted up. But fire once more lanced her side. She gasped again, tightened her grip on her side.

Okay, so that hurt.

She breathed through the pain, then warily looked down at her stomach. She wore a plain white, long-sleeved cotton shirt.

Holding her breath, she lifted the shirt up and ...

Panties, she was at least wearing panties—even if it was just them and the shirt.

She released her breath with a whoosh.

Gingerly, she raised the shirt higher, its loose fit making the task easier. On her abdomen, a red welt rose from her skin in a straight line. It extended from the bottom of her ribs down toward her belly button, maybe ten centimeters long. She reached around to her back, fingers searching the skin and, sure enough, touched a mirroring welt.

Holy crap. She'd been well and truly skewered.

Her stomach quivered and she lowered the shirt again. It was long enough that it met the bottom of her panties, but that wasn't saying much.

She glanced around the room. Several pillows, all stark white, were stacked on the bed. The silken walls met a floor that looked to be smooth, golden sandstone. A stone plinth stood in the corner, and on it sat a gem-green fern, its foliage draped over the edge of a copper-hued urn. The brilliant colors were all the more striking against the otherwise white backdrop. Their jeweled tones, the gold of sandstone, even the amazing indigo sky made the room one of the most exotic places India had ever been in.

But India didn't want to stay.

She needed to get home to the farm. Needed to get to Thrane—uh, except no, she didn't need to get to Thrane. She almost smacked herself in the head. He was the man who, by his own words, had used her—their attraction. Except, she did need to find him and ask one thing: why had he looked guilty when Evine had mentioned her father?

Was Thrane here, wherever this was? He'd said he'd follow Evine—his words were surprisingly vivid in her memory—and he was a man who stayed true to his word, one thing she grudgingly appreciated.

Her wound had healed, so she could go home when she figured out how to get there.

What to do now? India could call out and hope someone was nearby, but that didn't feel right. She looked up at the sky; the indigo had deepened as night fell.

A prickle itched along her spine, up to her neck. Where was she?

The prickle grew stronger.

This was going to hurt, she knew it, but she did it anyway. She swung her legs—first one, and then the other —over the side of the bed. The burning lanced through her again. She hissed but wasn't put off. After one more breath, she touched her feet to the sandstone. A warm tingle of awareness rose up through her soles.

Odd.

India levered her body up, keeping a grip on the bed in case her legs buckled.

They didn't.

She tried to pull the shirt down, but it was useless, so she folded both hands in front of her groin, and quietly, slowly, padded to the nearest curtain. She followed the ripple of the material, quickly came to a part, and slipped through.

She swallowed hard as she looked down a short flight of steps, where ornately scrolled sandstone pillars, wreathed in green vines, were spread out in a perfect wide row. More curtains billowed softly from an unseen breeze.

"Hail, India, child of the family of Freya," an unknown voice said from somewhere by the pillars.

India almost toppled and fought to keep her balance.

A feminine figure emerged. She was perfectly proportioned, with generous curves revealed beneath a creamy shift and an under-bust corset. Heavy straps of braided-gold wrapped around her shoulders and followed the lines of the corset. Gauntlets covered her forearms, and a forest-green cloak sat smoothly off her shoulders. A sword and scabbard, made from some shiny metal, rested on her hip. Her golden hair was piled messily yet elegantly on top of her head, and her delicate face featured gently arcing brows and emerald eyes.

"Careful," she said, gliding up the steps and standing on the same landing as India. "You may take a few more minutes yet to heal."

"Holy crap," India said. "You're ... well, you're absolutely stunning."

A throaty laugh met her words.

"That is a lovely thing to say. Thank you."

"Um, you're welcome?"

"And polite, too. Well, you are a truly lovely and

refreshing addition to this house." Her emerald eyes narrowed. "How is your wound? Is it still paining you?"

India found herself looking down at her side and drawing her shirt up—definitely not something she would normally do in front of a stranger.

"Ah, but I am not a stranger," the woman said.

That prickle itched along India's spine again. She dropped the shirt and backed away until she met the curtain. "The pain's okay. Manageable. Thank you."

"Please, take care. If you step past the curtain, you may fall and hurt yourself further. That would be a shame since you have healed so well."

This time the small hairs on the back of India's neck rose, straight and fast. She brought her magic up, ready to protect—

"Oh no, that is not needed in this place."

Her magic gently subsided without her will.

India studied the young woman. Realization struck. "Holy crap."

Emerald eyes twinkled. "Yes, child. I am Freya."

"Ah, hi—hello." What on earth was she meant to say now? "Um, have I been here long?"

"Not at all. Your time here has been of no parity at all to the healing you have undergone," Freya said, tilting her head. "Had you thought your healed wound was a sign of time passing? Ah, that must be a mortal thought process."

"So, *you* helped me?"

"Not at all. You came here with your wound on the mend. All I provided was a safe place for you to rest while your body took care of itself."

"Huh, I thought I was pretty much dying. And all the time I was immortal."

"Not at all. Your witchcraft is still finding its natural level," she said. "At the time you were wounded, you were mortal, child."

"Okay." She wasn't sure of the protocol when dealing with a god. Surely there was something she should do. Or say. Something better than *okay*. But she had no clue at all. Freya tucked India's hand within her arm, and India found herself effortlessly guided down the steps, along the pillared path.

"Come, child. Evine grows concerned for your wellbeing, and this is one stress I find unneeded."

India caught a whiff of magic right before the path of pillars changed, and then Freya and India were strolling along a track made from finely crushed shells. It led to a grassy square. Only the fact that the sky stayed dark with those amazing stars told India they were still in the Heavens.

Freya beamed. "You handled that wonderfully well. Most new immortals, even some who are older, take time to acclimate to the sensations of crossing."

"Crossing?" India asked.

"That is the term we use, for when we cross over land, or space, or worlds in an instant—or sometimes longer, depending on how far one is crossing."

"Huh, that makes sense. And I think that's the third time I've done it, actually."

Freya raised a perfect brow. "Third?"

"The second was when the Tree brought me from earth to—well, wherever we are. The first was a couple of days ago. I think I flew through the entire universe in the blink of an eye. It was astounding."

"Oh." Freya smiled again. "You will do brilliantly well as an immortal. Of course, you are a child of my family, so I suppose that is not such a surprise. Now, where is she? Yes, there," Freya said.

The tang of magic bloomed again, and then Evine, sitting at a copper-hued table and chairs, appeared in the distance. She'd changed her clothing since India had last seen her and wore a jade-green dress, caught off one shoulder and secured with ropes of gold braiding.

"Granddaughter," Freya called out softly.

Evine glanced up and India gasped.

"Oh, you were not aware that your grandmother is my granddaughter?" Freya said. "Well, it is a good time to learn about your family, I suppose."

"Freya." Evine dipped her head low as they approached. "My unending thanks for your assistance."

"Not at all."

India glanced back at Freya—her choice of words was surely no coincidence? Her twinkling green eyes told India she was right.

"Your granddaughter had begun to heal ere she arrived at my house."

"What?" Evine's eyes flew to India.

India shrugged. She didn't know why either.

"So now that we three are here," Freya said, "why don't you tell me what has brought you to my house?"

"I thought I was coming to the Heavens"—India barely paused when Evine sighed—"to have my fate written in your book."

"India," Evine said, her tone a mild rebuke, "has not had any education in the ways of the Higherworld or our family. Please excuse her lack of formality and knowledge."

"Not at all." Freya waved a graceful hand. "So, you are

here to visit the spinner's codex. That makes much more sense."

"So where is the book—er, codex, and how can I get there?" India asked.

Evine sighed again, looked pointedly at Freya.

"Worry not, Granddaughter, our India will come to learn the ways that are important. In the meantime, it is refreshing to have one so young and so honest in our house."

Evine pursed her lips.

"To answer your questions, India, our spinner's codex is held at the Great Library. The journey is one of considerable length and requires much energy, therefore might I offer you a crossing to take you there so you can complete your task? It would be lovely to help one so new to our family."

"Thank you, that sounds like a good idea." India bit back a groan. "Ah, any chance I can have something more to wear?"

33

Thrane, sitting astride Resilience, touched the World Tree. His only thought was India, and the Tree read his intention. He kept his eyes open during the crossing, arrived in the Heavens instantly aware of his surroundings.

The World Tree here was an ancient being, differing in appearance in all ways to the World Tree in the Mortal-world. Dozens of roots rose high out of the ground, coming together to form the solid trunk. It was over a hundred feet tall, and its twisted, gnarled limbs reached out to the sky with their spiked-leaf fingers. The closest specimen he had seen to it in the Mortalworld was El Drago Milenario, a Canary Island dragon tree in San Marco.

Steadying Resilience as she adjusted to the crossing, Thrane took the moment to run his hand over the trunk and whisper his gratitude. Next, he sent Resilience into a gallop along the trail that led away from the Tree.

He surveyed the land, picked out familiar landmarks in the deepening dark as they raced toward his destination. He was sure now of where Evine had taken India. After all, if you were going to get help, you might as well get it from a god. Particularly one who was your relative. Thrane sent a prayer of thanks to the universe—if anyone could heal India, it would be Freya.

Resilience ate up the trail in long strides, and in no time, golden stone columns rose in the distance. The nearer Thrane got, the clearer they grew and the taller they appeared, until they owned the horizon.

When they reached the base of a giant set of steps, made from the same material as the massive pillars, he reined Resilience in and dismounted.

Evine appeared at the top of the steps. She regarded him, then the horse. Her eyes widened before she darted down the steps.

"Why do you have Resilience?" she demanded, striding closer with each word, and Thrane was reminded that this woman was an extremely powerful Herald who was in no way grandmother-like in her physical capabilities.

"Jona gave me his mount to help me locate India," Thrane replied, glancing briefly at Evine before scanning the temple from where he stood. Was India inside?

"Jona would never give you his horse," Evine said.

"Then 'never' just happened." He peered closer at her garments. Evine already wore the traditional dress of the Heavens. Thrane had to swallow before he could speak again.

"Evine, where's India? Is she—is she—?" He cleared his throat "Tell me how she is."

"That is a demand, Keeper, and you are not in your world anymore. You do not demand things of me in my own family's house."

"This isn't your house. This is Freya's temple."

"That is irrelevant. I am Freya's family. Therefore this *is* my family house. And as none here outrank me, I have authority here. And you are not welcome."

Thrane wanted to shout, but he forced his voice to stay even.

"Are you saying Freya is not here?"

"Correct," she said, gently running a hand down Resilience's flank.

"Evine. You are the grandmother of the one for whom I hold a sincere and deep affection, and so I am tempering my response to you right now. But believe me, do not push me further on this. Now tell me, *please,* how is India?"

Evine looked at him with disdain, but all he cared about was that she appeared to be considering his request. Finally, she gave Resilience a last pat and turned to him.

"Evine."

"Growl at me not, Keeper. I knew India should not be in your company, and look at what happened. My family have lost so much for the Keepers. First Jev, and now India is at risk."

"By the gods, do you think I wanted to lose either of them? Jev was a lifelong friend, and India ... India is my everything."

"India did not die of her injury."

Thrane lifted his head. "What?"

"I acknowledge I owe you that, but no more will you get from me. Fair warning, Keeper—when I find her, I will do everything in my power to return India to *my* house and convince her that a life in the Higherworld is the best place for her."

"What do you mean when you *find* her? How could you have lost her?"

Evine shrugged one of her elegant shoulders.

"By the gods," Thrane spat. "*Tell* me where she is."

Evine was on him in a flash, held her small lethal-looking blade at his chest. The tip burned as she let it prick his skin.

"India was taken from this place by one of our gods, Keeper. So no, I shall *not* tell you where my granddaughter is now."

Thrane stepped even closer, and the knife's tip pushed to the point where Evine had to reduce her pressure or else risk slicing something important. He took the chance that she wouldn't risk a war with the Keepers by injuring him. That was not something she could afford to do if she intended to use the World Tree ever again.

Sure enough, she desisted, though kept her dagger held out.

Thrane batted it aside, seriously pissed off now.

"Save your dramatics, Evine. You and I might not agree on India's choice of family, but haven't you figured out yet that I'm only interested in helping her?"

"She doesn't need your help, she needs her family." Evine looked down her patrician nose at him. *India's nose.*

"So, no more information, then?" Thrane said.

"That is what I said."

Thrane didn't waste any more time talking. He grabbed Resilience's reins and swiftly mounted.

"Jona told me to return his horse to him." He turned Resilience around. "And that's what I'm going to do."

～

INDIA GASPED. Thankfully Freya still held her hand as they crossed over to a wide corridor inside what appeared to be a medieval castle.

India was clothed now, in a similar style to Freya. Her white shirt was covered by an under-bust leather vest, buckled through the front with heavy brass clasps. She wore leggings in the softest buff material she'd ever felt. And she had her own cloak, in the same forest-green as Freya's. The outfit was ridiculous and comfortable and made her feel powerful, all at the same time.

Freya gently squeezed her hand.

"India, know this—your fate can be formed before you are even a consideration in your parents' thoughts, or it can be set by actions you set forth. And sometimes, your fate can be something you choose. The codex is only a record, and even records can change. Do not fear this process. Allow us old gods this one formality, and then you can live your life. Come, child."

India walked along the corridor with Freya.

"Can I ask a question?" India asked.

A small frown puckered the perfection of Freya's face. India took that as a yes.

"Why all this fuss?" she asked. "I mean, yeah, I seem to have a lot of power as a witch, but I'm actually not that good at magic. It's more like I can read and influence the energy around me, not actually cast a spell. And okay, Thrane explained my magic could be very bad for the World Tree because of my heritage. But surely there are other witches like me?"

"You are right in one way, child. There have been others of your talent, and of your power, and even of your combined heritage. But never have I known of a being with all three traits. In this, you and your witchcraft are unique."

"I wish I knew why my mother hid it from me."

"Well, child, your very clever mother hid your magic so it couldn't be tracked. Did you know she searched for a permanent way to remove it?"

India gasped. "What?"

It was almost impossible to believe. Her magic was as much a part of her as her heart.

"Not all of it, child. Only the part that represented the worst of the danger to you. I know this because as she could not come here, she requested my assistance to search the Great Library—where we are going now—for her answers. But there was no way to achieve what she wanted. Your magic *is* you."

"Freya, do you know—that is, you're a god, so I'm hoping you might know—why she never lifted the spell that shrouded my magic?"

"Ah, child. I asked your mother that very question. She feared that if the spell was released before she found a way to remove the dangerous elements of your power, the strength of your magic would mean she could ever recast the spell. And then those tracking your magic could find you."

"But why? Why my magic?"

Freya sighed. "Do you know the story of the World Tree?"

"Yes. That is, Thrane—" India stumbled as she said his name. "Thrane explained a bit about it."

"Let me enlighten you further. We, the old and new gods, are elemental in our most basic form. Do you know that before the World Tree, there was no order, no sense of any purpose other than what we desired."

A shiver trickled down India's spine.

"No, I hadn't heard that," she said.

"I had imagined not. It is not a time even we gods reflect upon much. It came to pass that after eons of this, we, the old gods, created the World Tree through our combined powers. We each ceded a portion of our abilities to the Tree so that it would be our sole structured force.

"And then, one was born whose power talked to the very elements that created the Tree. And that one's power was so strong, it could be used for good—or evil, in the wrong hands.

"Child, these walls have stood for eons." Freya swept a hand before her. "My father, brothers, sisters—we all created this place, as we did many others, to both serve our purposes and serve ourselves. We have abounded in power, knowledge. Satisfaction. And yet, there are those of us who covet more, who would see the Mortalworld return to that time when the Gods had all of the control. And you my child, can give them that."

"So, I'm basically bait for the bad guys?"

"Oh no, not *only* that. But you must heed the possibility of your power." Freya's perfect face grew very serious. "Why did you stumble when you said Thrane's name?"

"Thrane? I don't even know where to start with him. Except to say he's a total asshole. An asshole who's more tight-lipped than—than—crap, I don't even know."

"Ah, child," Freya said, lips turning up in the barest of smiles. "Your Keeper was ever a soloist. And these last decades have forced him to rely on none other than himself. I have oft had a soft spot for him."

"He's not *my* Keeper."

"Apologies, child. *Our* Keeper. It was he, over one hundred and fifty years ago, who held the fate of your world in his hands. And since that time, he has in essence been alone in his mission. Do you know that supernatural beings bond for life? It is due to our immortality. Once we form a connection that touches our heart, there is something irrevocable in that, as if it's tied to our very soul."

"Nope. That's another thing I didn't know."

"Hmm, well, I was telling you about our Keeper. I gave him a mammoth task, one that required he commit to it alone. Beforehand, he was already a mighty warrior. Ruthless. Deadly. Afterward, the importance, the magnitude of all that he had lost and all he had to safeguard, sharpened his already bladed edges."

"Sharpened?" India said. "He cut me down."

Freya tucked India's arm in tighter. "I would imagine he felt he had no choice."

"Ha. No. More like he doesn't trust me."

"Oh, my child, I would not have thought that the case. Why do you say so?"

"Well, honest to God—no offense—he thinks that I'm a danger to the Tree. He brought his sword after *me*," India said. "And then, he tells me that all our time together—all of it—was basically a reason for him to stay close to me, in case he was right, and I'm this bloody-big grave danger."

"And the challenge there," Freya said, "is you have indeed been that—perhaps the gravest danger Thrane has ever faced. India, do you know much about your warrior?"

"I know he's not *my* warrior."

"Well, it's always a possibility that he's not *yours*. May I enlighten you while we walk?"

India frowned.

"Permit me this, child. It is not oft that I have the opportunity to enlighten one so new to our family."

"I'm pretty sure you're impossible to resist, Freya."

"You are right, there, child. Now, your Keeper—apologies, *our* Keeper. Throughout his mortal years, he never found love, never settled down, never sired any children. He was a unique mortal. And he was the finest warrior the Mortalworld had seen in centuries.

"It was no wonder the World Tree called to him. Then, as a Keeper, he had to see the loss of all those mortals—family, friends. It is a difficult thing to see those you care for pass the way of the earth. Perhaps that is why not many mortals are called to the Tree's service.

"And then, over a century ago, the World Tree came under a dire attack. It would have perished entirely if not for Thrane secreting one lone, little seedling away. And when the Tree fell in that battle, along with the other Keepers, Thrane was left alone."

A shiver prickled up India's spine. "Alone?"

"Alone. His brethren Keepers held off the Order long enough for him to get away, but they all perished for the cause. After that, bearing a burden so overwhelming that many would have broken under the strain, Thrane settled in your land. He watched over the Tree as it grew, and the communities around him also grew, such as your own family line. And he stayed there, resolute. I believe he has always held himself responsible, weighed down by the perceived possibility that, had he stayed at the fight all those years ago, perchance his brethren Keepers and the Tree would not have perished."

"Was that a possibility?" India asked, hugging her arms to her chest.

"Sadly, that outcome was always a certainty."

"And he's felt responsible for what happened for over a century?"

"Yes, and then you came along. Quite simply, you have the power, either at your own hands or at those who would kill you and steal your magic, to destroy the Tree. Destroy everything he has lived for, sacrificed for. That is a burden more heavy upon Thrane's shoulders than any other I can imagine. For along with the knowledge that your power can destroy the Tree, the connection he has established with you places him in a predicament as never before."

"Connection? No way. He used me. Lied to me."

"Well, he does have a rather important job to do. Yet he did not strike you down, nor made an attempt to remove the threat you pose, permanently. Tell me, did he harm you in any way?"

"Ah, no, not physically."

"Hmm. Perhaps there is one more question you should ask, but of yourself. Have you always been honest with him?"

India blew out a hard breath and gathered her thoughts. She wouldn't lie to herself. Not about this. And not to Freya.

"I didn't talk to him—or anyone—about the Tree. About how it ... well, how it spoke to me, called to me in my dreams. Not until last night anyway."

"Why not?"

"At first, I was scared they'd think I was mad. And when I realized the Tree was real, I was scared Thrane would try to stop me getting to it."

"Oh, child, fear causes so much dissonance in our

worlds. Well, you will choose your course with your—our—Keeper, but perhaps see things from his eyes if you can. And consider that his position was one of impossibility. Yet he spared you. And more, protected you. Perhaps his feelings towards you are further engaged than you believe."

Freya's words cast Thrane and his actions in a different light. Could Freya be right? Did Thrane really feel something for her? Beyond wariness that she posed a threat, anyway.

And had her secret been part of the problem?

"Well," Freya said, "hopefully you have the information you need. Now, we have arrived."

India looked ahead in surprise. Freya's words had obliterated the surroundings as they'd moved along the wide corridor. They stood before a giant pair of arched stone doors.

"Here you will find the spinner and her codex," Freya said. "Record your weave, child." She held up a hand, and the doors swung open soundlessly, revealing an enormous space filled with hundreds of people, either sitting at magically floating tables or in scattered overstuffed armchairs.

And they all stopped, watched as she and Freya entered.

Walls and walls of bookshelves, so many stories high India couldn't count them, led to a domed ceiling covered in paintings depicting scenes from every mythological story India had ever heard.

Ladders whizzed sideways and upwards and downwards around the shelves, people clinging to the rungs as they stared at India and Freya.

"How can there be this many books in the world?" India asked, stumbling to a stop. "And why is everyone staring at us?"

"Well, we are the gods, child, though they are not staring at me. But please, ignore their interest—they are simply unused to seeing those from the Mortalworld." Freya waved in the general direction of the cavern. "Let us focus on your reason for being here."

So, this was it. India was going to do this thing. She looked up at the walls of books.

Books. They were only books. And she loved to read, so why was she nervous?

"Where's the spinner?" India asked.

"Here." Freya gestured into the room, and suddenly, only one other person and only one table was in the library.

The other person, a stooped woman, old, with masses of curly hair in every shade possible, stood at the table. Her eyes were a kaleidoscope of colors, continuously inter-changing.

India smiled tentatively.

Out of nowhere, a little book appeared on the table. It was bound in brown leather and had gold carvings etched into the cover. Slowly, sibilantly, the carvings started to move, twisting and entwining, until they formed the figure of a serpent eating its tail.

The book fell open to a blank page.

India stepped forward, drawn closer to it. An image appeared in the page, at first like grains of parchment—colorless, but textured enough to stand out. Gradually, the grains took on the color of sand, began to move and grow. The shape built up and out of the page yet was still *of* the page itself.

Eventually, a three-dimensional figure formed—first roots, then a trunk, boughs and twigs, and finally leaves.

And in front of the image, color bloomed in the parchment where a sword emerged, hilt up toward India.

Freya picked up the book, and India succumbed to an irresistible urge to reach out and touch the image. A filament of parchment lifted from the page and stabbed the tip of her finger.

"Hey," India said, looking up at Freya in surprise. "No one said this was going be a blood sacrifice."

A bead of blood welled, dropped to the page. The book closed. Disappeared. As did the Spinner.

"Child, I should not have been surprised," Freya said. "You are, if nothing else, one of our family."

India blinked, as the room had filled once again with a multitude of bodies.

"Ah, what just happened? And why the blood?"

"The blood is to seal the fate. Although I have to say, it is rather an old ritual, and as I mentioned earlier, there have been those who have rerecorded theirs. However, as of now, the codex has confirmed that you are fated to be a Keeper, a warrior who will defend the World Tree and ensure its continuance within our worlds."

"I kind of knew that. The Tree spoke to me as I came through to the Heavens," India said.

"The Tree keeps us on our toes," Freya said. "But that is as it should be."

"So, what now?"

"Well, your grandmother Evine will be devastated to find out that you are not a Herald, or a Seer, or even only a witch." Freya winked at India. "But for you, child ... well, you have a choice to make."

"As in, right now? Right here?"

"It is but a small one," Freya continued. "You must

choose where you will Keep the Tree, as it is in all three worlds."

"Okay. I have to decide where to work, that's it?"

"Er, well, yes. You have put it in a term with which I am unfamiliar, though I can correlate it to your previously mortal existence."

India didn't even need to think about this one. "I know where I'll be going."

34

Thrane crossed to the Mortalworld World Tree to find rain drizzling through the forest canopy. He headed to his house first and tied Resilience under the cover of one of his sheds while he went inside to wash and change, then he nudged the mare up the hill toward Liz's farm.

Finding a free stall in the stable, he led Resilience in, quickly rubbed her down, and made sure she had fresh hay before striding to the house.

Liz met him at the kitchen door. It was obvious she hadn't been to sleep—her hair stood on end and her eyes blazed. Her face was pale.

"India is okay," Thrane said.

Liz swayed, and he reached out a hand to steady her.

"Where is she?" Liz asked.

"Freya must have taken her to see the spinner. That was hours ago though, so she could be anywhere in the Heavens by now. The fastest way to find her is not to run around. I'm only here to let you know that she's alive—now, I'm going to find her."

"*Anywhere* in the Heavens?"

"That's why I'm going to see an old friend. Someone who can find her."

Liz's eyes grew round with comprehension. "Is that the wisest choice? You were rumored not to be the most popular person there?"

"Doesn't matter. Going to see her is the fastest way to locate India."

"Remember, Thrane, we want you *both* back."

Thrane smiled, his first since India had been wounded.

"I know, Liz." He covered her hand with his. "How is everyone?"

A yap echoed through the house and the black pup barreled into the kitchen and over to him.

"This one has been the hardest of all to control," Liz said. "Nate brought him back here after ... after what happened at the Tree. The little monster has whined and whined, right up until you got here."

Thrane picked up the pup, who immediately licked Thrane's chin before nestling into his chest.

"Bah, look at him," Liz said. "Knows where his bread is buttered obviously."

Thrane gently scratched the pup's chin while he kept his gaze on Liz. "And all else is well?"

"Yes, all is well. Nate brought Oev and his father back here, they're sleeping now, then Nate went to patrol your land. You must have just missed him."

Thrane nodded, gave the pup one last pat before handing him to Liz.

"I'm heading off now," he said, "look after the little monster."

He took his medallion from his shirt, wrapped his hand

around it, and as he crossed to the Underworld, the pup gave a little whine and Liz cursed.

For decades, his training had focused on grasping his medallion, crossing into the Underworld, picking up his sword, and returning from whence he'd come in an instant. This time he took his hand off the medallion and stayed in the pitch-black cell.

The air was dank, musty. He stilled, heard no sound to indicate anyone else was nearby, so reached out till he found a ledge in the stone, felt around until he found a flint and candles, and a heavy iron key. Lastly he touched the medallion connected to his, the one that never left the cell, and laid it flat on the ledge again.

Lighting one of the candles revealed bare rock walls on three sides, and thick bars barring the opening of the cell. The hinged door in the middle of the bars was closed and padlocked by a chain as thick as his wrist.

But this chamber was designed to keep things out, not in.

He used the key to unlock the padlock, quickly left the cell, then after swinging the heavy iron gate shut and locking it again, he tossed the key back in. He couldn't risk the other half of his Connection being found by anyone.

He left his cell. It was one of many in a web of tunnels, carved out of the bowels of the mountain range that was the Lord Ursiel's home and domain, who he was going to see now. Because Serephena, Lord of the Ursiel, was also the best scryer on the three worlds.

As Thrane made his way through the warren of corridors, more cell doors appeared out of the darkness, but no sounds came from any of them, and he had no idea whether they were in use or not. Finally, he came to a steep, spiral staircase carved out of the mountain. He took off up the stairs at a run.

Many minutes later, Thrane ran into the main hall—a giant cavern carved in the top of the tallest mountain in the range. Massive vents, dug through the rocks and earth, acted as lighting, air vents, even cooling and heating—depending on the wish of the lord.

Serephena, midnight wings furled at her back, Valkyrie and Lord of the Ursiel, stood toward the side of the cavern at a series of long trestle tables, talking to a group of people. She wore the loose-fitting pants and vest of the Ursiel, but even so, her impressive curves were clear. Her hair, the same hue as her wings, was cut short around her face—far different from how she'd worn it when he'd last seen her.

"Thrane?" she called out, eyes widening.

He nodded, and she turned to the people she'd been speaking with, said something Thrane couldn't hear. Then she unfurled her wings and launched into the air, landing several paces in front of him in the blink of an eye.

"Serephena," Thrane called out, dipping his head in a brisk motion. "I have an urgent request for assistance. I need to find a witch—born to the Jones's house in the Mortalworld and also claimed by the house of Freya."

Serephena's lip curled. "From the Higherworld?" She waved one hand in the air, but her eyes narrowed. "What business does a Keeper have with a witch?"

He considered her for a moment, recalling Liz's words to be wary. "Keeper business," he replied.

"Really?" Serephena stepped closer. "It sounds like this witch is already the business of two families, neither of this world. And you expect me, a lord of the Underworld, to interfere on your behalf?"

"Serephena," Thrane said, rolling his eyes. "This is not the time for petty bias between the worlds."

One black eyebrow rose. "Have I given you leave to address me without my title?"

"Fine. *Lord Ursiel*, I have come to you with a genuine need for assistance. You did offer help should I ever need it."

"And did I not deliver that help by bestowing upon you the gift of a cell in my home—a cell that no other key but yours may open?" Lord Ursiel said.

"Fuck," Thrane muttered. "You're not making this easy."

That got him a throaty laugh. He'd enjoyed that sound once upon a time. Now it made him grind his teeth.

"Why, whatever do you mean, Keeper? Do you refer to the fact that when we parted, we did so at your request, not mine? Or do you refer to the fact that since then, every time you have visited my house you have managed to visit *me* precisely never?"

"My visits here have been, by necessity, brief."

"Tsk, tsk, Keeper. You and I both know you could have found time to say hello. After all, we were lovers once."

"Sere—*Lord* Ursiel—there's no time for this. Will you help me?"

Her eyes flashed, and her cheeks went red. But then she dropped her gaze, hid her expression.

"Fine, Keeper. I will locate your witch."

"Thank you." Thrane wanted to say more, but she whirled away.

"Follow me," Serephena called over her shoulder.

She picked up a lantern and led the way down the steps. The tunnels took them deeper and deeper into the mountain, and he wasn't sure how far they'd walked when she stopped at a cell. Not his.

Serephena withdrew a chain from about her neck and selected one of many keys from its links. She opened the gate and stepped inside, gestured for him to do so as well. As he did, Serephena hung the lamp on a stake that was driven into the stone. It cast enough light for Thrane to see that the cell was empty except for them.

"Why here?" he asked.

"I need a space where we won't be interrupted. And no one comes down here except for me. This cell will do as well as any. Now, I'll need something of this witch—a memory should do fine." She smirked as she touched both her hands to Thrane's temples. "This won't hurt ... much."

A knock hit his mind, and though he needed to answer it, doing so was hard. By the gods, let this be the right thing to do. But for India, he'd do anything.

He forced his mind to open up.

A grating, icy shiver racked through him, fingernails running down a chalkboard. He wanted to turn his head, escape the sensation, but again, forced himself to see it out.

He had no idea how long it took. One minute the touch on his mind was there, the next it was gone.

He opened his eyes. While his normally accurate internal clock had paused during that—that—mind search, the candle within the lamp had shortened considerably.

"Sere, how many of my memories did you see?" Thrane demanded, grabbing Serephena's arm as her hand dropped from his face.

"Enough." Her cerulean eyes stared into his. "You put *her* before the World Tree? You would not make time for me— an ancient, a lord of the Underworld—and yet you put a mortal before your sacred duty?" She gave a hollow laugh.

"Well, it appears you have indeed fallen in love, Keeper. After all these years."

"You've got what you need, so where is she?"

"Now, now. You know this may take some time. While I *am* the best scryer in the three worlds, even I have to search by land until I can pinpoint a location."

Serephena's wings unfurled, enough for her to fan them once—causing the air to stir—and then she was outside the cell. Thrane sprang for the door, but she swung it shut.

"Serephena! By the gods, what are you doing?"

"Well, I'm going to do as you asked, Keeper, and scry for your witch. I did find one interesting fact from your memories, however. You didn't mention your witch is of the three worlds. I wonder why?"

"Let me out of here, Sere. Ri'Kiant is still out there. India needs help."

"Oh, Thrane, I'm going to have a little fun while I find your witch. And if she *is* in the Higherworld, surely, she's safe from your nemesis. Not sure about the rest of the supernatural world, though."

Thrane growled. "I came to you in good faith," he said, feeling under his shirt for his medallion. "I won't be back for your help again. I—"

Where was it?

"Oh no, are you looking for something? This, perhaps?"

His medallion dangled from Serephena's hand.

"Now rest awhile," she said. "Your memories tell me you have pushed yourself for nigh on two days with no rest. I'll be back when I have some news."

He cursed as she once more fanned her wings and propelled herself away from the cell.

35

India accepted Freya's offer of one last crossing and returned to the Mortalworld. As soon as she arrived, she placed a hand on the World Tree's trunk.

Welcome, affection, and purpose filled her. Along with an awareness of the entire world on such a deep level it took her breath away.

"Whoa, slow down, that's a lot to process." She laughed but left her hand in place. "Why don't we start with baby steps, huh?"

An image of a toddler, wandering through the fields of Nan's farm, played in her mind.

"Hey, that's me, isn't it? Why—ah, baby steps. Of course. So you can really understand me?"

Warmth suffused her.

"And that's how we communicate? I talk, and you send me feelings, sensations, images, things like that?"

She laughed when, once again, warmth suffused her.

"Well, it looks like we'll have no problem communicating. I'm a pretty emotional kind of person."

India ran a hand over the bark, looked up into the dark brown, almost black, boughs of the Tree, and the dark green foliage that spread above.

"You look like the perfect place to stay and sit for a while. But right now, I have to get home and let everyone know what's happened. I can tell you one person who's going to be stunned—that may be an understatement—when he hears this news."

She waited for the warmth to come again, but this time an image of Thrane came to mind—his serious face stared right back at her. Was that her thought, or the Tree's? It didn't matter. She was going to find him straightaway.

But just because Freya's words had opened the door—a smidge—on the possibility that Thrane wasn't a total asshole didn't mean she was going to forgive him. But they did need to talk. He had to explain what had happened with her father.

Especially since they were going to be working together.

She ran her hand along the bark one more time

So how to get to Thrane's from here? The first time she'd come to the Tree she'd been following a trail of energy. If it had worked for her once, it might work again. She reached inside herself, brought her energy consciously to the forefront of her mind. As she did, the energy of her surroundings sprang to life. In the floral energy currents, a very specific layout was evident.

India set off in that direction. The energy pathway—technically, lack-of-energy pathway—easily took her between trees and plants, large and small, and unerringly brought her out of the forest into low scrub, and to Thrane's house.

She dropped her magic and ran the rest of the way to his

kitchen door. She knocked hard, waited only seconds before knocking again. She ran around to the front door, banged harder this time. She walked to the library windows—no lights were on.

Not even the pup yipped.

Of course he would've taken the pup to wherever he'd gone. He might have talked a good game about not wanting it, but judging by the way he carried it everywhere, Thrane was well and truly hooked.

Okay, he was probably at Nan's. But India didn't even have her phone so she couldn't call anyone. Well crap, looked like she was in for another walk.

Not wanting to waste any more time, she took off up the hill toward home, only slowing down when she reached the remains of the bonfire in the back paddock. Smoke rose in a lazy, swirling, translucent plume from the bed of embers to dissipate beneath the sky.

She remembered gathering around fires like this in her childhood, probably in this same place. Whole potatoes would be wrapped in foil and buried deep in the coals. Or the last of the damper would be packed onto sticks, and even the youngest kids would sit close and let the flameless fire toast the dough. And then would come her favorite part —cracking the crust of the damper. And her mother and father would be right there with butter and jam, cautioning her not to eat it while it was too hot.

She hadn't experienced it for eighteen years, and yet their little ritual was still so important to her. That's when it hit her. Her parents might not be physically with her, but their magic, their family rituals were still a part of her. Living in her memories. Her parents had given her a part of them forever.

She lingered only a moment more, let the emotion of those memories wash over, fill her up. With whispered thanks, she took off again.

India's legs were noodles by the time she reached Nan's stables. And she was thirsty. She wasn't sure when the immortality thing kicked in—hadn't Thrane said she could basically survive without food or water? It must still be evolving because she needed a drink badly.

Running through the stables, she almost barreled into Vera.

"India! My lord, when did you get—how did you get—? No, no, come here."

Vera grabbed India and hugged her tight. India smiled and returned the hug. Finally, she pushed herself out of her aunt's arms.

"Where's Thrane?" India asked. "I need to tell him and Nan what happened."

Vera's face puckered. She wiped her hands on her jeans, grabbed India's arm and said, "Come on, we need to find everyone."

Vera led the way into the house, yelling for Nate and Nan. Moments later, they were all in the living area, and Nan, Nate, and her Uncle Jack greeted her with hugs and kisses and welcome backs. Jona and Oev walked into the room, and India hugged her grandfather and traded nods with Oev.

"Where's Thrane?" India asked.

A frisson of awareness speared through her, and she recalled the image of him she'd seen when she'd been with the World Tree.

Oev sauntered into the kitchen, took two mugs from

Nan's cupboard and helped himself to two coffee pods. When everyone turned to him, he paused.

"What?" he asked. "I don't know where he is. I'm getting coffee for Father and myself."

Oev was dressed in normal clothes, as was Jona.

"Where did he go after I left?" India asked.

"Now, niece, I'm a Higherworld warrior, I give you that, but even I can't tell you where to find our illustrious Keeper. Last I heard he was going after you. Welcome back, by the way. You look much better than when we last saw you."

India looked around the room. Everyone's faces held varying degrees of comprehension and shock, but Jona's face was the most revealing.

"Do you really not know where Thrane is, Grandfather?"

"I have not heard or seen him since he took my Resilience and went after you. But I have to second my son's words. Welcome back. I am truly pleased to see you well again. Your injury ... well, it was significant."

India blinked. "Ah, why did he take your resilience?"

"Resilience is the name of my horse. Thrane took her into the Higherworld to find you. He was in a hurry, given the size of your wound and the amount of blood you had lost."

Nan gasped, rounded on Nate. "You said India was hurt, not that it was—what did you say, Jona—significant? Enough to cover Thrane in her blood?" Nan grabbed India's hand, looked her over. "Are you okay?"

"Nan, sh, I'm fine. Truly. Though I do need to tell you what's happened."

Oev took a sip of his coffee, eyed India closely. "I think we would all like to hear that."

"Then I'll have a coffee, thanks—with a little milk," India said. "And a glass of water."

"India, dear, sit down," Nan said. "Now. Show me where you were hurt."

"Okay, okay, Nan, I'll sit. But here—look, I'm really fine."

India lifted the bottom of her T-shirt, displayed her abdomen and the red scar that ran across it. Everyone crowded round to see her wound, now healed, and she had to stand to show the other side.

"See? I'm okay," India said, rolling her eyes.

"Spill, dear." Nan, her face pale, sank into the chair beside India. "Tell me everything."

India told them everything, watching Nan to see how she would take the news.

"India, are you telling me that you will be staying here, in our world?" Nan asked.

"Yes, Nan."

"So, your father's family"—Nan glanced at Oev, a little kindlier at Jona—"didn't claim you?"

"I still don't know how that would've worked," India said, "but it's irrelevant now. I'm a Keeper. Freya explained that anyone from any of the three worlds could be called to be a Keeper. The Keepers, who are integral to the continuity of the worlds, are considered a house in their own right. I'm still a member of our family and Dad's, but I have another family now too."

"And you're saying that Freya—the goddess Freya—healed you and has been looking after you?" Nan asked.

"No, the Tree healed me. As soon as I touched it. It still took me to the Heavens, because it took a few minutes to actually complete the healing." India squeezed Nan's hand. "Where's Thrane?"

"India, he went to find you. When he couldn't locate you in the Heavens, he went to an old ... friend, to see if they could scry for your location. She lives in the Underworld."

"Why did he go there? I wasn't in the Underworld."

"Oh, well, you see, he knows—knew—a lord of the Underworld who can scry," Nan said. "She's one of the strongest in all the worlds."

"So she'll be telling him that I'm here? How long ago did he leave?"

Nan looked at her wristwatch. "Over two hours ago."

"Elizabeth," Jona said, "did he go to Serephena?"

Nan nodded, and Jona turned to face India with a thoughtful look. "Granddaughter, I fear the Keeper may be the one who needs assistance."

"What do you mean?" India asked.

"Serephena is a lord of the Underworld," Jona said, "and she has complete dominion over her lands—they're a mountain range if I recall correctly. Your Keeper, some time ago, had a relationship with Serephena, and when they parted ... well, rumor has it she was unhappy with that outcome. Rumor also has it that she longs to repay that gesture with one of her own."

"So Thrane's gone to ask his ex for help, and she's what? Going to hurt him? Do something bad to him?"

"No." Oev gave a short bark of laughter. "She won't hurt him. Hurting a Keeper without an accorded reason wouldn't end well for her. But there's nothing in the accords that says she can't make it difficult for him to leave. And, she is an Underworld lord—they are a tetchy, uncouth lot."

"Uncouth? Tetchy?" India said. "I need a quick lesson in the Underworld, because it looks as if I'm going on a rescue mission."

"India," Nan said, "the Underworld is not a place of death, or despair, or *lacking*." She cut Oev a glance.

Oev snorted but continued with his coffee.

"It is actually the opposite," she went on. "It's the source of life. Remember what I said about a plant—how the roots are as important as any other part?"

India nodded. "Yeah, but what does that have to do with the Underworld?"

"Well, the World Tree secures the Underworld through its roots. When the Tree was first created, and the three worlds separated, many beings—including several old gods—decided to live in the Underworld. Over the ages, some gods moved on to different planes of existence, but their children, or children's children, still maintain dominion over their familial lands. Like my father. Now, it is my twin, your great-aunt, who is now lord in his place."

"But you said you're not immortal," India said. "What about others in the family? If we carry the genes, is immortality a possibility?"

"All of my children and their children have been mortal. Until you."

"Actually, Nan, Freya said I wasn't already immortal. It happened when I became a Keeper."

"That makes sense to me, dear. My belief is that the witchcraft gene we carry is too strong. And my sister's witchcraft is negligible. It was as if, when we twinned in our mother's womb, our powers were split at that instant. And I know that my sister would be more than happy to help you."

"Of course, she would." Oev rolled his eyes.

"Oev, India's fate has been decided—blessed by your own family god, I might add. And my sister will not interfere with a Keeper."

"So how do we call her, Nan?"

"She's my twin. With my witchcraft, we can communicate. It's a limited skill, but we can pass basic messages between the worlds. India, your witchcraft should be strong enough to help me pass a message through with more speed and accuracy, if you'll help me? We can arrange a distraction to help you find Thrane."

"Of course. But how can your sister help?"

"I have an idea," Nan said. "And this I do know—Serephena is formidable. She will not break with protocol, I agree with Jona on that, by risking permanent harm to Thrane. But I have heard stories of her—any help will be better than none. And you might want to learn one or two useful spells."

"Okay, I'm game. Which ones?"

"Let's step into the lounge, dear. We need to discuss something else."

India followed Nan into the lounge room.

"Are you really okay, India?" Nan asked, picking up India's hands.

"Physically, I really am well. Emotionally ... well, I'm better than I've been in a long time. But, Nan, do you know why Mum never told me about the protection spell, about Dad? About my magic?"

Nan sat down, pulled India onto the couch beside her. "Yes, India. I do know. And I'd planned on explaining everything after the bonfire—when I thought we'd be able to recreate the spell. After Jev was killed, Annie made me promise never to go find her, just in case the Order's trackers followed our magic to her. To you."

"That's why none of you came to the funeral?"

Nan's eyes filled, and she nodded. "It was the hardest

thing I've ever done ... stay here when all I wanted to do was say goodbye."

"Oh, Nan, I'm so sorry. It never occurred to me that you sacrificed being there."

"My dear, it wasn't nearly as hard as losing you would've been if we led the Order to you. And your mother didn't tell you anything because she was scared you'd search for us, for your father's family too. Annie's spell meant you had little magic to call on to protect yourself. She thought that casting the spell before your magic developed might stunt your magic from developing at all. We all thought the same until ... well, until after the spell ceased."

A lump formed in India's throat. Love. Fear. Hurt. Everything was so connected.

She cleared her throat. "Thank you for telling me." She squeezed Nan's hands before releasing them to gently wipe away the tears from her grandmother's cheeks. "Now, how do I help Thrane?"

Nan slowly nodded. "Do you know about Thrane's Connection?"

"His what?"

"Well, I'm sure Thrane would have told you this, given everything. It's how he travels to and from the place where he keeps his sword. Two pieces of the World Tree let him travel between them."

"So Thrane carries a branch or a twig with him all the time?" India asked.

"Technically, it could be, but no, usually the Connection is made into something—a staff, a rod, that kind of thing."

India bit her lip. Thrane always wore a medallion on a leather strap around his neck. Could that be it?

"So if Thrane has the Connection, presumably the Tree can take me to him?"

"Yes, in theory," Nan said. "But be careful—I'm sure that if Thrane had it, he would likely be back here already. It's possible that the Connection has been taken from him."

"Then I have to get to the Underworld—fast. What's this spell that'll help me?"

"It's a veiling spell, dear. With your strength, you should be able to enter Serephena's domain relatively unseen."

"Relatively?"

"Well, the spell only works when you're not moving. But if there are people around, usually they'll move on at some point, so you'll need to stay veiled until that happens. If you can't"—Nan frowned—"that's relatively."

36

India led the way to the World Tree, helping Nan through the hardier scrub and wending through the cool, quiet forest. Even with the weight of concern for Thrane pressing down on her, a small smile curved her mouth when the World Tree came into view.

She took a deep breath. "We're here."

A swell of warmth gently buffeted India, then moved past her. India sensed it stop and envelop Nan. Nan's blue eyes softened for a moment.

"Well, that was certainly a welcome," she said.

"Yep, it has a way with communication. Okay, Nan, teach away. What's this spell?"

"India, dear, this spell isn't an easy one. And you don't want to practice too much as you'll need your strength for the real thing. The spell will create a veil, like a 'shell,' around you—it can be half a circle, or a full circle, though that is much harder. The image of the veil has to make sense to whoever is viewing it. If you make a bright green veil and you're on the beach, then while *you* may not be seen, the veil certainly will and that'll be just as bad."

"Got it. No hiding behind a giant green ball on the beach. What else?"

"Once you have the image of what you want the veil to look like, you have to send your energy out and build it by drawing on the elements—air, dust, water—whatever is around you."

"That makes sense given how energy currents move," India said. "Let's give it a go."

She held her breath as the spell came together—until Nan clapped her hands sharply and shattered India's focus. The spell fell away.

"You had it, dear. Try to work on your speed, but otherwise, it was working. I only broke your concentration to save your energy. You really will need it later."

"Thanks, Nan." India smiled, but her heart steadily beat faster and faster.

"It's all right to be nervous. Nerves keep us on our toes. But remember—you are a witch. You are a Keeper. You can do this."

"Thank you, Nan. I—I love you."

"Oh, my dear, I love you too."

The words rang with a truth India couldn't deny. Somehow, in the last week, they'd established a true connection —no, they'd *re*-established their connection.

"And remember," Nan said, "we don't know how long Elaine's distraction will give you."

"Holy crap. Okay, well this is it. See you soon."

She squeezed Nan's hand then touched the Tree. Instantly, the Tree welcomed her with a wave of warm energy. An image of Thrane entered her mind. He wore a leather vest, with his medallion clearly visible on his chest.

India nodded her understanding of the message, but she still didn't know all the ways the Tree communicated, so she also said, "Yes, that's right, I'm going after Thrane. Can you take me to him?"

A quick blast of chill hit her, and she didn't need any lessons to understand that. But then another image of Thrane came to her, his medallion even more prominent.

"Ah, I get it. You can take me to his Connection?"

The warmth whipped her again, fast and sharp.

"Right, let's not linger?"

A curling tendril of earnestness touched her, and India didn't have time to say anything else before she was whisked away.

The sensation of tumbling weightlessness assailed her first, but she opened her magic up and caught her equilibrium fast. And then she was soaring through space—giant curves abounded around her, galaxies spun past, and then a moment's sensation of slowing down before her feet met firm ground, and she could breathe again.

Luckily, India kept her magic up because, suddenly, she was at the edge of a huge cavern. She quickly noted a plain rock wall behind her, and at the same time, she sent her energy out into the cavern—careful not to push too far— and then reeled it in, faster than she'd ever done before. The four elements came with her energy. Keeping the image of the rock wall present in her mind, India fit the elements to her image. A jigsaw puzzle coming together.

Finally, the spell was complete. Perspiration dotted her brow. And crap, she had no idea how long it had taken or what the veil looked like on the other side. But the few people sitting at nearby tables hadn't even looked up, so it would probably do the job. She exhaled and dropped her magic. Now that the spell was cast, she only needed to keep up a minimum level of energy to maintain it.

Veiled, she looked around the cavern.

A stunning, black-winged woman with black hair strode in through the nearest entry. She nodded at everyone she walked past, and they nodded or bowed to her in return. It *had* to be Serephena.

So, this was a Valkyrie? She was absolutely beautiful.

Thrane had been with her? Had left her?

A churning sensation hit India's belly. But she had no time to worry about how stunning Serephena was—she had to find the Connection, and the Tree had brought her to this location. It had to be close.

The Valkyrie walked to a table near India and picked up something from it that was attached to a cord. India's heart stopped.

A noise rumbled from the far end of the cavern.

The Valkyrie dropped whatever she'd held and swiveled, her amazing wings unfurled, and she shot up into the air, hovered in front of two giant arched doors, before India could blink.

"Holy crap," India said, then winced and bit her lip—her magic veil was visual only.

Luckily, no one paid any attention to her words. Everyone was focused on Serephena as she flew to a tall winged man who'd walked through the entry doors to the cavern. He was all arrogant grace, his body encased in black leather, with silver-tipped white wings furled tight and high at his back.

Could this winged man be her aunt's distraction?

India didn't waste another second. She opened her magic up again, and this time used it to trace Serephena's energy trail.

The Valkyrie's currents were obsidian diamonds—they spun fast in their orbit but were in absolute control. They trailed in a wake through the air to where Serephena, still hovering, confronted the newcomer. Remnants of Serephena's energy currents led to a doorway in the opposite direction of the action.

India could follow that trail—and hopefully find Thrane. Or she could try to find the medallion—*if* that was what had been on the strap Serephena had dropped. But the table with the strap also had people sitting at it, while Serephena's energy currents led away from everyone.

Okay, so she'd find Thrane first.

But how to get out of the cavern without revealing herself? The magic veil needed to move with her—except she had no idea how to make it do that.

At the other end of the giant space, the man in black leather unfurled his wings and slowly spiraled into the air. The lazy beat of his wings was mesmerizing—and then his eyes met hers and he winked.

Holy crap, had he seen through her veil? And why the wink? Unless ... was he Elaine's distraction?

Serephena swung over to intercept the winged man.

Okay, time to go.

India dropped her veil and backed into the doorway behind her A sleepy heaviness stole into her limbs, but she ignored the sensation. Rescue now, rest later.

The corridor she found herself in wound off to the right in one direction and to a darkened stairwell in the other. Serephena's energy trail led down the steps.

India recalled Nan's invocation for light, so she willed forth a little more energy, reached out a hand, pushed the air above it with enough force to cause friction, then whispered the spell.

The energy caught alight, and a small ball of glowing witch-light hovered above her hand. It was surprisingly bright, so she reduced her energy until the light had dimmed, only illuminating the dark of the stairwell enough for her to see the next step.

India set off downwards, following Serephena's trail.

Several landings came and went, but still the crystals led down. Many steps later, the energy crystals were tiny specks, but they finally departed the stairwell and led India into a dark, quiet tunnel. The witch-light showed rough walls, hewn from the very mountain itself.

India took a breath, settled her nerves. Okay, she could do this. It was only an endlessly long dark tunnel with—hopefully—one living warrior somewhere along it. Openings appeared, each set with thick black iron bars extending from the ground to the ceiling. Cells. They were cells. India tried to walk quietly, carefully—but nothing stirred.

Until the hairs on the back of her neck rose.

Thrane appeared in a sudden rush at the bars of the cell to her immediate right, the harsh planes of his face dangerous, as hard as the rock walls around them.

"India," he said, his voice a strangled rasp. "What, by all the gods, are you doing here?"

The golden fire at the heart of his eyes gleamed beneath her light spell, and she didn't hesitate, just came closer, wrapped her hands around the bars.

"Thrane! Holy crap, I found you. I didn't know if it

would work. I mean, I thought it would work, but I didn't know, and then I came here. Only now, how—"

"India, how did you—"

"—do we get you out of here?" India's witch-light dimmed. "Damn it." She pushed a bit more energy into the spell to keep it steady. "These bars look strong. Do you know where the key is?"

"Stop, India, stop."

The insistence in Thrane's voice made her pause. She took a breath, took in the face before her. He regarded her, too, and his eyes traveled from her hair to her toes. She let him look, waited for him to see she was well.

"India, how did you get here?" Thrane asked. "And why are you wearing that?"

"Holy crap, I have *so* much to tell you. And yeah, the clothes are part of it. But shouldn't we focus on getting you out of here first?"

"I have a feeling that getting me out of here is intrinsically tied to how you got in. So no, first I need to know *how* you came to be here."

"Huh, you're being a bit grouchy."

"Grouchy?" The blades of his eyebrows lowered. "The last time I saw you, you were covered in blood, remember? So please, tell me what, by all the gods, is going on."

"Yes, well, that was a very traumatic thing. I'll give you that.

Thrane's brows lowered farther.

"For both of us," she added. "Okay, here's the short version because I'm really not sure how long we have."

Thrane opened his mouth to speak again.

India quickly brought him up to speed, then looked at Thrane expectantly.

Thrane was silent but eventually said, "You *are* a Keeper." He stared hard at her. "You're immortal."

India shrugged. "I'm getting there."

A smile slowly spread on his face. His eyes fired up.

"What?" she asked.

But he just stared. And stared.

"Ah, so how are you getting out?" India looked around.

She willed the light-ball into the air. The cell's bars were easily eight feet high, and the cell itself looked wide enough to hold ten men of Thrane's size. A hinged gate in the very middle of the bars was secured with a bolted padlock.

Finally, Thrane shook his head, though the smile didn't leave his face.

"So no ideas then?" India asked.

"Of course I have an idea. I've been pushing against these bars for the last three hours. I can already feel a slight movement." Thrane braced his legs, and she could see his muscles bunch and push beneath his T-shirt as he pushed against the bars all of his strength. "It may take time, but I'm sure I can do it."

"Hmm."

India eyed him. The view was fine, but she had her own idea about how to get him out, and so she released the energy that was creating her ball of light.

"Hey, where's the light?" Thrane asked.

"Hush, I haven't done this before, and I need to concentrate."

She opened her senses fully. In the pitch-black, energy currents glowed as they swirled around the tunnel—Thrane's spun madly, likely from the immense sustained energy he'd exerted to shift the cell bars. Her own energy mingled with his. The other energies were those of the natural world around them—exactly what she wanted.

India focused on the iridescent air currents and tried to bring them in, but they were so fine they slipped out of her control. Crap. She calmed her mind and tried again, this time only gathered one strand of air energy and very gently cajoled, stroked, and reeled it in until she felt it inside her. She then found another and another until she had seven strands. She'd no idea how many she needed but gathering those seven had taken time and effort.

Lethargy swept in—her limbs grew heavy, and sticky cobwebs began to fill her mind.

Crap, she couldn't afford for her magic to conk out now. Shaking her head, she forced the fatigue aside, and pushed the first strand of air into the padlock. India was so finely attuned to the energy of the air, *she* was buffered by the pressure as it moved through the opening of the padlock, *she* met the cold iron barriers of resistance as the air-energy met an internal wall.

Taking a quick breath, India held that strand of energy in place, and sent the next into the padlock, until it too fit within the lock and could go no farther. Each time India reached a wall of resistance, she sent another current in, pushed in a different direction.

A dinging sound rang in the back of her mind, pulsed to the rhythm of the lethargy that wormed its way through her. She held her breath. She needed to get this done *now*.

On the sixth current, she met a dip in the resistance, and the lock snicked, disengaged.

Her breath whooshed out. Her magic went with it.

Pitch-black met her senses.

That heaviness hit her again, this time dragging her

limbs and body down. As she tried to ignite another ball of light, strong arms gathered her up.

"Tired. I'm tired," India whispered.

And then her head met a hard, warm chest and a reassuring heartbeat became her pillow.

37

Thrane gently eased down to the floor with India in his arms. They needed to find his medallion, then get the hell out of the Underworld, back to the Tree, back to being ready for Ri'Kiant. But what to do with India?

He held her tightly to him, oddly reassured by the thrum of her pulse, the warmth of her skin. Right before she'd gone limp, she'd said she was tired, but then she'd passed out.

Given what she'd been through, that was no surprise. Even immortals needed time to recuperate from injury, and as a newly minted immortal—hell, as a newly minted Keeper—her body would burn energy faster than ever before. She'd probably be hungry for months, maybe years, while her body settled into its immortality.

Thrane thought about leaving India asleep and making his way through the tunnels to find Serephena, but no. No way he was leaving India alone in the dark. And carrying her out of the cells as a deadweight, not knowing who or what might come at them, wasn't a smart plan. The only way they could escape was if India was physically mobile.

He shifted until his back was against the rough rock wall, ignored the digs of the jagged edges, stretched out his legs. Keeping one arm around India, her head to his chest and her legs draped over his thighs, he pulled her cloak tight to keep her warm.

By the gods, how amazing was this woman? She'd faced down the Order. Had nearly died. Had somehow held her own in the Heavens, and now, had not only found a way into the Underworld but had used witchcraft to open his cell.

He snorted, slightly chagrined that India had outperformed him in the whole rescuing department. Although, he would've shifted the cell bars ... eventually. But more than anything, he respected India. Her tenacity, her heart, her power.

This depth of—of feeling was totally foreign. Was something he hadn't been prepared for. Had never expected.

Certainly, he'd respected women, had been attracted to them, but he'd never had such a bond with another being. This bond, this experience with India, was like nothing he'd ever known.

Mine. Hers. Forever.

This was visceral, physical link. At least on his side.

Gods—what about India? Their last conversation before Ri'Kiant's attack had been fuelled by anger, distrust. Hurt had dulled her eyes. Desolation had made her body droop.

He never wanted to see her that way again. Even now the memory of her face in that moment, the memory of her distrust in him, of their intimacy—it roiled in his gut.

And then Evine had revealed the truth about Jev.

He needed to set the record straight. India deserved to

know. She also needed to know that his feelings weren't some light thing.

How would she react when he told her?

He rested his head against the cold, hard rock, and ignoring the discomfort, stared out into the darkness.

Earlier, he'd been chilled in the cell, but now that India slept in his lap, her vitality, her life force seeped into his body, warming him up.

And seriously turned him on.

He winced, shifting India enough so he could adjust himself. His erection wasn't going away, but at least the change in position reduced the risk of castration.

It was an hour later when Thrane sensed India's heart rate increase. She moved her head from where she lay on his chest, and for one moment, everything was silent and still, except for the beat of his pulse—of hers.

The warmth that mingled between them warded off the cool of the mountain's belly, and an urge to connect with her rose sharply.

Would she let him? Would she welcome him?

"India," he whispered. "Can I kiss you?"

Silence met his ears. His stomach dropped. She didn't want him—

But then she shifted, her body brushing his as she maneuvered to face him. Her lips pressed into his.

Her intoxicating scent poured through him, and in the dark, every other sense heightened. His blood surged, and he had to touch her, get into her—except, he couldn't.

"Gods, India. I want—need—more than this moment

with you. But we don't have time. Ri'Kiant will be back soon. There's so much I need to tell you, but first, I have to say this."

India's shaky breath echoed through the dark, then she brushed against him as she stood. He pushed to his own feet, stretched out muscles kinked from being a cushion for the last hour.

The cell lit up suddenly, India's witch-light once more in action. Thrane drank in the sight of her stunning face, gilded by the glow of her spell.

Gods, he had missed her.

He roughly cleared his throat. "Back at the Tree, what Evine said about Jev. You need to know she was partially right."

India's witch-light flickered.

"Wh—what?"

"Thirty years ago, the World Tree here in the Underworld came under siege. I was the only Keeper left, and my World Tree had been hidden for a long time. I asked a lifelong friend from the Heavens, a warrior renowned in his own right, to watch over it while I went to the Underworld." The familiar heavy chill sank heavy in his gut. He swallowed and blew out a hard breath. "By the gods, this is hard to say, India."

"Thrane, just say it."

"Gods, we don't have time for this. But you deserve to know. That man was your father. I stayed in the Underworld until the threat was removed. While I was here, Jev met your mother, and they had you. And then he was killed." Thrane glanced down at his hands. "So Evine is right. If I hadn't asked Jev to help—"

"Stop, Thrane," India growled. "You are not to blame for

what the Order did. And my father would never have blamed you for what they did. That's on them, not you. And I don't doubt my father would have been proud to fight, proud of any action he could've taken to help preserve the Tree. In any of the worlds. And the same goes for the Keepers who stayed behind so you could get our World Tree to safety. You're not responsible for any of it. You are the reason I—we—are all here, today."

Thrane's blood rushed through his veins. "You don't hold me responsible?"

"Thrane, I can definitely say that I don't blame you for my father's death. And those Keepers, they wouldn't blame you for theirs, either. Neither should you."

The remnants of guilt, a crushing weight he'd worn for years, began to weaken beneath India's fierce gaze.

"India, you leave me without words."

"Well, what about ideas? Do you have any about how we get out of here? And what do we do about Ri'Kiant?"

"Ri'Kiant," Thrane snarled. The urge to track the demon down, skewer him and burn his ashes, slammed through Thrane. He clenched his fists to stop his hands from shaking. Now was the time for precision. Control. "The demon is the reason we need to leave. At least the black moon has passed, and you're here with me."

"Why the black moon?" India asked. "Won't an ordinary new moon do? Nan explained that when the sun, moon and earth are aligned it enhances all magic."

"An ordinary new moon gives your magic additional strength, yes. But destroying the Tree takes extraordinary magic—like yours—as well as the intensification of enhanced power that only a second alignment brings. Thank the gods they don't come around often."

India turned to go, but Thrane grabbed her wrist. "Wait —there's one more thing. And the gods know we don't have long, but I have to tell you. And I need to get it right." He hauled in a deep breath. "You—being with you wasn't just for the Tree."

India stilled, and the light in her eyes burned brighter than ever. Finally, she reached out and cupped his cheek. "Thrane, I—I—"

Thrane pressed a fast kiss to her palm. "You don't need to say anything more. I just need you to know the truth. Now, let's get the hell out of here."

India's eyes searched, and his heart filled at the heat that shimmered in her gaze. Maybe he hadn't blown it after all.

"Okay, so how do we get out?" she asked. "Because, yeah, I want to have that talk."

"We need my Connection. That's how we're getting out of here."

"That's your necklace-thing, right?"

He cut her a glance. "It's not a necklace."

"Right. The carved-wood medallion that hangs on a leather strap around your neck."

"That's better."

"Well, the not-necklace must be in the cavern," India said. "That's where the Tree took me, and I saw Serephena drop something on one of the tables right before this winged and very hot guy flew in. Literally flew in—as in wings and all—and basically mesmerized everyone."

Thrane stopped midstride. He took India's hand that directed the witch-light and raised it closer to her face.

"Did anyone say who he was?"

"Ah, not sure. But he appeared to see through my veil."

India's eyes shone bright with green fire, her magic

enhancing their emerald glow. Twin urges—to make love to her and protect her—assailed him. That he could do neither right now had him grinding his teeth. He focused on her words.

"India, not many beings can see through a veil when it's done properly—any chance you didn't cast it correctly?"

He swallowed a smile when an indignant look flashed over her face and her little ball of light flashed red.

"I didn't mean you can't do it, only that if you're new to the spell, maybe you missed something?"

Her ball of light resumed its normal warm glow.

"I don't think so. It fooled everyone else." She raised an eyebrow. "Even your ex."

"You know about Serephena?" Thrane asked, studying the expression on India's face.

"Mm."

"Apparently, I misjudged the level of her unhappiness with me." Thrane gestured ahead of them. "Are you able to lead? We should use your light while we can to help us move quickly."

"Of course. She really is stunning, though."

"What? Who?"

"Serephena."

"India, she was a moment in time. You are ..." He tried to find the words, but couldn't even begin to shape how much India meant to him. "You are every moment of my day and night, India Jones."

Her eyes glowed.

"Now, we need to move as quietly as possible," Thrane said. "If we come across anyone, I want to use the darkness to hide us since I don't have my sword."

"Hey—isn't your sword here somewhere?"

"Who told you that? Liz? Did she say anything else?"

"Not about your sword," India said.

"You said before that Elaine was arranging a distraction?"

"Yep."

"And you think the winged man was her distraction?"

"It must've been, because it worked perfectly. Everyone was mesmerized—even me for a moment."

"Well, that would explain why he could see through your veil."

"Huh?"

"Were his wings white?"

"Yes, with silver tips, and he had long black hair."

"That sounds like Moyarn. He's a distant cousin of yours."

India shook her head. "My family keeps getting crazier."

"Well, you have quite a family tree. Makes sense that you're so special."

India stared down at him from the step a couple above his. A new look entered her eyes. "You think I'm special?"

"India, I've been to the farthest reaches in all the worlds, and you are the most special creature—mortal, supernatural, or otherwise—that I have ever known." He reached up and took her hand. The light-ball stayed steady as he ran his thumb over her palm. "I need to tell you more, but I want the right time and place to explain everything properly."

India's eyes widened, sparking with emerald fire. Even her little light-ball turned green.

"Come on, Jones. Your distraction might not last as long as we need, and we're almost at the level we need to be. Can you dim your light?"

The witch-light dimmed.

"Thanks. Right, time for me to take lead. Keep just enough light so you don't trip."

"What about you?"

"I'm not tripping on these steps, I promise you."

Thrane placed his right hand on the rough stone wall to guide his steps, then took off.

When he reached the level that led to the main cavern, he paused and India bumped into his back. He turned and whispered for her to bank her light altogether. The landing they were on was dimly lit from the light shining in from the cavern, and once she did, he allowed his eyes to adjust.

"I'll take a quick look in the cavern. If the way is clear to the table, I'll run through and grab my medallion."

"What if it's not?"

"We'll go to plan B."

"Do we have a plan B?"

"Not yet."

He stepped surely and quietly to the cavern's opening and eased through it. The cavern held fewer people than when he'd been here earlier, and most of them sat at the rows of long communal tables.

Serephena, clearly identifiable with her black wings, sat with her back to him. Though she seemed unaware of Thrane's presence, others would see if he made a dash for the table India had mentioned. And he had to hope India had indeed seen the medallion—and that it was still there. He was going to need her help.

He slowly melted back into the dark of the tunnel.

The medallion was key to getting India home safely. However, once in the cavern, it would take a mere moment for everyone to see him, and then it would come down to who was faster—he and his supernatural speed, or

Serephena and her wings. But India had a spell that might negate all of that.

"Time for plan B," he murmured into India's ear. "Can you recast your veil to hide the two of us?"

There was silence for a moment before India whispered, "I think so."

"Okay, so cast your veil inside the cavern. You'll need to hold it long enough for me to find the medallion. I can take Serephena on if needed—after all, she can't actually harm me. That's not allowed."

India sniffed. "Then what was with keeping you prisoner?"

"That was more like an impediment, not actually hurting me."

"So, you can take her on if you need to, but you don't want to?"

"Exactly." He had to grin when India rolled her eyes. "Right, I'm off. Stay back from the doorway. I'll be back in a minute."

"Can you cast a veil of the wall to the right of the doorway?" he whispered. "It extends all the way to the computer desks, so we may be able to make our way around."

India frowned.

"What's wrong?"

"The veil takes energy—a lot of it. I don't know if I can hold it long enough, or if I can make it move. That's, like, PhD level, and I'm at beginner. But I'll try."

"That's good enough for me." Thrane held out a hand. "If you need more energy, can you take it from me?"

"I have no idea." She took his hand. "But I can try if I need to."

"Then let's go."

38

India took a deep breath. She'd tested her magic faster than she'd ever thought would happen. But she'd gotten into the Underworld and had saved Thrane from that cell— no way were nerves getting in the way now.

She poked her head around the cavern doorway, quickly took in the expanse of rock wall she needed to cover, then ducked back into the tunnel.

"Holy crap, Thrane." She worked hard to keep her voice pitched low. "You know the rock changes, right? Because it's *rock*. It's not like it's one continuous color or texture. I learned this spell what—a few hours ago? Now you want me to cover two people, make it move, *and* change color?"

Thrane looked at her steadily.

"Fine, I guess I can try. But if this all goes wrong, don't blame me."

That got a small smile from him, but his gaze stayed firm.

India sent her energy out into the world, reeled it back in, and brought with it the elements from around them to create her veil image. Only this time, she cast the veil inside the cavern. Finally, it *felt* done, and she looked back at Thrane, took heart in his steady look.

Taking his hand, she led him into the cavern but skidded to a halt, conscious of needing to keep them both contained behind the veil. One person briefly glanced their way but after a moment turned back.

India held her breath and focused on staying still.

With her back pressed to the rock wall, facing the cavern full of people, she was close to terrified. Her human mind screamed, *they see you, you're about to be caught!* But her witchcraft sensed the veil, even if her eyes couldn't see it, and so she shoved the doubt out of her mind.

She squeezed Thrane's hand and gave him a look that said, *holy crap, look what I did!*

Movement at the rows of tables caught India's attention. Serephena's black wings were spreading out, and then the Valkyrie lifted into the air. A moment later, white wings unfurled too, and the black-haired winged man followed Serephena into the air.

Thrane bent close to India's cheek and whispered, "That's Moyarn."

India nodded. Wow, was she actually related to *him*?

Serephena spoke, though her words were too low for India to make out, and Moyarn replied. His face was languid, but India caught a familiar expression, and sure enough, his eyes cut right to her, then to Thrane.

His eye movement must have alerted Serephena because she spun around. Moyarn shot out a hand to grab one of Serephena's. He yanked hard, and the Valkyrie, clearly not expecting that move, tumbled toward him.

Moyarn covered Serephena's mouth with his, and while she let out a screech, she didn't push him away.

Everyone else scattered away from the tables.

India seized the opportunity and pulled Thrane along with her, ran to the wall nearest the table, eyeing the people around them for any sign of reaction. *Please, please let the veil hold.*

She looked back at the table, gasped. Crap, now their momentum was too strong, they were going to run into—

Thrane yanked her back at the last second, banded an arm around her waist and pulled her into him to absorb her momentum.

She hastily checked her spell. The magic and the veil were still there, but whether it matched the rock wall at her back was another story.

She searched the cavern again for reactions that they'd been seen. Wow, there was no need to worry about the veil —the massive space was empty but for the two winged-creatures making out hot and heavy in mid-air.

It was a scarily beautiful sight.

She glanced at Thrane to see what he thought of the scenery. She needn't have bothered—he was focused on the tables. Then *he* broke the veil, bolting for the farthest table, their hands still clasped. Before India knew it, he'd grabbed his medallion, and she careened through space, arrived at a pitch-black location.

Not even a breath later she was back in the cavern. Only now Thrane held his sword.

She blinked, caught her equilibrium.

"Thrane, that was so fast." She cut him a glance. "But why are we here, not back at home?"

He looked down at her, bared his teeth. "I need to have a word with Lord Ursiel. It'll be fast."

Serephena had broken away from Moyarn and was watching Thrane.

Crap! India realized her and Thrane's voices must've broken up the mid-air action. Serephena's electric-blue eyes seemed afire—but whether the sparkle was from making out with Moyarn or from being pissed off at Thrane's escape, India had no clue.

She wasn't taking any chances though and opened her magic up fully. As Serephena swooped toward them, India murmured, raising a wind that created an invisible wall.

The Valkyrie let out a short shriek when she hit the barrier, and as she looked from Thrane to the tables and then finally to India, comprehension bloomed on her face. She furled her wings and elegantly landed on the floor.

Looking over her shoulder at Moyarn, who was still aloft, she said, "Was this the reason?"

Moyarn shrugged, but India read the energy pouring off him as both arousal and delight. His face was a study of casual amusement, though, as he gracefully landed and lifted a brow.

"Why any reason for a kiss?" he asked.

"Serephena," Thrane said, "you have abused your role as host."

"Host?" India said, shooting Thrane a look. "You're kidding, right? She just held you captive, like a prisoner in her dungeon."

"Thrane was in no danger here," Serephena said. "Certainly, he appears to have come to no harm."

"Ah, but I came here looking for a fellow Keeper," he replied, lowering his chin. "You kept me from that task."

"You did not say she was a Keeper." Serephena slowly looked India up and down. "And I told you, it would take time to fulfill your request—I gave you no undertaking as to how long that time would be. Although apparently it was a task unneeded, given your current company."

"So, what next, then?" Thrane asked. "Will you continue to offer sanctuary to the Keepers through the safety of your cell?"

Hell no. India inhaled sharply, opened her mouth to shout her opinion when Thrane squeezed her hand. Somehow, she managed to bite her tongue, even though she wanted to yell at him for even thinking about working with the conniving—stunningly beautiful—Valkyrie again.

Serephena rolled her eyes. "Your precious sword may continue to reside with impunity under my roof."

"You can drop the wind, India," Thrane said.

"Are you sure? She looks feisty."

"Drop your wind witch-Keeper." Serephena laughed. "I will not harm you or your lover."

India gradually lowered the wind, though she kept her magic up. Moyarn swept over, setting down with slightly more grace, if that was even possible, than Serephena. He was as tall as Thrane—maybe taller.

He winked at India.

"Greetings, witch-Keeper. My lord says hello. And to let you know, you are welcome to come visit any time."

"Thank you," India said. "And it's very nice to meet you."

A tingle—small but diamond hard—hit her straight in the back of the neck. She brushed aside her hair. The thick mass fell forward over one shoulder, and she touched her hand to the sensitive skin at her nape. Nothing met her searching fingers, yet the tingle grew in both size and strength. She thought Moyarn spoke, but all her concentration was tied up in the oddest sensation she'd ever—

"India," Thrane said.

He too rubbed a hand against his chest. Right where his medallion now lay.

Their eyes met.

"Something's coming," she said.

Thrane shook his head. "Not something, some*one*."

"What are you two talking about?" Serephena asked.

"The Tree, here in the Underworld, has sent us a warning. And India felt it, even without a Connection." He glanced back at India. "How did you know?"

"I have no idea, maybe my witchcraft?"

"Well, in that case, you'll be the first Keeper to talk to the Tree without a Connection. That is brilliant," Thrane said.

Serephena clapped. "Keepers? What, *who*, is coming?"

Thrane ran a hand down India's shoulder.

"My best guess is Ri'Kiant. *How* he got here, I have no idea. The Tree would never bring him here. He must have access to a god, and that god must have a Connection."

Serephena's wings unfurled with a snap. "What? No one would dare breach my domain."

A knock tapped at India's mind and she almost gasped. "Thrane, I think the Tree needs to tell us something— communicate—or whatever it does."

She used her witchcraft to focus on the knock, and without any effort, the World Tree gently, yet with the weight of an entire universe, touched her mind. She sent a mental thanks, then focused on Thrane.

"It is Ri'Kiant. The Tree showed him to me."

"India and I are Keepers," Thrane said to Serephena.

"We must take this fight. Will you cede your dominion to me in this?"

The Valkyrie's surprisingly delicate features struggled to contain both rage and insult before they hardened.

"Yes, Keepers. The safety of the World Tree comes above all else. But only in this matter, and only should my own people not be in direct harm. How long do we have and what do you need?"

A hissing howl echoed through the cavern, and the giant space suddenly went dark.

As the Valkyrie demanded to know why the sun-vents had gone dark, India didn't waste any time before whispering her ball of witch-light into the air. Moyarn and Serephena, stunned, turned to look at her.

"Good work, India," Thrane said. "Serephena, looks like there's no time. Keep your people below but have your best fighters at the ready in the first entry. Moyarn, hold at the inner door. I—we—need you to watch. If something goes wrong, you need to spread the word. The World Tree cannot fall."

Moyarn placed a hand on his heart and nodded his head once. He cut India a last glance, then he and Serephena swept away, each with a forceful thrust of their wings.

India swallowed hard. "You seriously want me with you? To fight with you?"

"Yes." Thrane swiftly turned to her. "You are a Keeper, India. If *you* think you're up to it—and I believe you are— then we're stronger together than alone. This is our place, our reason for being."

"So ... you do trust me?"

Thrane's jaw clenched.

"India, I know it might be hard to believe after what happened at the Tree. But, yes, I trust you."

Warmth flew through her, thawed the last chill in her being at those simple words. He trusted her.

She took up the gauntlet. "I need a weapon," she said.

"You already have your weapon. Witchcraft. But you need to stay behind me. I'll place the demon at my front and keep him there. He's still coming for you. We need to use that." His eyes narrowed, and he searched her face.

"Ah, Thrane, why are you looking at me like that?"

"India, over a century ago I promised myself that never again would I put my people in harm's way. But I know—without doubt—you are up to this. Your magic can stop Ri'Kiant. So not only am I asking you to join this fight, I'm relying on you."

India swallowed. "You're that sure?"

"India, *you* can do this. *I* can do this. Together, we can stop him. No—don't talk, hear me out. We have an opportunity here. We let Ri'Kiant think he's got you. Remember, he doesn't know your abilities. We let him believe he's gotten through me, and when he comes for you, unleash everything you've got at him. Every single fucking ounce of wind to keep him blocked. As soon as his focus goes to you, I will be right there at his back. And I can end it."

The pain of her last encounter with Ri'Kiant rose in a flashback of white-hot fire. She pressed a hand to her side. India inhaled sharply.

"You're allowed to be scared, India."

"Are you mad? Of course, I'm scared. The last time I saw Ri'Kiant, I got skewered, remember?"

Thrane winced. "I will remember that for the rest of my existence, India. And I swore, after you were hurt, that I would end this. And this is where that happens." He placed one large hand over hers. "You know I trust you. Trust me?"

India searched his eyes. They held reassurance and a resoluteness that called to her own energy. He meant it. He was going to end this. And he believed she was capable of helping him.

Could she really do this? Could a mostly un-tried witch take on a demon in an Underworld cavern?

But India had already made her choice. She'd accepted the call. Everything she'd done from the moment she'd left Brisbane led to this moment. And today was apparently the day to help the Tree.

"I'm in," India said. "I won't lie—I'm about as scared as I've ever been. But as long as you're here, I'm in."

She took a breath. Tried to still her shaking hands. Thrane nodded.

"Being scared is sensible. I am too. But I'm even more certain that you can do this. Use your wind as a barrier. If Serephena, in her own dominion, couldn't get through, then no one else will."

"That's great for you to say. You've got a great big bloody sword."

"Your magic is more powerful than my sword," Thrane said. "Mark my words, I wouldn't do this if I thought you weren't up to it." He searched her face. "And I can't lose you again." He leaned down, kissed her hard and fast. "I *won't* lose you. We can do this. Now, can you split your light? Keep a dim light here, but in front of us so we're in shadow, and then have a bright light at the cavern doorway?"

India nodded. "And, Thrane, I'm immortal, remember?"

"Don't do anything foolish, India. You're still a babe in the immortal world—a serious wound could still kill you."

India grabbed his arm and pulled him down for another quick kiss. "Well, I'm not losing you either."

Finally, he smiled, then placed her at his back as she split her witch-light in two. As the brighter ball of light arrived at the entry, the giant doors smashed open. Their heavy weight bashed against the walls in a roaring echo.

"Thrane," India said, jumping.

"Hold steady, Jones. We've got this."

39

R i'Kiant appeared in the giant doorway, holding a long, thin sword in one hand. He shielded his eyes from the witch-light.

India blew out a steadying breath; they'd started well if Ri'Kiant couldn't see them.

But then the demon inhaled deeply and turned unerringly in India's direction. "The wind carries your magic stench, daughter of Jev," he said. "Know this, tonight I end your life. It is only fitting that *I* kill the daughter since I dispatched the father so long ago."

India inhaled sharply. *Wh—what did he say?*

"And the witch-mother, too, though much more recently," Ri'Kiant continued.

Ice flooded India's core, almost stopping her heart. She stumbled, and her witch-light sputtered, beams of light careening wildly around the cavern.

Was the demon telling the truth? Had he killed her gentle, beautiful mother?

She looked to Thrane.

"India. Control your magic," he said, then bared his teeth at Ri'Kiant. "The black moon has passed, demon, and your chance to destroy the Tree with it. Leave now while you still can."

"When my victory is nigh?" No longer shielding his eyes, Ri'Kiant withdrew a long, curved knife from his belt. "Oh no, I am going to kill the witch right here, and use her magic to take out every last member of her clan, from child to old. With all their magic, I shall *then* have the power to destroy the Tree, black moon or not. And not even you, Keeper, will stop me this time."

India tried to control her light-spell, but all she could see was her mum's face from that night ... her eyes closed as if asleep, her soft, rounded cheeks, the clear, unblemished skin of her forehead. Her gentle, gifted mother who had only wanted to protect her daughter.

"It was a stroke—and there was no Order mark!" India cried out, tears stinging her eyes.

"Her death looked natural, just as we planned, and I wasn't there to steal *her* magic. I was there to find you. Leaving our mark would only have tipped our hand. Once your mother's shrouding-spell for her own magic weakened enough for our trackers to find her, it was an easy kill. And the perfect way to bring you home, to me, exactly as we planned. And now I end this."

Ri'Kiant laughed, then sped at them.

"India." Thrane's voice shook, and he shielded his face as the witch-light lurched toward him. "India, your light! Listen to me, the demon's wrong, *we* are going to end this. And get justice for your dad, and your mum. Now, your light!"

Hauling in a shuddering breath, her resolve hardened, and her tears dried. *Justice*. Her parents deserved that.

India stabilized her witch-light right as Ri'Kiant reached Thrane in a flurry of dual strikes and thrusts from sword and knife. Thrane countered the blows with lightning flicks of his weapon.

Jagged screeches of metal on metal rang through the cavern.

Sharper, harder, India's pulse hammered with every crashing, shrieking strike. But she forced herself to look away and focus on her magic—she couldn't let fear for Thrane interfere. He trusted her. She had to trust him.

With her heart pounding, she started to call the wind but then paused—could she create a veil instead? It was the one thing she could do well. If she built it to her right and replicated the look of the cavern, she could use it for cover. Then, when she made the wind barrier, Ri'Kiant wouldn't even see her, let alone get to her. But then, he'd said he could scent her magic.

Okay, so she'd create two veils—one of the cavern, one of herself.

India dropped the wind and built a veil of the cavern. Thrane was still holding Ri'Kiant off, but the demon was striking so hard and fast. What if Thrane couldn't win the fight? Or what if her magic couldn't sustain so many spells?

Her stomach clenched, but she swallowed hard, shoved the doubt away. Focused on building her next veil behind the first. It was harder still because she had to recall her own image.

And then Thrane failed to deflect a harsh blow from Ri'Kiant, and staggered beneath the strike.

Ri'Kiant whipped in with his knife, struck in a sickening

arc across Thrane's side. Thrane grunted and blood welled across the wound. When he stumbled to his knees, India almost cried out. But she held her nerve. The plan. Stick to the plan.

The demon kicked Thrane in the back, sent him sprawling across the floor, then pivoted. Ran at full speed toward India.

She screamed and darted behind her cavern-veil. At the same time, she pushed the veil of herself to the left.

Please, please let this work.

Ri'Kiant rushed at her. Fire burned in his eyes, and the circle etched into the flesh on his forehead blazed a reddish gold. He yelled strange words, a tangle of sounds and syllables, and raised his sword, ran the blade straight through her veil.

"India!" Thrane wildly looked over her self-veil.

Ri'Kiant caught his balance and spun on his feet, looked incredulously at his sword.

"Oh crap."

Her veils worked from only one direction, and Ri'Kiant was now on the wrong side. He narrowed his eyes, bared his razor-sharp teeth.

"Fool me, witch? You are nothing," he snarled. "You will *be* nothing more than the meat I skewer to give my god her world."

Ri'Kiant raised his sword again, held the knife down low and rushed at her once more. She scrambled backward.

Thrane, with blood staining his shirt and his wild gaze locked on her veil, raced toward her. But he was so very far away.

Ri'Kiant cried out again, his yellow eyes flashed wide with triumph.

India's heart stopped. Her mind blanked. Every muscle froze for one crystal clear instant ... and then she screamed from depth of her soul. She tore open that part of her witchcraft she'd never before fully recognized—the tang of her magic bloomed more fragrant than ever before, and her energy currents poured out of her, held aloft on the echo of her cry reverberating around the cavern. And suddenly the world around her lit up in blaze of glowing energy—a combination of every energy current that existed.

And they were hers to command.

India's veils dropped. Her witch-light extinguished.

In the pitch-black, magic guided her unerringly as time slowed and every single energy flared to life in iridescent glory. She could even see the energy that made Ri-Kiant— the electric current that pushed his blood through his veins, the pulse of each synapse firing as thought created action, the energy discharging in the muscles of his arm as he raised his sword.

The crystal currents that were Thrane's energy raced ahead of his body, as he hoarsely cried her name again, as he desperately threw himself toward her.

India would've told Thrane not to worry, but all her focus was in her realization that she could see the energy of life. And if she could see it, she could influence it.

And she knew then why she was such—no, had *been* such—a danger to the World Tree. She could control the energy of the universe.

It was beautiful. Terrible. Terrifying.

She called up more of her witchcraft, ready for the final fight, only her energy was slow to respond. Icy fingers ran down the back of her neck.

She pushed again, forced more will into her magic. It sputtered in shallow bursts.

Her blood congealed. Her witchcraft was near exhausted —she needed to act now. She called on every energy current she could muster, forced them out to meet those of the demon. But they moved as if dragging through thick mud instead of gliding weightlessly as they normally did.

India screamed again—her physical energy transmuted into one last spurt of magic in time to see the glow of those eerie yellow eyes as they rushed at her. Steps away.

"Thrane—"

Something touched her hand—warm. Vital. She knew that touch.

Can you take energy from me? His words from earlier floated back to her.

She knew what to do. India stopped forcing her energy forward, instead let it flow backward. A trickle—all that she had left—met Thrane's raging energy currents.

Their force buffered hers. But after the initial impact, their energies met on such a symbiotic level that they flowed together seamlessly. His strength was her strength.

Energy currents abounded before her again, and the demon raging toward her was once more a being of energy. Iridescent sparks flickered as he lunged toward her, as he thrust his lethal sword at her.

India threw up her free hand as tiny drops of spit arced from Ri'Kiant's puffed lips and his alien language filled the air.

Burning white-hot heat stabbed through her hand. And then, somehow, Thrane's sword was there. He pushed the demon's blade back, his massive body sheltering hers as his heavy blade met the next thrust from Ri'Kiant.

Thrane grunted, and India desperately called up every ounce of her witchcraft once more. This time she used Thrane's energies, drew them from him through the touch of their skin.

And a new strength opened up to her. She had the ability, but Thrane had the might. The raw, untamed force of his nature enhanced her potential, allowed her to take her magic further. India pushed their combined currents straight at the demon. At the last second, she gripped Thrane's hand, jerked him back.

"Don't touch him," India cried out.

Thrane disengaged from the fight right as her energy met Ri'Kiant's.

India hauled in a deep breath, shouted with everything she had, "Cease!"

Ri'Kiant dropped to the ground, his thin sword clattering on the stone floor. His knife skittered away, and light filled the cavern again.

Holy crap—what had she done? The adrenaline that had flooded her suddenly died off, and a chill racked her body.

She stared at Ri'Kiant, now a tangle of limbs on the floor. Her magic detected no heartbeat. Energy was still there, although it was different now—no longer life, but a reflection of life. It lingered among the remains, then, in a silent rush, took off in a single stream.

"India, are you all right? India, answer me." Thrane shook her shoulders.

Startled, she looked up. Thrane's chocolate eyes narrowed on hers.

"Thrane. Yes, yes, I'm okay." She put her hands on his forearms. "You can stop shaking me now."

"I thought you'd been struck." He hauled her into his chest. "What, by all the gods, happened?"

His heat surrounded her, warming up that icy spot inside.

"Oh, the veil," India said. "I didn't think about you seeing it, too."

"Gods, India. You scared the life out of me."

"Crap, sorry, Thrane. I had the idea that I could make the demon think I was here, when really, I was there. And it worked—I made two real veils."

"Don't *ever* scare me like that again. But what did you do after that? How did you stop Ri'Kiant?"

"Truthfully, I'm still working that out." India took a shaky breath. "Thrane, I spoke to the elements that made him, to the energy that was his life, and told it to stop. He can't—won't—regenerate."

Thrane knelt and, touching Ri'Kiant's neck, felt for a pulse. "How? Are you certain?"

"Ah, yes. His life force left. After I killed—" India swallowed hard. "After I *stopped* his energy. Thrane, this is scary, but I'm pretty certain that if I wanted to I could move each and every element."

India looked down at the mass that had been Ri'Kiant. An oily slickness worked through her, and she dipped her head, breathed through the sudden urge to be sick. "I've never killed anything before."

Thrane regarded her squarely, then picked up her hand —the one that had been lanced—and ran a thumb ever so gently over the tender skin.

She hissed.

"Sorry." Thrane removed his thumb, but held on to her hand, kept his gaze on her wound. "When I thought

Ri'Kiant had struck you, that he might have done enough to kill you ..." His nostrils flared as he heaved deep breaths in and out, and his eyes blazed chocolate fire. "It was awful. I fucking hate that he even did this to you. I'd kill him here and now if I could. But, India, I've spent hundreds of years living with the knowledge that as protectors of the World Tree, there are times when we have to take a life. My choice to be a Keeper means I've chosen to be a killer when I need to be. You're right to feel sick, and that's not a bad thing— because it means you won't take a life without it being imperative. But just now, you did what had to be done. You saved the World Tree, and with it, the Mortalworld and everyone who calls it home."

India searched Thrane's gaze, and his belief shone back at her. Then the smallest smile touched the corner of his lips when he held up her hand.

"Look," he said.

The split skin of her palm, edges drizzled with blood, began to knit. It started with one filament of tissue, and then another and another, until the wound healed in a seamless line.

Part of her was astonished to see her skin knit, but it wasn't enough to keep her mind from what her magic had done. What *she* had done.

"How do *you* feel?" India asked. "I have no idea how much of your energy I used."

"I'm fine—maybe a little more tired than normal after a fight. India, how you stopped Ri'Kiant, I had no idea your magic could do that."

"I had no idea, either. But I do know I couldn't have done it without you. I was ready to tap out, Thrane. And then you, through the touch of your hand ..." She looked down where he still held hers. "This right here, the vitality of your skin. It let me in, and I used your energy to bolster mine. That's what gave me the strength to stop the demon."

"India. You are—"

"Terrifying?"

"Nay, never that. Not to me. But you are without doubt, a power unlike any other. And very, very special."

India went to speak, but Thrane stumbled. Fresh blood seeped through his shirt at his side.

"Thrane, should we get you some help?" she asked.

"He got me again before you shut him down."

"Will you be okay?"

"Yeah. Hurts like a son of a bitch, but it will knit soon." He raised his blood-soaked shirt. "See? Already closing."

"That's kind of like mine. At least we'll have matching scars."

"Sorry to tell you this, but I won't scar, and your hand won't either. Not sure about your abdomen, though. Any injury we sustain as immortals, providing we recover, of course, is regenerated to the time when we became immortal."

"Great." India peeked at her own torso, and sure enough, she still had the raised scar.

Thrane let out a laugh, hugged her close. "You are *absolutely* certain Ri'Kiant won't regenerate?"

From her position squished into Thrane's side, India looked at the remains at their feet. There were no energy currents at all, and the weight of the knowledge that it had been her doing bore down on her hard. Killing another being was such an alien concept, part of her was horrified that she'd even been able to do it, let alone with such ease.

But then she thought about the other possible outcome and looked within herself.

The taking of a life—or stopping one, to be accurate—was not something she would ever take lightly. But the truth was that she'd do it again if she had to. She would do whatever was necessary to protect Thrane, the Tree, her family.

She took a deep breath, finally sure of herself. "Absolutely."

"Then how about we head home?"

"That sounds perfect."

Thrane reached up and, with their hands clasped, touched his medallion.

40

As firm ground met India's feet once more, the familiar outline of the World Tree appeared against an indigo sky. The vibrant color reminded her of the moment she'd first awoken in the Higherworld, though the rest of her senses affirmed she was indeed home.

The pungent tang of loam tickled her nose, and she smiled at the hint of rain carried on a fresh breeze. Her heart sang at the echo of bird cries, the rustle of leaves, at the ghostly greens and misty blues of the forest in the deepening shadows.

There was a sense of welcome as well. The Tree knew that its Keeper—Keepers—had arrived home.

"You chose a very special place to bring your Tree," India said.

"Yeah," Thrane said looking around the clearing. "When I first came here, these hills looked as they do now. This may sound odd, but I was called to this very spot."

"That doesn't sound odd at all." India squeezed his hand. "On my first day back on the farm, I found this grassy place past the cottages, where the land spreads out like one of Nan's patchwork quilts in greens and browns and lilacs. It called to me then, and so did the Tree. So no, it's not odd that the land called you here, to the most perfect place you could find. You had a massive task to do, Thrane. But you did—are—doing it."

"What do you mean?"

"Freya told me that you've been alone for such a long time. You had to make a heartbreaking decision to leave the other Keepers in battle and find a safe place." India touched the Tree, too. "A lot of people, maybe most, wouldn't have been able to do it. You saved our world, Thrane. You might be maddening, and your ability to answer a question with a question drives me batshit. But you're an amazing man. The Tree, and our worlds, are lucky to have you. That's what I mean."

Thrane squeezed her hand in return. He closed his eyes, and when they reopened their golden inner fire blazed bright.

"India, *you* are the amazing one. Thank you for saying that."

"Do you know, when I came back to Victoria—came home—I knew I was looking for something. I thought it was to learn about my magic, but there was something else. I just didn't know it at the time. I do now."

"And?"

"Connection. It's all about connection. At first, I found it with my family—Nan, Nate, you know? But then there was Simone, and my aunts and uncles and cousins. I've even found a tie to my parents through my memories. The Tree." India spread her fingers over its cool, smooth bark. "Then there's you. This—you and I—is the deepest connection by far. It's a rope that tugs on me, pulls me to you every time you're near."

"India, I've never looked for or wanted a tie to anything or anyone other than the Tree. And I think that was in part because I wanted the Tree to be my only dependent—the only thing I could ever lose again. Having a bond, an attachment, meant more to risk. More to lose. Do you remember when we picked the pup up from the vet?"

India nodded, a low hum burning through her. Her heart began to thud.

"Well, you asked why I didn't keep him. The truth is, keeping a pet grew too hard—the attachment, then the hurt and the loss each time they leave. And that's with a pet. This —gods, this is hard to admit—but I've been avoiding loss for such a long time that it's been my reason—no, I'm going to be honest—my excuse for not letting anyone close. But then you came along. And, like a god's demand, suddenly this feeling—this connection, like you say—was here. It existed, and no matter how hard I tried to hold my feelings back, I couldn't. And I don't want to hold back anymore. I *want* to be with you."

For the first time since her mother's death, India's entire being relaxed. Tears pricked, she blinked, and Thrane was right there. He cupped her cheeks, his chocolate eyes searching hers.

"Was that too much?" he asked.

"No." She brought her own hands up to hold his. "That was definitely not too much. Of all the tears I've cried since Mum passed, these are the happiest."

Thrane gently wiped the tracks from her cheeks, lighting another fire deep within her. She leaned up, pressed her lips to his.

"If only we had a condom," India said, "this would be the perfect place to have our moment."

"Here?" he asked and nipped her lip.

India laughed, suddenly happier than she could remember.

"Why not?" She darted a look at his injured side. "Unless you need to wait—let that heal fully."

"What, this scratch?" He let out a chuckle that turned into a growl. "Come here."

Thrane pulled her hard, flush against him. Groin to groin. She moaned, his answering groan low and long as their bodies fit together. India relished the press of his hard chest.

"So are you saying that by some miracle you have a condom?" she asked. "Because I don't."

Thrane fished around in his back pocket, took out a slim wallet.

"I'm a Keeper. We're always prepared," he said, face deadpan, but his eyes gleamed.

"Thank the gods for that."

She couldn't contain her smile and rose up on her tiptoes, stared into melted-chocolate with a golden-fire heart.

Thrane's heat curled around her, drew her closer, closer until their breaths mingled. Her blood began to simmer, pound. Heavy heat pooled low in her belly. She pressed her breasts into his chest. Heat ignited, flooded her core.

"I need you," Thrane said, and his heart hammered solidly, vitally against her, matching the wild beat of her own. "Need you now."

He unbuckled the brass clasps on her corset and cupped her breasts.

The friction of the linen tunic against her skin and the heat of his palms as they shaped her flesh made her nipples tighten. She moaned, pushed harder into him, craving the pressure, the contact, *him*.

"Gods, India."

His eyes grew feral, and he whisked her tunic over her head. She barely registered the chill of the dusk air because those hot calloused hands were back on her. He thumbed her nipples, then leaned down and took one into his mouth. He laved over her sensitive tip, then sucked hard. Fire spiked, arced from her breast to her groin.

Thrane reared back, color high on his cheeks, and ripped his shirt off and over his head. India ran a hand over his abdomen, abstractedly noted the wound was almost gone. His eyes stayed hotly on hers as he yanked down his jeans. Grinning, she matched his movement, shook off her boots, wriggled out of her leggings.

They both laughed as they kicked their pants away. And holy crap, Thrane was commando. His thick length, proud and strong like him, jutted out—for her. Her mouth went dry. Her core clenched.

India kicked off her panties, then she also stood naked in the forest. She should've been chilled, should've been worried about someone intruding, but there was something elemental about being in this place that drove all other sensation and worry away.

Even the forest had gone silent, as if this moment was theirs and theirs alone.

No more laughter. No more words.

India soaked Thrane up, a visual feast that would feed a starving nation. Darkly tanned skin covering thick, bulging muscle from his thighs to his chest to his shoulders.

Heat and need blazed at her. For her. And that connection between them, the visceral tug that had linked her to him since the start, bloomed in her chest. India leaped for him. Pressed his massive body back until he hit the World Tree. She tasted his chest, salt and musk tangy on her tongue.

India ran her lips over one nipple, took a tiny nip. He hissed, and she laved the sensitive nub, said sorry with a flick of her tongue before moving her lips down, down farther, until she dropped to her knees.

"India."

"Sh. Let me do this."

She nuzzled her cheek against him. He groaned, hissed in a breath. She ignored the press of stones and twigs on her knees.

"Have you ever done this here before?"

"Nay." His voice was like gravel, weighted down with desire. "Never here."

Her senses delighted to think she could give him a first in his ageless existence. She eyed his thickness, moistened her lips. His fingers tightened in her hair.

Slowly, she leaned forward, tasted him. Thrane's unique spice hit her tongue and she hummed in approval. He swayed, and she kept her gaze on his as she took him into her mouth as far as she could.

"Gods, India," Thrane groaned, swayed again.

She moved up his shaft, kept her lips tight around the hot, salty skin. A shudder moved through his entire body.

"India," Thrane said, his fingers tangled in her hair. "Gods, I'm going to come if you keep going."

India released him and Thrane hauled her up by the waist, pinned her to the World Tree with his chest. She wrapped one leg around him, searched for and found solid purchase in a hollow in the roots with the other.

"I take it you liked that?"

A half-laugh, half-growl rumbled from within him. "Oh, yes. Please say we can do that again. But now it's my turn. Hope you're ready for the ride."

"I'm ready for whatever you've got," India said.

He hurriedly took care of the condom and then nudged her legs wide. His heat connected with her core. Then the thick, silken length of him slid between her sensitive folds. She moaned, and her head fell forward. He groaned and burrowed into the dip between her neck and shoulder. Pushed inside her.

"Thrane." She gasped as he stretched her anew. Hot and hard and strong. She moaned at the fullness, the tightness. The completeness. The spice of his skin, the heat of his hold, the sweat on his chest as he held her securely. The hot puffs of his breath in the curve of her neck, the shudder that racked his body as he settled inside her. And then he slowly withdrew.

"India," Thrane said, his voice a hoarse whisper.

He turned his head, pressed a hot kiss to her neck as he withdrew a little farther. Her inner muscles clamped down on him, as if her body didn't want to lose that amazing fullness either. He hissed, pushed back inside her, deep, hard. Rubbed along every single nerve ending until he once more filled her. Again and again, he pushed and withdrew.

Tension gathered, wound tighter, tighter, until finally her body exploded, and every nerve ending convulsed, and wave after wave of sensation crashed through her. Gradually, India's heart and breath slowed.

She managed to lift her head. "You haven't come?"

"Wanted you to get there first." Sweat beaded on his chest.

India almost purred in delight, still filled by his heat. "Thrane, do you trust me?"

His attention was locked on where their bodies joined, and he moved his hips forward, pushed himself inside again with a short, hard thrust that made her gasp.

"Thrane!"

"Hmm?" he asked, vaguely.

He moved once more and she moaned.

"Ah, well, firstly, do that again."

He did and she gasped, her head fell back against the bark.

"God, that's amazing." Her body tightened, another climax building. "I've got an idea." She hauled in a breath. "Let me show you."

She connected first with her own energy, then to the energy of the world around her. Thrane's diamond crystals spun at lightning speed, but their inner core of gold fire was almost white-hot. India reached out with her own green energy and lightly touched hers to his. Once again, they connected seamlessly. But instead of drawing on Thrane's energy as she'd done the last time, she caressed the diamond currents.

Thrane gasped. His eyes widened, and he throbbed hard deep inside her.

Her breath tore from her at the deep flare of sensation.

Thrane's chocolate gaze captured hers, his sculpted hips pulled back hard, and he let out a roar before pushing into her hard and heavy. He reared back.

"Gods, India, I can see you. I can see you and feel you

and you're a part of me." Wonder met lust in his deep voice. "Again, we have to do this again."

It was all she could do to hold on as his hips hammered into hers, his thick erection pushing into her, over and over. India climaxed hard, almost lost control of her crystals under the onslaught of sensation. He finally drove himself home one last time, shouted as he emptied himself into her.

Eventually, India took stock of her body—tiny internal flares of sensation, her crazed heartbeat that was finally beginning to steady, the discomfort of the Tree along her spine, twinges and scratches in unusual places.

She gulped air into her lungs, watched through heavy eyes as Thrane did the same.

He slowly leaned back, eased the pressure of his chest that held her up. As he did, her leg unwound from his hip, and she wobbled for a moment as her muscles unkinked. Thrane steadied her and she drank in the harsh beauty of his face. He placed the softest kiss on her lips, cherished her mouth for one long, gentle moment.

"That was out of this world, India." Thrane brushed aside her hair. "So, Jones, it's you and me?"

India looked into that melted-chocolate gaze, deeply inhaled his masculine scent of spicy musk. Knew exactly what she wanted.

"I'm game. Are you?"

He dipped his head, paused a breath away. "Count me in."

As she closed her eyes, India opened her magic, and an infinite loop of energy appeared—creating a bond that connected her to Thrane, him to her, and them both to the Tree. Warmth and acceptance, and a connection deeper than she'd ever thought possible, settled in her soul.

A WAXING crescent moon was on the rise when India and Thrane arrived hand in hand into the welcoming warmth and light of the farmhouse.

Nan, Nate and Sim all sat around the kitchen table.

Nan's hand went to her chest, and then she took in India and Thrane's clasped hands. A small smile played about her mouth.

"Well, you two," she said. "You've been gone for long enough."

Heat worked up India's cheeks, but she refused to drop Thrane's hand. She led him with her and used her other arm to enfold her grandmother.

"I'm home, *we're* home now."

Nan leaned back. Blue eyes misty. "And?"

India couldn't shake a smile at the imperious demand.

"Ri'Kiant is gone, Liz." Thrane said and let out a shuddering breath. "It's over—for now."

The End

THANK YOU & REVIEWS

Thank you for reading my debut novel, and the first book in *The Immortal Keepers* series. I hope you liked meeting these characters and their world as much as I did.

If you enjoyed this story, I would be very grateful if you would leave me a review. As a new author, every review helps me pursue my dream of a career in writing.

ALSO BY HM HODGSON

The Immortal Keepers

Book 2 Keeper Of My Heart

Book 3 Keeper Of My Desire

Relics and Legends

A Wreath Of Thorns

Anthologies

Mermaid Kisses

Guarded Hearts

FREE EBOOK GIVEAWAY

Can a cursed Merprince blackmail his way out of a fairytale nightmare?

Read now to enjoy this Beauty and the Beast retelling!

Get your free ebook now by joining my reader group.

ACKNOWLEDGMENTS

Only through the steppingstones laid by many people and organizations has this story found its way to you.

The Last Keeper was completed in 2018. Unsure of what to do next, I looked up the QLD Writers Centre and through their Writer's Surgery found the amazing Anna Campbell. Anna became a mentor and friend and is mentioned first because everything that's happened with my writing stemmed from Anna's advice – I can't include it all, but here are some of the highlights: join the Romance Writers of Australia (RWA), find my tribe, get a critique partner, enter competitions, read as widely as possible, and understand that writing is a long game (perhaps the hardest advice for someone as impatient as me!)

Attending my first RWA conference in Melbourne 2019, I found my tribe. Also through the RWA I discovered their online learning courses, two of which have been instrumental in The Last Keeper: Ebony McKenna's Self-Editing (Ebony also helped with an early draft) and Novalee Swan's Digital Self-Publishing (Novalee's insights and tailored suggestions for my publication journey were priceless). The RWA has email groups for writers in different stages of their career, and the Aspiring eLoop have been amazing – to D.D. Line and everyone on that loop, wishing you all the best for each of your journeys! I also started to enter RWA competitions and in 2020 *The Last Keeper* was a finalist in the RWA First Kiss Comp. I cried when I read that email, because it somehow validated that I *was* a writer – 19 agents had rejected my manuscript at that point, and doubt was beginning to creep in, but that competition changed everything in my mind.

Also at conference, I found my critique group. Melanie Pickering, Jennifer Westgarth and Jacqueline Hayley. These wonderful women & amazing authors are the absolute best part of writing—collaboration, honest feedback and friendship. And a special call-out to Jacqueline for her stunning cover artwork!

In early 2020 Rachel Bailey and Josephine Moon through their Sunshine Writers Lab introduced me to *Save The Cat* by Blake Snyder and the suggestion to completely rewrite my beginning. That weekend workshop turned my story around and I am forever grateful to both Josephine and Rachel for their insights and critique (and for an awesome workshop!)

To my first author-reader, M.L. Tompsett, thank you for your feedback & advice. I hope you enjoy the final version.

To editors Sarah Proulx Calfee and Libby M Iriks – your polish and craftsmanship have made a little idea and a bunch of words gleam. I am so grateful to you both for your advice, your effort and your care with my book baby.

To the friends who have listened to story ideas and pitches (so many pitches!) and always encouraged me on this journey – thank you.

And finally, for my family: Henry, your love and support *is* magic. No other way to put it. For my sister Julie and wonderful friend, Chantal—you were the first readers of this story back in 2018, I hope you love it now! My mum for her unending belief that writing is my gig (and never minding when I raided her Johanna Lindsay stash as a teenager). My father for his love of storytelling, humor and keen eye for typos. And every other family member who's read this story, helped untangle plot bunnies or joined a family chat to find another word for something ... like Julie's idea of crossing places (told you I'd give you the credit, Jules!)

So really, this book would not be here today, as it is, without four years of support. My thanks to you all.

ABOUT THE AUTHOR

HM HODGSON

Brisbane author, HM Hodgson, has always loved stories. Creating her own is the natural evolution of a passion for reading, a love for what makes people tick, and the fantastic places that can be imagined.

Today, she writes about romance (steamy scenes a must!) and magic. Magic that moves worlds and takes her to another place. When not writing or reading or reluctantly cleaning up after her children, she loves looking after her veggie patch and a little flock of chickens.

Keep in touch with HM Hodgson at:
www.hmhodgson.com

www.ingramcontent.com/pod-product-compliance
Lightning Source LLC
Chambersburg PA
CBHW020546120726
47903CB00001B/156